tang

Yuri Vynnychuk

Translated from the Ukrainian by
Michael M. Naydan and Olha Tytarenko
Translation edited by Ludmilla A. Trigos

Spuyten Duyvil
New York City

Acknowledgements

An excerpt from *Tango of Death* under the title "Wartime Stories of Galicia Past," co-translated with Svitlana Barnes, appeared in *Consequence Magazine* 7 (Spring 2015).

Chapters 1 and A of *Tango of Death,* co-translated with Olha Tytarenko, appeared in *Trafika Europe* 7 (March 2016).

I've borrowed, revised, and added to the biographical information of my introduction to this volume from my introductions to two of my previous books of translations of Vynnychuk's prose: *The Fantastic Worlds of Yuri Vynnychuk* (Glagoslav Publishers, 2016) and *Windows of Time Frozen* (Klasyka Publishers, 2000).

My special gratitude to my co-translator Olha Tytarenko for her meticulous work on this extremely complicated translation and also to Ludmilla Trigos for her terrific editorial suggestions on the final version of the manuscript. I, however, take full responsibility for any errors or omissions.

ISBN 978-1-949966-33-6

Library of Congress Cataloging-in-Publication Data

Names: Vynnychuk, I͡Uriĭ, author. | Tytarenko, Olha, translator. |
Naydan, Michael M., 1952- translator.
Title: Tango of death / Yuri Vynnychuk ; translated from the Ukrainian by
Michael Naydan, Olha Tytarenko.
Other titles: Tango Smerti. English
Description: New York City : Spuyten Duyvil / [2019]
Identifiers: LCCN 2019017373 | ISBN 9781949966336
Classification: LCC PG3949.32.Y73 T3613 2019 | DDC 891.7/934--dc23
LC record available at https://lccn.loc.gov/2019017373

This translation is dedicated
to the memory of Svitlana Bednazh Barnes,
who left this world all too soon.

A BIOGRAPHICAL NOTE ON YURI VYNNYCHUK

Ukrainian writer Yuri Vynnychuk was born in 1952 in Stanislav, Ukraine, which is now called Ivano-Frankivsk. His father was a doctor for the anti-Stalinist and anti-Nazi Ukrainian partisans during World War II, and his uncle on his mother's side Yuri Sapiha was killed by the Soviet secret police (the Cheka) in 1941. Vynnychuk was named in memory of his murdered uncle. In 1973 he completed the Stanislav Pedagogical Institute (now the Vasyl Stefanyk Precarpathian National University) where he developed the reputation of a prankster. At that time, he became involved in student publications as well as in the literary underground. In 1974 the KGB conducted a search of his house but found no materials that would have incriminated him with the Soviet regime. To avoid inevitable arrest, he moved to the larger city of Lviv, where he hid at apartments of several friends, constantly covering his tracks from the KGB. Until 1980 Vynnychuk was blacklisted and not allowed to publish in official sources. Till then he published works under the names of various other writers and ghostwrote books on occasion. He eked out a living from the honoraria from his various pseudonymous publications, a practice which, by habit and by design, he has continued to do. During the 1980s he held readings of his works in the apartments of friends and became well-known for his satiric poetry and stories about a mythical country called Arcanum—a land where, in the short story "The Island of Ziz," the streets are paved with fecal matter and everything is made of it. From 1980 on, Vynnychuk was allowed to publish his articles and translations in the Ukrainian periodical press. He made a number of enemies among the Soviet literary establishment for his merciless attacks against hack writers.

In 1987 Vynnychuk was instrumental in the creation of a singing and comic performance group "Ne zhurys'!" (Don't Worry!), which rose to swift popularity in Ukraine. Under Mikhail Gorbachev's *perestroika-perebudova* and subsequent Ukrainian independence in 1991, Vynnychuk emerged from the underground to occupy an eminent place in the new Ukrainian cultural scene. His collection of fantastic stories and novellas *The Flashing Beacon* (Spalakh;1990) sold out almost immediately. He also published a collection of poetry *Reflections* (Vidobrazhennia, 1990) and compiled and edited two anthologies of Ukrainian fantastic stories from the 19th century. His pulp fiction novellas *Maidens of the Night* (Divy nochi, 1992) and Harem Life (Zhytiie haremnoie, 1996) enjoyed extraordinary popularity. The former was made into a television movie. His love of storytelling and of his adopted hometown is reflected in several volumes—*Legends of Lviv* (Lehendy Lvova, 1999), *Pubs of Lviv* (Knaipy Lvova, 2000), *Mysteries of Lviv Coffee* (Taiemnytsi lvivskoi kavy, 2001), and *Mysteries of Lviv Horilka*[1] (Taiemnytsi lvivskoi horilky, 2006). His fantasy novel *Malva Landa* (the heroine's name) appeared in 2000, and a collection of fantastic tales *Windows of Time Frozen* (Vikna zastyhloho chasu) in 2001. His novel

1 The Ukrainian word for vodka that comes from the same root as "to burn," suggesting something like the Native American term "firewater" for liquor.

Spring Games in Autumn Gardens (Vesniani ihry v osinnikh sadakh, 2005) garnered the 2005 BBC Ukrainian Book of the Year Award. His collection of autobiographical works, *Pears a la Crepe* (Hrushi v tisti, 2010) also was nominated for the BBC Prize. His book *Tango of Death* won the 2012 BBC Book of the Year Award for Ukraine and has attracted an extraordinary amount of attention both in Ukraine and abroad, particularly in German and Czech translations. His most recent novels include: *The Apothecary* (Aptekar, 2015), *The Censor of Dreams* (Tsenzor sniv, 2016), *Lutetia*[2] (Liutetsiia, 2017), and *Blood Sisters* (Sestry krovi, 2018). The latter is a sequel to his novel *The Apothecary*. He additionally has authored two plays, sixteen anthologies, twelve children's books, a cook book (he's a culinary expert), several translations from Czech and German as well as a book of lyric poetry purportedly translated from Old Irish.

Vynnychuk was designated a Golden Writer of Ukraine in 2012, and in that same year was persecuted by the corrupt Yanukovych regime for his satirical poem "Kill the Mother" (*Ubii piderasa*), which became widely circulated on the Internet. Vynnychuk's name also was included in the recent and infamous "List of 47," which consisted of prominent Ukrainian cultural and political figures targeted for assassination by Russian-backed killers.

Vynnychuk continues to write incredibly prolifically and resides with his wife Myroslava and their son just outside the city limits of Lviv in the village of Vynnyky (yes, the name of his current home bears a close resemblance to his last name).

---

2 The name of the ancient Roman city that was the predecessor of Paris.

ON *TANGO OF DEATH*

Yuri Vynnychuk's *Tango of Death* comprises myriad sticky wickets for the translator. The stickiest may be the very colorful language that the author uses to create his powerful narrative about the fate of four close friends from the time of prewar Lviv, through wartime and postwar Lviv, to the present day. Multi-cultural Western Ukrainian Galician dialect, besides the core of standard Ukrainian, contains elements of Polish, Yiddish, and German along with "batiar" slang. The batiars were now legendary young movers and shakers in Lviv, who hung out together socially and tried to make money in legal and quasilegal ways under the watchful eyes of the police of various occupying forces controlling Lviv over time. Fortunately, for me as translator of such a text, my parents, who emigrated to the U.S. after World War II, had lived in Galicia (Halychyna in Ukrainian) not far from Lviv until 1942. Thus, some of the dialectal and period linguistic elements that Vynnychuk uses in the novel were somewhat familiar to me. I am particularly grateful to my co-translator Olha Tytarenko, a former long-time resident of Lviv, for sharing her expertise on the colorful Galician expressions found in the novel. She painstakingly looked up many dialectal words and expressions I wasn't aware of to enlighten me regarding their meanings. How to convey them in English, however, turns out to be an even more complicated matter. Most important for the translator is to somehow convey that almost magical language of Vynnychyk's narrative along with the unique manner of speech of the various colorful characters we meet over the course of his novel. In this respect, the novel reminds me somewhat of James Joyce's *Dubliners*, which is populated by unique characters from all walks of Irish life from washerwomen to priests to pub-culture intellectuals. *Tango of Death*, too, is populated by scores of colorful characters from all walks of life (from doormen to funeral parlor directors to shop owners to scholars) and numerous ethnicities (particularly Ukrainian, Polish, Jewish, German, and Russian). To get the full impact of the richness of the style of *Tango of Death* one does need to read it in the original (with help from the glossary located at the end of it).

Tango of Death is one of the first literary works of Ukrainian prose fiction to deal with the topic of the Shoah in Lviv and the atrocities perpetrated by the Nazis in the Yaniv concentration camp where it is estimated that over 140,000 Jews were slaughtered. While one needs to keep in mind that the novel is a work of fiction, it is based largely on historical facts and uses many historical personages such as the sadistic Yaniv camp commandant Vilgauz, who had many tortured and killed under his personal supervision, and the musicologist and co-director of the prison's orchestra Jakob (Cuba) Mund, who was among those executed there. The brutality of the Nazis and Soviets has been expressed in oral histories by survivors, in memoirs, and in photographs from those times. Many of the extant photographs of the pogroms described in the novel in Lviv in 1941 are available from Internet sources. A simple image search of "Lviv 1941" will yield many of the horrific pictures from that time. Some disturbing graphic pictures taken at the Yaniv camp can be seen at the following Ukrainian website: https://inlviv.in.ua/lviv/yanivskiy-kontstabir-pid-lvovom-abo-tango-smerti.

For his readers Vynnychuk importantly recreates the *personal* experience of living through those horrendous days, one of the bleakest times of Lviv's history. The novel itself is not a history per se, but rather an emotional recreation of the time and events with an attempt to provide as much factual detail as possible. Much of what Vynnychuk depicts actually did happen to Jews and to the other inhabitants of the city. For example, one can find pictures of Jews forced to crawl on hands and knees to clean the sidewalks with toothbrushes as Vynnychuk depicts in the novel, along with photographs of Jewish women stripped nearly naked and forced to run along the streets through gauntlets of gawkers (including the local Ukrainian population), who taunted them. The murder and mass graves of Jews, Poles, and Ukrainians are documented in pictures of the heaps of bloodied bodies. Lviv truly was a part of the bloodlands, to borrow the term from the title of Timothy Snyder's book *Bloodlands: Europe between Hitler and Stalin* (Basic Books, 2010).

The masterful narrative of *Tango of Death* develops in two time periods: in pre-war and World War II Lviv in Western Ukraine as well as in the chronological present. Numbered chapters from 1-31 are interspersed with twenty-six lettered ones from A to Z. The former occur in the present time, the latter in the past. The novel traces the fate of four close friends—an ethnic Ukrainian, Pole, German, and Jew—who grow up together, experience youthful adventures, misadventures, and love, and end up united in the cause to defend their homeland against invading forces. Their lives are not governed by the ethnic group to which they belong. Instead their lives remain steadfastly and intimately intertwined as they support each other in the best and worst of times in Vynnychuk's tale of a city—to borrow another phrase, this time from Dickens. In microcosm, their interactions and familiarity with each other's lives and culture breeds camaraderie, mutual respect, and love among them. Their microcosmic world is precisely the way the wider world should be. Vynnychuk's story line in the novel, however, is not restricted just to the bleak horrors of the war. Just like life, there are many moments of humor, of compassion, of love, of understanding. The line of the plot that can be described as magical realism (the search for a mystical book that holds the key to reincarnation for doomed souls) also allows for a corrective to the horrors of history that destroy individual lives. The missing musical notes of the "Tango of Death," a musical piece that was actually played by the camp orchestra during the executions at the Yaniv camp by the Nazis, end up being a source for salvation for ill-fated souls. Vynnychuk is a masterful storyteller, who takes his reader on a fascinating ride in this, perhaps, his most significant novel.

Michael M. Naydan
Woskob Family Professor of Ukrainian Studies
The Pennsylvania State University

TANGO OF DEATH

Dedicated to Yevhen Nakonechny (1931-2006), the author of the books A Stolen Name *and* Shoah in Lviv, *the guiding soul of the Vasyl Stefanyk Academic Library, who many times persistently and sympathetically inclined me toward this subject, for suggesting numerous sources to me, and for sharing his personal reminiscences.*

High above snow is falling, ravens are crowing, the trees are cracking from the cold, and somewhere far away snow is crunching beneath the boots of the killers. You can perceive their approach in everything—somewhere off in the distance you can hear the threatening barking of the village dogs, which is different from their regular barking; the barking increases in intensity, while the crows, cawing loudly, dart into the air and fly off. Four young men are sitting in a hideout, listening to the barking; then, glancing at each other, they burn certain papers; smoke crawls out of the vent. Then they change into clean shirts and pray. They don't pray together, but each one separately, and their prayers are in different languages. Three of them sit down around a small plank table; a bundle of grenades lies on the dark smooth surface; the hands of all three of them are placed nearby. They wait silently. There is no fear in their eyes. Each one thinks his own thoughts.

The fourth one takes a violin into his hands, stands next to them and listens closely. The sound of the dogs barking is already above their heads; the fire in the hideout is burning out, and tiny sparks jump across the burnt documents and disappear in the air. Upstairs, the command demanding surrender can already be heard. The men don't react; their eyes are riveted to the grenades. They shudder only when they hear despairing women's voices appealing to them, cursing them, imploring. The voices force the tears out of their eyes, but they refuse to give in; they know all too well what awaits them.

A hand with a bow touches the violin, and the melody of a tango resounds. Now the barking of dogs and human voices are forced to burst through that melody, and not only through the melody, but also through the singing—the four men are singing something really quietly. And then one of their hands stretches to the pile of grenades....

1

When we're young, we're all nobodies, not even the greatest geniuses whose careers and recognition await them in the future come into this world overly suited to life, that's why it's not unusual that after we get married, we find ourselves in certain ordeals that rarely end happily, but instead more often in the parting of ways. This was exactly the trap that young Myrko Yarosh fell right into after he got married to the sweet and warm Roma after graduating from the university. He used to read the poetry of great poets aloud to her, and she pretended to listen, even straining her eyes and pursing her lips. Her face became so inspired that he fell in love with her more and more, thinking that she, in fact, had been created to listen spellbound to everything he would say, that entire heap of words, which he was falling in love with and which he was sinking into, as though into a quagmire, greedily swallowing air. When during those readings she snuggled up to him and tickled his ear with her hot breath, he thought that the idyll would be eternal, and that both of them simply were destined to be married to each other. Feelings overpowered common sense, and from the moment they married, they started to live at Roma's parents' place, and that was the beginning of the end.

Two years of teaching and then part-time graduate school boded no joy, because if there wasn't any money, there'd be no money, and Roma's parents never denied themselves the chance to remind the young couple on every occasion that they were mooching off them. In the evening, after putting their little son to bed, Yarosh, with his books spread all over the kitchen, was writing his dissertation about the literature of Egypt, Babylon, Assyria, Sumeria, Arcanum, and the Hittite Kingdom. But the deeper he delved into the topic and dug up sources, the more his work seemed to be hopeless, because certain sources gave birth to other ones, and those to yet others. It was endless, forcing him to get lost in the labyrinths of different versions and often to draw conclusions by groping about in the dark; though everyone working on this topic was not dealing with the complete panorama of literary life back then, but just with fragments that miraculously managed to make their way to us, that miraculously had been decoded and read, but not all of them, because no one had completely figured out the Arcanumian[3] language, however an opinion about their literature had been formed from Hittite and Hurrian sources. It was the latter issue that excited Yarosh so much that he cast aside all the remaining ones and took to decoding Arcanumian texts. Many scholars had tried to do this before him but failed. Arcanumian cuneiform was unlike any other.

Finding time for his scholarly work just in odd moments, Yarosh seriously began to contemplate the meaning of his

3 The Merriam-Webster Dictionary defines Arcanum as "mysterious or specialized knowledge, language, or information accessible or possessed only by the initiate." http://www.merriam-webster.com/dictionary/arcanum. Additionally, it adds: "The word *arcanum* (pluralized as 'arcana') comes from Latin *arcanus*, meaning 'secret,' and entered English as the Dark Ages gave way to the Renaissance. It was often used in reference to the mysteries of the physical and spiritual worlds, subjects of heavy scrutiny and rethinking at the time. Alchemists were commonly said to be pursuing the arcana of nature, and they sought elixirs for changing base metals into gold, prolonging life, and curing disease. The frequent association of the word with the alchemists' elixirs influenced the use of 'arcanum' for 'elixir.'"

family life. The stupid routine of work in school oppressed and tormented him; he was surprised at how it came to be that he had become a teacher despite the fact that he had hated that profession when he was still in school. He would come home tired, and the only thing that could motivate him to do scholarly work was wine. The first glass took away his daylong tension, the second freed his thoughts, tore off all their chains, and then his pen would begin to fly across the paper as though it were mad. True, it lasted for not more than about two hours, but then tedium would fatigue him, and he would fall asleep with his head filled with ancient hieroglyphs, clay tablets and papyruses. The complete disdain of his wife and in-laws of his scholarly work added to this feeling; they considered his work nonsense, a waste of time, well, he would never complete his scholarly work, and would therefore be destined to pass through life as a simple school teacher. It became a kind of obligatory ritual to tear him away from his work and to send him to the store for bread, to carry out the trash, to fill up the water in the portable cistern when the water pipes would be turned off, to awaken him before dawn so he could occupy a place in line for milk, kielbasa, cheese, sugar, and flour—it made no difference. He was the only one who was made to run after everything, when in the 1980s there was a shortage of nearly everything. People turned into hunters for goods, scurrying through the city and saving places in several different lines at the same time so that in each of them they would manage to buy a kilo of sugar or a packet of laundry powder, because they wouldn't give each person more than one. And he also had to keep vigil over the bookstores, where once a week they used to deliver new books; only a limited circle of people received information about that, so for at least an hour before the bookstore would open up after the "delivery of goods," he would occupy a place in line, and then dash into the place ahead of the crowd and be the first to grab a Kafka, Camus, Akutagava, Cortazar, Marquez, Borges. Their number was endless. For the sake of his sacred goal, Yarosh even started up a platonic love affair with one of the bookshop salesgirls. He wasn't able to do anything more because she was one of those spinsters, who, as a result of years spent in loneliness in their everyday life, become intolerable, capricious, and boring. Inviting her out for coffee, Yarosh was forced to listen to her expound on her life motto, an entire heap of those cunning prescriptions, with which she surrounded herself from every direction like warning flags. Overall, her entire wardrobe, which was designed to hide all the protuberances of her body like a nun, was a warning flag, because she was waiting for "serious relationships;" "flirting didn't interest her," but "Mr. Myrko[4] is a very pleasant person," "you can trust him," "it seems to me sometimes that we've known each other for a really long time"—and a long, promising smile, one more little flag that began to gleam on the horizon, more, with a telling caution: "No one, no one, no one—just him alone." Yarosh looked at her pale white arms, covered with fine little strands of red hair, and began to imagine that her legs might be covered with the same fine hair, and this even elicited the desire in him to research this as yet unstudied continent with all its hidden nooks. The mere fact that he had far too little free time saved him from that research, so only going for coffee

4 Galician Ukrainian often uses the term "Pan" (Mr.) or "Pani" (Mrs.) with a person's first name in addressing someone as a sign of respect or unfamiliarity with that person.

with her was entirely sufficient to sustain friendly relations and to acquire information about the arrival of new books.

Once when he finally went to sleep long past midnight, leaving his papers on the kitchen table, which late in the evening served as his office, and in the morning finding a hot, grease-spattered frying pan on his papers, from which his father-in-law was scarfing down an omelet, liberally covered with scallions, and blocking himself from the world with his newspaper, it was the last straw for him. With unceremonious boldness, which he had never dared before, but with an obliging "excuse me," he plucked his papers from under the frying pan, shook them over the table in front of the astounded and delirious eyes of his father-in-law and left. Now he realized that he was standing before an inevitable dilemma—he must sacrifice something: either his family life, or his academic one. He chose the former. One morning, so as not to arouse any suspicion, he left the house to go to work the same way as any other day, although he still had to take his son to daycare as one of his regular duties. Parting with his little son was particularly painful for him. He knew he would be losing many pleasant moments in the future, because what he had planned would certainly ruin his current lifestyle once and for all, but he saw no other way out. Waiting for the house to be empty, he returned, and slowly, without rushing, gathered all his things, packed his books and papers and wrote a letter, in which he announced that he was going away forever. He'd send alimony at the beginning of every month. Then he phoned the school where he worked and announced to the principal that he was forced by virtue of various circumstances to quit his job.

"You can't just leave in the middle of the school year!" The principal was justifiably indignant.

"I have very serious reasons."

"Can I ask what they are?"

"Illness."

"An illness?" The principal grew concerned. "Is it that bad?"

"Unfortunately, the diagnosis isn't satisfactory," he repeated a phrase that he had heard in a movie and sighed.

"Well, that's to say... while you're undergoing treatment, we'll keep your job open...."

"No, no, treatments are useless... the illness is incurable, understand? There's no point."

"So where are you going? Do you have a new job?"

"No. I just want to live out the rest of my days to my own satisfaction. Do you understand what I'm talking about?"

"Of course. That's very sensible. And really, why work like a mule... but you can leave your work service record with us... so your term of service remains uninterrupted... oh, what kind of work service there is now!... but all the same, so you don't have any problems... because if you end up at the police station, and they take an interest in your place of work... they'll tack on social parasitism... it's safer this way...."

"Of course. Thank you very much for your concern."

"You're welcome. And remember that our entire staff always took pride in you. And the children loved you. It will be hard for them without you."

After that he called a taxi and ended up on the other end of Lviv in Mayorivka.

The day before he found himself accommodations at a reasonable price with a retired couple. The room was kind of small, and he couldn't even lay out all his books, but on the other hand no one bothered him. In the morning he would set off to the research library and work there until five, then would return home, on the way back, buying a few buns filled with liver for four kopecks apiece, then he would fry the pies in a skillet and eat them with his tea. He got used to managing with little. But on the other hand, he could now completely devote himself to his scholarly work. To earn a living and to pay his monthly alimony he published literary reviews and translations. For a not overly wealthy, yet not miserable existence two or three publications a month were enough. And the most important thing was that no one get on his case.

In Yarosh's family his mother's elder never married sister Aunt Lucia was still alive; her fiancé had gone missing in the war, and she continued to wait for him even after the declaration of independence, when all those who survived Siberia returned home. She had a spacious house in Kryvchytsi and repeatedly called for her nephew to live with her, but he made up every possible excuse, knowing that auntie would give him no peace, she would yearn for conversation, attention, and finally the desire to take care of him would surface. But Yarosh had no need of care, he sought only privacy. Besides, he often visited auntie, bringing her food. He even supplied her with interesting books and patiently listened to her stories. Auntie was an enormous woman with a sagging neck. She had thick legs, and she walked, waddling like a duck. She smelled of Validol, although in her youth she used to be very attractive.

She received the greatest satisfaction when she managed to sit her nephew down at the table and feed him something.

Then she sat down across from him and looked at him with adoring eyes, gratified that he thought the meal or cake with berries was tasty. Every August she set about cooking preserves from different berries and fruits, although she very rarely ate them. Yarosh did not have a sweet tooth, so the jars of jam increasingly took up all the shelves in the pantry, since there was no longer any other space for them. But every August the very same procedure took place—boiling down the berries and mixing them with a wooden spatula in a large bowl. At that time auntie resembled a sorceress who was preparing some kind of magic potion. She was focused and serious, and every fly that dared to flutter into the kitchen at this sacred time, immediately fell into her field of vision and onto her swatter's rubber flap. The scent of the softened, loose berries intoxicated and infused the walls and furniture so powerfully that the house and everything in it looked like candy—as if it were made of marzipan. Any attempts to convince auntie not to putter around her preserves failed. She just couldn't kick that habit and didn't want to, because her beloved was terribly fond of sweets, and many times she nostalgically remembered feeding him with a teaspoon. He would lick up everything clean, drops of red or yellow jam glistening on his lips and tongue, and afterward she herself would taste those droplets. Every time she set about puttering around the jam, these recollections would spring up in her memory and remain there until this process was complete, and then little by little diminished and dissipated until the next August.

One such summer, when the heat was stifling, and a breeze hovered over the trees, Auntie Lucia, having exhausted herself by the stove, sat down in an armchair and dozed off, forgetting to turn off the gas under the pot with the hot preserves. The fire happily continued to lick the metal; the berries frothed, boiled, bubbled, and rose, and reaching the edges of the top of the pot, overflowed onto the stove and put out the fire, but the gas continued to flow and filled the kitchen with its sour smell. Aunt Lucia smiled in her sleep, stretched out her hands to meet someone, and whispered: "Finally ... you've come back...."

Yarosh returned in the evening, and the house no longer smelled of marzipan. He instantly flung open all the windows and doors, turned off the gas, and called for an ambulance. But it was already too late; in the end the preserves finally killed her.

Auntie, as she promised, bequeathed the house to her nephew, and not long after the funeral Yarosh moved to Kryvchytsi. The house was surrounded by an old still fertile orchard, along the length of the fence were untidy gooseberry bushes; red, yellow and black currants; white and black grapes snaked through a metal frame. Flower beds stretched beneath the windows, large sunflowers, hollyhocks, and dahlias proudly stood sentry. On the ground floor there were two spacious rooms and a kitchen, and on the second—a large loft with wide windows where he set up his study. The house was cluttered with auntie's things, an endless amount of different stuff, which for auntie probably held immense value. In particular, he was surprised to come across a full uniform of a Polish policeman, carefully packed in a linen bag, and when he unfolded the uniform, he saw a bullet hole and traces of dried blood. What the heck was that all about? They didn't accept Ukrainians into the police—so, was her fiancé a Pole? Was he wounded, then fled and hid out at Lucia's? Maybe after that he changed into civilian clothing... What happened to him after that?

For several days he worked to clear out his living space, burning some things and throwing out others, though not immediately, as some things he found required closer attention, like a box of old watches, alarm clocks and clocks, which his grandfather had tried to fix. All these dead mechanisms from Lord knows what times amazed Yarosh, so he tossed out only some of them in the trash and placed several of the old timepieces on his shelves. His auntie, who fortunately survived more than one war and more than one misfortune, remained the same even in peacetime. With her reserves of cereals, sugar, salt, flour, soap, matches, and various homemade preserves, one could manage there for many years. In the pantry the shelves were adorned with many jars: preserves, obligatorily including rose petal jam; they were lined up according to the degree of ripeness of the fruit and vegetables, but they weren't sealed with metal tops, but rather with a special glass paper, which, after moistening, auntie applied to each jar, after which it hardened and created a tight cover; in the pantry itself she also placed a small circle of glass paper, soaked in alcohol, so it wouldn't grow moldy; candied fruit—orange, lemon and tangerine skins boiled in sugary syrup, and additionally—paradise apples and quince; dried mushrooms, apples, plums, and pears; jars with marinaded mushrooms, plums, gherkins, and pickles. Each jar carefully had the date and the name of the products. And in dark bottles, berry juices plugged and covered with wax. Coal and firewood were still kept in the cellar even though a gas line long ago had been connected to the building, but auntie had her own views on life. Yarosh was not even surprised when close to the top of the ceiling in the cellar he found some smoked hams that were resting in stockings. When he pulled them out to taste, he became convinced that nothing was wrong with them, just that they had dried out a bit, but cut into thin strips, they were fantastic for sandwiches. Little bundles of garlic, onion, red hot pepper, dried dill, and caraway along with little bags of nuts were hanging on the walls of the cellar. Apples and pears lay on the shelves in straw. A large plywood box filled with sand stood in the middle of the cellar, and in it there were carrots, parsley, celery, and beets. He could make use of all of it other than the preserves, just because there were too many of the latter. Yarosh made wine from them, adding them to grapes instead of sugar.

One other cumbersome thing of his aunt's remained—an old Austrian piano, it looked imposing and functioned as a safe for Yarosh, where he kept money and documents. On top of the piano lay a small album, which usually in older families is called a "memento book" or a "Stammbuch." Here house guests would inscribe greetings, good wishes, poems, and also draw something. Every young girl could boast about such an album, sometimes several of them. Yarosh flipped through several pages. Among the variety of patterns—mostly butterflies, little birds, little flowers, and curly stems—there were calligraphic handwritten poems or such clever maxims adorning the album: "Who loves you more deeply, let him sign below me!" The last two notes were signed with the name "Yas":

Na górze róże, na dołe fiołki, My się kochamy, jak dwa aniołki.[5]

5 In Polish with poeticized English translation immediately following.

(Roses on the mountain, violets in the valley, We love each other like two angels who don't dally.)

Ile razy jedząc zrazy, trafisz na cebulę, Tyle razy bez urazy wspomnij o mnie czule.[6]

(When you eat meat patties and bite into an onion, Remember me fondly with no hard feelings.)

6 In Polish with poeticized English translation immediately following.

A

"My little sparrow," mom chirps, "are you awake? Then run quick-quick to have a bite to eat, because the kasha will get cold." My mom's gentle chirping accompanied me all my life, and even now, when it's not near, I hear it, the gentle modulation of these sounds, these affectionate baby-talk phrases that awakened me every morning. And then I'd sit down at the table where my cream of wheat with raisins and nuts was waiting for me. I'd gather up a full tablespoon of liquid May honey and in a really thin stream trickle it on the surface of the cream of wheat, drawing fantasies, which looked like castles and mountains, forests and meadows, rivers and impassable swamps. And all this only in order to gradually, spoon by spoon, destroy this fairyland, each time imagining that the mountain, the forest, the river, the castle was disappearing in my mouth.... But even before I awoke to the affectionate words, mom fired up the stove, and through a dream I heard wood crackling, the sound of a little shovel scraping in a bucket of coal, the slight clanging of pot covers in the kitchen. And in winter, when the doors to my bedroom carefully opened, the oven door rattled, paper or straw rustled, matches were struck, flames joyfully covered the firewood, and the quiet soothing hum of the stove plunged me back to sleep, I suddenly became even more comfortable than before, it seemed that it wasn't the stove, but that my mom was pouring warmth into the room and I contentedly purred... but after that I couldn't doze very long, because the dairymaid already was knocking at the door and together with the latest news poured fresh milk into jars. In a few minutes the aroma of coffee brewed in a white porcelain machine with a bit of "Frank" chicory wafted over, and the dream then shattered, dissolved and disappeared....

I knew my father only from photos, because my dad Oleksandr Barbaryka died on November 22, 1921 when I was four. Preserved in my memory is a still hazy recollection of someone large in a long overcoat and shaggy pointed cap who takes me in his arms, and I cry with fright and reach toward my mother, and that is all. Having fought in countless battles for the Sich Riflemen, in the army of the Ukrainian National Republic, at Kruty[7] and at the Motovilivka forest, he eventually lay down his tempestuous head near Bazar,[8] among the 360 rebellious soldiers shot by Kotovsky's forces, who before that had savagely killed all the wounded who were lying on carts with sabers. All my life I missed my dad, with each year more and more, and then I became a momma's boy, a beloved little flower, a little golden sparrow, her little sunshine, a cute little frog, a baby hamster, and a little snail... But I wasn't the only one who couldn't accept the death of my father, for there, near the village of Bazar, the fathers of three of my friends Yosko, Yasko, and Wolff died: Leopold Milker, a Jew, born in Galicia in 1901, the son of a teacher, who studied in Vienna, a pharmacist in charge of a field hospital pharmacy during the campaign; Bronislaw Bilewicz, a Pole, born in 1895 in the village of Hvizd of the Novohrad-Volyn district of Volyn Province, a villager, in the army of the Ukrainian National Republic from 1919;

7 The battle at Kruty occurred on the 16th (in the Julian calendar the 29th) of January 1918 near the train station of the village of Kruty.
8 On November 17, 1921 the Volyn group of the Army of the Ukrainian National Republic under the command of General Yuri Tiutiunnyk was defeated by the Bolshevik army at a battle near the village of Bazar in the Zhytomyr Oblast.

Ernest Yeger, a German, born in 1890 in Prague, graduated from the Polytechnic Institute and officer training school in Vienna, a lieutenant in the army of the Ukrainian National Republic from 1920.

They all died for Ukraine, but what was Ukraine to them? No one had an answer to this question. For each of us, Bazar remained something mythical. The warriors who went on that tragic campaign grew in our imagination to the grandeur of the Argonauts, who set off for the Golden Fleece, for they also set off for the Golden Fleece of freedom, but every last one of them died for Ukraine. Before their execution by firing squad the Bolshevik commissar made the following offer to the doomed 360: "If any of the convicted repents and swears to join the Reds to fight against the Ukrainian gangs, he will be pardoned!" But in response to his call Lieutenant Colonel Mytrofan Kuzmenko darted out and shouted to the villagers, whom the Bolsheviks had herded to the spot of the executions, "My Ukrainian people! Listen to the voice of your faithful sons! At some time in the future you will pay back for us! Long live...." The enemy's bullet cut him off in the middle of his last word and knocked him into the grave. Several voices struck up the national anthem "Ukraine is Still Alive!" An entire chorus joined in with everyone singing: Ukrainians, Poles, two dozen Russians, the Jews Yakiv Krutokop, Josef Yendryk, Zahar Atnabunt, the German Josef Krantz, the Belarusian Mikhail Malevich, and even the Chinese Mon Za Lit. Our fathers also sang, bravely standing before the swarm of machine-gun bullets, and then they were covered with earth—both the dead and still living—and the villagers long afterward would mention how the earth kept stirring.

The tragedy at Bazar was described in many Galician periodicals. It was included in school readers, where the executions of the unpacified Kozaks[9] were also illustrated, and we remembered in detail how and what happened back then, and we looked at the picture, guessing where each of our father's was. And even later, when we learned that the artist painted this painting from imagination and simply could not know what these heroes really looked like, everyone still managed to choose "his" father, who at least looked a little like misty childhood memories and like those photos that remained for us. But we could not come to terms with the fact that our fathers had not resorted to guile to save their lives and refused to agree to cross over to the side of the Reds, though not for real, but only temporarily, and at the earliest opportunity to escape and join up with the rebels of Kholodny Yar (Cold Ravine) to avenge the defeat, and then return home in glory, because the borders then were not yet guarded so closely. Each of us put himself in his father's position and tried to imagine escape, revenge, and a return home. But one interesting detail that we also learned from the newspapers stirred our imagination the most: that night one of the wounded soldiers clawed his way out of the grave, crawled to the peasants' houses where they treated him, and later helped him cross over the Polish border. Who was that Kozak of the Kyiv 4th Division, who managed to survive and save himself? And what if he's one of our fathers?

I have often asked myself the question: if my dad died for Ukraine, then for what did the fathers of Yas, Wolff and

---

9 I am opting for the transliterated Ukrainian spelling of Kozaks, the powerful fighting force in Ukraine and freedom fighters, rather than Cossacks, which sometimes in English has the connotation of marauding bandits or Russian troops.

Yosko die? They themselves also didn't know, and that tormented us the most.

Our mothers—Vlodzya Barbaryka, Golda Milker, Yadzia Bilewicz, and Rita Yeger—became acquainted with each other on the tenth anniversary of the battle of Bazar after meeting at the symbolic grave in the Yaniv Cemetery. Since all four were born and raised in Lviv, they quickly became friends and began to visit each other more often, and we kids were happy about that because we had three Christmases and three paschal celebrations—Catholic, Greek Catholic, and Jewish—and gladly visited each other, relishing red Kozak borsht topped with golden fried onions, in which mushroom dumplings floated, then—stuffed fish, which Golda decorated on top with grated horseradish and fanciful cut-outs of cooked beets and carrots, then—pastry pies filled with sauerkraut, then sour stuffed cabbage with grated potatoes, then Bavarian-style sausages, then fantastic layered tortes, sheet cakes, and strudels and pretzels, whose aromas completely filled the house and tickled the nostrils.

We also walked together to school, even though we weren't the same age, but we always kept together so that no troublemakers could cause us harm, and we all lived pretty close to each other. My mother and I and Mrs. Golda and Yosko on Klepariv Street, Mrs. Yadzia and Yas on Brayerivska Street, a floor below Dr. Lem's apartment, and Mrs. Rita and Wolff on Horodotska Street. We always met up at St. Anne's Cathedral, and with a wave, we went off wherever we wanted from there.

Of the four of us Yosko was the youngest in age and smallest in stature. Besides that, he was skinny, wore glasses, and carried a violin around with him. You can imagine the sight as he idly wandered with that violin that was almost bigger than he was. So, we took care of him, because everyone wanted to insult the little shrimp. If I caught sight of him somewhere on the street, and if he weren't my chum, I myself would've had the impulse to stretch out my hand, tear off his cap, and throw it on a branch. But he was our friend, and you wouldn't find quite a character like him. When we first started to try smoking, it was none other than Yosko who brought us cigarettes that he stole from his music teacher, though he didn't smoke and was a very obedient child. It was not for nothing Mrs. Golda would say: "My Yosko honey! He's a golden child! It's too bad his dad can't delight in him." Yosko's daddy was a pharmacist and was in charge of medications for the Ukrainian People's Republic army, that's why the neighbors called Mrs. Golda "Mrs. Doctor Lady,"[10] and she was very proud of that fact, and when we wanted to cozy up to her, we also used to say, "Mrs. Doctor Lady." She didn't rebuke us for our antics, but instead brought us the most delicious onion flatbread or salty ladyfingers with caraway seeds; even when we got into her washtub filled with clean sheets that she had just taken off the clothesline and were pretending we were sailing on a pirate ship, and she had to wash those sheets again.

Wolff was a hefty guy, two years older than me, as short and fat as he was tall, with such chubby, apple-red cheeks

10 In pre-Soviet Galician society, it was common for men to be called by the name of their profession such as pan profesor (mr. professor), pan doktor (mr. doctor), pan inzhener (mr. engineer). The wives would also share the same appellation as their husband but with the feminine form when appropriate: pani profesor (mrs. professor), pani doktor (mrs. doctor), or pani inzhener (mrs. engineer). Since they are not actual names, I am leaving them without capitalized letters.

that his ears were not visible, but on the other hand he was really strong. It was superfluous for him to demonstrate his strength; it was enough for him to come up when he saw that a fight was beginning and to gently snort and squint, then everything settled down immediately and everyone took off. Even older guys were cautious around him, but in his heart, he was good-natured and wouldn't even hurt a fly. He would often pick up a little sparrow that troublemakers had hit with a slingshot, blew at him, stroke him, and even bring him home to be nursed. We repeatedly made fun of him, asking whether he cries when he sips chicken broth, because a chicken is no worse than a little sparrow. In response Wolff laughed and patted himself on the stomach, repeating that all the chickens that he consumed were all there in his stomach, and there they are cozy, warm, and happy, and whoever doesn't believe it can put his ear to his stomach and listen to them happily cackling. We pressed our ears to his stomach and really heard some kind of clucking, similar to a chicken's, and Wolff laughed, and his belly twitched. Wolff was a master of all trades and knew how to make a sailboat and an airplane with a motor. During the winter he made tiny mangers, the kind with three kings and such a life-like tiny baby Jesus. A tiny donkey, a tiny ox, and a tiny horse lowered their heads. When Wolff pulled a string, the tiny baby Jesus waved his tiny arms and legs and whimpered "Be-ee!" Mrs. Rita said that it was a sin to mock the baby Jesus, but we couldn't understand what she meant, because what kind of mocking can be going on there. Because it was an infant, it couldn't preach the Word of God, so it says "Be-ee!" We went caroling with that tiny manger and to the Zamarstyniv and Lychakiv cemeteries and had incredible success everywhere. Even Yosko went with us, and although he didn't sing carols, he played along on his violin. We sang carols in three languages and even went to Vynnyky, which was a German settlement, and caroled for the Germans. They couldn't have been happier, because already just mostly older people were there, because their young people had gone to the fatherland, and there was no one to carol to them in their native language until we did. Oh-hhh, we stuffed our bellies there! They even gave us some for the road.

But Yas was a thin pole. He had long legs, long arms, and climbed trees like a monkey, and there wasn't any ditch that he couldn't jump across, so we were not surprised when he boasted that he had even jumped the Poltva River, though we had not seen that miraculous wonder. So, it was everybody's dream to be like Yas. When from time to time his mother locked him in the house so he wouldn't knock about and study his lessons instead, he would crawl out through the window. Yasko and I were hooked on adventure books and at first wanted to be pirates, then cowboys and Indians, but in the end, we would turn into a Kozak and a hussar and fought with swords like Bohun and Skrzetuski.[11] Our sabers were wooden, but all the same, sometimes we'd end up with injuries. In addition, we drew maps that indicated where buried treasure was and hid those maps in boxes and tossed them in someone's cellar and should anyone find it and realize it was a treasure map, they'd set off on a search. Though this was fun for us, we really did want to find some kind of treasure.

---

11 Ivan Bohun (d. 1664) was a Ukrainian Kozak, who fought with Bohdan Khmelnytsky against the Poles in the Polish Uprising. Jan Skrzetuski was a fictional character in Henryk Sienkiewicz's novel *With Fire and Sword*. Both characters appear in his novel.

As for me, I wasn't anything special. I was neither tall nor a shrimp, neither fat nor skinny. I inherited my father's long face and sharp eagle nose, and blue eyes in which girls would drown. We liked to walk around different winding lanes and narrow streets where houses were swaddled in drowsiness and wild grapes, and window sills blossomed in gillyflowers, nasturtiums, and lazy cats that basked in the sun. We liked to catch the scents that poured out from the kitchen windows, and to guess what they would be having for the midday meal there today. But we didn't love the circus and the zoo, even if it had come all the way from Warsaw. Once we went and saw an eagle in a cage who was sitting squinting and frowning on a dry branch. His eyes were so sad that it seemed like he was no longer alive, though he kept on living, but he didn't see any meaning in life. He was dying like an ember, and he looked as if he had been bespattered with white lime and was all pockmarked, but it was not lime. Tiny sparrows were sitting on top of his cage that had only bars and no roof, and they were crapping on him, gaily chirping and fluttering their wings. Evidently this pursuit provided unusual pleasure for them, and the eagle, resigned to his fate, only blinked his eyes sadly and sometimes just shifted his weight from one foot to the other. Looking at him, we wanted to cry, but we didn't. Instead at night we snuck into the zoo and quietly opened the cage door wide open, but the eagle didn't move. Then Yas took a stick and poked him. The eagle startled and looked at us, and then Yas kept poking the eagle, and he retreated to the edge of the branch, until he jumped down, but he would not leave the cage. Maybe his wings are clipped, Yosko said. Then I answered we'll take him away with us. And finally, Yas chased the eagle out of the cage. He jumped to the ground, looked around, fluttered his wings, as if he were shaking off all the sparrows' crap, and then soared up into the sky. The next day all the newspapers reported the news, and then from that time on the management of the menagerie had to hire better guards, instead of the old granddad, who dozed in the kiosk at the entrance.

As I'm writing this, it's spring outside, something disturbing can be sensed in the air, and I want this spring never to end....

2

In 1988, when Lviv was buzzing with meetings and different cultural societies were beginning to be set up, Yarosh suddenly felt the spirit of rebellion inside himself and rushed headlong into politics, but on the eve of the first democratic parliamentary elections he noticed a strange and unpredictable thing—the vast majority of candidates at all levels were narrow-minded people, poorly educated, and sometimes close to the all-powerful KGB, which had to have its cadres everywhere. It planted them even among the democrats. Dark creatures from the other world began swarming around the most prominent leader of Ukraine's independence movement, bizarre bastards, exiled by the KGB, for whom they conveniently remained to pull strings, reaching into all areas of the liberation movement. Various blockheads made their way to the top, who in everyday life couldn't string together a few clever words, but, after getting a hold of the podium, tossed out slogans at the heads of the masses starving for freedom. All these dropouts, primitives, and secret agents very quickly squeezed out those like Yarosh, leaving to them only the backyard of culture, which since then never rose above its beggarly condition. When Yarosh saw who began to run the show in this masquerade of a new life, he left politics and again focused on his research.

The two years he spent in the revolutionary struggle, writing pamphlets, speeches and newspaper articles, were not all in vain because his name became known. He was offered a teaching position in the Department of Oriental Studies, in a year he defended his candidate's thesis, and after five years received his doctorate. Hordes of students packed his fascinating lectures. His textbook and dictionary of the Arcanumian language, published in London, became a sensation in the scholarly world. Finally, the Arcanumian language's many mysteries were revealed, its cuneiform fully deciphered, and the world began to learn its still unknown history and literature to a much fuller extent. Then another sensation exploded: it became clear that the mysterious fifteenth-century Voynich manuscript, over which innumerable scholars struggled, could finally be read thanks to the Arcanumian language. Several times Yarosh traveled to international conferences, but soon realized that he could fritter away his entire life with this kind of travel and contacts, without ever managing to achieve his goals, and limited himself to sending articles. From time to time he allowed himself a discreet little romance, just to jettison some accumulated semen, but he never allowed anyone to get too close, having built between himself and the rest of the world an invisible wall. As soon as he felt his bed partner beginning to show a deeper interest in him and cooing something about her feelings, he either disappeared or took their relationship to such absurdity that she would dump him. The most important thing in all this was not to explain anything, not to elaborate, not to see any tears, and not to hear any complaints. Female students often tried to flirt with him, and although he could not help but admire youthful attractions, with all this strength Yarosh quelled his passion, fearing a flood of feelings that, drowning him, would take away precious time devoted to his research. However, he wound up in scandals twice. The first time was when the girl he dumped tried to commit suicide. First

Rusya wrote a wordy poem, in which she spoke about her feelings and about how hardhearted he was and laid it on the table in the kitchen. Then she carefully spread out wet towels under the door, turned on the gas on all four burners and in the oven, sat on the floor, popped open a bottle of Georgian wine, and began to drink. The alcohol and gas entered her slowly, and she wasn't in a rush, because she knew that her mother was just about to return from work. Her mother was a doctor and she's saved more than one little soul gone astray. It happened that way this time. They took Rusya, tipsy not so much from the gas as from the wine, to a psychiatric hospital. It turns out they take all the failed suicides there. In her medical history it was recorded that she attempted it because of an unhappy love affair, and only Yarosh could release her from the loony bin, taking responsibility for her. Yarosh had no desire to go there and couldn't understand why he should, they had nothing tying them to each other, what kind of responsibility could he take for her—marry her or something? He attentively read the farewell poem that Rusya's mother had given to him and saw that all this was just a game, for show. She tried hard to get him back, though he didn't give her any hopes, because it was just a purely physical thing between them. For Yarosh it was convenient to run over to her place during a break between lectures because Rusya lived near the university, and in return he involved her in a journal that he edited. While sitting at home she could earn decent money, a part of which was his own, given to her in the form of honoraria. What other than that could he do for her?

His visit to the historical institution called Kulpark, that had nothing in common neither with culture nor a park but was just a corruption of the German name Goldbergerhof, made a lasting impression on him. The hospital itself was located in picturesque surroundings, among trees and flowerbeds; ravens nested on the trees and loudly cawed. It had been two weeks since the attempt to end her life. The suicide greeted him with a joyful smile, as if nothing had happened, as if she were not a patient, but a nurse. Her smile was not even so much joyful as lustful. It seemed as if she were about to swallow him, sucked all over like a caramel candy. She looked fantastic; even though she was in a bathrobe, but she was carefully coiffed and made up. Rusya took him by the hand and led him upstairs to a dead-end hallway where there wasn't a living soul, then she leaned against him, and they came together in a long passionate kiss, during which her hand slipped into his pants. Yarosh tried to resist, not because he didn't want it, but that place terrified him. The voices of patients echoed below, there were screams, the clanking of the lunch cart, the clanking of pots and bowls, the scent of the hospital's soup, which always smells the same and which you never can cook at home. All this was not conducive to an amorous mood, but the girl decided by any means to get her satisfaction. She wanted to have him again. When she turned her back to him and lifted up her robe, saying only a few words to him: "I missed you. Let's do it," and under her robe she was completely naked, Yarosh dutifully fulfilled her desire. In less than three minutes Rusya began to moan and quiver, breathing heavily, then she deftly turned around, sat down and did what she always did, what he liked the most. She was ready to take him into her mouth anytime and anywhere, even in a bus. All this was happening behind a small window that looked out onto a park, where patients were walking in pajamas. From time to time doctors or nurses crossed the space, but Yarosh was calm, he knew it was impossible to be seen because of the sun's reflections on the window, and he also knew that what was happening was happening for the last time. He wouldn't be with her any longer, and he would probably never again meet another girl who would do it on the spot anytime or anywhere. This was still a farewell kiss, which he wanted to delay as long as possible, so he looked out the window at the trees, the crows' nests, the dog, running in the park. He looked without pangs of conscience, because she herself had ordered him: "Don't come!" This wasn't the first time she had organized this kind of marathon. Once, so he could distract himself and delay orgasm as long as possible, she gave him a volume of Marcel Proust and insisted he read it aloud, while she methodically kept pumping and pumping, expressing with her entire body, with all the sounds she was able to extract from her mouth, that she was doing this not so much for him, as for herself, that it was a thrill, as if she were under the influence of drugs, and Proust served the role of a kind of background for this penetrating playing of the flute. This time there was no Proust, and Yarosh, so as not to come too soon, shut his eyes and began to recite his translations of Arcanumian poetry to himself. He recited them softly, but the girl with her shouts of "yes" encouraged him, until he didn't have the strength to endure, and he released from himself everything that he had kept trying to restrain. She didn't tear herself away from him, didn't abandon him, but stopping her movements, just kept him inside her, in her hot lips, until he grew smaller and tumbled out. Yarosh felt like a drunken man, the world spun topsy-turvy, his head was buzzing, he felt like sitting down, though there was nowhere to sit. Rusya was tired. She leaned back against the wall and watched him triumphantly, as if she had been victorious in heavy gladiatorial combat. Her wet lips were moving as if she were sucking candy, swallowing saliva, her lips continued to move, savoring and swallowing, and then she stuck out her frolicsome little tongue and licked her lips slowly and seductively, as if she were provoking him for a second round. But there couldn't be a second round right away, and she understood this, so she stretched out her hand and guided him downstairs. In the lobby patients scurried about. Those who had "minor" issues, could move freely, go to the park, and watch TV. Yarosh had yet to meet with the physician in charge to sign a commitment that he would take care of Rusya. When he made his way to his office, a beautiful girl with luxurious blond hair intercepted him, the robe on her chest opened up, exposing her full breasts. A mysterious fire burned her eyes and she started to mumble: "You must help me. They are bullying me here—jabbing me with illegal drugs. Write about all this. We're all experimental guinea pigs here." While saying this, she pressed closer to Yarosh. Her hands were in the pockets of her robe, and with them she lifted up her hem, but Yarosh didn't have time to notice what kind of surprise was waiting for him because Rusya arrived just in time and pulled the girl away from him.

The chief physician questioned Yarosh for a long time, asking him what his relations were with the "sick woman," if he felt guilty over what happened, if he'd take care of her so as to prevent future recurrences. Yarosh agreed to everything in order to rid himself of all this as quickly as possible, then signed some papers, and only then did they let him go. The next day Rusya called and joyfully reported that she was at home and that he could visit her, adding: "You know, of course, what's waiting for you? I'm hungry and thirsty. If you don't feed me, I'll die." Yarosh didn't come, but she didn't stop calling. During every conversation with her it felt as if his member was standing at attention, and he barely restrained himself from dashing off to Rusya's. What's more, she spoke with him not in her usual manner, but in such a seductive, languid tone, as if she were lying in bed, luridly describing where was holding her left hand and what her middle finger was doing. But Yarosh understood that if once again he gave in to that temptation, it wouldn't be so easy to break out of it. Rusya was an excitable girl, she often had bouts of hysteria. She slapped him twice, and once even tried to pour boiling water on him. Yarosh barely managed to duck out of the way. Although after that dousing, as always, everything ended with passionate lovemaking right on the floor. But things could not continue this way any longer, and he chased away any thoughts about her. After that she made other phone calls, with threats to burn down his house, to douse him with acid, to go to the dean's office and tell the truth about him, accusing him of sexual perversion and creating a scandal for the whole university, "I'll stand in front of the university with a sign saying you're a dangerous sex maniac and a pervert." Yarosh was convinced that she was capable of this and, whenever he got closer to the university, he looked all around in fear to see if the angry fury was there with a sign. However, it passed. The threats were suspended in the air but never realized in life. Soon Rusya found herself another victim, true, though again among the faculty, and thus she didn't end up out of Yarosh's sight.

B

We didn't lack entertainment in childhood, any innocent morning could begin with sensational news. I remember one day we were eating breakfast with my mom. I was eating cream of wheat with raisins and honey, and mom—scrambled eggs with brisket. And suddenly:

"Mrs. Les! Mrs. Les!" I heard the voice of mrs. watchman,[12] who maintained Lviv's ancient tradition of calling women by their husband's first name, even if he happened to be deceased. Since my father Oleksandr was nicknamed Les, my mother's name thus came out as Mrs. Les. "Run as fast as you can to Sprecher's,"[13] Mrs. watchman puffed and panted. "Some darn nitwit just jumped off the roof onto the pavement."

"Yoy!" Mom cried out and began hurriedly to pile the brisket onto her bread to make a sandwich, which meant that in an instant she would be ready to fly out of the house. "What's happened to her?"

"This is whats! A potato pancake with brisket!" Mrs. watchman stuck her head into our window, gasping for air with each word, like a fish that had just been pulled out of a tub of water. "I've just come from there. I ran over especially so's to tell you and am running right back. So that brisket, did you smoke it before Easter?"

12 "Shimonova" in the original. According to Galician tradition she is called by the feminine form of her husband's profession in Ukrainian, a watchman or doorman. Her husband would be "shimon." Since these are not actual names, they are not capitalized in Vynnychuk's Ukrainian usage.

13 According to an author's note, Jonasz Sprecher was an architect in Lviv who in 1921 built one of the tallest buildings in the city at 8 Mickiewicz Square, which still stands to this day,

"That one-that one, you already tasted it. After all, I did give you a big chunk—half the length of me forearm, didn't I?"

"It was half the length, really?"

Mom wasn't listening but was quickly putting on a dress and looking for her shoes. Finally, my mom planted a wig on her head, with which she never stepped out of the house. She was never separated from it ever in public. But the wig was so tall that mom always had to be careful in the house, so she didn't hit the doorpost. Once I said, "Moms, why do you have such a tall wig, it's like a stork's nest," to which moms replied: "Shut your trap and don't yammer stupidly. I'm so short, I have to wear high heels or a tall wig. I choose the latter." And then we ran along Klepariv Street and mother kept shouting somewhere into the heavens:

"Golda! Golda! Golda!"

From the window on the opposite balcony Mrs. Golda stuck out her head in curlers:

"What's the hubbub?"

"We're runnin' fast as we can to Sprecher's, some nitwit jumped off the rooftop onto the pavement."

"Yoy! I'm already running!"

A moment later Mrs. Golda, holding Yosko's hand, is racing with them, she's completely disheveled with her head still in curlers, she even had different shoes on her feet—one red and the other white. Running along Horodotska Street mother kept screaming:

"Rita! Rita! Rita!"

And Golda on Brayerivska Street screamed out:

"Yadzia! Yadzia! Yadzia!"

When the disheveled heads of Yadzia and Rita popped

out of the windows, then mother and Golda informed them about the incredible news of what had happened near Sprecher's, and for a moment we heard the stamping of their feet, and not just Yadzia's and Rita's, but also Yasko's and Wolff's, for how could you have this kind of event without them: a jump from the Sprecher skyscraper without a parachute!

Not too long ago we had a fantastic spectacle when the Human Fly came to Lviv. That was in 1929. All the newspapers wrote about the famous acrobat-tightrope walker who was to cross over the roofs of stone buildings on a bicycle from the Hotel George to the Square of Academicians, and he planned on crossing the space between buildings on high wires. People gathered—masses of them, and there when the acrobat passed along the wire between two buildings at the beginning of Horunschyna Street. Then to the stormy applause of spectators, he jumped onto the roof of the stone building, where Mrs. Telychkova's famous bed and breakfast was located on the main floor, then slipped and fell onto the pavement and died on the spot. The roof turned out to have been wet after the rain. But Lviv wouldn't be Lviv, if a street ballad had not appeared after that:

An acrobat-fly had come to the city
He crawled onto Telychkova and let go his spirit.

Near Sprecher's so many onlookers had gathered that you couldn't elbow your way in, but mom hastily elbowed through the crowd, straining angrily through her teeth: "Medical Service! Medical Service! Medical Service!" and dragging me along, and Golda, Yadzia and Rita along with their little munchkins within a step of them, repeating those same magic words, and soon they saw it all sweetly right before their very eyes.

"Too late," my mother sighed while taking the sandwich out of her handbag. And she was right, because they already had covered the body with a sheet, out of which only a few thin streaks of blood could be seen.

"But when they'll be taking away the body, maybe they'll remove the sheet?" Mrs. Yadzia said hopefully.

"They never remove it," my mother said in the tone of a seasoned witness of countless suicides. "They think this way they'll spare our nerves. But in fact, I would be much calmer if I took a good look at everything.

"Oy, don't tell me about it," Golda sighed. "I'm completely numb."

"It's a pity that we don't have the kind of bridge they have in New York," said Rita. "They jump into the water there almost every day."

"The poor Poltva,"[14] mother sighed. "If they hadn't walled it off, we'd have something to look at."

Policemen kept order and waited for the orderlies to come from the morgue. Some man with a hat in his hand and a thoughtful mien lifted up his head, as if trying to measure the height of the building, and he was not reassured until some varmint-sparrow decorated his bald head with a playful splat. The man swore, took out a handkerchief, and began to wipe off his bald head.

"I wonder if it's a man or a woman," mom asked some merchant woman standing nearby.

"A girl," she replied and with a colorful scarf wiped the corner of her dry eye. "She's so young... They say over a tragic love."

---

14 The Poltva River now flows under the city of Lviv. It was paved over during the times of the Austro-Hungarian Empire because of the stench of sewage running through it.

"Come on! Such things still happen?

"It happens, it happens. He made a baby with her; then he dashed off to the army.

"I'd show him the army!" Mom shook her head. "Oh, I'd give it to him! I'd go to the staff headquarters, to the Minister of War, all the way to Pilsudski, but I wouldn't allow it. Nope, no way."

"For us something like this is impossible," said Golda. "Everyone would condemn such a man."

Meanwhile, orderlies arrived with stretchers, the whole crowd suddenly tensed up and moved forward. The policemen spread out their arms and shouted that no one should even dare to approach, but everyone waited for the orderlies to take off the sheet. Alas, it was in vain, because they carried the covered body to the car, and the throng sighed heavily with disappointment.

One other time my mother and I witnessed a suicide. It was on Copernicus Street. We noticed a strange man, who several times rushed out onto a balcony, looked down, disappeared, looked around, and again ran out.

"Oy, something must be happening here," my mom said.

And in a minute that man actually appeared with a rolled-up cord. He tied one end to the balustrade, and then, whistling, masterfully made a noose out of the cord.

"Is he going to hang himself?" I asked.

"It looks like it. But it won't be a particularly pleasant sight."

"Why?"

"Because the muscles relax and then everything in his stomach will come out of him, smelling terribly."

The man was moving very nervously, but at the same

time had as cheerful an expression as if he had won a hundred zlotys[15] in the lottery.

"In his place I wouldn't be so happy," mom said.

"But why?"

"Because that balcony is in its last days. I know that place well—mr. barber Pompka once lived there. Once the entire balustrade on his balcony collapsed. But in order to sell the home at a good price, he repaired the balcony in a slipshod way, and they made the balustrade from plaster. There's no metal rod there.

"Oh, so we have to tell that man," I became sincerely worried.

"Well, go ahead and try. Though I don't have faith in such young dandies. Give him advice, then he'll call you a fat toad.

"Pardon me, sir!" I shouted, cupping my hands around my mouth. "Wait a minute, don't rush. That balustrade is made of plaster, it won't hold you."

"What? Don't stick your nose into somebody else's business. You're a putz!"

"My son is telling the truth," mom interrupted. "Mr. barber Pompka bamboozled them and made a new balustrade out of plain plaster. But if you tie a rope to the iron lantern above your head, it will be much more secure."

"Shut your trap, you fat toad!" The man barked out angrily.

"Didn't I tell you so?" Momma sighed and with sincere sadness watched him throw the noose around his neck, shake his head back and forth, as if fitting it to his neck most comfortably, and jumped down. He had to fly a little longer

15 The main Polish currency,

than he expected, because the plaster didn't hold up and cracked. The balustrade crumbled, and the man slammed onto the pavement and broke both legs.

"See?" Momma sadly nodded her head. "Now you've got incredible trouble. You have to lie several months in the hospital and who knows, maybe for a lifetime walk with a limp. And if you had listened to me, right now you wouldn't be moaning and hissing in pain. Let's go, son. I can't look at these ungrateful sons of bitches. He thought he'd make life better for someone. And now his poor wife will suffer with him all his life instead of nicely burying him and getting married again.

3

A female student who later grew up to be a writer came to him and announced that he simply had to help her with her senior thesis; she didn't have a topic, she didn't like anything, and she desperately needed his help. Yarosh advised her to write on the works of émigré writer Emma Andiyevska. He had several books that the writer herself had given him. Nadya immediately jumped at the idea, took out a copybook, and began to write down the wise thoughts of mr. professor for her future thesis. At that time, it was turning to dusk. Yarosh suggested having a bite to eat. It just was roasted chicken, and of course it wasn't proper to eat meat without wine. They consumed two bottles of champagne and a bottle of wine with it. Nadya went to the tape player, turned on the music, and began smoothly and dreamily to move in some dance that only she knew. Yarosh didn't even notice how he ended up beside her, and they continued to move together, and then their lips met, and at that time when their bodies pressed much closer, his right hand lay on the girl's breast, and his left on her pliant bottom. It ended with both of them in bed, and because he was intoxicated, Yarosh couldn't reach orgasm for a long time, so Nadya did the same thing as Rusya, and Yarosh thought that fortune had smiled on him again—when something's lost, something else is gained. After this a period of passionate love ensued, which took place in the summer. Nadya lived at his place for weeks, until Yarosh learned something unpleasant. It happened when Rusya invited him to her birthday. He wasn't planning on going, but a colleague, her new beau, got mixed up in it and convinced him to go.

Yarosh may have made a mistake, or maybe not, in taking Nadya with him. In any case, thanks to this something was revealed that he could have learned too late, for example, if they had gotten married. At the party a pretty young girl stuck to him and didn't move a step away, and in the meantime Nadya danced with a man the same age as Yarosh. From time to time they went out on the balcony for a smoke and chatted up a storm without stopping. When it began to grow dark, Nadya said to Yarosh that she was feeling ill and was going home, and her new friend would walk her home because he lived nearby. Yarosh didn't see anything bad in this, and once they disappeared, the pretty girl suddenly detached herself from Yarosh and occupied herself with someone else. Yarosh suspected something strange but didn't attach great importance to it all. He got bored and went home. The next day Rusya called and said that she had planned everything at that party and urged her girlfriend to keep him occupied, and her male friend with Nadya. She advised Yarosh to ask her how she spent time.

"So, what?" He asked in as an indifferent tone as possible.

"She provided full service! That's how!" Rusya laughed with satisfaction. "Don't believe me? I know you don't. What about the mole on the right side of her stomach? It's a rather big mole, the size of a cherry. Once for such a little thing she could have been burned at the stake. The sign of the Devil! And a carefully shaved gorgeous pussy? Does this say something to you? Smooth just like a young girl. Just the kind you like.

"So where did they do it? On the street?"

"No, at his place."

Yarosh put down the receiver and felt rage boiling in him

but it was anger at himself for so stupidly being caught yesterday in a cleverly placed snare. A mole, a gorgeous shaved pussy... Nadya had spent the previous night at his place; last evening she asked to borrow his electric shaver, and then revealed her unique beauty, then they kept on making love... Yarosh fell asleep, his hand covering her smooth white bosom. He still felt the warmth of her skin on his fingers... But for someone to make such discoveries it wasn't absolutely necessarily to make love. Anywhere at the gate he simply could have pressed up to her and felt under her skirt. But when he called Nadya, no one picked up the receiver, though she had to have been home. He finally got through at three in the afternoon and heard her soft, barely recognizable sleepy voice. Of course, she was asleep. She felt so bad. She drank too much. Her beau stopped at a restaurant on the way home, and she got sloshed there.

"What were you doing at his house?" Yarosh said.

The girl remained silent. He repeated the question.

"I went to his place to call my parents to tell them I was coming home so that they would keep the door chain unlatched."

"What was the point in warning your parents when you were just one block from home?"

"I was drunk. I had to sober up."

"But you're not afraid to talk to them in a drunken voice. And when did you come home?"

"Sometime around one in the morning."

"And you slept until half past two in the afternoon? Somehow I never noticed your ability to sleep fourteen hours."

She remained silent. So, did he. After a minute Yarosh put down the receiver. It was painful for him, but time showed that he would have suffered even more disappointment if their relationship had continued because the stories about her love affairs that subsequently reached his ears showed the ease with which Nadya approached her intimate life, collecting lovers. Ten years passed since that time. She published several books and in one of them he recognized himself among the characters, and although there were many fabrications and outright female venom, the scene where they made love in a field among stalks of corn touched him. He remembered the way it was and even felt gratitude for the fact that she reminded him of those sweet moments. At the same time, he was surprised that she still couldn't forget him, trying to settle scores and placing signs in different parts of books, by which perspicacious readers might recognize whom it was about.

C

When two hats decorated with flowers and feathers meet in the middle of the market, it's a familiar and widespread event; a passerby would never pay attention to it, and until four hats converge together, oh-oh, then everyone looks at this scene, with a gaping mouth, and even tries to catch individual phrases, because the eyes under those hats seem to be on fire, and their female owners mutter without catching their breath, choking on words and impressions:

"Mrs. Golda, how do you do!"

"*Sehr gut*, *gut*, Mrs. Vlodzya. My elbow's been hurtin' me all day. And here's Mrs. Yadzia! Mrs. Yadzia, what're you buyin'? The cauliflower today's gots a crazy price!

"It's not the cauliflower gone crazy, but people. How's can you overcharge so much!"

"Mrs. Rita! You're here as well! How nice that we've all gotten together, no?"

"I bought two oxtails, a bunch of dill, and some parsley."

"Will you be making sour dill pickle soup?"

"I nearly bought spoiled carp. I ask the merchant woman if it's still alive, and she answers, "Yoy, ma'am, I don't know whether I'm alive in such difficult times, how should I know if the fish is alive?"—"And maybe," I say, "it croaked?"—"Ay, there's no way it croaked? It's sleeping"—"Sleeping? I smell something reeking from it." And she says: "Ay, Mrs., when you're asleep, do you keep good control over yourself?"

"Oh, get out of here!"

"I speak to her in Yiddish, and she to me the same, and she still lies right to my face! And my elbow is so sore!"

"Rub on some alcohol at night and wrap it in a washcloth. Who would have thought: a kilo of beef is already sixty cents! My neighbor, who has a postman husband, buys a kilo on Theodore Square for thirty cents, but such cuts, that only her husband can chew it."

"And a kilo of bread is fifteen cents!"

"And a darn egg is three cents!"

"Mrs. Rita! You have a super fashionable jacket."

"Ay, how's it fashionable? I repurposed it from old curtains. Do you see the tassels?"

"What will you be buying at the market?"

"Plums. My little guy asked for knoedels. With plums.

"Oy, we need to get together somewhere soon. So much news!"

"Only at my place!"

"Mrs. Vlodzya, we already met at your place the last time. I'll invite you over to my place."

"Oy, Mrs. Rita, why have that bother for you."

"I won't take no for an answer. I'll bake strudel."

"Well, then till we meet again."

And finally, the hats scattered in different directions and dissolved among the stalls of Rynok Square. There, too, everything is already bustling, buzzing, a downpour of voices splashing, spreading, turning into a multi-winged cacophony. And among all of it one could distinguish the voices of the women merchants, who can chide anyone and aren't afraid of anyone either. During the war they would snap at the Germans and the Russkies, for they were proud of their amazing gift—an extremely nimble tongue. It's been said that when a merchant woman stood between a windmill and grinding mill and began to yammer, the windmill stopped, and there was no more water in the grinding mill. But the old woman kept on talking and talking, and not a single merchant woman has died from tuberculosis thanks to this continuous training of their lungs. It wasn't for nothing that in the morning for breakfast she drank a quart of hot punch to strengthen her chest and to keep her voice from wearing out. I always admired those highly regarded women; most of them outlived their first husband and then were quickly married off to another one as if they were unspeakable beauties, although most were so corpulent that they walked like ducks on their elephantine legs, waddling from side to side. A fat puffy beet-colored face, weather-beaten and baked in the sun, extremely lively insightful eyes that could instantly assess any customer from head to toe, swollen hands with fleshy sausage fingers that deftly hide money between the two enormous balloons of her breasts. Whom could such a beauty attract? However, a widowed merchant woman wasn't seized with loneliness for too long, and the reason obviously lay in her industriousness, her ability to earn bread for both herself and her children. Here I listen to a squabble and hear a merchant woman sneering at some lady: "Look at her! Lo, here's a buyer for me. She's got a single zloty in her pocket and wants to buy the entire bazaar. Behold the lady from Busk Hollow! She's wide in the shoulders, narrow below!" And in the meantime, here's another: "Well, good woman, I have to pay for goods too, run around, present bills, defer, promise: tomorrow, tomorrow, but at some point, even I need to pay, no? And taxes? Who will pay them for me? Well, I'm a poor Jewish woman, I have a sickly husband and many *tsores*.[16] Do I lay those eggs or make the cheese myself? I'd have nothin' against it, but it's not the way it is."

16 The Yiddish word for "woes" or "troubles."

4

During this time his son Marko grew up and entered the university. Nowadays they saw each other more often, but usually his son would run to the department office to "borrow" a few hryvnias[17] and immediately disappeared. After all, this kind of relationship satisfied them both.

Inspired by research and the translation of Arcanumian texts, Yarosh ascertained that Arcanum had its own *Book of the Dead*, which was distinct from the Egyptian and Tibetan ones. True, it was not as well preserved and had significant lacunae, but several songs from that *Book* were striking in their exquisiteness. The ancient Arcanumians believed that every person has two souls, one mortal and another immortal, the latter of which migrates to another person. Songs from the *Book of the Dead* were performed not after death but before, that is, while the person is still alive, but is dying. These songs would facilitate the transition to the netherworld; what's more they would not only facilitate it but would serve as a guide, to lead the immortal soul of the deceased through all the ordeals of the afterlife and to return back to life. These songs were performed in a dance to the accompaniment of a tambourine and reed-pipes. In the Arcanumian language, the dance itself is called—oh miracle!—"Dan-go mrah," which painfully called to mind the familiar word "tango," which comes from the language of Ibibio Nigerian tribes. Here Yarosh remembered that Arcanumian kings in their campaigns of conquest repeatedly had penetrated deeply into Africa and reached Nigeria where the Ibibio tribe lived. Who borrowed these dances from whom

17 The main denomination of Ukrainian currency.

was not so important, but "dan-go mrah" literally meant "dance of death" or rather... "tango of death." Of course, this dance was not like the tango: each dancer danced separately without touching the other dancer but with his or her hands spread wide as if embracing someone—thus in this way each of them could perform the imaginary dance with the dying person's soul.

Suddenly he found yet another clue for his research in the *Book of the Dead* when his son said that he's dating a girl who's attending Yarosh's special course dedicated to ancient literature and is really interested in Arcanum. Yarosh immediately realized about whom he was speaking, because twenty to twenty-five students attended the special course at different times and one girl in particular stood out, not only for her beauty, but also for her determination. She had not missed a single class and later announced that she would defend her senior thesis on Arcanumian literature. The young lady's name was Danka. She was tall with a longish face framed by naturally dark brown hair, which was slightly curly and fell to her shoulders. She had a sharp aquiline nose that gave her a grand appearance, and when she strode with her long even legs, she held her back stiffly, and in her stride a certain majesty also manifested itself. Her voice did not appear to be overly feminine, it was deep and expressive without superfluous sweetness.

"You've probably noticed her," Marko said. "So, there's no need to introduce you, but I'd like you to get better acquainted. Do you mind if I bring her over on Saturday?" And when Yarosh shrugged his shoulders, he added: "She's so enthusiastic about your lectures that she's ready to retell them to me by heart for hours. Though I get very little of it. But it's good, different interests just serve to promote intimacy."

D

From my earliest childhood days, I perceived and soaked up Lviv by its smells; they are countless, and you can recognize the season by them without even leaving the house or looking out the window. Autumn keenly smelled of pickled cucumbers, flavored with fragrant dill, garlic, and horseradish. From the outskirts the melancholy scent of burnt potato stalks reached the city. The transition from autumn to winter was marked by the scent of sauerkraut. In winter just before Christmas Eve the scent of smoke filled the air, since almost all of Lviv smoked sausage, ham, fillets, and briskets, and in all the courtyards, even in the central part of the city, metal vats were installed with tin tubes leading up to them and a fire lit near their hole so that the smoke would go into the barrel and surround the meat, so it would just be smoked, and not cooked. It was the sacred duty of mr. watchman, who also had to get the firewood, chop it up, and arrange it in a pile, and then respected mrs. watchman, dressed in four skirts, four sweaters, and four scarves, sat on a little stool right by the fire and watched to make sure the fire did not go out nor that it get too big. When enough embers had already accumulated, mrs. watchman poured some of them into an old pot and pushed it between her feet and covered it with her skirts, so now she was so warm that she could even take a nap. The tenants of the building also brought her meat, which she smoked, and then from each she took a piece of ham or brisket. Right before the Christmas holidays it already smelled of fritters, fish and honey; in the Jewish quarter the scents of goose fat, fried onion, pepper, and "gryf"—bran cooked in the milk from an udder—were added. In the spring just before Easter the brisk scent of smoke and smoked meats again flew into the windows. Again, mr. watchman dug in a barrel, attached tubes to it, and chopped wood, and mrs. watchman carefully noted in her crumpled copybook all the meat that was brought to her, but this time she did not have to keep warm with a pot of embers, because even though it was still chilly before the holiday, the sun was shining brightly. Sparrows excitedly chirped on the trees, turtledoves cooed, and magpies screeched. Additionally, around Easter the scent of different baked goods, Easter breads, and fresh violets knocked on doors and windows; and in the summer, mushrooms and strawberries dried in the sun, which were sold right on the streets. And when summer was coming to an end, the entire city drowned in the heady aroma of preserves made of berries and hollyhock.

The city changed its demeanor beyond recognition during the day. At dawn, when it was still asleep, carts laden with vegetables rode into Rynok Square,[18] and other carts heavily rattled along cobblestones, distributing barrels of beer and various goods, and the bells of the trams started ringing, carriages began to jingle, brooms began to swish. After seven o'clock, grade school students walking to school began to appear on the streets. The city was now completely awake—shutters began to snap, blinds rattled on the stores' doors, windows were being opened, and then Lviv resounded with hundreds of voices, and those voices echoed in every direction. The pretzel sellers shouted: "Pretzels! Pretzels!" Used clothing sellers made their appeal: "Used

18 Ploshcha Rynok or Market Square is the central square of the old town of Lviv.

clothing, used clothing, used clothing, we sell and buy!" Metal repairmen—Hutsuls and Lemkos—wrapped in wires and with mousetraps, walked around shouting out: "We fix pots! Do you need something wired?" And the coopers: "Do you need something hand beaten?" And the sand sellers: "Sand needed? Anyone needs sand? Saaaaand!" And scrap sellers: Booones! Raaags!" At the Viennese Coffee Shop, at the hub of several tram lines, it was always really crowded—some people were waiting for the tram, others hurried off somewhere or were gaping. Next to the station, fire-roasted sunflower and pumpkin seeds were sold. Jewish women offered hot roasted chestnuts, Turkish and English walnuts in bags made of rolled up newspaper. In the same spot they baked the chestnuts on a tin sheet with depressions and little holes, beneath which there was a metal box with smoldering coals, and on the top, it was covered with a second tin lid. The Jewish women yelled out: "Heisse Maroni[19]! Gebratene![20] Frische![21]," and those who were selling hot bean fritters: "Heisse bobele!" Pretzel makers carried big baskets hanging on straps of fresh fragrant pretzels, strung on sticks that stuck out of baskets. Some pretzels were sprinkled with poppy seeds, others with salt, but the most famous ones were the "May" pretzels—golden, crispy, filled with meat and cabbage and densely covered with poppy seeds. They melted in your mouth. Jewish men also sold pretzels, shouting "Egg Pretzels!" And when they passed by some Ukrainian groups, their bad command of Ukrainian elicited roaring laughter from the customers: "Pretzels on an egg! Pretzels on an egg!" We loved to tease them and

19 Hot chestnuts in German.
20 Roasted in German.
21 Fresh in Yiddish.

also shouted back: "Pretzels on an egg! Pretzels on an egg!" or "Eggs on a Pretzel! Eggs on a Pretzel." Old mustachioed villagers from Korchiv in the Pidliasshya region carried baskets of onions right on their heads on top of sheepskin hats. Garlands of onions hung from a basket and from the old man's shoulders, falling on his chest and shoulders. The way they hung from his belt made the old man look like a fairytale creature in golden garlands. His exotic appearance aroused both delight and fear at the same time among young children who accompanied him yelling "Onion man! Onion man!" and who instantly scattered in every direction as soon as the old man began to stare at them angrily. "The Onion Man will come get you and take you away," mothers used to say to scare their naughty children, and many times my mother pointed to the Onion Man from our window, saying he could turn a rambunctious kid into a garland of onions. And when she bought onions from the Onion Man, she hung a garland in the kitchen on the wall. I looked at it with fear, wondering who the naughty boy was who had turned into the onions, and whether blood would gush from the bulbs if you bit it. So I didn't eat those onions raw and asked my mother not to do anything with them, because what if the magic spell could be broken at any moment and the garland of onions again became a little boy, but then he'd be a cripple—without legs or arms, without an eye or without an ear. In any case, his mutilation would be on our conscience, but my mother didn't listen to me and boldly sliced up the onion for a salad. Potters in clanking garlands of pots and pitchers, cried out "Earthenware pots! Pans! Skillets! Wire binding! Repairs!" Brush makers sold various brushes; straw makers—straw and reed mats that ladies of the house set out on their thresholds; sieve-makers sold sieves and since this particular product was light, the sieve-maker hung sieves and strainers all over himself, so that it was almost impossible to see him. Poultry sellers carried birds in cages on long sticks. Coal sellers transported their coal on carts, shouting out: "Coooooal! Coooooal!" Water haulers every morning transported water in troughs; and mail was delivered by the postman's covered yellow carriage, which always played the same tune on a curved horn. The iceman announced his appearance with a bell; upon hearing it all the maids and ladies of the house ran out with flat tubs and troughs, into which the iceman placed cut pieces of ice; the sand carrier brought sand, shouting out "Saaand! Saaand!," which the ladies of the house used for scouring the pots and for strewing on the floors and stairs for them to dry faster.

We loved to run to Rynok Square to look at the black-hatted Hutsuls, in coarse linen trousers tied up with belts and linen shirts, densely embroidered with small red and black crosses. They sold bowls, goblets and jugs made of clay, wood or copper, handbags, leather belts and shoes, colorful toys, Hutsul kilims, cloth shoulder bags, wood office supplies, ink, and frames signed with the names of localities—Skole, Kosiv, and Zhabye. The Boykos had long mustaches and a mandatory curved pipe in their teeth and sold apples, pears, dried Bosnian plums, walnuts and hazelnuts, chestnuts. The Boykos sold all this cheaper to children so our mothers sent us to the Boykos, and we were just happy because the Boykos also gave us tastes of their most delicious goods. The old merchant woman Valakhonyova, as broad as a barrel, sold blood sausage, glistening from fat in a big pot sitting on charcoal. She stirred it with a ladle and hollered, "Extra bombshell fricassee! Braised kishka!" And the portions were so big that when you ate them, you wouldn't need to eat again till evening. For that reason, the representatives of such respected professions as butchers, loaders or drivers considered it a great honor to be among the steady clientele of old loudmouthed Valakhonova, although on the streets of Lviv you could buy not only blood sausages, but also patés, gingerbread, fried sausage, polenta, Kulykiv[22] bread, crusty Kaiser rolls, and salty bread sticks.

Every Saturday loud reverberations like gunshots rolled through the entire city, though no one was shooting; it was the ladies of the house beating the dust out of carpets, runners, quilts, and pillows that were hung outside on railings. Once a month the kitchen turned into Africa—it was the Great Laundry Day, when the laundress became queen of the kitchen. In general, doing the laundry took an entire week: they would boil on Monday, starch on Tuesday, dry on Wednesday, darn on Thursday, and iron on Friday. On the eve of Great Laundry Day, in the evening they would push together two large kitchen tables, onto which they placed a huge tin vat and into which they poured hot water with liquid soap. In it they soaked bedding, towels and nightshirts. In the morning, when the laundress, a robust girl with coarse hands and feet, came to us. Then tropical temperatures overtook the kitchen, steam swirled from floor to ceiling, the windows were covered with mist, it was impossible to see anything through them, but on the other hand it was convenient to draw various faces on them. The fire in the stove became red hot, and two big vats stood on its burners.

22 The village of Kulykiv in the Zhovkva region is approximately twelve kilometers from Lviv.

The laundress took Shikhta factory soap, put her wash on the "washer" or "washboard"—a wide board made of corrugated tin in a wooden frame—soaped it up and went from top to bottom across the furrows—shur-shur-shur! It soon foamed in the vat from the soaping, and I couldn't resist grabbing an entire handful to enjoy the fluffy weightless ball that shimmered with the colors of the rainbow and winked at me with tiny little eyes. But soon everyone who remained there for more than a few minutes began to be bathed in sweat, because after the first wash they took out the clothing and boiled it in large pots. The stifling air finally chased me out of the kitchen. And I loved to watch as they added bluing in small muslin bags to the water. The water becomes a bright cobalt color, but the wash doesn't become azure blue, but even whiter after this bluing. The bluing dissolved in the water in small clouds that stretched in thin fibers and feelers, resembling a monster with countless long thin legs. Blood ran and dissolved in water in the same way, when you place a cut finger into it. It was no wonder that the clouds in the sky seemed to me, a little guy, like featherbeds that swam in the dissolved bluing. The starch was viscous and sticky. It made the water thicker, sheets rinsed in it crackled, starched shirts were made rigid and were ironed while still wet, and then the gluten burned by the iron smelled of burnt cookies. Heavy irons were filled with hot coals. We had to make sure that they didn't leave strips of soot. The coal had to be a special kind—made of wood and well burnt, because the iron would smoke from unburnt coal, and then my mom would complain of a headache.

During the warm months when Sunday came, all the windows on all the city streets would be opened up, virtually all the windows, and people would lean out of the windows, mostly curious women, old and young, leaning their elbows on pillows. Some shouted out, others silently observed passersby, others waited for what would not come, and a smile played on everyone's lips. Whoever had a balcony would sit on it and also smiled and looked at passersby, and everyone felt like one big family. Strangers could even speak to strangers without any unnecessarily polite mannerisms; it seemed as if they had known each other for years, because not only the people but also the entire city was smiling and joyful.

But Lviv appeared the most attractive during the evening when the streetlamps were lit up, when bright neon signs and ads blinked, when shop windows were lit, and when music wafted from the restaurants and coffee shops. Then the hundred-meter distance from Hotel George to the end of Academician Street was crowded with people, beginning at six in the evening and continuing until after nine—ladies in hats, gentlemen in black bowlers, military men in uniforms, students in school hats. In fact, rendezvous often took place here and they all walked back and forth, from time to time running into friends, tipping their hats, stopping to say a few words, or even gathering in a larger company to go to a restaurant. Along that hundred-meter promenade you could meet all of your friends, and it was like this every night, except for Sunday, when hordes of people came out after Mass at noon to promenade. After strolling on the right side of Academician Street, the throng immediately returned on the left side and crossed to the right side again and repeated the same walk several times, and then scattered among the coffee houses and confectionery stores. If you found yourself among this crowd you were floating slowly as if caught up in the flow with everyone else, without increasing your speed or slowing down your gait, and you felt quite comfortable. Only on occasion did this human current form small traffic jams: parents and children always stopped at Klyaften's shop window with children's toys. You couldn't help but stop when there was a real battle going on in the store window, miniature soldiers were preparing for an attack, cannoneers froze near the cannons, generals examined the battlefield with binoculars. Also, passing Khorunschyna's, you didn't have the strength to stay away from Mrs. Telychkova's Tavern and not pick up a few delicious sandwiches to snack on; and farther along, Zalewski's confectionery store's fabulous shop window—where you could see a miniature confectionery store—awaited the people who were strolling. Tiny dolls in white robes performed their important work. One was mixing dough, a second one rolled out the dough, a third one poured something into a pot, a fourth one grated something in a small clay pot, a fifth one was putting the dough on a baking peel into the oven. They were all moving, powered by an electric motor. Right before Christmas and Easter the store display window changed. It became a holiday table with chocolate and marzipan products that looked like holiday dishes—Easter breads, dyed Easter eggs, ham and entire piglets. There were also bunnies and baby rams in baskets decorated with fresh periwinkle. And the tiny little tables were adorned with tiny little bottles of liqueur with tiny little glasses tied to their long necks. Those windows were changed so often that every child's little heart was drawn to them as soon as they found themselves on the hundred-meter promenade. But after nine o'clock, the streets began to empty and everybody hurried home because at ten p.m. the watchmen locked the entrance gate to the buildings, and later to enter the building, you had to ring the bell and pay the watchman a tip of 25 or 50 groszen[23] for the service.

I used to love going with my mother to the Krakidaly Bazaar[24]—a wonderful world that began behind the Opera House and attracted people to it just by its name, in which there lurked a great mystery because crocodiles would immediately swim into your imagination, though there were no crocodiles there. It was just a strange corruption of the name of the Krakow suburb, where bazaar passions seethed and the flea market, or, as Jews called it, the Tandmark, whirled. Perhaps the Near East's legendary bazaars look the same: shops were located around the square and in front of them and everywhere you cast your eye, there were booths with various goods, especially clothes and shoes. Krakidaly truly was a Jewish dominion; here you could see dignified gentlemen and gentlewomen, well-dressed in the European manner, and bearded Hassidim with long sidelocks in black full-length robes and hats, and Jewish women who, having pulled various grease-spotted duds on themselves, resembled cabbage. In the middle of these tightly-crowded countless booths, myriad sellers and crooks loudly praised their wares, and among all this there were little smoking stoves on wheels with simple snacks steaming on them. Most importantly—you also need to remember that just as in the bazaars of Istanbul, Tangiers, Marrakech or Cairo, you can and even must haggle to bring down the price starting at

23 The Polish unit of currency in coin form. One hundred groszen comprise a zloty,

24 The local nickname for the bazaar, which historically was located on Krakivska (Krakow) Square behind the Lviv Opera House.

half. Next to the Jewish commercial traders, Ukrainian and Poles bustle about. Everything is in constant motion, and a loud cacophony of sounds drones in the air.

Here some cunning con artist shows a bottle of vodka with water and the figure of a quite large diver inside it, though he obviously couldn't have crawled in there through the neck of the bottle, so the con artist asks: "How is it that he got through this thin bottleneck?" And looking over the crowd, explains: "It be done like this. To's the bottle ya needs to put in the thin shkeleton of the diver. And then you sprinkles in some magic powder. Then the water becomes white like milk. Then place it on a cabinet first, and then after an hour the water's again clean and clear. And there you have it! And then everyone's can see how such a fat diver crawls through such a narrow neck." The crowd around him grows and the shyster finishes with his last claim: "It's not a toy, please ladies and gentlemen! Nooo—children shouldn't play with it, it's an indispensable thing for the household. Cause that diver shines all day like a star, and at night is lit up so's you can read newspapers next to it, embroider, and even eat dinner. And what's do ya think? How much does this kind of happiness cost? You won't believe it! This peachy birthday present or wedding present costs just twenty groszen! And twenty groszen—that ain't real money, no?" He surveys the gathered crowd again and in a moment goes on from where he began: "How is it that he got through this thin bottleneck?"

But for us elementary and gymnasium students, Krakidaly was valuable for the fact that at book stalls, besides books and school textbooks, you could buy "bryky" [plot summaries]—various booklets with translations of Latin and Greek texts and abridged synopses of classical novels that freed us from having to read a work. The "bryky" were strictly prohibited by the school authorities, not only for bringing them to school, but even for reading them at home. Although they made a pupil's life easier, they devalued independent study of the classical languages. However, after looking around really well to see whether or not some teacher was nearby, we often visited the booth of pock-marked Nukhym, who loved lads like us, and for a purchased "bryk" always added some useless thing with it—an old worn detective story or an illustration of a battle with the Boers, torn from somewhere—that we could throw away later. We always had to accept this gift with feigned gratitude, because it guaranteed us favorable treatment in the future. And there we bought the works of Karl May about Winnetou, Old Shurehand and Shatterhand, passing them from hand to hand, hiding them in class under tables. Karl May was the best of all the writers of adventure stories because his works awakened and captured our imagination.

5

Outside it was still a warm autumn, crows were flapping around in the trees of Kleparivsky Park, shaking off the morning dew. Old Josef Milker was standing there, leaning on the windowsill and absorbing that gloomy, unfriendly landscape with his eyes, as if he were trying to take pictures of it. But in reality, he admired that location, which for him was unbelievably dear. His childhood and adolescence took place there. Hytsel's Mountain[25] witnessed so many events, all these trees with crows, they were there even then... when Jews from Klepariv were expelled from their homes and forced to resettle in Zamarstyniv, because the ghetto had the very same character as sharkskin, and then he so longed for this landscape, for the elms, maples and ash trees whose branches were full of ravens' nests and mistletoe, because from the windows of his new dwelling he saw only a railway bridge, where from time to time military and freight trains rattled past. It was called the Bridge of Death because there was a barrier and a sentry standing in front of it, like at the gates to hell. They let some out and allowed others to enter, and sent off some to unknown places, to the mysterious sands in Lysynetsky Forest. But there, on Hytsel's Mountain mistletoe bloomed, not in the spring, but in February when there was still snow. And it was right then that he felt in exile, how dear the mistletoe

25 *Hytsel'* (Gizel) means dog-catcher and comprises the origin of the name of the mountain. Dog-catching was a dishonorable profession since the times of the Austro-Hungarian Empire because dog-catchers would often cruelly kill the cats and dogs by skinning or strangling them. Thanks to Olha Tytarenko for bringing this to my attention.

was to him, that its pale pink blossoms were missing there in the strange house, where six of them had to huddle together in one bedroom, trembling from every roar, from the loud stomping of feet, from the sounds of the detachment of soldiers, from the clicking of triggers. But the shots... the shots no longer scared them so much, the shots were heard in the distance, they all got used to the shots... even when they were in the Yaniv concentration camp. The tape of memories then broke off, black unintelligible frames began to flicker, and Milker already saw himself again in his native Klepariv, in his parents' house. Many things had disappeared in the time he was absent. The Germans took something, the liberators something else, and his neighbors yet something else, but some things remained. Nobody wanted the old furniture, and under the cupboard beneath the floor he had managed to hide the most valuable things—a violin and albums with photos. Milker often looked at these photos, which depicted his entire large family, his friends, his beloved girlfriend; all of them died a long time ago, but he still remembers their voices and with his eyes shut, he can recreate them. That's his mother calling from the window: "Yossel! Yossel! Come home now! Your teacher's arrived!" Oh, how could one forget Mr. Katsenelenbogen with his jarring and guttural voice? He's all in black, like a raven, his long skinny arms seem as if at any moment they'll flap in the air, and he'll fly off, and from above will start beating secret knowledge into unlucky Yossel's head with his beak. And here's his sister Leah and Ruta,[26] his girl, they're collecting flowers in the Kaiserwald and are bursting into resounding contagious laughter, which it was impossible not

26 The Ukrainian version of the name Ruth.

to give in to. And there, his friends were having a picnic on a burlap blanket and it seems that even the smell of roasted meat on a spit is wafting from the pictures... Beneath the floor he managed to hide the china, and most importantly—a cup in the form of a plump chubby little boy. He used to drink milk from it as a child, but he no longer drinks anything from it, and the cup sits behind glass in an old credenza. He associates it with his deceased mother, who used to pour warm milk into the cup, adding a spoonful of honey, and would bring it to him every night, and when he was ill, added both butter and baking soda to the milk. He'd screw up his face, but he drank it, and now when he was looking at that cup, it seemed that childhood was still living in him, and when he closes his eyes, he hears the voices of his friends who call him to go outside and play ball.

He lived modestly, giving private music lessons. He had enough money to live, but Milker was a booklover. He maintained relationships with second-hand booksellers from Kyiv, Moscow, and Vilnius, and since he didn't have enough money to buy old books, he also engaged in speculation, as they called it then, because he visited illegal book bazaars monitored by the police. That's why because of conspiracies in the 1970s-1980s they had to frequently change the booklovers' gathering place. When the police conducted a raid, everyone ran instantly, sometimes even leaving the books behind. One time they actually gathered on Hytsel's Mountain around a monument to executed Polish insurgents. Milker recalled how during the winter the police rushed up the mountain from every direction; everyone took to their heels, slipping on the snow that children had sledded on. Some fell and rolled down. The books scattered in every direction, but Milker didn't lose his wits. Sitting on top of a bag full of books, he rode on it like a sleigh. Spreading their hands wide, the policemen tried to catch him, but he dashed past them like a whirlwind, stopping just outside his gate.

Yes, he had many memories of Hytsel's Mountain, because there, at the very crest of it, he first kissed Ruta for real, not on the cheek the way they had kissed before. And he also remembered a legend that he heard from his grandmother about the origin of the name of the mountain. For it's there, right near Hytsel's Mountain in a mountain ravine completely overgrown with elderberry, that a really cruel dog-catcher lived in a clay hut, who would catch dogs and cats and tear off their skins. And once he caught Mrs. Budyonovka's favorite cat and was about to kill it, when suddenly right before him a woman appeared in a green dress with loose green hair. She grew incredibly angry at the dog-catcher, snatched the kitty from his hands, and in a single instant the slopes of the ravine closed together, forever burying the dog-catcher and his hut. Since then sometimes at night at the foot of Hytslev's Mountain it was as if you could hear the desperate cries of the skinflint and the barking dogs. Milker smiled, remembering how many times he tried to listen attentively, but only from a distance, because all the children were wary of that mountain in the evening.

He so loved Ruta that after the war he couldn't venture into a new passion. Ruta stood before his eyes. He was convinced she would appear any day, and he must wait for her, like Leah, as many waited for those whom fate had separated. He turned ninety before you knew it, and the memories now were the only thing that warmed him. To live at that age isn't easy when you've completely lost your entire family and friends, and even those who were younger than you and who could have been your sons and daughters, but their voices still continue to resonate in memory, and their traces still live on individual objects. And there are still books, cabinets full of books, and among them there are still unread ones; looking at them, he joked to himself, "Well then, I'll read you and then die." Besides the unread books were also ones that had been read that he wanted to reread, so the number of unread books decreased very slowly.

The old man walked away from the window, took a bottle of water that sat overnight and began to water the potted plants. There were many flowers, and the flowers were unusual; rarely did anyone cut them for bouquets, because they lose their bloom too quickly, and no one had heard of them being potted in homes, but it didn't matter to the master of the house. He not only watered them, but also continually talked to them, and he would even kiss one flower with his dry lips and gently wink at it, as if he were wooing and trying to seduce it, and the flowers answered with a coquettish trembling of petals.

It was still very early in the morning, and the old man steamed himself some green tea, cut himself a slice of rye bread, placed a slice of farmer's cheese on it, slightly salted it and had breakfast. He had been doing this for many years. He deliberately went to the Krakow Market to the same saleswoman for cheese twice a week, sometimes buying sour cream from her too. Then he made a salad for himself with cheese, sour cream and finely chopped greens and onions. For lunch he ate vegetable soup and then potatoes or buckwheat kasha with salad. He ate meat just once a week.

Milker wasn't planning on dying. He regularly drank beet kvass and Hawthorn berry tea for his blood pressure. He felt quite all right. He had a definite goal that tenaciously kept him alive and would not release him to the other world.

E

I used to love to go with my mother to the Atlas Restaurant at Rynok Square where a very interesting public gathered, all of Lviv's bohemians—writers, painters, musicians, actors... They gave great concerts and improvisations, which were spontaneous but were expected by everyone. My mother and I used to sit in the corner sipping tea and just watched and listened to everything that was happening. No, we were in no way embarrassed in front of all those celebrities. And why would we be embarrassed, because my mother was also an artistic person, she often liked to say "we, artists" because no one better than my mother was able to come up with poetic greetings for birthdays or weddings. And that's not all—my mother also thought up wonderful epitaphs for gravestones, true masterpieces that would leave no one indifferent.

Sleep, dear grandpa, and don't worry,
We'll lie down with you but not in a hurry.

Or one like this:

Dear grannie, under the weeping willow
You've found your own eternal pillow.

Mom would create these poems in three languages—Ukrainian, Polish and German—depending on who ordered them, and when it was necessary to resort to Yiddish, then Golda would come to her aid, and they would make up rhymes together. I was proud when I could read in several of Lviv's newspapers: "I make up verse greetings and gravestone inscriptions in all languages. Please contact me by telephone... Ask for Mrs. Vlodzya." You might think that such an announcement might seem too impertinent—"in all languages!" But there was never a case that someone asked us for a poem in a language other than the four mentioned above. And my mother had incredible acting talent, to tell you the truth. There was the promise of a great future for her, although she played just one role, depicting the fourth deadly sin in church. However, she decided just to focus on one thing and chose poetry.

Generally, the cemetery united Mrs. Golda and my mother not only through the gravestone poems, but also by the fact that Mrs. Golda spoke with the dead. What's there to say—inhabitants of Lviv liked to go to the cemetery, chat a bit with their dearly departed, some in their minds and some out loud. But this contact was one-sided, though there seemed to have been exceptions since one could often see some granny, moving her lips and nodding her head, as though she were agreeing with what she had heard. The majority of the living, however, although they spoke to the dead, telling them the latest news, didn't hear what the deceased would say in response. Golda was an exception—she heard voices from the other world. Her clients were mostly widows or inconsolable mothers. They all would come to her home, and Golda, falling into a trance, would inform them of something that would drive out their despair and tears, and their sorrow would become less unbearable, and the poor women would leave her with a light heart. Golda would take special customers to the cemetery and would speak with the departed directly, bending her ear to their grave.

"What-what is he saying?" A despairing widow would ask her.

"He says that it's difficult for him to lie there, because he doesn't feel your grief."

"Yoy! This is nonsense! I was flattened like matzo bread! It's not enough that he nagged me all my life, he's even doing it after death!"

"He said it'd be easier on him if you'd chip out some nice gravestone inscription that would display your grief."

"Really? He said that? Ah *gut*! I'll do that. But what inscription?"

"I'll give you the address of a certain Mrs. Vlodzya. She'll advise you."

Yes, my momma worked in tandem with Golda, and not only was Golda useful to my mother, but my mother, completing an order for another epitaph, helped her interests:

"Wouldn't you want to talk with your husband?"

"How?" The widow became frightened.

"Yes, live. Through a medium."

"Oy, that's surely a sin!"

"Why would it be a sin? Didn't Jesus talk to the dead? I'll give you the address of a certain Mrs. Golda. You'll even thank me and keep thankin' me."

And though besides holding séances, Golda also told fortunes with Tarot cards, by reading coffee grinds, and by rabbit bones, which she called the bones of St. Martseliy, all the same, her conversations with the dead were the most popular.

Inasmuch as my mother and I considered ourselves creative people, we eagerly hung around bohemian circles, and although the bohemians didn't hang around in our circles, it didn't stop us. In the afternoon my mother and I visited the "De la Paix," nicknamed "De la Payes,"[27] because during the day Jews gathered in the restaurant in their dark black frock

27 "Payes" is the word for the sidelocks that many Orthodox Jewish men wear.

coats and hats and gave advice about great matters. Maybe they didn't just sell wood or corn, but also ran the world, decided the fate of the US president and the Japanese emperor. From the moment they left, the waiters opened all the windows and balconies wide and aired out the strong odor of onions and garlic, which hounded Jews from the moment of birth to their last moment on earth, hovering above them like an insidious evil spirit that with its inexorable presence pointed its finger at them, announcing to everyone: "This is a Jew!" In the afternoon the bohemian crowd converged and played the piano. When my mother and I dropped by, you had to see my mother putting on airs, majestically wearing her wig and thrusting out her breasts as if she had a pole up her butt, because she belonged to those women who in the evening look like they're twenty-six but in the morning they're forty. I didn't look too bad either, because my mom foresightedly tied a colorful scarf around my neck so that it was evident I was a poet, painter, or a musician. Mom nodded first at one guy, then at another who was sitting at a table, explaining to me that it was—Syasyo Lyudkevych[28] himself, a prominent composer, and there—the writer and artist Edzio Kozak.[29] And the brothers Kurdydyk, thin as rails, who packed all the periodicals of Lviv with their ditties, were hanging around with them. When momma finally floated out like a sailing ship to the middle of the room, each time she hooted: "Servus,[30] Syasyo!" Then Mr. Lyudkevych leaned over to Edzio Kozak and asked him who she

28 The Ukrainian composer Stanislav Lyudkevych (1879-1979). [author's note]
29 The artist, humorist, and caricaturist Edvard Kozak (1842-1992). [author's note]
30 A typical Galician greeting to friends from pre-Soviet times.

was. Learning that she was some kind of crazy woman who writes ditties for gravestones, nodded his head, and again immersed himself in the symphony that was reverberating in his head.

When in the evenings we happened to visit the Atlas at Rynok Square, mom would also behave there as if she was the one for whom they were waiting. I even imagine at that moment she heard cries of delight, air kisses, and welcome speeches, because, walking, no—not walking, but floating—she briefly but rather regally bowed to the left and to the right, and she greeted some people so that the entire dining room could hear. "Kornel sweetie, how do you do?," she hollered to Kornel Makuszyński,[31] who a few days ago had entertained the entire public with the fact that, after flying into the tavern and kissing the hands of the ladies, he even kissed the tiny, dry, wrinkled hand of the aged bathroom attendant. To Genio Zbierzchowski,[32] who was sitting near the piano with a glass of wine and a cigarette in his mouth, she tossed out: "Genio, get serious—your mug is the face of Lwów,[33]" the stunned Genio leaned over to Kornel and asked: "Who is that elegant lady who greeted me so unceremoniously?" And Kornel explained, "she's some crazy lady who writes gravestone poetry." One time, when a film actor had come to Lviv—and what an actor he was—the star Mieczysław Cybulski!,[34] an enormous crowd of overexcited young ladies who dreamt of getting an autograph gathered right in front of the restaurant. Then Mr. Edzio Tarlerski,

31 The Polish prose writer and poet (1884-1953). [author's note]

32 Henryk Zbierzchowski. Polish poet, prose writer, and dramatist (1881-1942). [author's note]

33 The Polish spelling of Lviv.

34 Polish actor who often played the role of a leading man (1903-1984). [author's note]

the owner of the Atlas Restaurant, said: "Do you know what just happened? They just peed in their pants from excitement. I'm not exaggerating—I saw the stains on the sidewalk!" But my mother didn't even have to stand in line for that autograph. With one hand she pushed aside the waiter who was standing at the door maintaining order. She went inside and, paying no attention to anyone else, walked right up to the table at which the famous actor was having his midday meal, and then she looked at him coquettishly and said, "Miechik, sweetie! My you're quite a rascal! How you beguiled that Countess! May lightnin' strike you! Just slap down a few words for me on your photo!" Still in shock, his mouth full of hunter's bigos, Miechik gave her his autograph. When he managed to swallow what he had been chewing, he asked her, "Lady, do I know you?" My mother's ship filled her sails and, leaving the port named Cybulski, spit out in farewell: "Don't trouble yourself, Miechik sweetie! I've forgiven you for that night!" Countless surprised looks flew at her, but of course, the strangest was the look of the actor himself, because his painful attempts to recollect "that night" were not crowned with success; instead they spoiled his appetite and caused him anxiety and uncertainty about all the subsequent nights, for which he could still be forgiven, or perhaps not.

In the Shkotsky Tavern[35] of course mother had to bother Professor Stefan Banach,[36] a leading mathematician, though my mother and I had the same relationship to mathematics as frogs to bird migration. But it was impossible to deter my

35 The Scottish Tavern, which was known as a meeting place for famous mathematicians. [author's note]
36 A mathematical genius and professor (1892-1945) [author's note].

momma when passing by the table where university professors solved mathematical problems every day. She shouted: "Stefan sweetie! Oh, what a real rascal you are! Were ya partying all night again? What bags you have under your eyes!" And then she said to Stanislaw Ulam,[37] "Stas! Hide your claws! Auntie Bandzyukhova's[38] greeting you!" Then Stefan Banach leaned over to Stas Ulyam and wondered who the crazy lady was, and Stas nodded back to him that he wasn't mistaken, it was indeed precisely that crazy lady who writes gravestone ditties, and that's how she got her looniness. But no, my mother was not a crazy lady, she just liked to laugh and loudly to demonstrate her involvement with the bohemians. Although the bohemians never accepted her into their group, mother did not suffer too much. She knew more about each one of them than his friends, and sometimes even more than he knew himself, because she knew how to analyze and draw conclusions. And I'll tell you, not everyone has it, this gift from God—to analyze and draw conclusions—not even one out of a hundred thousand, that's why my mother felt like a big fish in a small pond among them all.

---

37 The Polish-American mathematician (1909-1984).

38 A popular figure in street songs and cabaret performances [author's note].

6

Even on weekends Yarosh got up early, when the horizon was just only beginning to blaze, and timid rose-colored flashes penetrated the windows. The skylight was always open, and the chill of the pleasantly cool morning permeated the nostrils, airing out the remains of a dream, and only the birdsong barely disturbed the silence. On such mornings he liked to work at a table, surrounding himself with books and papers. Actually, it wasn't just one table but three lined up in a row along the windows. On one table, he wrote something by hand, on the second one he typed on the computer, and the third was covered with books and folders, from which slips of paper stuck out. Under the tables were boxes filled with periodicals, clippings and various notes. In a separate big box there were crumpled scraps of paper, sentenced to death; they were balled up or torn to shreds. When the box got filled up, Yarosh carried it out into the garden and burned the contents, so no one's eyes would see his jottings again, but one time the wind picked up a sheet, tossed it up, swayed it, and gracefully whirling it, wafted it down to his neighbors' farmstead. Yarosh grew numb, having realized that the sheet contained a draft of his translation from Arcanumian. The text was erotic and from a young lad's perspective, and nowhere was it noted that it was the translation of a literary work, so it would turn out to be a great embarrassment if his neighbors read it and thought that their neighbor was a pervert. Yarosh hastily screwed some wire into a stick, pushed the stick through the fence and, and jabbing the paper, managed to get it. The curtain in the neighbor's window swayed and

Yarosh, removing the sheet from the wire, waved it in the air, as if he were apologizing for his invasion. From that time on he never threw uncrumpled paper into the box.

But even before sitting down at the table, he went to eat breakfast, boiled coffee, added milk, then added a spoonful of honey and drank it with a cheese sandwich. Then he could go out into the garden, walk among the trees, pick an apple or a pear, and then eat it, scaring off forty frightened magpies that loved to peck at apples. The orchard evoked a special meditative mood in him. Most of the trees were old, having been planted before the war; at the very end of the orchard stood a mighty, wide-branched walnut tree, that scattered a good half of its crop beyond the fence, and there, children or passersby picked it up. Yarosh never picked up anything that fell beyond the fence, because what he harvested in the orchard was enough. As he walked through the orchard, he listened for children's voices, so that he wouldn't frighten them while unexpectedly approaching the fence. His neighbor, Mrs. Stefa, was also an early bird. As soon as it began to dawn, she sprang out into the garden and started digging near the flowerbeds, and upon seeing Yarosh, informed him about the news on the street—for example, that "Mr. Kotsiuba died yesterday because the ambulance arrived late, and Mrs. Potsiluyko's billygoat kid broke his leg, and now they have to put him down, and the Krytskys are marrying off their daughter to a black man, and the world, probably, was going to hell in a handbasket, because what will their children be like, although the black guy speaks Ukrainian. And, listen, yesterday he walks past me and says, Glory be to Jesus, and I said—His Glory Forever—and then I went numb and became mute, and I wasn't able to do anything other than look at him walk away. And last night my late husband, whom you may still remember, came to me and patted me on the head and said, dig up the dahlias because there will be frost, well, and I rushed to dig them up, because he planted them, he won't forgive me if they freeze." And then Mrs. Stefa for no darn reason can ask, "Have you ever been to Znesinnya? [39] No? Then don't go there. You never know what's waiting for a person there. I saw people there who recognized and greeted me, but I couldn't remember them, and then I glanced at them, but then I saw they were looking around, smiling and affably nodding their heads at me, but I didn't venture to approach any of them, even when I heard, how do you do, Mrs. Stefa."

His neighbor inspired Yarosh with the idea that every resident of Lviv must have known in his or her life a lady like Mrs. Stefa, or several of them, because in childhood, many such Mrs. Stefas swarmed the house of his parents since his father was a dentist. Every Wednesday when he had a day off and could see patients at home, people crowded into the house. Dad remembered all his patients. When the next old granny came over from the village of Tuchne and said that Marika, who had married Misko from Pechykhvosty who works at the combine, advised her to come to Mr. Doc, father immediately knew about whom we are talking, because not only did he make Maria's teeth, but also Misko's, who got them knocked out in a nearby village club when he had gone over to Marika's. When Marika's sister brought her father-in-law, then father shocked him, by asking about the

39 Originally, it was a village in the Lychakiv region of Lviv but now is the largest park in the city. The name means "Ascension."

sick woman who ended up in the Kulpark because she had got up in the middle of the night and wandered through the village wearing only a shirt. Then there were some patients who could come to their house at any time, they were Zamarstyniv's elite, the crème de la crème, the undisputed leader of which was the bailiff's wife Mrs. Khomyk, a fat lass with fat arms and legs, large breasts and the kind of voice that when the Lord needs a trumpeting voice for the Day of Judgment, then without a doubt He would resurrect Mrs. Khomyk first because you could heard her at both long ends of the street. Mr. Khomyk was also a janitor, but a delicate man, thin and quiet. When he overdid it at the tavern, then Mrs. Khomyk would easily pick him up and carry him like a sack of potatoes, but out of male solidarity dad called him nothing other than Mr. Director, and Mrs. Khomyk—Mrs. Director.

"Mr. Doc!" Mrs. Khomyk whooped from the street, waddling onto their lawn. "Haves you heard the news? I have to make a list of everyone who's not goin' to work and who's sittin' in the house all day. What the heck's happenin' here? In every house there's grannys and grandpaps who're pensioners, then what, do I needs to make a list of 'em? And why does I need to open a can of worms? Cause, ya see, they wants to list 'em as parasites. And I should list all of 'em? I know 'em all. Does I needs to make myself an enemy, by doing such mean things to people? I still haves a conscience. I've seen even worse before. Since those first Soviets didn't they tells me to make a list of everyone who got Ukrainian newspapers? But I tells 'em I can't read. I can count money, but don't know how to read. So how can I know who reads Polish and who reads Ukrainian newspapers, and who doesn't? So, they gave up on it. And then the krauts came and told me to make a list of all the commies and Jews. Well, I wasn't as good to the commies since they settled in those empty houses after people were taken to Siberia, let em' know they can't have a party on other people's bones. As everyone left, then they could also have set off to the east, but no, they stayed because it was a pity to leave such luxurious rooms with furniture and china. But the Jews? Who? That Izya, who whenever he would meet me, would always take buckets of coal from my hands and would say: "Mrs. Khomyk! I'll help you, because you are a lass and it's not fitting for you to carry that!" Or that Khana, who always gave me some clothes 'cause she put on weight quicker than me? Or Mr. Kohn, who lived right above me, and used to say: "Mrs. Khomyk! When I hear your voice at dawn, it's like I drank half a liter of strong coffee and I's ready to work hard. Thanks to you I'm saving on coffee, may God grant you health so you can wake me from my deep sleep." Do you know, Mr. Doc, what deep sleep is? Aha, that's what I thought... No, not that I loved the Jews, no—but I loved those Jews of ours from Zamarstyniv. I swear I loved them. And what of that? Didn't I take Hannah's daughter into my house? Didn't I hide her? She lived at my place, like in God's bosom, I fed her, did her laundry. I took care of her like a relative. I brought her books so she wouldn't be bored. And she went to Palestine and could've sent me a panorama picture of Jerusalem! Or an olive branch so I could sprinkle some holy water on my Shteftsyo with it when he comes homes drunk. There's thanks for me, no? Maybe in that time that I hid her, I could've fed a dozen piglets! The Shalays, ya hear, also hid Jews, and they done give 'em a small bundle of gold. So, they built themselves a new house, and their Jews left, and now every year for the holidays, they send postcards. And these are respectable people, no? But that's fine, I'm not regrettin' for anything, in the other world I'll be repaid a hundredfold, they've made a warm place in heaven for me a long time ago. Well, Mr. Doc, pour me ten grams 'cause I've caught a chill. Is that your caraway seed liqueur? Oy, it's fine! I don't want kielbasa, cut me a little piece of *salo*.[40] Oh, it's super. I don't know how you can chase horilka with anything else. *Horilka*[41] with *salo* and bread is our trinity—I'm telling you, may God forgive me. Aya, one is there in heaven, and the other one on earth. Bread is—the Father, *salo*—the Son, and *horilka*—the Holy Spirit, forgive me, Lord. Add some onions to that—the Immaculate Virgin. Oy, it's so good! Just one more shot and I'll be going. It's cold today, the wind's so bad my teeth are chatterin'."

He really never had been to Znesinnya, though he had been all over the place in Lviv, but the words of Mrs. Stefa ate into his brain, and on a certain warm day in August, when the sun shone brightly and was creating mirages, he started wandering. It was not far from Kryvchytsi to Znesinnya, the small houses didn't block out the sun, and light poured from everywhere. Yarosh was so stunned by the bright intoxicating light he had to squint, and he made a shade for his eyes with his hand to be able to discern anything in more detail. It was midday, everywhere drowsiness prevailed, trees dozed without any breeze, cats and dogs

40 *Salo* is an almost pure white smoked pig lard and is considered a national delicacy in Ukraine. For a discussion of it see the following: https://www.theguardian.com/world/2015/mar/06/salo-ukraine-national-obsession.

41 See footnote #1.

lay curled up like bagels, sparrows weren't tweeting, only here and there chickens lazily clucked, but very weakly and briefly, and grasshoppers chirred. At the beginning of the 1990s you didn't hear such a menacing and brutal roar of cars. Lviv's suburbs were bathed in pristine quiet, as if one's head was immersed in a warm bath. It was noon, and Yarosh remembered Ivan Franko's poem "Beware the midday demon," which is more dangerous than the midnight one because it fatigues and subdues you, creating apparitions that are difficult to distinguish from reality. He recalled that Lady Midday appeared to villagers at noon with a sickle in her hand and lopped off the heads of those working in the fields during that time. Midday instilled fear, perhaps, because at midday in the heat life grew still, the sun became menacing and insidious. You'd be better off at that time taking a snooze somewhere in an orchard. But there was another problem—midday dreams induce certain unpleasant images and horrible visions. Walking along a narrow street between houses made of burgundy-colored Austrian brick without stucco, Yarosh saw an old man walking toward him holding hands with his grandson and chatting about something in a lively way. The old man was dressed in a white shirt and vest, from the pocket of which hung the silver chain of a pocket watch. He wore a black hat on his head, and his waxed black mustache protruded. The little boy was in short pants with suspenders and brown gaiters. The two looked strange. Yarosh had seen these types only in old photographs. It even seemed to him that he had gone back in time and he rubbed his eyes. When the grandfather and grandson approached without paying any attention to the passerby coming from the opposite direction, Yarosh barely restrained himself from speaking to them. He had a strange, unconfirmed feeling that he knew them, and that he knew them very well, but he couldn't remember from where. But they passed by him without even looking up. After a few steps Yarosh looked back and noticed that the little boy made a movement with his head, as if a moment before he also had looked back, although he could have imagined it. For some reason he wanted the boy to look back, for then he would have been emboldened to approach them and, perhaps, they would have remembered together where they had seen each other. From the window of a house the head of a woman leaned out and a voice echoed: "Where have you been? Lunch is on the table," and that voice also sounded familiar, as if it had made its way through the thicket of dreams. Suddenly, Yarosh really wanted to become that little boy and run into the house with loud laughter. Suddenly a longing for his parents, who recently had died, constricted his throat until tears appeared. And he felt sorry for himself as never before. His footsteps began to quicken, and he kept repeating "the demon of midday... this is the demon of midday... this is a phantom, this is not real, neither these houses nor this little street," and in a minute he turned onto another street, from that one to a third and wandered his way right to a tram stop.

That evening, when he was picking plums in the orchard, Mrs. Stefa said to him, but in a whisper:

"Were you at Znesinnya?.. Go to confession tomorrow. It'll help."

She again bent over her flowers, as if she had not said anything.

F

Our grandmother also had an occupation. She used to cry, but no, not like each of us does. She would perform an artistic lament. No one lamented the way our grandmother did. Listening to her, even a stone would have started to weep if it were able. Even someone who didn't plan on crying would start to sob and howl and would wave their hands. It happened that even a malicious neighbor who had even been unrelenting in quarrels with the dead man also was unable restrain himself and began to gulp down sobs, cry, and then further would moan and groan, and sniffle. For if grandma was crying, she cried not on her own behalf, but from the family, not as a whole, but from each individual separately, instantly reincarnating herself from an inconsolable widow to despondent brothers and sisters, and finally in the image of daughters and sons, of grieving grandsons and granddaughters, and one time, when she was asked, in the name of a favorite doggie. That time, she whimpered so truthfully and got so worked up that all the dogs from the surrounding streets picked up on her canine sobbing and the entire city began to howl. Thinking that it was a siren, passersby rushed in fear to look for a bomb shelter, underground toilets, and basements. This is what our grandma, a professional lamenter, was able to do. That's why people vied to order her for a funeral, and there were days when she hadn't finished crying herself out properly at one funeral and had to run to a second. So that's why there was confusion on more than one occasion. Thus, she begins to sob for a deceased man, until it turns out that it's a deceased woman. But that's nothing, our grandma always knew how to extricate herself from a situation. Once it happened that Mr. Apeltsyner, the owner of a notions shop, came over to our place and ordered our grandma for his own funeral. Grandma was surprised, because Mr. Apeltsyner, the owner of a notions shop, was still in perfect health and smoking expensive cigars. But he explained that he wanted to hear grandma lament him, because he wants to pay in advance to decide whether or not to order our grandma. When our grandma asked why he doesn't hire a Jewish woman, who could lament in Yiddish, Mr. Apeltsyner, the owner of a notions store who smokes expensive cigars, replied that he doesn't give a shit, because he doesn't understand Yiddish, and although he'd be already dead, his soul probably would like to enjoy for the last time the lament of his relatives, those near to him, and a professional weeper. And grandma fulfilled his wish with such enthusiasm and fervor, with such passion of feelings, that when Mr. Apeltsyner heard grandma lament in the image of his wife, he started to sob himself, and when all six of his daughters started to sob in turn, then he got all stuffed up, and when his sons-in-law joined in the performance of grandma, he then choked on the smoke of his expensive cigar and cried for a half hour more after grandma finishing lamenting, and then paid her the money, returned home, drank up some tea with rum, lit an expensive cigar and died, because he liked that lament so much he wasn't able to wait for his last minute.

My mother also had a brother, a priest, who had a parish in Zamarstyniv, whose name was Father Myroslav, but I just called him "unks." People came to listen to his preaching not only from all of Zamarstyniv, but also from Holosky, and Pidzamche, and even from Brukhovychi. Troublemakers usually stood alone in the first rows and eagerly caught every word, choking from laughter, because they loved unks above all else, calling him father-troublemaker, and unk's sermons were really remarkable. After one of those sermons people discussed it all the way home to try to get to the meaning of it. One sermon sank do deeply into my soul that I learned it by heart, just like the Our Father:

"Of what will I speak to you today, brothers and sisters!" Father Myroslav began to preach one Sunday. "I'm going to say that God—is the highest wisdom. He thought about everything to the smallest detail, giving life to flies and mosquitoes, and butterflies living a single day, and snails, and people. And we, ingrates, sometimes complain that life is short, and some would like to live forever. But imagine that our dreams came true—and people were to live forever. Each would then have not only grandfathers and grandmothers, but also great grandfathers and great grandmothers, and even great-great-grandfathers and great-great grandmothers, and great-great-great-grandfathers and great-great-great grandmothers. Imagine that a certain girl decided to marry a decent guy. In order to do that he'd have to ask for permission from her mother, and her mother—from her mother, and she—from her own mother all the way to her own great-great-great… grandmother. What if they all lived in different villages and cities, this process would drag on for years and years. But let's say that the oldest great-great-great grandmother, dried up in old age like a splinter and resembling a crooked branch that was kept on the windowsill among the flowerpots in order to remember to water it, that oldest one agreed with the choice of her great-great-great granddaughter. Then the good news would have to roll back from whence it came, and years after years passed again, and the bride meanwhile had already aged prematurely, and her young lad from nerves found himself some other damsel. Isn't that awful?"

Mother's second brother Uncle Lyodzyo was a member of the Ukrainian Insurgent Army. Several grenades were always hanging on his belt under his shirt. He promised to blow himself up if the police tracked him down. My mother forced him to take off those grenades and hang them on a wardrobe in the entryway, lest one of them might blow up accidentally. Uncle had nothing against it. He took me on his knees and said:

"Look, when you grow up can we assassinate somebody together?"

"What's assassinate mean?"

"An attempt on someone. We'll blow up some Polish minister."

"Why?"

"What do you mean why? Because we'll get an order. You have to execute an order. If they call me to the main command post and say, "Now you have to jump with grenades under express train number 368 / 2, which will be at Pidzamche at 19:30 hours," then I just touch my cap as a salute and exclaim "Yes, sir!" And I'll run right on the track. And without hesitating for a moment, I'll fall right under the wheels. Fiery victory will burn in my eyes, and the words will echo from my lips: "It's not time, not time to serve the Polaks or the Russkies."

"What are you teaching the child?" Mother shouted from the kitchen. "You want him to repeat that in school?"

“Nawwww,” uncle wagged his finger near his nose. “This is a terrible secret. So you don’t dare give me up to anyone, hear?” I nodded and felt my little heart grow still from fear. “You’re the son of a hero and the nephew of a hero, that’s me. That’s why you have to prepare yourself for heroic acts. But don’t say squat to anyone.

And so, I prepared myself.

Uncle Myroslav, Uncle Lyodzyo, and my mom had one common treasure—grandpa Lucilius, their pappy. His father, my great-grandfather, was a teacher of Greek and Latin, and named his son Lucilius, but he did not follow in the footsteps of his father but rather joined the army. But before that he got married and made children. On the Italian front he got shell-shocked and returned home, and after some time he began to sink into an incomprehensibly deep stupor, sometimes just freezing in the middle of the room or at the table while he was eating soup. When grandma would take a fly swatter and smack it on the table, my grandpop would suddenly shudder and emerge from his mental stupor, as though from the depths of the sea, saying, “Well, so-so... and you’re saying...” with a look as if he had not sunk anywhere, but was telling us something and now just completed his instructive tale.

Although grandfather had a good pension for his military service, his soul yearned for something more and, when the director of the nature preserve on High Castle Mountain,[42] who was also a veteran, offered grandpop work as an echo, he gladly agreed. All of grandpop’s work in that

42 Vysoky Zamok (meaning “high castle”) is the highest point in Lviv, a wooded mountain peak overlooking the city that is a popular spot for locals and visitors to the city. In the thirteenth century, there was a castle on top of the mountain.

job consisted of sitting in a cave, listening carefully to all the exclamations of tourists and echoing the endings of words. Tourists really liked this kind of game very much and they sometimes yapped there until midday, inventing more and more clever words, the endings of which turned young and older ladies' faces beet red. "Who can't sleep on a night of evil (*lykhuyu*)!" The tourists would yell, and grandfather immediately picked up in his sepulchral voice the last five letters [*khuyu*, meaning "prick"] and with inspiration rolled them, slowly growing silent. Rascals invented even clever phrases like "From the windows the preacher men (*popy*) blew (*zduvaly*) the flies," and grandpa, shrewdly catching the subtle subtext, did not just repeat some letters there, but he drew out both of the last two words [*popy zduvaly*, meaning blew butts] and dragged them deep into the cave, like some female captive. And as he got older and feeble, he became hard of hearing and could no longer repeat the tourists' shouts precisely, and so he began to improvise. It would turn out even more interesting but had little to do with what was actually said. Suspecting fraud, tourists began to make their way into the cave and grandpop was saved only by the fact that none of them could get more than three meters deep into the cave, because they would slip on grandpop's droppings, falling into that puddle in the middle of the cave with such a desperate cry that the rest of the tourists would vanish into thin air. Grandpa lost his job. We now had our own echo in the house, because grandpa repeated the end of all of our sentences and got on momma's nerves.

"Go bring in some water," she asked grandfather.

"...water," grandpa repeated but didn't move from the spot.

"Why are you repeating?"

"...peating," grandpa smacked his lips but didn't move from the spot.

"Jumpin' Jehosaphat, what's this?" Momma exploded. "Why are you making a fool of yourself?"

"...self," grandpa nodded and didn't move from the spot.

"If you don't bring some water, you'll gets bupkis instead of soup with dumplings!"

"...umplings," grandpa agreed and didn't move from the spot.

"That's it!? Momma whooped. "My patience is shot, I'll go myself for the water!"

"...water," grandpa rejoiced and then grabbed the bucket and flew off like a shot.

Half the town knew our grandpa, because he always announced his return home from the tavern at night to the inhabitants of Lviv with his loud singing, which had little to do with singing and was undistinguishable from the bellowing of long-horned steer. It was not rare that some window of some house would open, and curses would rain onto his bald head. Grandma tried to shame grandpa in the morning, and called him on the carpet for a long time and patiently explained to him what shame he was bringing to the family, but grandpa just silently nodded his head and in the evening disappeared from the house and turned up where the city's darkest elite gathered—hobos, rascals, drunkards, ruffians, and robbers, in a word—the kind of mob with which it was dangerous just to sit at a table. But our grandpa felt wonderful among that riffraff. All the drunkards treated him like a friend, and because they loved him, they enthusiastically pulled various pranks on him, stuffing the pocket of his sport coat with condoms, ladies' cigarette butts, curlers, old stockings, and once they even crammed into his pocket large pink ladies undies that were called bloomers. Besides that, they smeared his sleeve cuffs and collar with lipstick, and sprinkled them with eau de cologne. In short, grandma had fun emptying those pockets and groaning over the smudged shirts. Those pink panties with a green patch between the legs knocked her out of whack. Grandma first showed them to the entire family, and then went out on the porch and began to wave them like a banner, crying out in a genuinely poetic voice for some peace in her lot, which her husband was so shamefully defiling. She rolled her eyes to the heavens and, addressing the Lord, begged for Him to come and take her away, because she didn't have the strength to endure anymore. "I'm ready to go away to that world at any moment," she appealed to the heavens and her female neighbors sympathetically nodded their heads and rubbed their eyes with handkerchiefs, "Nothin's keepin' me here. I just think about what'll happen to the old goat, it's driving me out of my wits, but I have to keep on livin' just to spite him! Unks at this time was calmly having breakfast, his mustache concealing a mysterious smile that might have been able to attest to the truth of all my grandmother's suspicions and give irrefutable proof of his guilt, if not for grandpa's advanced age. He never justified himself, never defended himself, and accepted all grandma's charges, because he obviously preferred to be thought of by everyone as an incorrigible rake than an old fart. Sometimes grandpa didn't come back by himself, but good friends would carry him home in a burlap blanket and lie him down on the threshold. Grandpa would peacefully snore until someone came out onto the porch, then grandma would grab a ladleful of cold water and pour it on grandpa. He would jump up on the spot, snort and shake his head, while shouting out commands: "Forward! Follow me! Pound the enemy! Draw your bayonets! Not a step back!" The second cup of cold water brought him completely to his senses, and licking and smacking his lips, he wondered what was for breakfast, to which grandma reported without fail that he would eat dog shit in béchamel sauce.

Right after grandpa died, my grandma sighed with relief. But right before that, clearly, she performed her unforgettable lament, in which, however, there was not a word about condoms, lipstick, or ladies' underwear, but it was such a lamentation that Yaroslavna[43] falls short compared to her:

"God, my God, how much I suffered because of him, and what didn't I find in those pockets!" She sighed among the family and neighbors at the funeral repast table. "I just had some rest when he was taken to the war. I never knew where he disappeared to, what he was doing, who he was meeting with. He never would tell me anything. I wasn't sure on any given night whether I'd even expect to see him by morning. Finally, all that's over, I don't have to worry anymore. Now I know where he is and that all is good with him."

Afterward everyone present sank into reveries about my grandpa, and for the first time I heard about his provocative nature, because from what I remembered he didn't seem to be a hell raiser. But in his youth he also loved to pound down beer, not in respectable pubs but in dilapidated dives, where you rarely get by without adventures. He boldly

43 Yaroslavna's lament from the famous epic poem "The Tale of Ihor's Campaign."

broke into his first best fight and calmed down only after he left it with a black eye, a bloody lip, a torn ear, or a torn tuft of someone's hair in his fist. Grandpa tried to cover up his dissolute ways by going to a reading room for auditions for a play, and one time stumbled his way home in the morning and shouted out to the entire courtyard:

"Goods day, me loverly!"

"I'll show you, loverly!" Grandma answered. "You first tell me where you were all night."

"I er was at the reading room. Yesterday was an audition and then the poolice came and caught us all in the act, and we all had to sits in jail, a course!"

"Yer a liar! Liar, liar, pants on fire![44] May all yer teeth 'cept one fall out so it aches your whole dang life! I'll give you a reading room! I'll give you jail!"

"I swear, may I be damned if I'm not telling the truth! And so's we're not to blame that he came, you know, the one's an agent, the other's a cop, and they took away a bunch of us."

"And also took the girls with you?"

"What girls? There weren't no girls. Why do you cling like a leech to me? I went straight from work, from the mason's to the reading room... well ... and you see what adventures we had!"

"And what about Ira? And Stefka? Were they also at the rehearsal? Not a step to the reading room for you no more!"

"And you know, you um can't not go to da reading room... Go with me once, cause yi'll see, there ain't no bad work going on... there's educational work there fer us."

---

44 She literally says here: "You should melt like a candle! And you should swell up like a thread!"

Reminiscences of the "educational work" caused friendly laughter without fail, especially the mention of how grandma one morning first discovered on his shirt cuff a poisonous red lipstick and created such a scandal that all the neighbors long remembered it. It's possible that the scandal was not without basis, and grandpa truthfully "jumped into some buckwheat" (meaning he was getting some on the side). And my grandma ran out with his shirt on the balcony and delivered a fiery speech in which she let rip and scolded to high heaven not only her husband, but also Itzhak Spukh's tavern on Sonyachna Street, including the bloated Itzhak Spukh himself, where decent men fall into the clutches of promiscuous sluts and lascivious seductresses. The intrigued neighbors tumbled out of the windows, poured out onto the porches and balconies and listened to that tirade with unabated attention, while grandpa quietly snored on their marital bed. But at a certain moment into his sleeping consciousness came words and expressions that undoubtedly struck his manhood and honor, so he jumped out of bed, rushed to the balcony and grabbed grandma—who was then a young bride—crosswise, bent her over the handrail so that she waved her arms like a chicken trying to take flight, and her large round breasts dangled out of her blouse. Now she was crying out a single word "Help!" And grandpa, holding her neck with his left hand, with his right hand doled out such resonant slaps on her buttocks that the sounds echoed every which way.

7

Nothing special differentiated that Saturday morning—breakfast, a stroll in the orchard, Mrs. Stefa's monologue, this time about the night wind, about apples knocked off, about branches that fiercely whipped the window panes and kept her from falling asleep, and about her prayer to St. Anthony, who will calm a storm. And Yarosh remembered that in the middle of the night he really did hear the din of the wind and the rustle of the branches. In the garden he saw fallen apples and began to gather them; they won't keep there for long, but you can squeeze out the juice. After carrying a basket of apples into the basement, he started off to a store where they sold Italian and German food. He bought spaghetti, parmesan cheese, tomato sauce, and also grabbed a few bottles of red and white wine. After cleaning up the house and freeing the table in the living room of books that had the habit of capturing increasingly wider territories like nomadic conquerors and suddenly appeared in the most unusual places—such as in the bathroom, on the stairs, on windowsills—he pulled out china, which he did not use himself, but which a former lover once washed perfectly and packed in a box, carefully examined them against the light and placed them on the table. God knows why he felt a strange anxiousness. It was as though it wasn't his son, but he himself who was bringing a girl home for the first time. This feeling never left him all day. His relationship with his son was far from ideal. Marko was raised without him as a father and kept a certain distance, including never calling him dad, and when he had to address him, he used words like "Listen!" Or "Do you hear?" Each lived his own separate life, and the building of bridges wasn't an inner need, but rather the maintaining of a tradition, though they lacked a closer relationship, where he could hug his son or tousle his hair.

After tidying up everything, he sat down on the couch next to the window and opened the New York edition of the Thomas Pynchon's novel *Gravity's Rainbow*, which he had been reading a few pages a day for a month. This reading always had a soothing effect on him, it allowed him to dissociate himself from the outside world, and the multiple polysemy of English words and phrases evoked cascades of associations that swarmed in his head like bees. When his cell phone rang, he jumped up as if he had been scalded. It was Marko calling—they were already driving up. Yarosh stepped out into the yard. The path that led to the wicket gate was strewn with half-rotten plums that had fallen overnight from a tree when the wind had been gusting. He quickly grabbed a broom and started to sweep them away. Marko and Danka found him doing that.

"Did you do that specially for us?" His son laughed. "You don't have to do that, it's even more pleasant to walk on a soft surface. I'm not going to introduce you, you already know each other."

During lunch they talked about different things that actually interested them little, but are obligatory at such meetings, and gradually the ice broke. The wine helped. Finally, the girl, slightly flushed, was emboldened to ask what the professor was working on right now. And Yarosh told her about the *Book of the Dead* and strange songs with dances.

"Tango of Death?" Danka asked. "That's interesting. There really was that kind of tango... During the war."

"Really?" Yarosh became more animated. "I've never heard of it."

"This tango was created in the Yaniv concentration camp during the war. My grandma told me about it. The Germans ordered several Jewish musicians to put together an orchestra and play different melodies for those condemned to the firing squad. Among those melodies was the tango, which was called the 'Tango of Death.'"

Yarosh didn't hide his surprise. Strange—how did he miss this?"

"They composed this tango themselves?"

Grandma knew one of the musicians who had studied with her at the conservatory. He survived and managed to escape. And he said that that they composed the melody based on some old manuscript."

Yarosh felt his heart beating rapidly, and the foreboding of a fresh sensation gripped him. He grew tense like a greyhound on the hunt. It turned out that the old musician might still be living somewhere in Klepariv. At least two years ago he was at Danka's grandmother's funeral, so her parents should have his phone number. Danka promised to get it for him. Then the conversation switched to the anthology of Arcanumian literature that the professor was compiling, and the girl said that she herself had translated some things but was just too embarrassed to show them.

"You should be more confident," Yarosh said. "For a young woman it's particularly important. And don't hesitate to consult people. I understand I'm supposed to be your scholarly advisor? Well, I'd be happy to look over your translations at first chance. You obviously must be using my Arcanumian-English dictionary, but soon I'll finish my work on an Arcanumian-Ukrainian one."

"That would be great. Of course, I haven't learned the Arcanumian language well enough yet to translate from the original, that's why I translate from your English interlinears. But it's also complicated because not only are English words polysemic, but also the Arcanumian hieroglyphs each have several meanings. What do you think: do I have the wherewithal to learn Arcanumian?"

"Why not? If you gain an understanding, it's much easier to learn than Chinese or Japanese. In the Arcanumian language the majority of hieroglyphs were phonograms and signified the coalescence of two or three consonants—pr, pl, vkr, pt, etc., or single consonants—24 in total. The hieroglyphs never noted vowels at all."

"Just like in Egyptian."

"Yes. And just the same as in Egyptian, there were ideograms among the hieroglyphs—symbols that corresponded to certain words and concepts. The Arcanumians combined ideograms and phonograms according to certain rules with the fact that phonograms prevailed. In sum there were three hundred most commonly used Arcanumian hieroglyphs."

"That's two times less than in the Egyptian."

"But in time among the Egyptians, especially in the Greco-Roman era, the number of hieroglyphs had grown, while among the Arcanumians nothing changed until the decline of their state. In addition, you'd be surprised how many similarities there are with the Ukrainian language. Practically every second word. Pta—*ptakh* (bird), escles—*skelya* (cliff), strh—*strikha* (eaves) and *stryh* (garret), dm—*dym* (smoke), ehta—*khata* (house)...."

"How do you say, 'my darling' in Arcanumian?" Marko interrupted. He had evidently gotten bored during the course of their professional conversation.

"Me elele."

"I don't see any similarity."

"Don't you know the word *lele* (beloved)?"

"And the god of love is Lel," Danka added. "You just don't understand how exciting it is to plunge into ancient languages."

"Oh-h, writing computer programs is also exciting. But since I don't understand anything in your conversation, then I think you won't mind if I at least watch the second half of the game since I've already missed the first."

Marko moved to an armchair in the corner and turned on the TV. Yarosh had never been interested in soccer, but the conversation with the student interested him.

"If you have a flash drive with you, I can copy the files I've already finished for you from my dictionary," he said, and when Danka gladly agreed, added: "Let's go to my study so we don't bother Marko."

Marko smiled and indifferently waved his hand. In the study, cluttered with books, periodicals, folders, clippings, and manuscripts, at first glance a mess seemed to rule, but Yarosh oriented himself perfectly in that mess. Turning on the computer, he quickly transferred the files to the flash drive and handed it to the girl, but her visit to the sacred office did not end here. She couldn't tear herself away from the books and, pulling out one after another, she leafed through them and unable to restrain herself from showing delight, she sighed. Yarosh knew well what impression his library made on intellectuals, so Danka's reaction didn't surprise him, but something else did surprise him. From the reverence with which she took individual books into her hands it was evident that she was familiar with them from a bibliography, but in the scholarly libraries of Lviv they were absent, since they were published abroad.

"What compelled you to learn a dead language?" She asked.

"Immortality. After all, it becomes materialized in words, the word has a magical power. God created the world with the help of a word. And when I start to speak Arcanumian, inside me thousands of Arcanumians come alive. Arcanum hasn't died, it has been resurrected and lives in those who study it."

"Immortality compelled you, and you compelled me."

Yarosh smiled, guessing the intimate desire of his guest, because he never lent books from his library, and first and foremost this especially applied to young ladies. Women treat books differently, often as blouses, shoes, or earrings borrowed from friends. Young ladies with whom Yarosh had romances never returned the books to him after the romance ended. True, the books he lent didn't have a high value. They were some kind of fiction, so there wasn't much to regret. On the contrary, Danka belonged to a completely different type of young ladies. She was interested in scholarship and books that interested just a few individuals on this planet. And there was another important circumstance—Yarosh didn't have a romance with Danka. So the girl managed to coax one book from him. But this time Yarosh sensed that he should give in, because to train a talented novice is also a responsible task. Additionally, the recognition of the fact that it was he who encouraged her to study the Arcanumian language won him over.

G

In contrast to my friends I had absolutely no desire to study. More precisely it wasn't quite like that, I had no desire to study in scholarly institutions, but rather preferred to study myself, mostly by my own trial and error. I moved gropingly, but confidently. I loved to become self-absorbed, and if I imagined a good place for me to work, then it would be a small train station where I could live and work as a watchman, meet the trains that would never stop there, but for which from time to time I needed to change the track switches, and I would have a kitty and doggie, and a chicken that would provide me with an egg every day, and a goat and that's it, no one else. I wouldn't even need paper, because I'd write my reflections on the sand, and on the snow in the winter .... But Yosko studied in the conservatory; he played the violin and bandura. You're surprised, really? A Jew playing the bandura is as strange as a Hutsul strumming a balalaika. But Yosko's father, Mr. Pharmacist, said that his son would play the bandura. Well, so his mom was forced to carry out his last will, and Mr. Pharmacist really loved the bandura, he loved it so much that he would have become a bandura player for the sake of that bandura. Though that dream didn't come true, on the other hand, he did die for Ukraine, so it turned out practically the same. Yosko's sister Leah wasn't as lucky because she was born after her father was no more. He couldn't leave any instructions about her future lot, but Mrs. Golda decided that the little girl also would study music, and when she appeared to have vocal abilities, she took her to audition for Professor Jan Rasp at the music conservatory, and he promised that he would definitely take her on when she finished her schooling. From that time on Mrs. Golda regularly bought raw eggs for her daughter and forced her every morning to gulp down an egg on an empty stomach before she started off for school, after which Leah had to sing out loud, like a nightingale to the whole dang courtyard. On weekdays that didn't bother anyone, but on Sunday, when many people wanted to sleep a bit longer, that singing got on your nerves, and then swearing and curses echoed from the window, but Mrs. Golda didn't give a rat's ass.

One time on Friday I found Yosko at home sitting on the floor, cutting paper with scissors into equal-sided squares. I was surprised, but he explained that tomorrow was Saturday, and they're not permitted to do anything on that day except for putting out a fire if one broke out in the house, so he was there preparing toilet paper.

"Yosyo, you plannin' on shitting all day long, or what? Why's it you need so much paper?" I asked in surprise.

"I'm doing it not so much for myself, but for my mom and sister, and two aunties and two uncles, and Grandpop Abeles."

There was nothing else to say—I sat down next to Yosko and helped him cut up the toilet paper. And soon Grandpop Abeles sauntered in with a live chicken under his arm; he took off his frock coat and hat, and then stepped out into the yard with the chicken. It was the first time I saw a chicken killed in a kosher way. Grandpop took it with both his hands and began to violently shake it about so its head filled up with blood, and when it had already become as red as a ripe tomato, grandpop pulled a hatchet out of his pocket and in a single stroke lopped off the head and waited for all the blood to drain out.

"We're forbidden from using blood in food," Yosko explained to me, and I just nodded my head in sympathy, understanding that Yosko would never ever try a delicacy like kishka, filled with blood and buckwheat groats, not to speak even of ham or headcheese.

Right at that time Leah arrived, and upon seeing our efforts, she burst out laughing.

"What, Yossel? Have you hired yourself a shabez goi? Maybe we can also make kluski dumplings for tomorrow?"

"What's a shabez goi?" I asked.

"When a Jew can't do certain work on Saturday, then he calls a non-Jew to help, and that kind of helper is called a shabez goi," Leah explained. "When you finish up your clever work, will you help me make the kluski?"

"Other than a snowman and spit balls made of bread, I've never made anything."

"That's nothing, I'll teach you. You'll thank me some day."

So then, Leah and I later made kluski from potatoes and cheese, grandfather Abeles plucked the chicken, and Yosko's mother kneaded the dough for a sweet pastry while poor Yosko was sweating over his studies. Because Golda had hired a Hebrew teacher for Yosko, Mr. Katsenelenbogen, who always wore a black frock coat and a black wide-brimmed hat from which in every direction his sidelocks dangled, even during sultry summer days. Because poor Yosko, while studying Hebrew, had to have a covered head, Mr. Katsenelenbogen brought a hat for him, which clearly was too large. That's why it wasn't sidelocks, which Yosko didn't have, dangling out from under it, but his mother Golda's curlers. Sweat flowed down his face in streams, and toward the end of the lesson he nearly cried. We kept peeping into the window and waited until his torments would end to go play soccer. Hebrew was really difficult for Yos, and he couldn't fathom at all why he needed it when he wanted to be a musician and not a rabbi. But his mother Golda was stubborn, deeming that Hebrew was a sign of intelligence, and who knows, perhaps, someday her baby boy would travel to the land of his ancestors. So we started to think and figure out how we could help our poor Yos. And then the idea came to Wolff to follow Mr. Katsenelenbogen's entire route from his house to Yosko's. So we did that, but we didn't notice anything useful save the teacher's firmly established habit to stop by the stand on Legions Street and drink a glass of lemon-flavored sparkling water. But that one detail greatly interested Yas, and, shouting out "Eureka!", he remembered that Mr. Rubtsak, whom he knew very well because he was his neighbor and on more than one occasion had helped him after school, worked at that stand, and it would be simply marvelous to pay a visit to him right then when Yosko's tormenter would be passing by there and toss a purgative laxative into the sparkling water. You can have no doubt at all that we really took to that idea. So we bought some powder at the drug store, and Yas set off to Mr. Rubstak's stand, and we watched from a distance. And right then Mr. Katsenelenbogen shuffles over wearing his black hat and carrying another just like it under his arm, leaning on his umbrella, from which he never parted, no matter how baking hot it was, and stopped as was his habit near the stand, placed the hat on the counter, hooked his umbrella over his elbow, and asked for a glass of sparkling water with lemon syrup. At that moment we ran up and one after another started yammering at Mr. Rubtsak to give each of us an ice cream, and really fast because we were rushing to school. Mr. Rubtsak nodded to Yas for him to pour the water, and he began to portion out the ice cream into paper cups for us, and I said to mr. teacher that he had a white feather on the back of his frock coat, that there must be some blonde girl wooing mr. teacher, and that blonde girls are really rare among Jewish girls. Then mr. teacher became alarmed and immediately began to inspect his frock coat and, grabbing the unfortunate blonde hair or rather feather, crumpled it up and with an expression of disgust on his face threw it at his feet and stamped on it. In the meantime they poured him his lemon-flavored sparkling water, above which yellowish droplets were jumping in the air, playing rainbow-like in the sun, and Mr. Katsenelenbogen with delight tasted the soda water, feasting his eyes on the sunny day, then pulled out of his pocket a checkered kerchief as large as a tablecloth, the other end of which, by the time he had wiped his lips still remained in the pocket of his frock coat, took the hat under his arm, and shuffled on, waving his umbrella. We moved further away, licking our ice cream, and in a minute Yas met up with us, and then we hid on the wrap-around porch outside of Yosko's windows. We watched Mr. Katsenelenbogen place the hat, in which Yosko's head immediately sank down below his ears, on Yosko's head. But his mother Golda propped up the hat with her hair curlers, and again we could see Yosko's sad eyes and lips pursed, ready to cry. Mr. Katsenelenbogen began to read some kind of mysterious words from the textbook, and Yosko repeated them. This lasted maybe ten minutes, when suddenly the teacher straightened up on his armchair, twisted his head in various directions like a rooster on a hill, then took off his hat, and after that violently threw off his frock coat and flew from the room into the hallway, where there was a common lavatory for several of the rooms. However, he failed to make his way inside because the water closet was occupied. Wolff was sitting there, and to the despairing screams of mr. teacher answered with an expressive moan, delivering along with it all the appropriate sounds, which he had been practicing for nearly half a day to perfect his performance.

Mr. Katsenelenbogen had already grabbed his stomach, dancing away a "tumbalalaika,"[45] and a hissing flew out from his lips when momma Golda ran out into the hallway to see what had happened to mr. teacher. When she found out what an unpleasantness had befallen him, she knocked on the door of the water closet, but also heard the moaning and unseemly fartissimo, then she rushed back into the house and carried out a pot and told mr. teacher to do his obligation in the pot. Mr. teacher waved his hands and whispered that it was unseemly to do such things in the hallway, but Mrs. Golda promised that she would stand on the steps, so that no one would catch mr. teacher in such an awkward situation. Then Mr. Katsenelenbogen took off the suspender straps from his shoulders, and began to take off button after button, loop after loop, but not quite as quickly as he had hoped, and in an instant, we heard a booming rumble, which reminded us of a landslide in the mountains, and together with the rumble, a shriek of both despair and relief echoed at the same time. Mrs. Golda flew to that rumble from the steps and quickly covered her nose, and mr. teacher stood there sobbing with his pants in his hands, not knowing whether it was from happiness or from grief, when

45 A Russian-Jewish folk or love song performed in Yiddish.

the door of the water closet opened up and Wolff jumped out, choking both from laughter and the odor. Mrs. Golda flung out choice curses in Yiddish, but even we understood her, and we took to our heels.

Yosko told us what happened further. That is, Mrs. Golda had to remove the teacher's clothes, heat up the hot water boiler, and bathe him in a wash tub, and then also wash his pants and underwear along with two shirts, not to mention his socks, garters, and even his shoes. Mr. teacher was morally broken and crippled upon figuring out the trick the damned kiddies played on him. He sat on the couch, wrapped in a bed sheet, and mumbled some kind of words of wisdom to himself under his breath. Tears flowed down his face and sorrow ate at his soul, and Mrs. Golda cursed us to holy hell, but she cursed Wolff the most, especially when she noticed we were peeking in to see her hanging mr. teacher's underwear on twine. The teacher didn't utter a single word, and to all the replies of the lady of the house answered just "uh huh: or "uh-uh." And then Mrs. Golda grabbed a straw broom and began to chase Yosko around the house, though he wasn't guilty in the least before God and had no clue about our operation. Having seen that he was hiding from her and defending himself as much as he could, whereas in all other instances when he had committed an offense, he obediently got a whacking, his mother believed his innocence in the end and sent him to meet Leah at the music school, so that she could stay till late evening at her aunt's until mr. teacher's shirts and trousers had dried, and he could get out of the hideous bed sheet.

From that time on Yosko stopped studying Hebrew. Mr. Katsenelenbogen would avoid Mr. Rubtsak's stall like the plague, and Mr. Rubtsak couldn't stop wondering why mr. teacher stopped liking sparkling lemon drinks so suddenly. After that incident, Yosko didn't see Mr. Katsenelenbogen for a long time, but when he met him in 1940 when Lviv was already under Soviet rule,[46] he politely greeted him and tried to apologize for the regrettable mishap. But Mr. Katsenelenbogen patted him on the back and said to him with sadness in his eyes:

"It's nothing, never mind, soon the time will come when you will envy those who have died, and more than anything, those who haven't been born."

When Yosko related that to us, we couldn't fathom at all what mr. teacher had in mind, till the beginning of July 1941, when our eyes were opened, because we saw mr. teacher among those Jews who were carrying out corpses from the prison on Lontsky Street, corpses that already had begun to stink, and that heavy stench struck your nostrils, corpses of people whom the Soviets had shot in all the prisons of Ukraine when they were retreating from the Nazis. There were corpses of young girls, raped and mutilated, and there were corpses of seminarians covered in dreadful bruises everywhere. All the Jewish people were in tears while they were carrying them and didn't turn up their noses like all the people standing to the side, covering their noses with handkerchiefs to avoid breathing in the stench. And later I

---

46 The Soviet Red Army occupied Lviv on September 17, 1939 and abandoned the city on June 22, 1941 before the arrival of the approaching Nazi army, which occupied the city on July 1, 1941 and which began a systematic eradication of the Jewish population over the next three years. Soviet forces retook the city in July 1944, and the city and much of Western Ukraine was annexed by the USSR.

saw Mr. Katsenelenbogen crawling along the pavement in front of the Opera Theater and scrubbing it with a toothbrush, and next to him other Jews crawling on all fours and also scrubbing the pavement. The math teacher Leo Feld, the musician Hershel Shtrauss, and the owner of the production shop Jakub Iker, and even the inveterate card player Itzhak Kon, who didn't fit in such dignified company at all, were also there. Nearby SS guys were just standing there laughing, and the crowd was laughing, darting glances at the Nazis, so as not to miss the next wave of laughter and join in with it in time, because that laughter drew them closer, raised them above this Jewish mob, above this rabble, that once was so full of itself, and today crawls along the ground in their suits and shirts and cravats. That laughter made them equal to the daring Goths and gave indulgences for their survival, for if you didn't laugh, then right away you found yourself on the other side, among these black bedbugs with long side curls. Without them there was no place for you among the representatives of civilized Europe. And I saw tears roll along the sunken cheeks of Mr. Katsenelenbogen, and he moistened his toothbrush in them and cleaned the pavement, tile after tile, and his cuffs had already gotten dirty, along with his knees, and someone in the crowd even kicked him from behind, and mr. teacher fell stomach-first onto the pavement. His spectacles flew off, and he groped around for them. Then I became so disgusted, so pained by the fact that we had caused him such misery, a poor lonely man who had never hurt anyone, he was just carrying out his teaching duties. I couldn't restrain myself. I bent over and gave him his glasses, and the crowd irately began to boo me. Someone pushed me and I flew against the wall, and the

SS guy gestured for me to come over and wanted to know if I was a Jew or not. Assistants immediately appeared and volunteered to tear off my pants to determine whether I was a Jew, but right then our school receptionist darted out from the crowd and lashed out:

"You back off! That's Leska Barbaryka's son! What kinds of people are you! I've known him since he was a tot!"

One of the SS guys translated the receptionist's words, then smiled, nodded, and shooed me away with his hand to let me know I was free to go, and I left, preserving the image of the poor teacher in my memory along with all the others who were crawling, even the card shark Itsyk. I saw Mr. Katsenelenbogen for the last time at the pharmacy. They had banned selling medicine to Jews, but the Teacher had not yet heard about that order and asked for heart medicine drops. The druggist didn't know how to answer so as not to insult the Teacher; he finally said that they hadn't delivered them yet, and the Teacher stepped out of the drugstore and moved in the direction of another one. I caught up to him and explained that he couldn't buy medicine anywhere but that I would gladly do that for him. He was surprised, but agreed to it, and when I handed him that medicine and didn't want to take money from him, he asked who I was, but I didn't tell him that I was carrying a sin against him in my soul, and I didn't say that I was friends with Yosko, because then he would have put two and two together. I just smiled and joked:

"A good Samaritan."

8

After leaving his father, Marko put his hand around Danka's waist and asked:

"Well, what do you think of my old man?"

"He's not all that old. By the way, I noticed that you didn't call him 'dad' even once."

"I grew up without him. That's understandable."

"Don't you feel sorry for him?"

"No. I know the way everything was... They constantly nagged him, my mother and granny... They didn't see any sense in his scholarly interests and insisted that he be engaged in tutoring, which brought actual money in. He eventually had enough of that and left.

"So, you'll never call him dad?"

"I don't know. I barely manage to address him with an informal you."[47]

They got into the car, and Marko pressed on the gas pedal.

"Should we go downtown for some champagne?"

"I've had enough. I've already had a lot of wine. Drive me home," she said dryly, watching the gray evening haze descend onto the street.

"It's still early."

"What of it?"

"Nothing. So, maybe, let's stop somewhere in a quiet spot."

"What for?" She said in such a frosty tone that he looked at her in surprise, and then put his hand on her thigh and laughed:

---

47 Like the French *tu* and *vous*, Ukrainian has an informal *ty* and formal *vy* form.

"For just a little of that."

But Danka pushed his hand away:

"You'd better hold the steering wheel and not my leg."

"What's wrong with you? Don't you feel like it?"

"I don't feel like doing it in the car."

"Would it be our first time doing it in the car?"

She didn't answer. She just looked straight ahead and pondered something, and when they passed the Church of Sts. Peter and Paul, she crossed herself, and her lips moved.

"Did you say something?"

"No."

"Are you talking to yourself?"

"I do that often. It's strange that you noticed it just now," she uttered, and in an instant was already somewhere entirely far away in her thoughts. Near the Lyalka Puppet Theater she barely restrained herself from asking him to stop the car and get out, so she could go somewhere in the quiet, narrow streets to continue talking to herself, but she remembered that she had an extremely precious treasure in her bag—a book, which she would still dive into that evening, about which she had dreamt. And her hand groped throughout her bag involuntarily, as if she were double-checking to see if the book had disappeared.

H

Wolff had studied medicine with Professor Weigel and Yas had studied philosophy at the university. Well, with me, it was the same as in the fairytale: there are three clever brothers, and the fourth one so-so. Though my colleagues didn't take me for a fool, my mother constantly agonized over that problem and couldn't decide at all whether her son was a dunce or a genius, because you know, geniuses are also a little screwed up. I personally was inclined to believe I was a genius, because nothing puffed me up as much as extraordinary ideas that simply demanded that I jot them down for eternity, so that future generations, thanks to me, would have the opportunity to improve themselves. And, since my mother had confidently established herself in the literary world, I also decided not to lag behind. Having acquired a large thick notebook, with numbered lines, I wrote on its cover "Reflections and Fantasies. Volume One." I had seen these kinds of notebooks on store counters, and shopkeepers entered all kinds of stuff in them, for example, "Mr. Littlebutt bought a kilo of meat on credit" or "From Sknylivsky's mill—four sacks of finely sifted flour." In five hundred years these kinds of notebooks would be an invaluable treasure. Too bad the stupid shopkeepers don't understand that, so can one doubt the immense value of my "Reflections and Fantasies?" To be honest, though, I started this notebook not so much for myself as for my mother, so she wouldn't try to push me into taking some job. The notebook was a marvelous excuse. It always lay in front of me on a little table, while I was picking inside my ear with a pen, scratching my forehead and trying to give birth to some kind of reflection or some lifeless fantasy. During special moments of inspiration, I even managed to scribble an entire page. I never doubted that one day it would be an epoch-making work, because an epoch-making work is the kind that rises above an epoch. More precisely—it generally says to hell with the epoch, holds it deep in its ass, shits on it, that's what an epoch-making work is. That's why I always carried a notepad, into which I entered my epoch-making thoughts that foamed and burst out of me, like boiled milk. When it was no longer possible to contain them, I jotted them down hastily, so that later in the sacred silence of home, having rolled about every such thought like a candy on my tongue, I could write it down in my notebook and in this way engrave it forever and ever. That's why it's not surprising that I really hated it when my mother would bring me out of my transcendental state. On a few occasions she was trying to find out what the heck I was scribbling in sacred silence, and quietly, snuck up on tiptoe from behind me so she could peek over my shoulder to recognize the unrecognizable, to perceive the imperceptible, to grasp the ungraspable. But because her heavy breathing would always give her away, I would snuff out her impulses with an explosion of incredibly grand indignation. She got lost in her simplicity and completely forgot why she had snuck up on me.

"Mom," I said. "Don't you have anything better to do? Have you already swept the dust from under the kitchen cupboard? It seems to me that a ball of powder is forming there that's ready to explode at the first opportunity. Have you baked the walnut tart with dried fruit that you promised me last week? Have you chatted with your neighbor friend, whose dead cat came to life and, digging itself out of the grave like Lazarus, returned home? Or maybe you've already finished working on the little inscription for the grave of Mr. Puppyman? And have you found our grandpa's false teeth, the ones he forgot in Mr. Snoutsky's pub? Your head must be splitting from the all these problems, and you sneak up to me like a fox to a henhouse!"

"It's me who's a fox?" Mom grew indignant. "It's me—to a henhouse? I cook for you, I bake for you, I do the wash for you, I iron for you, and look at you! A sponger! What good fortune that your father isn't around to see this disgrace! And he wanted his son to become a human being!"

From that time on I locked myself in my room and used to lie on the bed, lost in my thoughts and fantasies; at least I was able to memorize the ceiling, which you couldn't say about the textbooks that were scattered under my bed. Afterward I jotted down: "Even a genius needs companionship. Even a genius can be unfaithful to his wife. Even a genius washes his own socks." The mention of the socks that my mom always washed provoked associations with other parts of my closet, and my next thought was: "The fact that someone wears underwear doesn't mean that he will end up in paradise sooner than someone who doesn't wear it." I suppose everyone in his life can find someone who didn't wear underwear. I knew at least four such people. There was old nutty Mrs. Skorobetska, who in 1894 became famous for lifting up her skirt and exposing her bare ass to the first Lviv tramcar that ambled its way to Lychakiv Cemetery. Little has changed since that time, because although Mrs. Skorobetska has completely come to look like a mushroom and dried up, her bare ass has continued to remain the final argument in any debate. The second and third persons without underwear were two wheeler-dealers on Rynok Square, who showed their bare behinds to each other as the final weighty argument in a lengthy dispute. I wasn't the only witness to this historical scene, a whole bunch of people were, too, so, this famous occurrence even ended up in the newspapers. And the fourth person without underwear was Leah. From childhood she didn't wear panties, though she was an incredible neatnik and, going to the water closet, she always grabbed a washbasin with warm water, so she could wash up immediately. We found that out from Yosko, but I myself once ascertained it when we played hide and seek. Leah was eleven then, and I was fourteen. Her eyes were like two embers, and her luscious cherry lips looked as if she had just drunk a quart of blood, and there in the really thick elderberry bushes, where she and I had hidden, Leah sat on the grass, bending her knees in front of her and grabbing them with her hands, and I laid down on my back. Both of us were hiding and didn't say a word. It was just then that between the lowered hem of her dress and the grass, I saw her bare bottom with a small mysterious slit that reminded me of a smile which I had not had the opportunity to see before. Thin, little hairs just barely were beginning to curl around her maidenhood. I couldn't take my eyes off her and grew still, not breathing, as here the hem of her dress pushed up, leaving bare even more of that landscape of wondrous beauty, to which, against her will, her hand stretched and covered it with her palm, as though she were protecting it from all the misfortunes of the world, and her palm sensed the swelling warmth, which was radiating from her. This warmth moved upward along her arm, passed along to my chest, and I already sensed such a hellish heat behind my breastbone that I suddenly leaned back. And Leah, as if nothing had happened, lowered the hem of her dress and said: "It's time to come out now. They won't find us anyway." From that time on a certain invisible gossamer thread of feelings, still unformed and not comprehended fully, began to unite us, but when, like my peers, from time to time I plunged into solo-action, I summoned Leah's maidenhood in my imagination, and then warmth again penetrated into my hand and stirred in my chest. There was good reason, because Leah was becoming more and more beautiful over the years. She was already as beautiful as a doll as teenager; black curls framed her head, and a captivating spark appeared in her eyes and a blush on her cheeks; moreover, her breasts grew full, each of which you couldn't fit in the palm of your hand. Later her hips became rounder, and her bottom began to thrust out so much that I had to turn my eyes away. For quite a long time we didn't have the opportunity to be alone again, but always, when we happened to end up next to each other, I touched her palm with my pinky. And she responded with the very same barely noticeable touch, with which a warm current penetrated me, making my heart beat faster. Sometimes I managed to catch her pinky and hold it for several minutes under the table, sensing her react each time to my touch with her thin little fingers, without betraying herself with any movement of her head or her voice; and such clandestine mysteriousness enticed me even more, compelling me to seek out every opportunity to touch her. But when she turned sixteen, we were no longer compelled to hide. I would meet her at the high school and would walk her home, and along the way we would stroll holding hands in the Jesuit Gardens[48] or on High Castle Mountain, and for a long time still I didn't dare kiss her. In fact, I was bolder when I was younger. I don't know how long it would have continued, if not for one time when we were sitting on a bench on High Castle Mountain, and there wasn't a living soul all around other than squirrels. Leah didn't press my head to hers and didn't kiss me, but I pressed my lips to hers, and though we were doing this for the first time and really slobbered all over each other, we both liked it. I even grew emboldened and put one hand on her knee, and she covered it with her hand, and we sat there that way, leaning against each other silently, because I didn't have anything to say. I completely froze up.

Things with girls went as smooth as silk for Yas and Wolff. The sexiest nymphs would cuddle up so close to them, you'd be blinded. I was dazzled by Leah, but Yosko had problems on the love front. He was a small, scrawny, big-eared four eyes. He liked Ruta, who studied with him at the conservatory, but she was quite an arrogant girl and taller than Yosko. I couldn't even say what she wanted, maybe a knight on a white horse. Ordinary guys surrounded her, but she didn't want ordinary. Moreover, Ruta had been baptized, she was a Ukrainianized Jewish girl, and her father worked for a Ukrainian magazine and wrote articles on historical themes, in which he genuinely sympathized with our poor, unfortunate, shabby people. We decided to help our friend, so we gathered together in a pub, and I said:

"Yosko, you know that we're friends forever and we're ready to make any sacrifice for you." Yosko nodded sadly.

48 Now called Ivan Franko Park in front of the entrance to Ivan Franko Lviv National University.

"So let's do it this way. Go over tomorrow to Ruta's and say that you have something important to tell her and invite her to Jesuit Park. You'll go for a stroll with her. On your way there wag your tongue about whatever you want. Once you find yourself in the park, three hooligans will harass you. They'll try to hug Ruta and hold your arms. But you'll break away and toss them off like sheaves of wheat."

Out of surprise Yosko blinked his eyes, dropped his jaw, and gaped at us.

"Me? With these hands?" And he displayed to us his thin pale palms with long fingers.

"Don't be afraid. Those hoodlums will be us."

"You?" He couldn't believe it.

"Yes, us. Why are you surprised? We have to rehearse it with you several times so everything goes smoothly."

"But... but...," Yosko wiped his forehead. "Is this really chivalrous?"

"Yosyo," Wolff put his hand on his shoulder. "Open up those peepers! When you meet a lion it's best to be a lion. But with a woman you always have to be a fox."

We finally managed to convince him. After several attempts Yosko distinguished himself not too badly. He got so into the role that one time he smashed me in the chops. When I looked in the mirror, my busted lip on which a drop of blood was shining elicited in me a very timely idea.

"Yosko," I said. "You have to take with a single ripe cherry, and when you're slugging it out with us, toss into your maw without anyone noticing it, and bite it in a way that the juice leaks from your lips, then spit out the stone."

"Why?" Yosko didn't grasp it.

"My, aren't you astute! Like Berk's pants inside out. So

it looks like blood. As soon as she sees it, Ruta will immediately pull out a handkerchief and clean you up. Can you imagine what a heroic look you'll have then?"

"That's awesome!" Yosko was pleased. "But why just one cherry? I'll take a handful with me!"

"Are you crazy?" Wolff exclaimed. "If you released too much cherry juice, then she'll figure out it's not blood."

"What guarantee is there that together with the juice cherry skin doesn't come out of your mouth?" Yas noted quite rightly. "She might think you tore off a bit of your tongue as well. It has to be a thin red trickle."

The next day we hid ourselves in the jasmine bushes. It was the midday hour, and it was very humid. The park, which from early morning was filled with nannies pushing carriages and senior citizens, was now completely deserted. We didn't have to wait for long before we caught sight of Yosko and Ruta. He was babbling something animatedly, waving his arms like a windmill, but Ruta was listening to him inattentively, looking to either side of her and admiring the little birds and flowers, because she was the kind of girl who knew the value of words and the value of nature's beauty. We pulled our caps low over our foreheads, tied handkerchiefs around our faces, and unexpectedly jumped on the path.

"Stop!" Yas barked and turned to Ruta: "Give me your bag!" In the meantime, we rushed up to Yosko and grabbed his arms, but he deftly wriggled and kicked me in the knee. May a dog bite your nuts! We didn't agree to that! I really squawked in pain and then I saw Ruta smack Yas on the head with her bag. There were probably books of great wisdom in the bag, because Yas also curled up. Yosko and Wolff fell into the bushes as planned. There Wolff loudly began to groan and, pretending that he had barely escaped from Yosko, took his belongings under his arm and rushed to escape, and we after him. I'm limping and Yas is holding his head; blood was gushing from his ear. When we ran far away enough and examined our wounds, it turned out that we really got nailed. Ruta hit Yas so well that she tore his ear, I had a gashed knee, and Wolff's nose was dripping, like a gutter.

"Holy smoke!" Yas sighed, putting a handkerchief to his ear. "That girl can kick anyone's butt by herself!"

"And Yosko! What a swine he is!" I shook my head. "He put on boots instead of summer shoes. Do you understand? Boots! With thick soles! When he kicked me in the balls. I was seeing stars. That wasn't our plan!"

"We were just supposed to roll a little in the bushes and *schluss* [that's it]," Wolff grumbled. "But for some reason he socks me in the nose with his fist! And then gives it to me on the back! With those little fists of his! With those tiny little fingers! And who would have thought that he's able to do that? But then *campa* [a fight]!

In the evening we waited for Yosko at our prearranged spot at Zimmerman's Tavern on the corner of Yanivska and Kleparivska Streets. On the table in front of us there were mugs full of beer, *kvargli*[49] cheese fritters, salted pickles, bread, and a bowl of cracklings. Yosko came in all blossoming, smiling, and was very surprised to see our dark expressions. When we stated our concerns about his bad conduct,

49 Fried molded cottage cheese patties mixed with eggs, onions, and spices. Thanks to Olha Tytarenko for enlightening me about the culinary delicacy. She also found the following recipe online for making them: http://panistefa.com/zglevilyj-syr-kvargli/.

he justified himself by saying that he got carried away and too into the role, got overly excited, and anyway, everything needed to look as realistic as possible, so he tried as best he could, and those efforts paid off handsomely, because Ruta not only wiped the "blood" from his lips, but also gave him a little kiss. Yosko was in seventh heaven from happiness, and when he said that we could order ourselves anything we wanted, and it would be his treat, we finally defrosted, though we regretted that we chose such a cheap tavern and didn't go to the Roma.

Now everyone had his very own girlfriend, and we took strolls already as four couples. We often made our way to Kortumov Mountain and would hold picnics there, admiring the city from up high, but down below tumid gardens roasted in the summer sun.

"Look," I said to Leah. "There's your house."

"Yeah, and Mrs. Gell is beating her carpet," she smiled.

"You're fibb... ! You can't see that, because it's not visible."

"You're blind as a bat! I even hear the echoes of those sounds. Oh! Listen!"

I listened but heard just the singing of birds and the rustle of leaves.

"And over there in the garden Anelka's sunbathing," Yas picked up.

"Where?" I didn't believe it but looked closely."

"Stark naked."

But where?

"At home in her yard...," Wolff said and peered with his hand shielding his eyes. "Do you see—there... under the cherry trees... There a butterfly sat on her butt."

"Yeah sure," Leah nodded. "A red one."

9

The old three-story building on Kleparivska Street still retained the pre-war odors that tenaciously ate into the peeling plaster, into pockmarked windowsills and frames and creaking stairs that with every step resounded in a plaintive moan. Oh, they've seen so much in their lifetime. German soldiers trampled them searching for Jews, Cheka[50] secret police trampled them tracking down the underground, and then under the rattling of machine guns, both led people out to their execution, and the steps sympathetically sighed and sobbed and coughed. And for a long time, the window panes held onto the turbid reflections of missing people, their fearful faces, their terrified eyes, all their despair and fear and rage and irreconcilability. And on the walls, their fingerprints took a long time to fade away.

Yarosh walked up to the very top, to the third floor, where there were two doors to the dwellings, and metal doors to the attic overhead. The doors to the dwellings had narrow apertures covered with brass plates with the inscription "Letters," into which once newspapers and letters were easily pushed to plop instantly onto the floor. But only on one door's right jamb was a brass case the size of a little finger nailed diagonally. This was the *mezuzah*, into which a verse of Scripture written on parchment in calligraphy was placed into a tube. Upon leaving home or returning home, every devout Jew pressed two fingers to his lips and then to

50 The Cheka (*Chrezvychainaia komisiia* in Russian, meaning "extraordinary commission") was established by Vladimir Lenin in 1917 and was the first of several iterations of the Soviet secret police.

the *mezuzah*. At eye level you could see a round peephole, and under it a long frame in which you could insert a card with the name of the people who lived there. It's empty now. On the doorpost the massive bell recalled a breast with a firm nipple that invitingly beckons an index finger to touch it. Yarosh pressed the bell, a sound echoed as though from deep in the bowels, and after it, the unhurried shuffling of slippers. The peephole flashed open and someone's eye carefully examined the guest, and then a hoarse voice asked: "Who is it?" "Yarosh. I called you earlier." "Oh, yes..." The scraping of a key, the clank of the chain, the door opened, and there, hunched in the shadows, was a really scrawny, tall figure.

"Come in, come in... You don't need to take off your shoes, there's no mud in the street...."

The voice resembled the creaking stairs, its particularly Galician manner of expression and its guttural "r" sounded like the roar of a prehistoric creature made. It's not surprising, because the older Galician Jew is as wondrous as a dinosaur. It's not possible to see him alive now, you can only dig him up. Yarosh's excavations were crowned with success. He managed to procure from oblivion old Josef Milker, whose phone number Danka had given him.

"Please come on in," the old man took him along a long corridor to a spacious bright study chock full of shelves of books, which the owner of the house obviously did not allow to plunge into a pleasant nap, from time to time moving one, taking one in hand, turning the pages, and moving it from one spot to another. Yarosh's eyes slid across old bindings, recognizing inscriptions in Yiddish, Hebrew, German, Polish, and Ukrainian. Many books flaunted white tassel bookmarks, like scholarly regalia—we're read and studied! One more thing impressed the guest—vases with poppies. For the first time he had the occasion to see such a variety of poppies in a private home. Additionally, these poppies were unusual—they were not just red and purple, but white, pink, yellow, and burgundy—and they were significantly taller than those grown in a field or in a garden. Some of them reached the ceiling with blooms larger than the size of a head. Some were past their prime, others just had released their buds.

The old man invited me to sit in an armchair, he himself sat down comfortably opposite me and put his dry, wrinkled right hand on his scrawny knees. Instead of his left arm, there was an empty sleeve, tucked under his belt.

"Poppies—they're my weakness," he smiled to his guest.—I've been breeding them for a while."

"I've never seen such big, tall poppies."

"Poppies are very sensitive. I speak to them, turn on music for them, read aloud to them... Solitary men, you know, sometimes have their eccentricities. But this eccentricity of mine has been fruitful. So what exactly interests you about the Yaniv camp?"

"The "Tango of Death." The text, the music, and the authors. As far as I know, you were one of the musicians."

"Yes. I played the violin. It's strange that anyone else is interested in it."

"Did all the rest die?"

"You might say that."

"What do you mean by that?"

"A death isn't always a death. Sometimes it's just an amazing staging, a performance. The 'Tango of Death' at first glance is a melancholic melody, full of nostalgia. It seems it's nothing special. Have you heard it?"

"Of course. It's the same melody as the tango 'Milonga.'"

"It's a bit similar, but in fact the closest to the 'Tango of Death' in sound was the 'Tango-Macabre,' during which lovers shot themselves. Imagine—a despairing young man goes to a restaurant, pays the orchestra, requests a tango, and after downing a few glasses, shoots himself at the table in front of everyone. That's why it's called the 'Tango-Macabre,' but it actually had an entirely peaceful title—'That Last Sunday.' However, I must say that this similarity is only ostensible. To the layman. A musician immediately notices the difference. Three of us wrote the score of this melody—me, Professor Shtriks of the Lviv Conservatory and Cuba Mund, [51] the conductor of the Lviv Opera. Before the war, I played with Shtriks in the Bristol Restaurant where he conducted the orchestra. When we ended up in the ghetto, I showed them the amazing notes... More precisely there were twelve notes in all... They came from an old manuscript... The author of that manuscript was Lviv pharmacist Johann Kalkbrenner... In 1640 he escaped from Kraków to Lviv and brought the Latin translation of an ancient manuscript that was written in a language not yet known...."

"Arcanumian?"

"Yes. How did you know?" The host's eyes flashed. "Do you know anything about Arcanum?"

"To be honest, I should have told you everything before. I have been working for a long time on the culture of the

51 The stage name of Jakub Mund (1905-1941), who was a violinist and musical director in in the Lviv Conservatory. He was killed during the Nazi occupation of the city at the Yaniv concentration camp.

Near East and in particular on Arcanum. I wrote a textbook of the Arcanumian language, compiled a dictionary, and right now am working on translations of literary works."

Then he spoke about the Arcanumian "Book of the Dead" and the dance of death, the "dan-go mrah."

"That's really very interesting," Mr. Josef shook his head thoughtfully. "Then you should hear something else. That is, Rabbi Nathan Spira of Krakow, a kabbalist and Talmudist, produced that Latin translation of the Arcanumian manuscript in the early sixteenth century. The pharmacist wrote a book, not preserved in its entirety, that consisted of translations of ancient texts, including the translation by Nathan Spira, and the remainder of it comprised his own comments. And then individual pages from the manuscript were found by my childhood friend in the Ossolineum Library.[52] When we started to read it, we discovered an astonishing theory. The human soul, after leaving the body, after some time—and it could be a year, or twenty or forty years—is born again in a new body, but it remembers nothing about its previous life. People who have experienced great love, meet again in a new life and experience it again. Inseparable friends very naturally and unobtrusively become acquainted in a new life and are friends until death, parents meet their children... But none of them can remember anything, they don't even realize that they can remember something... True, there are sometimes cases when due to stress dormant human knowledge awakens in a person, and he or she begins, for example, to speak in a language previously unknown to him or her or to communicate in detail something that happened a long time ago. In any case, you can

52 Located in Wrocław, Poland.

imagine how much easier it would be for people to die if they knew that their soul, embodied in another person, had not lost anything from his or her previous knowledge and feelings. But in fact, we still remember nothing. But here the pharmacist discovered in the manuscript a secret that can awaken that previous knowledge in us and sort of prolong our previous life. To do this, right before death you need to absorb a special melody...."

"Absorb a special melody?" Yarosh repeated.

"I'm afraid I'm explaining this in a really primitive way... By the way, I was right—you don't listen to but absorb it. With your entire body, your entire being. The fact is that the tone of the sound of any musical note corresponds to the tonality of the sound of a corresponding organ or parts of the body. In other words, our soul is a musical composition that an entire coordinated orchestra of internal organs performs. Do you understand?" Upon seeing the wonder in Yarosh's eyes, he continued: "Johann Kalkbrenner discovered that the human soul is a self-contained symphony, the period of sound that lasts is not only from birth to death, but even longer, maybe even forever. You just have to change the composition of the orchestra. That manuscript also contained his treatise about the way in which you can create the score of exactly such a life symphony for any person, so that he or she by strictly following the right notes can live as long as possible and see where danger awaits and can avoid it in time. Every person is a separate tuning fork that is very sensitive, and when the specially selected sounds pass through a person, then a special way of seeing will be revealed. You just need to let the sounds fill you."

"But what is the link with the 'Tango of Death?'"

The old man rose up:

"Pardon me, I have to take some pills. My orchestra's already belching." He pulled the pills out from the drawer, swallowed them with mineral water, and asked: "Would you like some tea or coffee?"

But Yarosh refused, he didn't want to be distracted from the exciting conversation.

"The link with the 'Tango of Death' is that the tango became the melody that played the role of a tunnel for the soul's new reincarnation. Those fated to die at the Yaniv camp died specifically to this melody... More precisely, almost to this melody, because what we played had some subtle nuances without which the transformation of the soul could not occur. We played the tango that is known by everyone, but which had twelve notes from the manuscript fit into it. Without these notes the tango would lose all its power. The notes that were in front of our eyes had certain signs that were only understood by us, it could be some dots, little splotches or underlining. A musician not initiated in their meaning would play the melody without any consequences. Thus, the soul's new birth happened only to those who heard our orchestra right before their death. Hence they were resurrected and lived, and perhaps still are alive... Only they don't realize it, and those who knew them before cannot recognize them now. Although I have not yet lost hope to meet them."

"Then I don't see the point in this reincarnation. What's the difference if my soul will live in another body if there will be no ME? It will be a different person with other interests and hobbies. It won't be ME."

"But a person can awaken the memory of a previous life under one condition: if that person just before his or her death heard the melody from Kalkbrenner's treatise. And you can do this only one way: a person needs to hear that melody again."

"That is, he or she will remember only the life that they left upon hearing this melody? It doesn't apply to all previous lives?"

"Exactly."

"I read somewhere in Oscar Wilde that music gives us our own past, about which we never suspected up to that moment, forcing us to regret losses that never were and actions for which we are not to blame."

"Apparently, you've sometimes even encountered such feelings that this or that has already happened to you, or a person you see for the first time reminds you of someone you know, but when it was—you're unable to remember. Sometimes in dreams you see streets that don't exist, but the dream keeps coming back again and again... you know these streets and homes by heart, you even have the desire to find them... although you understand that it's just a dream. Dreams elucidate lost memory from us, but we remember little from our dreams. If we tried to analyze our dreams, to delve deeply into them, to move in search of ghostly streets and people that we dream... Of course, certain efforts are necessary... Some kind of impetus. The people you have contacted in a previous existence can be right nearby, because former friends attract old friends and former loves attract former lovers. Of course, they don't even suspect it. But people who just before death hear the melody of the 'Tango of Death' carry it inside themselves in their next existence."

"Where does that impetus come from?"

"Maybe they'll get it from hearing the melody of 'Tango of Death' again or, maybe, just as Rabbi Spira explained it."

"Unfortunately, I'm not familiar with his works."

"Then I need to tell you something. For the pharmacist in his commentaries based what he wrote precisely on the theory of Rabbi Spira,[53] who looked at the whole world as mist that conceals mystical substance diverse in its manifestations. Not just the Torah—the whole universe in his eyes was one great mystery. Everything material—man and animal, fire and water, bushes, trees, rocks—were for him filled with profound symbolism. The visible world is just the shell of wandering souls seeking the realization of a higher purpose. Spira and his teacher Yitzchak Luria knew the secret of these souls, their path into the world, their beginnings, and all stages of their past and future reincarnations. For them, it was enough just to look people in the face to know immediately whose soul had been transformed into it. They were endowed with the ability to reveal the source of the souls of all the biblical, Talmudic and post-Talmudic righteous. Whether wandering with their students in the countryside, along meadows and forests, or sailing the sea—everywhere and in everything, in the lapping of waves, the rustling of trees, the flutter of wings, in the chirring of grasshoppers, in the croaking of frogs, in the shuddering of branches, in the shimmering of air, and in the singing birds—everywhere they saw swarms of souls who sought perfection and redemption, heard their voices, their whispers...

Yitzchak Luria called this doctrine, which became the center of his entire Cabbalistic system, "Oylom a-tikun," which means "World of Perfection" or "World of Purifica-

53 Hasidic rabbi Chaim Elezar Spira (1868-1937).

tion." Rabbi Spira further developed this doctrine. All souls, he taught, in all their forms were initially concentrated in the progenitor Adam at his appearance in the world; some of them nested in his head, others in his eyes, in all his pores and in all the members of his body. In these primordial souls the source of goodness dominated, but after the Fall "good and evil became mixed together," and now the world is full of pure souls, mixed with sparks of evil and impure souls, wicked, mixed with sparks of goodness and holiness. Chained in its bodily shell, the soul suffuses its divine juices into the impure shell, behold, like a tree trunk passes its healing juices to its fruits, leaves, and bark. The second coming of the Messiah depends on this process of permeating the body with the soul. It will happen only when the process of cleansing souls, the separation of good from evil is finally completed."

Mr. Josef got up, went to a bookshelf and pulling down some old book, opened it where it was marked.

"I need to look at the treatise of Rabbi Spira. My memory is already escaping me. Thus, two paths lead to the differentiation between good and evil: "Gilgul[54]" (transmigration of souls) and "ibur" (the interrelationship of souls). "Gilgul" is a transmigration of the soul that has happened on earth into the body of a newborn baby; from birth to death the soul is doomed to share with the body all the troubles and hardships of its fate. "Ibur" is the embodiment of an additional soul into a living and even mature person, similar to a new life being born in a pregnant woman. Therefore, two souls are imprisoned in a person: one—from the moment of birth, the second—in adulthood. There are two types of

54 A Hebrew word and the kabalistic concept of reincarnation.

"ibur." The first is the soul that originated in an adult and abides in it for the sake of itself, inspired by the need to fulfill the commandment—a *mitzvah*, which it did not fulfill on the path of its past reincarnations. And in the second type—the soul is infused in a person for the sake of that person's salvation, to maintain and direct him or her onto a righteous path. The first soul fills the person's entire being as its main spiritual substance and remains in it until it is able to attain its purpose and fulfill its sought-for *mitzvah*, and once it has done that, it can leave the body. The second soul is free from mandatory involvement in the sufferings and hardships of the body. Without having a certain lifetime in this body, it remains until a person goes on the righteous path of good, and the more righteous a person is, the more closely it is linked with his or her soul. But when a person turns onto the path of sin, the soul leaves him or her and goes away. Thus, in these two ways of "gilgul" and "ibur"—the separation of good from evil occurs as well as the filtering of good itself. So when the shell of evil falls from the kernel of good, that's when the Messiah will come."

"This is very similar to what I discovered in the Arcanumian "Book of Death." Tacitus wrote that "great souls do not break down along with the body." Buddhists believe that each of us has lived an endless number of lives, but they have never tried to find a way to transfer the experience and knowledge of a previous life into a new one. The Arcanumians tried to do this, and their "Book of Death" is a confirmation of it."

"Like the 'Tango of Death.'"

"But you haven't yet found definitive proof. You haven't met any of those for whom you played your tango."

"I haven't, but I'm still hoping to. I will not die until I meet one," Mr. Josef's smile was sad, and the eyes that looked at Yarosh squinted and fluttered their eyelids, as if suppressing an unwelcome tear. After a minute he continued: "There were four of us, inseparable friends. A Ukrainian, a Pole, a German, and me, a Jew." Noticing Yarosh's surprise, he said: "Yes, a Jew (*zhyd*). We didn't call ourselves anything different here in Galicia. That was in 1939, when the liberators came, then they ordered us to call ourselves *evrei* (Hebrews). But *evrei* was insulting to every *zhyd* (Jew). It was a dirty word. Calling someone *evrei* was the same as calling someone a stray animal, garbage, worthless. But after the Germans exterminated the *zhydy* (Jews), only *evrei* (Hebrews) settled in Lviv. So here, I want to give you a manuscript that miraculously survived. One of my three dearest friends Orest Barbaryka wrote it. It describes all our adventures, and most importantly for you—you'll find out how Johan Kalkbrenner's manuscript pages were found."

The old man got up and trudged his way to a writing desk, pulled out a drawer, took a folder out of it, and handed it Yarosh.

"I kept it for a long time in the cellar in a glass bottle so the mice wouldn't get at it. And to disguise it, I covered it with wheat. As you can see, it is well preserved, even though it's written by hand, but the handwriting is quite calligraphic. Orest had an obsession with writing. Unfortunately, his other notes have been lost."

"And what was the fate of your friends?"

"When we were surrounded by the NKVD [secret police], we blew ourselves up with a grenade in our hiding place. They all perished. I got a concussion and lost an arm, but I survived. Maybe it was because I wasn't sitting with them but was standing next to them and playing the violin. I was playing the "Tango of Death."

I

My mom didn't want me to grow up a dolt. It didn't surprise me, because what else would you expect from the average writer-mother other than an attempt to push her son out into the world. So, she pushed me as much as she could, trying to set me up with work so that I'd be like everyone else, forgetting that brilliant children can never be like everyone else. She always held up my friends as an example, how good they were in school, they'd become someone, but I—a healthy dolt, don't want to study. I patiently listened to her emotional speeches and defended myself with just the fact that she didn't know me, didn't have a clue about my life and what would become of me, because she only sees my shell, which is incredibly deceiving, but inside, woo-hoo, I'm not so simple.

At first my momma pushed me to work at Mr. Zhabsky's[55] store, who sold imported produce from the colonies. There on the sign it said, "produce from the colonies," and in the showcase window sat a chocolate-colored Moor, and around him lay small boxes of tea, coffee, cocoa, cinnamon, cloves, and all kinds of spices from overseas. Beautifully arranged among them were carved wooden and painted bananas, pineapples, papayas, coconuts, and other bupkis.[56] Behind the back of the Moor were shelves adorned with exotic drinks: liqueurs from the Gdansk factory, "Marachino di Zara," "Girolamo Luxardo," "Guille Goldwasser," "Persico," "Curaçao," "Grand Chartreuse," the tangerine liqueur from

55 The name comes from the noun "zhaba" meaning frog.
56 Literally "figy z makom" means "figs with poppy seeds." I've opted for the figurative meaning here.

the Abbey Fécamp in France, the Dutch liquor "Wymand Focking," and also—Bendsdorp cocoa from Amsterdam, and "Frank," "Rosmanita," "Fig Sultan" and "Fig Royal," chicory coffee drinks in colorful cans. Children walking from school always stopped in large crowds near that window display and with impatience kept looking for the Moor to wink at them or smile, or maybe even beckon with a finger, and later the children would bring their parents to the store and would buy halva, sherbet, fried sugarcoated nuts, dates, and raisins. I don't know if you guessed already, but that chocolate Moor was me, because if there was one thing I loved the most, it was to sit idly like this. Sometimes I used to sit there from early morning when the children went to school until they came home in the afternoon, and also on Sundays, as people trudged from church, still savoring the sweet taste of Greek Catholic or unleavened Catholic communion on their tongues.

The worst was when my chums would come to the window and make funny faces to make me laugh: Yosko would puff out his lower lip with his tongue and with his big ears sticking out would look like a monkey. Wolff would stuff both of his thumbs into his maw, pulling it apart as much as possible, and with his index fingers stretched his eyelids down. Yas would press his snout to the window and showed his flattened nose. Turning my eyes away, I held out and thought of lofty things. I endured this job for a month, because when a troublemaker climbed into the shop window and tried to bite my ear, thinking that it was made of chocolate, I exploded into righteous anger and poured an entire bag of cocoa on his head. Mr. Zhabsky did not put up with this kind of outrage and gave me a different task—gluing stickers onto various boxes of goods, while a different Moor ended up in my former spot. I don't know why the shopkeeper decided that I needed to stick on at least a hundred labels per hour. It was immediately evident that he was devoid of creativity, because I had a certain philosophical vision of this task. I did not just generously smear glue on every label but put my soul into it. The process of putting in the soul lasted at least a quarter hour, so I could stick on no more than four labels per hour. I thus considered that haste merely harmed the aesthetic direction of the matter and if I had my own way, hourly I'd glue on no more than one sticker. Thus, the box would radiate all the love of my heart and warmth of my soul, but Mr. Zhabsky had a different opinion and asked my mom to take me away from him, or more precisely, "out of harm's way," apparently hinting at his quiet desire to kill me, cut me up into bits, and sell me in the form of dried dates.

"Reflections and Fantasies": "Never buy dried dates from Mr. Zhabsky—they might be the mutilated body parts of his former employees."

I did not become an ice cream vendor, though I tried very hard, because on the very first day when I went to the city with my cart holding a bucket of ice cream between pieces of ice sprinkled with sawdust, I was immediately surrounded by my chums. Not only Wolff, Yasko and Josef, but also about a dozen teenagers from our parish began to help push the cart, though it was completely unnecessary, because the cart rolled on its own, bouncing on the cobblestone pavement. But they didn't step aside, and then began to demand that I treat them to ice cream: "Say what—did we push it for nothin'?" I tried to explain that I didn't need their help, but they didn't listen to me, lifted the lid, and each one piled up as much ice cream as he wanted in paper cups so they could eat the ice cream with small wooden spoons. After the first portion they also wanted a second and a third, and I didn't even try to defend myself, remembering the commandment "if the house has burned down—then let the barn burn down too." After that it made no sense to do any more vending, and I dragged the cart, which I no longer had anyone to help me roll, back to Mr. Tsap,[57] who was very surprised to see that there were no earnings. I couldn't tell him the truth and so explained I was attacked by bandits who had pointed a pistol at me and took the ice cream. He stared at me with astonished eyes, and then said that he never had heard anything like that before and asked again:

"Pointed a pistol?"

"Right here—at my forehead," I touched it with my finger.

"Okay, but how could they carry off so much ice cream in their hands?"

"They had a bucket with them."

"And they didn't take any money?"

"What money? I didn't have time to sell anything."

He took a look—a little white spot of ice cream glistened on the bottom.

"And that's all that's left?" He asked in a tone that sounded like I had offered him seconds from my bowl of potato dumplings.[58]

"It was just thanks to my courage, because I rushed at them like a lion," I said proudly. "In fact, I nearly died, they could have killed me."

57 The name means billy goat.

58 Often known in the U.S. by the Anglicized Polish word pierogies and in Ukrainian as varennyky or pyrohy.

Mr. Tsap took me by the arm, led me out onto the street, and pointed somewhere off into the distance:

"Go, boy, and don't come back. If you come back—I'll kill you. Do you have anything to say against that?"

Smiling, I stared at his right shoe, then I shifted my gaze to the part of his sock that could be seen from under his pant leg, afterward onto his frayed knee, rising higher and higher, as if I was counting all the buttons on his vest, all the way up to his nose. On the tip of it I saw a red pimple. My gaze stopped on the pimple, and I said to him, "No."

If someone thinks I really suffered, they are mistaken, because again I got the opportunity to sit with my notebook, though not for long, because my grandma took the matter into her own hands and went with me to Mr. Irzha Knoflyk, who had a funeral parlor near Lychakiv Cemetery and with inspiration sent off his clients to better worlds. Indeed it was whimsically called "Charon" and competed with the corresponding establishment of Mr. Antoniy Kurkovsky called "Concordia," although competing with Kurkovsky was incredibly difficult, because he had several wonderful glass catafalques with four lanterns. The figure of a knight in armor and helmet with a lowered visor and black feathers towered on the catafalque intended for officers. Catafalques for girls and children were white with azure blue and yellow, and harnessed to white horses with ostrich feathers, but that still wasn't all, for Mr. Kurkovsky even perched an entire army of hired mourners, male and female, who were dressed in the robes of the Spanish Grandees, or for a change, in the uniforms of the Hungarian haiduks.[59] At the head of the procession, a master of ceremonies was

59 Peasant mercenaries elevated to noble rank following their ser-

marching in a Napoleon hat, emphasizing every step with the stroke of his marshal's baton. At both sides of the catafalque were his attendants, four on each side, with gloomy, stone faces, holding lighted torches. Mr. Kurkovsky himself looked quite cheerful, his pink face decorated with a thin mustache, resembling a roasted piglet at Easter. During the formation of the funeral procession he only looked on from the side with his watchful eye, to be sure that everything was in accordance with established instructions. When the funeral march started to move in the direction of the cemetery, no one could miss such a grand theatrical spectacle, and the procession grew in size with random bystanders, and swelled and expanded like a snowball.

No doubt you've noticed that my entire family is somehow connected with the netherworld. Even our living room resembled a morgue—on the walls were photographs of countless deceased aunties, uncles, grandfathers, and grandmothers together with their deceased male and female friends, who might have as well been mistresses and lovers, who knows. Therefore, it's entirely natural that I ended up at Mr. Knoflyk's firm, where you can buy not only wonderfully comfortable coffins in which even the living would be content taking a nap (just like the half-deaf carpenter Bouchek often did after drinking too much beer in Kuchek's pub) but also wreaths, ribbons, sculptures of weeping muses, carved hearts and large candlesticks, as tall as a person. And Mr. Knoflyk also had a black catafalque, to which he hitched four raven-black steeds and drove them himself, sitting on the box in a black frock coat and black top hat. Both of them—the owner and the carpenter—were Czechs

---

vice in early seventeenth-century Hungary.

and talked very loudly because the carpenter couldn't hear very well. Apparently, he was not aware of this, convinced that everyone was deaf except for him, so he shouted like a Hutsul in a meadow. Catching sight of my grandmother, Mr. Knoflyk was as happy as if she had brought him not me, but a fresh client, whom he could bury with full honors.

"Praise be! Who is it I see? The siren of the Poltva River! The golden voice of the afterlife! Please, please, watch your feet." And then he shouted deep into the parlor: "Bouchek, stop scraping with your wood plane, we can't hear anything!" But Bouchek continued to scrape, mumbling some song under his breath, and Mr. Knoflyk sat us down near an oak coffin, decorated with paper flowers and lined with white velvet, and said: "Mrs. Patroness is supposed to lie here today. You see that soft bed? I doubt she had one softer in her life. Will you go tomorrow to lament her?"

"Oy, I'll go, I'll go," granny sighed. "I have three funerals tomorrow."

"Whoa!" Mr. Knoflyk slapped his hands together." "Three of them! What joy! And I just have one. And those two must be Mr. Apeltsyner and Mr. Strus? Ai-yay-yay! The Patsyurky brothers snatched them away from me. Where is the justice here, eh? They'll pass off pine coffins painted like oak to them, but I give real oak ones. Oh, do you hear?" He tapped his knuckles on the coffin. "Do you hear that sound? You can make violins, banduras, trembitas,[60] and contrabasses from this kind of coffin. When you're there, tell them who's the real coffinmaker. Maybe somebody else will die, then they can come to me. I give a discount of ten percent and candlesticks for free. I'll even tell you how to

60 A long wooden alpine horn used in the Carpathian Mountains.

say it delicately. While you'll be mourning, you only need to add in these words: 'Oy, wha-at kind of a coff-in have they pu-ut you in? This coffin's not an oa-ak one, but a pi-ine one!' "Eh? But I interrupted you. You have some business that concerns me?"

And granny told him about her beloved grandson, who just dreams about a funeral establishment, and even since childhood used to make coffins out of match boxes, in which he interred various bugs and buried them with honors in the ground, and put up crosses with wreaths, which he himself wove from blades of grass. Mr. Knoflyk immediately began to think about where to set me up, because it was out of the question to refuse my grandma, who often supplied him customers, and now will be obliged to help him in his business.

"Oh, I already know," Mr. Knoflyk snapped his fingers. "He'll carry the cross in front of the catafalque. I'll give him a black coat, a black hat, and black shoes. And in his time off from funeral processions he'll assist Bouchek in decorating coffins. As a representative of such a highly artistic family, he must have outstanding aesthetic taste, I bet.

"Don't hesitate," granny comforted him. "Even when he puts potatoes on his plate, he forms really nice little piles, decorating them on top with dill, and sausages he never cuts crosswise, but only lengthwise, cutting them into straws. An aesthete to the marrow of his bones."

"Moreover, I'm in debt to you, because you don't betray me with that foppish Kurkovsky. Have you seen his procession? A whole flock of his paid mourners that shuffle their feet along the catafalque, they have beet-red noses, and when I see their eyes filled with tears, the thought doesn't leave me that he puts some kind of eyedrop crap there. And an unusual smell wafts from out of their mouths, pure spiritus!"

So that's the way I started working for Mr. Knoflyk. Most of all I liked to dress up in the black waistcoat and top hat and walk in a slow pace ahead of the catafalque with the cross in my hands, sensing admiring glances of passersby. It's true though, that my chums also worried the heck out of me and at whatever cost tried to make me laugh, doing various idiotic things, but I walked gritting my teeth like a mummy come to life, and looked only straight ahead, right at the cross I was holding in my hands, and in order to better focus, I even drew a little speck on the cross and didn't take my eyes from it.

I treated the aesthetic ornamentation of the coffins with creative inspiration. I entwined with prickly shoots of blackberries and thorns the coffin of Mr. Adam Tsehelsky, a veteran, petty official and worthless lush, who every day chugged down sixteen mugs of beer (which he carefully counted, undoing one vest button at a time after each mug, and since there were only eight of them, then he would button up one at a time for the last eight, and only then would leave the tavern, bowing to the innkeeper). When the family expressed their surprise, I explained that those thorns symbolized the suffering of the deceased, his readiness for the sake of the Fatherland to overcome any obstacles, and they agreed that I was right, and the son of the deceased even gave me a zloty tip.

"Well-well, Mrs., just take a look," I said to the widow. "Did your husband look better when he was alive? Turn your attention to this fresh expression on his face, to these good and happy smiling lips, from which obviously no false word could fly! You will carry the memory of this happy smile through your entire life!"

And the moved Mrs. Tsehelsky also shoved a zloty at me. Another time, when Mrs. Dupska-Kotsipinska[61] began to object because of the coffin's overly expensive trim, pointing her fingers at real flowers and interrogating me over why I didn't use artificial ones, I explained:

"Don't you understand that artificial flowers are a symbol of death, but a death without return, a deadly death, a symbol of decline and decay, they will never be resurrected for a new life, the Lord does not speak to them: 'Stand up and go!' on Judgment Day!" Here I raised my index finger, and Mrs. Dupska-Kotsipinska's entire body trembled, and Mr. Bouchek stopped scraping with his block plane and opened his mouth wide. "Artificial flowers are unnatural, perverse and obscene. This bright paint that fades in the sun and after the first rain turns them into monsters and ruins your mood. And the scent—the shameful scent of a wet rag! Phooey! I'm already nauseous! On the other hand, real flowers, even when withered or dried, will never lose their dignity, they will maintain contact with the deceased, pass along your final regards to that other world with their fragrance... And on the Day of Resurrection of the Dead these flowers will come alive together with your husband, and you just imagine that huge crowd of resurrected people... Those millions of millions... How do you think you will manage to find your husband in the midst of the countless

61 The name, as often is the case in Vynnychuk's prose, is humorous in Ukrainian. The first part of her hyphenated name suggests "dupa" (ass) in Ukrainian. And "kots" suggests woolen blanket or horse blanket.

masses? And I say: by the scent! By the scent of these very flowers! Here, take a whiff—gillyflower!—it can awaken the dead from sleep! Incidentally, it's awakened more than one. Yes-yes, don't be surprised. In the case of lethargy, the gillyflower gives us the opportunity to be absolutely sure." At those words, the inconsolable widow fearfully looked at Mr. Dupsky-Kotsipinsky to see whether he, by chance, might not be planning to really wake up from his lethargy, but the nauseatingly sweet odor of the corpse caused by the summer heat, eased her pained little soul, and she, sighing, in relief, nodded:

"So let it be already... But ... but why didn't you put his right hand like his left alongside of his body, but instead stuffed behind the lapel of his sport coat?"

"Because that would be tacky! Arms by the sides! What could be more stupid? He has to appear before the Lord, and not before a jury, no? His hand behind his lapel is evidence of his businesslike character, commitment and obstinacy. For he was like that? Wasn't he? So!

And Mr. Torba,[62] who owned a hair salon expressed his profound surprise that his late wife, still not an old lass—just imagine—was lying in her coffin, with her hands placed behind her head. Well, how can you work with these kinds of customers? They have no imagination whatsoever, no creative zeal.

"Mr. Torba"—I said, taking him by the arm. "Your wife was happy and full of joy, have you ever in her life seen her lying in front of you with her arms lowered? That didn't happen because it could not be. She didn't even sleep that way at night."

62 The name means bag.

"But it's common practice...," Mr. Torba timidly stammered.

"And you are right," I said, because I never argued with customers. "It's common practice. But in relation to whom? Shriveled old grannies and old coots! Your wife departed to a better world full of strength and energy; her body, despite her illness, smelled fragrantly of health! Yes-yes, I'm not afraid to say this—smelled fragrantly of health! She has not died! This is a delusion! And now, you should know, she is next to us!" Mr. Torba looked all around in fright. "She's here, I feel her breath, her contented whisper." Mr. Torba pricked up his ears and listened attentively. "Look at her—she's resting the way she used to relax in your garden in the afternoon when it's so pleasant to stretch out and lie in the shade of apple and cherry trees, placing her swanlike hands behind her head. She's lying there as if she's alive. You see these dimples on her cheeks? And this blush? I did my best. Even her lips are outlined with lipstick to show us the barely noticeable smile of a person content with life.

"Li... li...," Mr. Torba got choked up. "What kind of li... life?" Well, yes, sometimes I get carried away.

"Mr. Torba, don't you believe in eternal life?" I bowled him over, and he, wiping away tears, shook my hand. This is what I call the 'magic power of art.'"

Mr. Knoflyk purred with satisfaction. He liked my approach and the fact that I could quickly find a common language with clients. But he once remarked that I too obviously enjoyed looking at the exquisite body of a beautiful young lady who poisoned herself out of desperation because her beloved abandoned her in her third month of pregnancy. I sighed and said that it would have been better if she had had an abortion or had even give birth to it, than to perish this way too young and to pack such beauty into the ground: such full breasts, such a smooth belly where you can't even pinch an inch, such round, shapely thighs, and between them— this fancy threshing floor, this flower, which she obviously with great diligence tended to lovingly, over which she enchanted and meditated, caressing playful curls and trimming disobedient ones around these full puffy lips that grew still in their seriousness, like the lips of Mona Lisa. Mr. Knoflyk tugged at my button with his fingers and said:

"Our first rule is: we bury clients, but don't talk about them. Our second rule is: we bury all to the highest standards—whether it's a murderer, an innocent young girl, or the slut from the Levandivsky Bridge.[63] At our parlor, each one of them will find a cozy oak or pine abode furnished with white lace with tassels and flower garlands.

Truth be told, he was not entirely honest here, because all the same, the funeral ceremony differed depending on the client's wishes. My grandma was the regular professional mourner, but there were some customers for whom one professional mourner was not enough and so they ordered an entire choir. And just me in a black coat and black top hat in front of the catafalque was not enough, so they ordered eight sullen men in the same black suits. They all looked like ravens with their sharp curved noses, longish narrow faces with dark shadows under their eyes and thin nearly dark blue lips. Just their mere appearance instilled the fear of death.

---

63 A bridge in Lviv where criminals used to gather before WWII [author's note].

Mr. Knoflyk had a beauty of a wife much younger than him. She reminded me of the Venus de Milo, only with both arms. Sometimes when she walked, it seemed that she was not the wife of a funeral director, but an empress, because she didn't walk, but carried herself with a seductive rocking gait as though she were riding on horseback. It was impossible to take your eyes off her. Unfortunately, she spent most of her time in Krakow in sanatoria, taking therapy for some mysterious female diseases. But Mr. Shtrouba had another theory:

"Maybe she's taking therapy, maybe not," he said, shaking his head—but probably not with doctors, no... Such a lavish lady? She has to have some fop. But Knoflyk—he's an honorable man, but he's not skilled in young ladies.

Mr. Shtrouba owned a sawmill in Bryukhovychi, and Mr. Knoflyk bought boards for his coffins from him. They knew each other for years, so what reason was there for me not to believe him? Moreover, Mr. Shtrouba never changed his views when someone pointed out to him that there was a mistake on the door of the sawmill on a sign hanging there, "Coffins for Boards," while it should be "Boards for Coffins" instead. He said that it was even better because it attracts attention, and everyone who noticed the mistake would immediately hurry to tell him about it, and to do this they would have to at least go to the sawmill and chat with Mr. Shtrouba about it. I thought to myself, why such an injustice? Mr. Knoflyk always tells me such nice things about his wife, misses her, and even hung her portrait above his desk, and she, a floozy, roams around God knows where. In late June 1937, she came back, tanned and smiling, and she looked just like a doll, or maybe like the Virgin Mary, and just as sad, though smiling, because her smile was not overly happy, but rather despairing. Obviously her heart was still where she had come from, but now try sometimes to be cheerful when your husband is engaged in such grim business, no? But Mr. Knoflyk was very happy, and the work was going full blast. And when he drove the catafalque, holding the reins in one hand and in the other the whip, in appearance he resembled an Egyptian pharaoh in a chariot. It seemed right then and there the order would sound out of his mouth to advance to the final decisive battle against the Roman legions, and in measured steps I carried the cross at the front of the procession like a flag, making sure to be four steps from the heads of the horses, having learned to determine the distance by their snorting. Sometimes Mrs. Vlasta Knoflyk cried out somewhere in the crowd and gave a friendly wave, and Mr. Knoflyk then happily snapped the whip and clucked at the horses, and the horses shook their black manes. I always took pleasure in looking at Vlasta, because she was all illuminated and sunny, and she had a deep voice sweet as honey, and when she appeared in our office, it seemed that instantly the number of windows increased, because it became brighter and fresher. When she served us coffee, Mr. Bouchek's hands always trembled, with a loud thud he dropped his plane to the floor and took the coffee from her, and you could hear the spoon tinkling. I admired her extremely thin thumbs with pink petals of fingernails; it seemed those lovely nails had just fluttered from a flower, and I felt like touching her fingers, taking them into my hand to feel their elasticity, and then leaning over them with my lips and breathing in their smell. Sometimes I managed to touch them when I took the cup from her hands, and a certain incomprehensible trembling like a mild electric charge ran through my body. In any case, I kept a straight face, at least so it seemed to me, but every time in such instances Vlasta glanced right into my eyes, and the corners of her lips quivered either from the desire to smile or to say something, but that quivering of her lips spoke nothing to me, though Mr. Shtrouba had a different opinion.

"A floozy's a floozy," he sighed over a mug of beer while we were sitting and eating chitterlings in a pub, which because of its proximity to the cemetery was called "Under the Corpse." "Oh-oh, the things I've heard about her! I'd better not even repeat them! This kinda woman will waste all kinda money... sure, sure, she's getting treatment... I know that kinda treatment... Two more mugs!.. And Knoflyk—he's a decent guy, whatever he does, he's lucky everywhere... just not with his wife...."

And right then and there Mr. Knoflyk came in, sat down next to us, and ordered a beer.

"Tomorrow we have a doozy of a funeral, the great poet Bohdan-Ihor Antonych just died. He lived just twenty-eight years... How much more good the man could have done, but... it just wasn't his fortune...."

"I have his books," I said. "Tomorrow for sure there'll be an incredible swarm of people, no?"

"For sure! They're burying such an important man! I've already got orders for three dozen wreaths. It'd be even more, but most recently in Ukraine the fashion has taken root that instead of spending money on a wreath, they give money to a magazine or to some foundation and announce: 'We are giving such and such amount instead of a wreath for a grave, and such and such for this or that.' God forbid that I disparage this, but how can I survive in this situation? Not only the Patsyurky brothers steal customers from me, but now another fashion has spread among Ukrainians: 'You buy your own from your own people.' Now the patriots, when they have a choice, go only to Ukrainian stores. But what do coffins and a catafalque have to do with this? What's that, your own from your own? For a coffin? Will I, a Czech, bury someone worse than a Ukrainian? During the war I was a medic and also had to bury people. Sometimes twenty or thirty corpses a day. Mr. Lieutenant said to me: "Oh, Irzhyk, more than once they'll come to you in dreams." But nay, none came. They all died courteously, and I buried them courteously. Why would they come back?"

"Eh-h, don't say, anything can happen," Mr. Shtrouba sighed. "Two years ago, they buried the merchant woman from Lychakivska Street. She was a tough woman, healthy as a bull. You should see the kind of sacks she'd carry by herself, and sometimes even her drunken husband from the tavern! She wasn't really very old yet. But one day she went to bed and never got up. And about six months later her husband kicked the bucket too. There wasn't anyone in the middle of winter to carry him home from the tavern, and he froze to death. So, they buried him next to her. And when they dug up the grave, what did they see? The lid on the coffin was pushed aside, and she was lying sideways, and all her nails had been chewed off!"

"Holy-holy!" The innkeeper Mr. Salomon, who had just brought us beer, was dumbfounded. "The poor woman chewed them up from hunger!"

"No way from hunger! From being dumbfounded! Imagine that you wake up in a coffin! A pile of earth on top of you! Ha? Who wouldn't go crazy?"

"I've heard, I've heard about that," said Mr. Knoflyk. "She even turned gray in that coffin."

"Yes indeed, it ain't so bad if people die sometimes, no?" Mr. Tavernkeeper asked. "Because what would happen if everybody suddenly came here? At least, just those who I remember. I'd have nowhere to sit 'em, or any way to serve 'em... Just take Mr. Kuternoha alone!"

"Aya-ya," Mr. Knoflyk agreed. "A meter eighty in length and eighty centimeters in width. He was an enormous guy! The four of us barely were able to move him to the coffin."

"Yes, yes," Mr. Shtrouba nodded his head. "The same fate awaits all of us. Fours boards and a little bit of earth...."

"Ay, no way fours of 'em!" Mr. Knoflyk waved his hands. "It took six whole ones! Pure beech! But keep talking...," he nodded to the innkeeper.

"Mr. Kuternoha," the innkeeper continued, "could drink two dozens a beers and gobble up a whole roasted goose. And on top of that, he could scarf down a plate of cabbage with sausages and about a dozen large knoedels with gravy."

"Excuse me, but with what kind of gravy?" Mr. Shtrouba asked.

"Sour cream-tomato-onion," the innkeeper recited and licked his lips.

Mr. Shtrouba and Mr. Knoflyk just as greedily licked their lips and uttered nearly in unison:

"And could you bring us...."

"I could!" Mr. Salomon was overjoyed. "That what clients means, who have style! I'm bringing it out right away!"

While the innkeeper was preparing the knoedels, I was watching his pretty daughter behind the counter and recalled how quite recently Yasko, Yosko, Wolff, and I were making a pass at her, but her daddy really got angry and wouldn't allow Rebekkah to serve us, so he chased her behind the counter to wash glasses. Unable to find any other way to get revenge, we held in our anger to direct it at the innkeeper. Once I called him:

"Mr. Salomon, I want to ask you how long your telephone wire is."

"Long enough."

"But precisely, in meters, we need it for statistics."

"About three meters."

"So, go hang yourself with it!"

Another time Wolff phoned and wondered if Mr. Salomon had hot water.

"I'll check right now," the innkeeper said, and returned in a minute and said that he did.

"Well then, go wash your feet and go to sleep."

That's how we played our game, maybe for a week, until we got tired of it and lost interest in Rebekkah. Mr. Salomon, of course, had no idea who was mocking him, but his daughter figured it out and always glanced at me suspiciously, as if she were waiting for the next trick. Then they brought us the knoedels with gravy and, breathing in their intoxicating aroma, we emptied our tankards at once, and then set down to the food. Mr. Salomon stood over us like a mountain, crossing his short thick hands on his stomach and satisfyingly nodded his head, admiring how we greedily downed his goodies, and we nodded to him and signaled to him that it was super, first class. Mr. Shtrouba, with a satisfied smile, smacked his lips:

"How nice it is to sit like this in a tavern, drinking beer or *horilka*, eating *kvargli*,[64] cracklings, knoedels and, to

64 See footnote #49.

think about nichts. Not to think then about how often we'd enjoy that kind of happiness."

"And, you know what," Salomon looked up at the ceiling, "if you live long—not often, but if you live for a short time—then often."

However, we didn't manage to understand the depth of Salomon's wisdom or eat up all the knoedels when the stableman flew into the tavern and began to move his lips like a fish soundlessly, as if he were out of breath. But from the movements of his mouth you could guess he was saying two words "Mrs. Vlasta," and Mr. Knoflyk jumped to his feet: "What? What happened?" But the stableman just waved his hand, and we all ran to the funeral establishment. Mr. Knoflyk ran so hard that Mr. Shtrouba and I could barely keep up with him, and from a distance we already could see that a crowd of people had gathered. When they made a path for us, we flew inside. Vlasta was hanging on a cord thrown over a beam, and some papers were lying on the table. As we learned later, it was her case record from the hospital where she had been treated, with the diagnosis "lung cancer." I saw Mr. Shtrouba sniffle and wipe his eyes; he was ashamed of what he had been saying up until now. And Mr. Knoflyk tore his hair out and screamed: "I'll bury you all! All of you!"

With the death of Vlasta the funeral establishment almost went to the dogs, because Mr. Knoflyk, who saw thousands of deaths, buried thousands of people and could talk about death as something quite as ordinary, so to speak, as the weather or the horse races, he still was unable to endure the death of the person dearest to him and started drinking. Mr. Bouchek and I barely managed with great difficulty for a month, but then Mr. Knoflyk pulled himself together and returned to work, though he lost not only his good humor, but also his smart elegant look because of it all. He stopped shaving every day as he did before, became shaggy and let himself go, and became silent and withdrawn. He would often suddenly start screaming and raving out of nowhere, exploding in anger and with a downpour of despairing words. Deaf Bouchek couldn't care less, he just agreeably nodded his head, while I finally had enough of it, and I quit the job that I had managed to learn to love.

10

Reading the manuscript, Yarosh repeatedly felt a strange and incomprehensible sensation. Very clear images and bright visions of what he had read suddenly appeared in his imagination. The Barbaryka family became increasingly close to him, and that strange world that disappeared without a trace together with the people who lived there began to entice him, the world that fell into the depths of time, like Atlantis. But when it came to the surface again, then it already looked different, having lost all those colors, sounds, and smells that reigned there before. No one could revive them, no matter how much they try. Fantastic visions began to haunt him; sometimes he heard voices that made their way through him like the wind through leaves. Perhaps they were not addressed to him, but it was as if from the depths of the night those voices called someone by name—whose name was it if not his? Far, far away against the backdrop of a clear moon the silent figure of a woman could be seen moving slowly, and the rustle of her silk dress reached his ears. Mysterious voices uttered her name through him, through the leaves, the grass, and sand, her moist and warm name spread like milk on the lips of the grass, creaked on the teeth of sand, dissolved in the warm night. The black butterflies of daybreak nervously fluttered their wings and black ambrosia poured in her tracks, but before she came close enough to be able to see or recognize her, her body dissolved in the gloom.

In the evenings he read the manuscript, and the next day walked around under the impression of what he had read. Lviv appeared to him in a completely new light, unknown and fantastic. Now, strolling along those streets described in the manuscript, he stopped and looked around carefully, trying to recognize something out of what he learned. Sometimes the sound of Lviv's dialect would reach his ear, he immediately stopped and searched with his eyes to see who it might be, but it was just a few words or a single phrase, tossed out in the course of a conversation, and he disappointedly moved on, espying new and newer objects. With particular pleasure he went into the streets that he earlier had passed by without even looking at them. He examined buildings, each courtyard, he looked at the windows and at the pots on the window sills, as if trying to find at least a trace of old Lviv, that vanished world which would never return, for those who left it will not return. Lviv is my Arcanum, he thought, there was only stone left, and everything else—people, language, culture—all this disappeared and became a dream. One day he decided to start off toward Kortumov Mountain, the place where the four friends loved to walk. He already entered Horodotska Street, when suddenly he came face to face with Danka. They nearly collided with each other because they both were in some kind of daydream. They were both incredibly happy about meeting, though they tried not to give themselves away, became flustered, and spoke some kind of nonsense just to prolong their unexpected conversation, which at any moment could break off with the phrase "well, time to go, ciao." Still it was not interrupted but continued on, supported by whatever suddenly came to mind, until finally Yarosh gathered up the courage and said:

"I want to thank you for having brought me to Mr. Josef. I received a very interesting manuscript about old Lviv from him. And now I can't deny myself the pleasure of going to those places about which I've been reading. So, I decided to wander over to Kortumov Mountain. Imagine, I'm a Lviv native, but I've never been there."

"Me too," she said with all her naïveté and spontaneity, having abandoned all the phrases mandatory for young ladies that would demonstrate her indifference, her independence from anything that she might come across, and leaving him a good opportunity for the quite logical invitation to go with him. In another instance, instead of such a simple and undemanding prompt, she could have said "Really?" However, then there would be the risk that the conversation might come to an end, and she felt he did not want that. She also suddenly had the desire to take a stroll to Kortumov Mountain, and she was prepared to say, "I'd also go with you," but Yarosh, overcoming embarrassment, blurted out:

"Great! Let's go together. There are supposed to be wonderful spots there. We'll have a picnic. Like the heroes of that story."

With a sigh of relief, she nodded, slightly blushing. They came to Klepariv Street, and then hopped over to the Krakow Market, where there was a stand that sold Italian products, and where Yarosh had been shopping for a long time. There he bought two bottles of Sicilian wine, a chunk of parmesan cheese, a slice of gorgonzola, and green olives. Near the Church of St. Anne, they boarded a streetcar and got off near the Yaniv Cemetery, and then started their way up, passing the cemetery. When they made their way to the top of Kortumov Mountain, they saw a really wild expanse, overgrown with thickets, which was settled with rickety little dacha buildings made of veneer and wooden planks not long ago, but which were now abandoned with gaping holes, and when the wind blew through, they howled and rattled. Wild apple trees, pear trees, plum and cherry trees, eaten by lichen, overgrown with witch mistletoe, intertwined with wild grapes in small black bunches, which, like an octopus entangled their feet and hands. They were living out their last days; everywhere you could see just one thing—unrestrained dying. But that dying was special, unusual, autumn did everything to make it beautiful, and turn those dried up, twisted trees into colorful paintings which riveted one's gaze and beckoned. The disheveled grass tripped them up; at times they slipped on rotten apples and pears, but it didn't hinder Danka and Yarosh. They looked all around, pointed out to each other some interesting things and it was evident that both were enthralled by this amazing landscape exhibition in autumn's free gallery. The weather was warm, from far off wafted the scent of burnt potato vines, which Yarosh always associated with childhood, potatoes baked in a campfire, gray fog and a sad nostalgia for long-gone days.

Then they made themselves comfortable on the concrete foundations of an unfinished dacha and spread out their food and refreshments.

"My God, I never thought that it would still be possible to find such a wild location in Lviv."

"Me, too. By the way, there used to be a concentration camp here. The famous Yaniv concentration camp."

"Really? Why you didn't you tell me right away? This is where they played 'Tango of Death?...'"

Danka gazed at her surroundings and said:

"Honestly, I felt some kind of pressure right away... The kind of impression that...."

When she fell silent and got lost in thought, Yarosh asked:

"What?"

"No, I...," she shook off her thoughts like drops of rain. "It's strange... here where everything happened, people planted potatoes, tomatoes, cucumbers, then gathered them... and ate them... and the dead... the dead were fertilizer for them?"

"Don't exaggerate... These people didn't have the foggiest idea about the concentration camp. Just a little farther, where the slope is, that was the Valley of Death. There were firing squads there. After the war when they began to dig up the ramparts that were formed after the burial of prisoners, they found only ash. It was a clean job. When they began to distribute the land to workers for orchards and gardens, attention was drawn to this wasteland. They dug up the ramparts with ashes and evened them to the ground, then broke up the land into plots and distributed it. The summer visitors to the dachas usually were not local people, but rather state officials, the military, veterans. Nearly all of them spoke Russian. This was because all the Galicians have family in villages; they don't need any summer cottages. So Lviv bears no responsibility for all this. We were a constituent part of the colony. The colonizers decided everything. On rainy days streams gray from ash flowed out of the Valley of Death. They also built garages all over the Valley of Death. Excavators, leveling the ground for the building of the garages, from time to time stumbled on bones, but no one paid attention to that anymore."

"That is, right where we are now, there are no dead beneath us?" She asked in a tone as if she needed to find out from a doctor whether she had stomach ulcers.

"No," Yarosh reassured her. "There only were wooden barracks here."

"Well, then," Danka sighed, subdued. "Then... Then we can have a drink."

Yarosh poured out the wine, cut the cheese with a knife, and opened a jar of olives. The wine was white and slightly carbonated. Something began to rustle in the grass; they saw a field mouse that was picking up crumbs and they grew still, having conspiratorially exchanged glances and making an agreement not to frighten it. At this moment a certain spark passed between them that brought them closer to each other, but they continued to communicate, maintaining a certain distance and pretending that that spark was not there.

"Do you know who enticed me to take an interest in dead languages and literatures? Jorge Luis Borges."

"Really?" Danka opened up her mouth wide and theatrically began to blink, clapping her hands. "Borges? Incredible!"

"Why are you so surprised?" Yarosh couldn't understand. "Borges touches on that topic so many times that...."

"No, no, not for that reason... It's just me too! Do you understand? Me too!"

"You too were enticed by Borges?"

"Uh-huh!" She was incredibly pleased by this discovery and did not hide her enthusiasm. It seemed right then and there that she'd rush into the professor's arms so that they could both say that magic word "Borges." "We have to drink to this. I've read everything that's been published here. I've read individual stories and essays several times and continue to read them again."

Yarosh poured out the wine and noticed that his hand was trembling. Something suddenly began to creep into his subconscious, something vague, but exciting. He felt a secret joy because of what just happened, because now that spark that passed between them already had become clearer and shone like a star.

"I read Borges first in Polish and Czech... and only later in Russian and Ukrainian. I revered him and was very happy when I had the opportunity to visit Buenos Aires. There was a scholarly conference dedicated to ancient literature. In my free time I strolled around the city, trying to find traces of Borges on my own." He noticed then that Danka was looking at him wide-eyed and continued: "Buenos Aires evidently was built on the pattern of an ideal chessboard, but over time the side streets began living their separate lives and rushed helter-skelter, getting tangled up and disappearing in the artful design of a spider web, or on the contrary, hitting up against a dead-end wall. These dead-end streets quickly become a real trial for the traveler who decides to take a stroll alone. Actually, they lay in ambush for me when I myself tried to find on the map house number 994 on Maipú Street where Borges lived for over forty years in an almost monastic cell...."

"...that was separated from his mother's bedroom by a wooden screen," Danka interrupted, demonstrating her knowledge of Borges' biography. "In his cell there was barely enough room for a bed and a desk."

"Yes, however, that apartment has not survived. But across from it, the bookshop remains where Borges went every morning to dictate his works after he became blind. And the National Library on Mexico Street is still there, where he worked as a modest librarian...."

"... So modest," Danka picked up again, "that the library staff didn't even know it was the same Borges, whose books they lent out to readers...."

"'The streets of Buenos Aires,'" Yarosh recited, "'are streets with a delicate and sweet flavor of memories, streets where the haunting memory of the future roams in the name of hope, inseparable, indelible streets of my love. The streets which without unnecessary words manage to get along despite our lofty sadness for being born here. The streets and buildings of my city, may their breadth and warmth never abandon me.' But inexorable time has made its own adjustments, changed, mixed up everything where the foot of the genius stepped. The 'Literary Coffee House' with the writer's books is now located at number 840 Tucuman Street where Borges was born. The only thing that remains untouched is the gate that leads to the patio—an inner courtyard—and the patio itself with tables under umbrellas. But the street slowly and steadily over the years has slipped down to the river. Who knows how many years will pass, maybe a hundred, maybe two hundred, and it will all end up in the river along with the 'The Literary Coffee House.' In the coffee house on the corner of Chile Street and Taquari Street, Borges wrote love letters to the young woman who consistently rejected all his advances and marriage proposals, not even the dedication to her of his book *Aleph* helped."

"I know... Cecilia Ingenieros ... She was the daughter of the philosopher and essayist Jose Ingenieros."

"She wrote something herself but entered into literary history only because Borges loved her. Just like Likera, whom Shevchenko loved. There are very few women willing to sacrifice themselves for an artist or a scholar. Usually it's not those women, for whose sake a great man is capable of some mad exploit in an explosion of passion, nor those whom he attains, before whom he stifles his pride; more often it's women who are as beloved as a mother or sister, without fury, without an excess of emotion. The way Vynnychenko[65] loved his Rozalia."

"But you have in mind women who don't share their passions and activities with their husbands and are not themselves artists and scholars, right?"

"Of course. Women who have the same likes and passions do not have to sacrifice themselves. They just complement each other."

"And what happened next? Remember, Borges did find a someone willing to sacrifice...," she said, looking somewhere off into the distance, where the landscape of the city unfolded. She spoke in a tone in which Yarosh sensed sadness, though perhaps it only seemed that way to him.

"He did find one. A certain young Japanese woman became a companion to him during his old age. He appeared everywhere accompanied only by her. But was there passion between them? It's not known."

"And would you like someone to bring herself as a sacrifice to you?"

"Ideally, I want something else... In any case, not sacrifices...."

"And if that something else is not there? Then what? Then—a sacrifice?"

Now she just looked at him right in the eye and a smile quivered on her lips. Yarosh shrugged his shoulders and said:

---

65 Prominent Modernist Ukrainian writer and political figure Volodymyr Vynnychenko (1880-1951), who was married to Rozalia Lifshits.

"Then—a sacrifice. However, it's possible to make a mistake here. At least that's what I've already experienced."

J

But my mother didn't let me go astray and dragged me to Mr. Tsapsky[66]—director of the famous "Ossolineum." Our grandma had mourned his mom with great inspiration, and in a Homeric style (not to be confused with *homerychny* meaning grand) my mother sang her praises in her obituary. Mr. Tsapsky was very pleased when he saw my mother in a light green knee-length jacket and a red beret, which coquettishly covered my mother's left eye. For a long time he launched into compliments about her literary talent, to the point that I even thought that it wasn't his mother who had died but his wife, and that having been widowed, now he's hitting on my mom, but when he even began to kiss her hands, then I started coughing, although I didn't feel bad. Let him slobber not only on her hands, but not in front of me, because I'm a well brought up child, lacking in perverted fantasies, Oedipal complexes, and those, what are they called?... But Mr. Tsapsky interrupted my deep generalizations:

"A-a-ah! So, this is your sonny boy!"

Sonny boy! I should think not! I'm already nineteen, and I'm still a sonny boy? I wanted to explain to Mr. Director that I'm not merely a sonny boy, but a philosopher with a sharp vision of the world around us, and the first thing I noticed was—perfect order on Mr. Director's desk, where all the folders lay inside each other, and sharpened multicolored pencils neatly stuck out of a wooden pencil holder. When my mother while talking about all my hidden talents took one such blue pencil, twirled it in her fingers back and

66 The name comes from the word "billy goat" (tsap) in Ukrainian.

forth and laid it on the table, Mr. Director instantly picked it up and put it in the same place between the red and green, so they stuck out again evenly like lattices in a picket fence. Thus, the conclusion one can deduce from this is disappointing: Mr. director Tsapsky is a damned awful person who belongs to a breed of crazy pedants, fastidious and boring, and if he has a wife, she's long been howling at the moon or sweeping leaves in the park next to the Kulpark hospital for the insane. So my first impulse was to grab my mom by the hand and shout, "Let's save ourselves!" and scram from here as far away as possible. But suddenly Mr. Tsapsky got up and, rubbing his hands like a butcher anticipating joyful interaction with a plump little boar, approached me. Turning his head decorated with thirty-two hairs and smiling at the level of my chest because he was such a shrimp, he spluttered out: "Very pleased to meet you! I have the honor to invite you to work in our wonderful institution," and then took me by the hand and led me to show me my new place of work, and my mother shuffled in short steps behind and couldn't be more pleased with what respect Mr. Director treated her sonny boy.

"Don't overburden him there at the beginning," she clucked, wiping her tears with a handkerchief, "he's a dreamer with a philosophical turn of mind. It runs in our family; his father died for a better future, and he's an orphan. Everywhere that he previously worked, they still remember him with tenderness and warmth."

Luckily, she failed to specify where they remembered me with affection and warmth, because I sneezed too expressively. The library was a kind of labyrinth of very tall stacks, among which one could get lost easily, and at first, I even liked it, because in advance I foresaw this need to be alone that I used to get from time to time, to hide in a little far-off corner and sink deeply into my thoughts and fantasies. Mr. Director took me to some old bat dried up into a sliver and said:

"This, Mrs. Konopelka, is our new employee, I mean librarian—Orko Barbaryka. He has a golden mother, a golden grandma, and a golden heart. And his momma—here she is, right in front of you." And then, turning to us: "Mrs. Konopelka is the chief librarian, she recently turned a hundred, but she still has her strength and sound mind; not for anything do we want to send her to retirement, because in her head she maintains the entire catalog of our library. Mrs. Konopelka's head is a national treasure."

Mrs. Konopelka's head nodded at this like a porcelain Chinese doll, and it was difficult to imagine in what order the entire directory could be kept if she was bobbing her head like this all the time. At that moment the door opened, and the draft picked up Mrs. Konopelka's dry little body, lifted it into the air and slightly swung it over the table, gently lowering it back into a chair. But with all this she didn't release the folders with documents in her hands and continued to flip through pages with her bony finger.

"Despite her venerable age," Mr. Director continued, "our Mrs. Konopelka has a falcon's eyes, and stepping out onto the porch, sees people drinking coffee on the terrace on High Castle Mountain, and a tram that's gone off the tracks up on Lychakivska Street. I have no doubt that Mrs. Barbaryka will immortalize Mrs. Konopelka in her profoundly talented poems. Especially because Mrs. Konopelka personally knew Emperor Franz Joseph II and carried in her hands

Crown Prince Rudolf and Wilhelm, singing them lullabies. Adam Mickiewicz himself asked for her hand, but upon being rejected by her, died soon after. And Cyprian-Kamil Norwid?[67] He knelt on his knees and begged for a kiss!"

"Oh-oh, Cyprian! Boy was he a rascal," Mrs. Konopelka nodded her head without raising it from the papers.

—And Teofil Lenartowicz?"[68] The director would not stop and winked to my mother.

"Oh-oh, Theo! I used to call him Filyus. He clambered up to my window once and nearly fell off."

"And Kornel Ujejski?"[69] Mr. director rejoiced and nudged my mother with his elbow.

"Nelko? I just pointed him to the door. Poor guy, like a grasshopper!"

"And Adam Asnyk,[70] with whom she went to school? Maria Konopnicka even slapped her over Asnyk! Is that right, Mrs. Konopelka?" Mr. Director nearly choked from laughter, and my mother listened, with mouth agape, and didn't know whether to believe it or not.

"Oh-oh-oh, that Maryska!" Mrs. Konopelka shook her head without raising it from the papers. She was a nasty woman! She jumped all the way into my eyes for Adask, but I just laughed. Because everyone thought that I'm a femme fatale, but no one knows my greatest secret."

"Which one?" The director asked. "Till now I thought your greatest secret was that Yuri Fedkovych,[71] jumping from the window of your bedroom, nearly landed on Dra-

67 Polish poet and artist of note (1821-1883) [author's note].

68 Polish poet (1822-1893) [author's note].

69 Polish poet (1823–1897) [author's note].

70 Polish poet and dramatist (1838-1897) [author's note].

71 The famous Ukrainian writer, translator, and folklorist from Chernivtsi (1834-1888).

homanov,[72] who had just come to the city to see you. As a result, Drahomanov called Fedkovych out to a duel and shot him through the ear. And meanwhile you were chugging along in a train to the resort of Abbazia[73] in the company of Count Tyszkiewicz."[74]

"Of course!" Mrs. Konopelka mysteriously smiled. "I was young and rash. But no one knows my biggest secret."

The director feigned a sigh and finally, sufficiently satisfied, took my mother by the arm and said:

"Well, we won't keep on distracting them, let's go, Mrs. Vlodzya. And you, Mrs. Konopelka, familiarize Orest with his new responsibilities."

When their footsteps outside the door had grown quiet, the old woman raised her head, looked around, and asked conspiratorially:

"Who was that?"

"The director and my mother."

"Really? The director? I thought he died long ago," then she looked at me carefully and added: "Very strange things happen here sometimes. There are some people who appear, then disappear, and then appear again. Just so you know," she switched to a whisper, "more than one person has been lost here in the paper jungles, so you should watch out and move strictly following the arrows, never wandering off from the designated route, otherwise you might find your way to a place from which there is no return. Somewhere there," she waved her hand, "even my husband got lost,

72 Mykhailo Drahomanov (1841-1895), the famous Ukrainian civic and political activist.

73 A popular resort in the Austro-Hungarian Empire now called Opatiya in Croatia [author's note].

74 Michal Tyszkiewicz (1857-1930). Count, diplomat, journalist, artist, and philanthropist [author's note].

rather not my husband, but my fiancé, who disappeared like snow at Easter time, and I'm still waiting for him, that's why I can't die. If you lay your eyes on him sometime, then bring him here, because he probably can't make his own way, weak and blind, and also deaf. Though you might ask, why would I need a man like this, but I'll tell you—actually this is my biggest secret—such is my fate, I've still kept my chastity for him, and I am not sure if he'd be able to take it from me or not, but he would be able to make sure that it's been maintained. And it would be the greatest happiness for me. Then I'll finally toss all these papers and folders that have muddled my mind out of my head. I'll air out my head and quietly croak. But no, not like most people in bed or in the hospital, no, I'll go to distant corridors, the most remote nooks and there I'll wander off, disappear, melt among these bookcases, and when after a hundred or two hundred years someone comes across me, I'll already be so dry and flat that they'll take me for an old manuscript, put a number on me, and put me on a shelf. And this will be the pinnacle of my happiness, do you understand?"

"So how then should one understand all your romantic adventures?" I asked timidly, but the old woman surprisingly calmly informed me:

"And do you, young man, know how many holes a girl has?"

I nodded, though I was not certain that I knew, and she continued: "Exactly. And I've treasured one as a valuable gem."

And I thought to myself, here I am already nineteen and I know what that valuable pearl looks like, but still haven't tried it yet.

All employees were given a library map, according to which one should move among the shelves, with red crosses marking the dangerous places. Mrs. Konopelka even said to me that a spirit was living in the library that frightened people at night and pulled pranks during the day, and that he repeatedly lifted up her skirt. This is why she now wears narrow, long skirts all the way to the ground. Every morning upon arriving at work, I received a task from Mrs. Konopelka, with whom I had to share the same office, to find such and such a book that disappeared who knows where, and in its place was another book with the same call number. I had the whole day to do these searches, because I had to rummage through several book cases, climbing ladders and sneezing from dust, and then, when the book was found, she had to write a new call number for it and in her calligraphic handwriting fill out a card for the card catalog. Once I really did notice some apparition behind a bookcase that scuttled upon seeing me. I didn't dare follow after it, but since then, whenever I started off in search of a book, I always took a stick with me, though I was not certain whether I was dealing with a spirit or Mrs. Konopelka's fiancé.

Mr. Director rarely dropped by, but every time Mrs. Konopelka reacted in the same way:

"You saw him? Really saw him?" She nodded her head. "My Sweet Lord, I'm still in my right mind considering him a spirit. He's long dead."

"Our Director?"

"Uh huh... Since Austrian times. I even brought a primrose blossom to his grave. He hadn't appear for a long time, but recently started up again. Why such a calamity for me? So, you say you saw him? That's good. But I want to ask you, this is a very discreet request, you understand, I want to ask that you never give yourself away, and knowing that he's dead, you should speak to him as though he were a living person. Okay? I've already been doing this for years and as you can see I've suffered no harm from him. Once the draft blew a card off my desk, tossing it at Mr. Director, and the card flew right through him, really pierced him, but it was as if he didn't notice anything. And I also pretended that I didn't notice anything. Since then he doesn't give me too much work. If my fiancé had died, then Mr. Director would be the only mediator between us. So, I really appreciate his friendliness. Believe me, he'll have the same good attitude toward you, if you keep to certain conditions."

"And how about the rest? The rest of the library staff?"

"Have you seen anyone else other than me?"

"No."

"Well, it's like this. They sit in their offices, and some even spend the night there and eat, because sometimes the smell of pea soup, sauerkraut and sausage with garlic wafts over to me, but frankly, I greatly doubt they're all alive and not ghosts. In any case our relations are peculiar. Every morning, in the hallway over there on the small table with the telephone I leave them tasks that they are supposed to complete over the course of the day. They take them, and by evening they neatly assemble the filled-out cards for the general directory on the same table. The library is the hereafter, Hades, and you, like a young Orpheus, have descended into this abyss for Eurydice, but there is no Eurydice, because I can't be your Eurydice. And this is our tragedy.

For a long time, I didn't see anyone from the library staff other than Mrs. Konopelka, although sometimes the voices and smells she spoke of wafted to me, mostly kielbasa with garlic, pickled cucumbers and fried onions, and once I even caught the smell of potato pancakes and my mouth watered. I couldn't imagine that in the library, in this temple of knowledge, there was a kitchen where pancakes were fried, but I couldn't find the kitchen even by following the smell. It would have continued like this if not for one event which gave me the chance to see the entire library staff—and that was rape. On that day, Mr. Director convened an urgent meeting, and I saw a whole flock of people of all ages and both sexes who had one thing in common—they were dressed as if they had emerged from the good old Austrian times of the last century—black worn frock coats, comical cuffs, ties and orange blossom boutonnières in the buttonholes of men's' jackets, long black dresses with necklines of white lace on the older ladies, and bright dresses with buttons on the back of the younger women. It seemed if you inhaled the air more deeply, the smell of naphthalene would suddenly make you feel dizzy. The Director tapped a cane on the floor and said:

"You, perhaps, do not know what an awful event happened here this morning. On her way to the women's restroom, a female worker from the cataloguing department was raped by a man whom she could not recognize. He had women's' pink panties on his head, with openings cut out for his eyes. He dragged her between the bookcases and held a carved wooden knife to her throat. It was the kind we usually use to slice open uncut pages of magazines and books. She learned about this later because initially she thought it was made of steel. Therefore, she didn't make a sound. Most outrageous was that because of the victim's short stature, he forced the poor woman to stand on the immortal work of Adam Mickiewicz, namely the thick edition of *Pan Tadeusz*, which had been published in Paris—a great rarity!—Then he ordered her to bend down, and still things didn't work out, because now she was too tall, then this fanatic grabbed *The Eneida* by Kotlyarevsky, published in St. Petersburg and, standing on it, parked himself sweetly there and implemented such a mind-boggling act of violence on the poor young miss, who guarded her chastity to that moment like a gold incunabulum.[75] As a result of this, two tiny droplets of blood even fell on our prophet Adam's face, engraved on the cover of his immortal work, and which until then took pride in maidenly innocence and purity; the poor *Eneida* was embellished with white spots of a known origin, upon which I don't consider it necessary to expand here. Of course, we could call the police and entrust them with investigating this shameful crime, this blasphemy in regard to our classics, but I believe we will cope on our own. Miss Milya agreed to help us with this, though she did not see the face of the villain, she took a close look at the tool of the crime... I would even say the instrument ... that in the process of the rape a few times feebly fell as the result of the rapist's overly nervous arousal, and at his request was stimulated by the hand of the victim. Thus, her hand well remembered all the peculiarities of this... a-ahem... this... tool of the crime... So, now an investigative experiment awaits us. Miss Milya will sit down over there behind a screen, and all the men, myself included, will come up to her and, unbuttoning their pants, will show his... er... his own... in short, everybody knows what....

75 A rare book or pamphlet printed in Europe before 1501.

"Excuse me, Mr. Director," responded Dundyakevych, who was as old as the hills, "Do I have to go through this er–execution? Cause this, you see, at my ninety years of age, fer sure it might be a little ridiculous. I couldn't even rape a hen, much less Miss Milya," and he, blushing, giggled into his fist, and after him, everyone else did too.

"Yes, Mr. Dundyakevych, you can go, the director nodded. "And you, too, Mr. Telepinsky also go, because you're shorter than Miss Milya, not even the *Eneida* would have helped."

"And me?" Mr. Tsundel asked timidly.

"Oh, and you even more so! Miss Milya recounted that in no way could it be somebody Jewish. Go with God."

I won't say that the groping of my dick was a disagreeable procedure for me. Miss Milya did it very delicately, though without clear knowledge of the matter, thus she looked at me with her eyes, in which the suffering of the entire world was reflected and asked:

"It wasn't you, right?"

"I would have kissed you first," I said, "just like this," and I leaned over and kissed her lips, which opened to meet me, and she continued in the meantime to hold my dick and did not let go even when I straightened up and intended to go.

"The rape," she whispered, "wasn't so unpleasant... He did it delicately...."

"And the knife?" I asked.

"What knife?"

"The knife that he put to your throat...."

"It wasn't a knife, but a latch... an ordinary latch... a copper one... he pulled it off the door, so no one would walk in on us... he was so nervous... he couldn't shoot his wad at all... I helped him... I made that up about the knife... if it was you... I won't tell anyone...."

And she continued to hold my dick. I pulled it out, buttoned up, and said:

"*Pan Tadeusz* and *Eneida* are the pinnacle of literature. I would never dare besmudge them."

In general, this entire procedure went to the dogs, because Miss Milya could not recognize anyone. The last one fulfilling their civic duty was the director, who stayed there even longer than me, and came out covered in red spots. Mrs. Konopelka made an observation in my ear:

"Look what a vampire! He's already drunk up her blood. I wouldn't mind fattening up myself like that after death."

After that everyone dispersed to their offices and book repositories, and the director led Miss Milya to his office to once again listen to all the particulars of the crime in detail.

"How fragile and wounded is a woman's lot," Mrs. Konopelka sighed when we got to our office, "especially here in the library, where there are no beaten paths. I'd hang a warning sign on some bookcases: 'Danger: Do not enter. You may not return.' Whoever raped her disappeared among the books, they'll never find him. I've already said that there are strange things happening. In the antiquarian books department, I've often heard whispering, an anxious whisper that grew in intensity, then subsided... The whisper did not belong to a human being, although individual words could be understood, but I did not understand them, someone was whispering in an unknown language. For some reason, I'm sure it's not a human being... And once I slipped and almost fell, and when I bent down to lift what fell at my feet, I then discovered with horror that it was a handful of seaweed. It was fresh and smelled of the sea... and wet footprints went deep and disappeared into the darkness where I did not dare intrude... Do you understand? In my younger days I've been to Abbazia and have seen the sea, the smell of it still lives inside me... But you need to ride at least two days to get to the sea in Croatia or Slovenia... Maybe it was brought in a bucket of seawater... But why? To toss it on the floor? But that's not all. About four years ago I climbed on top of bookcase number 188, where we have still uncatalogued manuscripts and where no one had been for years. Suddenly I felt something wet slap me in the face one time, and then again. I nearly fell off the ladder, but managed to firmly grab onto a rung, and the third time, can you imagine what I caught with my fist?.. A fish tail! A slippery cold fishtail! Of course, in an instant, it slipped out of my hands and disappeared among the books, and I came down off the ladder with a wet face, went to the washroom and looked in the mirror: on my cheeks was a trace of red and three small scales... Later I showed them to a professor, and he determined that they were scales from an ocean fish. Oh, and they smelled of the sea!"

She bent down, pulled out the bottom drawer of the desk and, removing a small box, opened it:

"Here, take a look... This is dried seaweed and scales... I keep them just in case. You never know... Don't think I'm an old idiot, like our dearly departed Director sometimes allows himself to think. I'm telling you this, so you'll be vigilant. In a few days I'll send you to bookcase number 188. Then you'll have to remember my story."

11

Sometimes in the evenings Milker went to the city center and took a stroll but he only got as far as Rynok Square and walking around city hall, never went beyond it to promenade where the unrestrained torrent [of people] once roared. It seemed to him that, upon ending up there, without fail he'd meet countless ghosts of that old non-existent Lviv. He'd hear their voices: "How do you do, Mr. Maecenas?"—"I kiss your hands, Mrs. Engineer!..."[76] He didn't wander off to his former Jewish neighborhood because he had the suspicion he wouldn't come out alive, he wouldn't survive the onrush of feelings that would overwhelm him when those whom he knew and loved would show themselves from the windows, and different voices begin to call: "Ay, Yossel! Yossel! And where are you headed? Come over here!.. Yossel, tell mother that Ida's getting married! Let her come to us and help with the cooking!.. Yossel! My you are so big! Probably running after girls?" Just one attempt to imagine this picture moved him, and he shook off those visions like cherry blossoms. A lot of tourists always hung out at Rynok Square. Upon seeing them, the old man slowed his gait, and even stopped for some time to carefully look around, as if he were seeking someone. He didn't have a single friend with whom he could go for coffee and sit at the table on a warm evening, so usually he drank coffee by himself until someone sat down at his table. He never ventured into conversation with anyone and listened to the chitchat of others with an indifferent look. He could sit like this for an hour or two with one coffee,

76 See note #6.

perhaps even ordering a slice of strudel or poppy seed roll. He especially liked the warm, silky autumn evenings; they wrapped him in gray recollections. He bathed in them, like in warm water.

"Mr. Milker, can I sit next to you?" A girl's voice awakened him from his thoughts. The old man looked up and saw a girl with luxurious curly hair and fiery eyes. Large full lips smiled, showing pearly teeth. He nodded and watched in amazement as she sat down at the table, nodded to the waiter and ordered coffee, cherry liqueur, and an apple pie. Milker remained silent, waiting for the girl to explain something, but when she began to speak, he felt his fingers begin to tremble and his entire body tensed up.

"Excuse me, maestro, for disturbing you. I've been hoping to meet you for a long time."

Maestro? It had been a long time since Milker heard that word; it seemed it had come to his ears from the depths of years. He gulped but didn't say a word.

"My mother studied with you... she's told me a lot. I also play the violin, but my mother said that your lessons were one of a kind. And when I began to find out more about you, it became clear that you no longer give lessons."

Milker nodded.

"That's true. I don't. I taught as long as I had hope to educate a genuine virtuoso, a great violinist. But I happened upon ignoramuses or students for whom music was not something vital... something for which they would sacrifice their personal lives, because art, like a pagan god, always requires sacrifice. And one who does not make these sacrifices dissolves in space. Such is the law. What's your mother's name?"

"Oryslava Hornytska. And my name is Yarka."

"Oryslava... Orysia...," Milker got lost in thought. "Yes-yes... one of those who didn't dare to make the sacrifice. She chose quiet family happiness instead of music. In order to play just for her husband later. Mostly on his nerves. Music doesn't forgive such behavior. Will you be the same?"

"No. Never. I made my choice. I told my mother that music is the main thing for me, and that she should stop managing my life. And then she told me about you. She said that only you can make me a virtuoso. That you know the violin's special secrets that you're not in a hurry to disclose until you're sure you've met someone to whom it's worthwhile to reveal them."

"If you've come just to find out my secrets, it's useless."

"No, I want to improve my playing. And receive some more knowledge only when you believe in me."

Milker had a sip of coffee and pondered. Something in this girl was winning him over. He saw in her eyes a fire, and heard in her voice a thirst for knowledge, but something still was missing, was it faith—or what?

"Once all art belonged to the gods," he articulated. "It was for the gods that temples were built, that music was composed, icons were painted; it was for the gods that people danced and sang. And for whom you want to play?"

She didn't hesitate to answer:

"For the angels. Not for those painted in churches or on prayer cards, but for the angels that we carry inside ourselves. For a person has an angel in herself or himself, not a guardian angel, but an angel that moans, imprisoned in the darkness of the soul of each of us, and which rarely, very rarely we manage to free from the chains and give him freedom to take off, fly up, and then... then..."

"...then together with him our soul rises up, the soul of each of us," Milker continued and added: "You're quoting Mircea Eliade...."

"These words are mine too. That is, they have become mine. They became my credo. I don't want to betray this angel at any cost."

"If you are saying this sincerely...," the old man lowered his eyes. "In addition, a person who reads Eliade can't escape my attention."

"Oh, believe me," Yarka put her hand on his—her thin delicate hand with narrow pink nails onto his dry and wrinkled one, onto his bony fingers with long neatly trimmed nails. She placed it on his hand and felt the cold of his hand, the throbbing of a deep blue vein, and the hope that he was beginning to trust her.

"I've already decided everything for myself. You won't regret that you've made me your pupil."

K

I liked work in the library. I had more than enough free time and could rummage through old books and manuscripts, or making myself comfortable on the ladder, jot down some words of wisdom for my "Book." One day I came across a treatise on the mirror, little-known but by the prominent scholar De Selby. You'd think, the mirror, big deal... But there is no other thing in our life that is more enigmatic, mysterious, and insidious. I've admired it since childhood. Stretching out on the floor and setting up a mirror opposite me, I slowly lowered the upper part of it so that the floor beneath me seemed to be running away somewhere down, and then I moved toward it—into an unknown abyss, into something terrible and irreversible, perhaps even to hell itself. Fear overwhelmed me. I felt warmth envelop my feet, and in an instant the heat would burn them. I quickly lifted up the mirror, then the floor was lifted up with me, and I rapidly risked flying down again, but headlong. This could be repeated countless times, but it was even more interesting when I turned out the light. The mirror then showed mysterious abysses, strange slinking shadows, and with the help of a second mirror I penetrated into boundless labyrinths, in which I completely sank, breaking up into countless individual portraits and shrinking to the size of a poppy seed. I like this diversion even now, especially when I reached the conclusion that the mirror shows the appearance of person at a younger age than in reality. Because the light travels with a precisely calculated speed, this means, that before the reflection of some subject will appear in the mirror, the first rays of light need to fall on this subject, then reach the mirror surface, reflect from it and return to this subject, in the given case to the human eye, which means that between the moment when a person casts a glance at his reflection in the mirror, and the moment when the reflected image is reflected in his eye, a very specific period of time passes that can be measured. Of course, this period is so small that hardly anyone would consider this phenomenon as a problem worthy of serious discussion, but I found proof of this theory in De Selby, who succeeded in understanding these very same conclusions three hundred years ago. That is, take note, I came to comprehend this on my own, and I came across the treatise of De Selby much later. The scientist proposed to reflect the first reflection in the second mirror and observed that in this second reflection it is possible upon careful examination to detect differences in comparison with the first. De Selby even created a system of parallel mirrors, each of which reflected in an infinite row his entirely diminished and diminishing face, which he placed between the mirrors. Then De Selby asserts that he very carefully "with the help of a powerful telescope" examined the reflection, distanced incredibly far from the original in an infinite row of parallel reflections. The description of what he saw in the telescope was striking. De Selby asserts that in proportion to his reflected faces going to infinity, they became increasingly younger and younger, and the last reflection that he was able to examine—to see it with the naked eye was totally impossible–was the face of a boy about twelve years old "of exceptional beauty and nobility." He failed to get to the reflection, in which he would have seen himself in the cradle, "because of the curvature of the earth's surface and the limited capacity of the telescope."

This discovery shook me to the depth of my soul. I thought that De Selby's forgotten treatise should immediately be published, and the industrial production of telescopes and an accessible system of mirrors should be started so that every person could look back at his youth, not limited just to photographs. Moreover, reversing the mirror in the opposite direction it would be possible to look into one's future, to see how the appearance of this or that person changes, and thanks to this to foresee illnesses and death. But another discovery made an even more powerful impression on me: if I had come to this theory myself and if the human soul is traveling the entire time from body to body, it would not be surprising if De Selby's soul had settled itself in me. When I finished reading his treatise to the end, I discovered one more thing: De Selby in his experiments relied on the conclusions of the medieval Persian scholar Al-Mu'tasim,[77] whose name translates as "Seeker of Blood" or perhaps "Bloodseeker." And what do you think? I immediately felt like my soul had aged several more centuries, and I would have almost begun to prattle in Farsi, if Mrs. Konopelka had not brought me out of such real closeness to Al-Mu'tasim, ordering me to put bookcase Number 188 in order immediately. The books there lay in disarray, mostly well tattered editions from God-knows-when, among which I came across eight faded and dried sheets. Reviewing the numbering, I saw that four more were missing. It was as if someone had torn them out of an unknown book. The sheets were copied musical notes, and between the notes there were some strange signs and drawings—I recognized a mandrake root, gallows with a noose. There also were

77 See Borges' 1935 story "The Approach to Al-Mu'tasim."

plants, birds, and animals, but kinds that never existed in nature, and various organs and parts of the human body. The individual drawings and lettering were so tiny that I decided to take those sheets with me to try to examine them more closely with the aid of a magnifying glass. I hid them under my shirt, and, barely managing to wait to the end of the work day, carried them off, not home, but to Yosko's, because it was he who was studying at the conservatory. He would be able to get to the bottom of it sooner, to find out what's what. Yosko's hands began to shake when he saw these ancient musical notes. He sat down at the piano right then and there and tried to play them, but some awful cacophony came out. Yosko said that those notes are probably encrypted, that is, arranged in a completely different order, but in which order—It was a riddle, though... here he armed himself with a magnifying glass and examining more closely, saw between the lines of notes a Latin inscription:

"This music is somehow connected with medicine. It is written here that the tonality of the sound of any musical note corresponds to the tonality of a corresponding organ or body part."

"The tonality of the sound of an organ or body part?" I was surprised. "I've never heard anything stupider."

However, Yosko made copies and photographs of the mysterious sheets and aimed to decipher them. The next day I showed Mrs. Konopelka the sheets, and she was really surprised:

"It can't be! It's Kalkbrenner's lost treatise, which so many people are after. In 1640, Johann Kalkbrenner, Lviv pharmacist and medical man, composed music, which upon hearing allowed a person to remember all the details of his or her previous life. However, only under the condition that he or she had heard the same music before his or her death."

"Since when are pharmacists creating music?" I was surprised.

"Kalkbrenner was a multitalented man. However, his treatise disappeared. Only mentions of it remained in other scholars' writings. And who knows whether these sheets come from that treatise. But this is only eight pages, where are the rest?" After these words she beckoned me with her dry twisted branches and led me into the depths of the hall between the sheer cliffs of bookcases and stopped next to old folios, bound in leather, on the backs of which one could not see any inscription other than embossed letters and numbers. "Here, take this book into your hands," she pointed to a manuscript in a black binding, "and open it up to page seventy-seven."

The book was heavy as if it were made of lead. On page seventy-seven light glimmered, something shined over and over. I could sense the sound of rain, the light in the book first extinguished, then lit up. A gust of wind shook the pages and the smell of the breeze, crow's nests and wormwood blew right into my face. it was as if a lightning flash had sewn in the pages, not allowing them to fly away. I turned the page and the sound of the wind became louder; on page eighty it already drowned out the words of Mrs. Konopelka, who tried to explain to me that it I shouldn't flip the pages any further. Actually, I guessed this from the expression of her face and her nervous movements, and I slammed the book shut and put it back in place.

"In this book, it rains, thunders and flashes," Mrs. Konopelka said. "And in that one there's rustling of the woods, it smells of pine needles and you can hear someone's steps, the crunching of dry branches, in that one the winter sun rises, and in this one—it sets... Never take a book into your hands in which the sun sets, because it might be your sun....

12

Having come upon this spot, Yarosh was surprised he remembered his translation of the works of the Arcanumian poet Lucilius and also a description of the latter's library collection, made by one of his friends. Among those books were:

The Book of Advice

A certain odd Book that the blind Eudokia presented to Lucilius consisted of advice. In the preface, an unknown person promised great bliss to anyone who would politely heed the book. But blind Eudokia warned that the Book cannot be read just for the hell of it, just for fun. The book will still influence the reader and will destroy his soul. Unless you flip the pages with a knife, which has been blessed twelve times, and just before reading it, it must be sprinkled with blessed poppy seeds.

And yet Lucilius was emboldened to read a few pages, arming himself with a blessed knife.

"If the devil appears to you, try to convince Him that you do not have any hostile intentions toward Him," it was written in the book. "But do this carefully, without haste, because the Devil is a creature who thinks slowly and can incorrectly understand you.

It is best to begin with the eyes. Take his hand (usually topped with a huge black claw) in both of your hands and gouge out your left eye. In the meantime, do not touch your right eye so as not to make mistakes in all your subsequent actions. So, then, without letting go of the hand of the Devil, knock out your teeth with it. Don't pay attention to the blood—sooner or later it will stop gushing anyway.

Then let go of His hand and bow to Him. With a stone that you've always carried under the front of your shirt, strike yourself in the chest. If the first time you break your rib, then consider yourself an extraordinary bold person, and you can be proud of your agility. Extract the broken rib and give it to the Devil. This act is particularly important, and you must treat him as seriously as possible. After accepting your rib the Devil will create a Bright Maiden, who will give birth to you. However, you will come into this world not alone, but in the form of twins, one of whom will be left-handed, and the second—right-handed.

Now after you have secured your future, you can behave more boldly. The Devil undoubtedly will like this. Most importantly, do everything with laughter and song so as to show in this way that you are a daredevil.

Strike yourself again with the stone, deeper in your chest, pull out your rib and fling it down to His feet. Your children, who will glory in you, will grow out of them. Tear at yourself mercilessly.

The Devil will be extremely touched when you ask him to make balloons out of your guts. He'll blow them up, and you'll burst them with a pin. Here you'll see Him happy at every 'Pop!'

And for you it's fun.

Place the last intestine—the thickest—to the Devil's ass and ask him to fart. When the intestine is filled with gas, float up with the balloon into the blue heavens and become an angel."

The book *The Fish Trap*

This book was so thick that it was even hard to hold it in one hand. On the first page there was a drawing of a regular fish trap that's set out to catch fish in a river, and nothing else, but after turning this page, you could encounter a text that forces you to think whether it's worthwhile to continue flipping the pages of the book.

"Dear reader," it was written there. "Keep in mind that when you are emboldened to read the book *The Fish Trap*, with each page read you will lose weight, becoming smaller and smaller until at the very end you completely become a sequin, possibly physically unable to turn the last pages. But if you managed to read the book to the end before you disappear, then suddenly you'll come back to your original state, and in addition, will also acquire eternal existence. So, you need to read as quickly as possible, striving, however, not to miss a single page or word, otherwise all your work will be in vain. If you try to look inside in the middle of it, you'll lose your sight. You need to flip page after page, and when you reach the second half, you will come across the tiny squashed corpses of your predecessors. Let them be a warning to you and hasten your reading.

"This is all that you are allowed to know about this book."

Lucilius started reading this book only when he felt that it was time to die, for some reason he was confident that he could predict it. Death in the book seemed to him incredibly exciting, much more interesting than dying in bed.

The book *The Anthill*

This book could irritate anyone, even as patient a reader as Lucilius was. And only his reverent attitude toward books did not permit him to toss it into a fire.

The fact of the matter is that the book had its own secret. Upon opening it, you can see only an anthill of letters that creep and crawl away further from your eyes, fleeing from page to page without allowing you to catch a single word. But if someone turned out to be agile enough to open this book so rapidly that the letters would be unable to scamper away and, in this way, could catch just a single word (it's no difference even which one), this would immediately vanquish the book, and it would allow itself to be read.

But all Lucilius's attempts to catch the letters in a state of order before they scattered proved useless. He was never able to catch them off guard. It was as if the letters constantly were on alert and at any moment were ready to turn the text into chaos. No doubt, this was their way of existence, and it made them satisfied.

Lucilius was very interested in who the author was and how he was able to write it. But it was impossible to make out the author's name. Nothing, not a single word.

Is such a book worthy of existence? Well, if no one has burned it for hundreds of years before me, Lucilius thought to himself, then I won't burn it. What if someone succeeds in taming it!

Words that have Disappeared

Among Lucilius's books was one with blank pages. You couldn't read anything there other than a single Word. And that Word was so powerful that it often forced Lucilius to open the book at any page and read it. This book had power over Lucilius, such power, that perhaps no book lover has over a book, and it turned out that it was not Lucilius reading the book, but it was forcing him to do so. It was not entirely necessary for his eye to catch sight of it, it was enough for the word to arise in his memory, and then nothing could restrain his desire to take the book in his hands.

The question is, why read it at all when just a single Word is written on every page, and one that Lucilius knew by heart? The fact of the matter was that the Word, depending on your mood or certain external circumstances could be perceived differently; in addition, it still seemed to Lucilius that there would come a time when he would read something else besides that single Word after opening the book .

Despite its power over Lucilius, the book did not show any aggressive intentions and did not harm anything for a long time. Reading it, Lucilius always felt like the Word was saturated with certain mysterious meanings, but reluctantly subjected itself to the explanation of these meanings. The Word itself seemingly enjoyed being in this state of polysemy and mystery. Perhaps the Word was afraid that when it would be understood completely, it would immediately die, become a set of sounds, already unfit for daily reading and meditation. This fear, obviously, gained in strength over time, for the book's desire to be reread gradually became curbed, and it beckoned its owner to it less frequently than before.

However, once Lucilius opened a book that stood on the shelf to the right of that book with the single Word and became horrified. The book, which originally contained the collected parables of the East, had also become a book containing just a single word. The Word was different, but that still didn't provide any comfort, because so many great works were lost. Lucilius looked into the book that stood to the left and became even more horrified—this book too was transformed into a single-word one. It seemed like an epidemic. The Book infected all the books that were on both sides of it. Lucilius began to leaf through them and saw that certain pages were also infected with singlewordedness.

What could be done? The first thought was immediately to burn all the one-word books before the epidemic spread to the entire library. But the poet hesitated—these words... they might still be useful to me—but at the same time he asked himself: is it really so hard to remember them? Even if each of these words can be the quintessence of each book, he still wouldn't want the entire library to become a collection of quintessences.

In the end, Lucilius burned all the one-word and partially infected books. And right at the moment that they turned to ashes, he forgot all the words that appeared on their whitewashed pages. He didn't even remember the first Word, which he read so attentively for so many years and from which the epidemic spread to adjacent books. From then on, he always had a thirst for those lost words. He wanted to retain them within himself, and now with a certain special thirst he threw himself at books, hoping to come across and recognize at least one of those words. He searched for them frantically even in his own manuscripts, but much to his incredible surprise he found nothing similar at all. But he stubbornly believed that he'd find them all the same. For this reason, he wrote hundreds of pages, hoping that some of those words would pop up from his subconscious.

They didn't pop out. But the number of works kept growing and growing.

Is it possible to cover with writing such a mountain of paper and not once use even one of those words?—Lucilius wondered. Then he recalled that there are dozens, even hundreds of words that, though he knows them, he will never use them, but all the same they exist: “vigor,” “excitement,” “creative contribution,” “in creative inspiration....” These words elicited disgust in him, but which emotions did those former words elicit in him? He started reflecting, maybe it would help him remember them. Only one thing was indisputable: those words sparked his desire to write.

The odd thing was that their absence elicited in him even more the desire to write, for in this relatively short time he produced immeasurably more than in previous years. You can compare this, for example, to air and freedom. When they are there, you don’t notice them. When a poet doesn’t have enough air, he dies, and when he doesn’t have enough freedom, he turns into a prophet.

L

"I brought you here not to boast of our treasures," Mrs. Konopelka continued. "Kalkbrenner's treatise was located on the top shelf, you see there's an empty space between the books? In the place where the book was that disappeared, a small board was inserted so the neighboring books wouldn't press together, for each of these books has its place and it can't be changed, otherwise its amazing properties also would change. The date when the book disappeared was written on the board: "Anno Domini 12. 12. 1812." Now take me where you found these sheets.

We again moved among the stacks, and although I was walking fast enough, the old woman shuffled after me, not falling behind by even a step, and sometimes passing me somehow, she would unexpectedly stop in front of me, and allow me to go in front of her, so I could lead her until I finally stopped near the familiar stack. She ordered me to climb up and carefully inspect the wooden shelf. The ladder, vibrating, screeched mercilessly and bent under my weight. Just in case, I held onto the shelves instead of the ladder. It was good that I had grabbed a flashlight, because there right under the ceiling darkness reigned. I illuminated the dark shelf, which, although it had been smoothed by a plane, had badly cracked over the years, and I began to examine it inch by inch, until I saw the cracks that did not look natural, and man-made scratches, and when I reported this to Mrs. Konopelka, she ordered me to climb down, take a clean sheet of paper and a pencil, and climbing up, to place the paper on those scratches and trace them with the pencil. Then she grabbed that paper and clumsily walked so fast that I barely managed to keep up with her, flitting swiftly among the stacks, grunting and giggling with satisfaction. After I ran into the office, the old woman already had placed the paper on the table, and armed with a magnifying glass, she squinted with her eye. What I saw even without a magnifying glass looked like this: a circle, and inside the circle several numbers.

"What do you think?" The old woman asked, tapping her finger on the paper. "Finally, we're on the right track. But where does it lead? This circle... It must point to something." Then she began to draw circles next to each other with the pencil. It seemed it would last until she filled the entire sheet, but she suddenly stopped, raised her head and smiled to me: "Circle! What's that in German?"

"Ring!"

"Exactly! Ring! Or should we think Rynok Square! Eh?"

I shrugged my shoulders. Well, the Rynok... But Mrs. Konopelka had already guessed it:

"Rush right away to Rynok Square and walk past the buildings with the numbers inscribed here," she pointed her finger at the numbers, "and copy the writing on the buildings for me."

"Do you mean the signs?"

"The signs, seriously, dunderhead? Nothing is as short-lived as signs. Copy the Latin inscriptions! And don't miss or mess up a single letter."

I was stunned, thinking that Mrs. Konopelka finally lost her sanity, but obediently took a pencil and a few sheets of paper together with the copied numbers and lumbered over to Rynok Square. I set to my task with my usual conscientiousness, so I returned to the library three hours later.

During this time Mrs. Konopelka got incredibly antsy and she flew at me with a wet towel and berated me for being a Mr. Slowmotionsky[78] like the world has never seen and that if it wasn't for her poor eyesight, she would have tackled this task in half an hour. Then she grabbed the sheets with trembling hands, setting herself down in a chair, and began to read and take notes.

"Yes, Rynok Square, 2 ...Bandinelli Palace... 'A 1739 D: 28 AVG'... This is abbreviated, and the full version is: «ANNO 1739 DIEI 28 AVGUSTI». That is the "Year 1739 of August 28." But we are interested only in the numbers, so let's write only them down. 1739 and 28. First—the stack number, the second—the number of the shelf. Rynok Square 4 ... "MA SR", and below—"MD CL."

"What kind of hocus pocus is this?"

"MARTINUS ANCZEWSKI SECRETARIUS REGIS MEDICINAE DOCTOR CONSUL LEOPOLIENSIS." That is "Martyn Anchevsky, secretary of the king, doctor of medicine, Lviv counselor."

"But there are no numbers here."

"You're mistaken, there are. These letters—are also Roman numerals. C—100, L—50, D—500, M—1000. In the top row we have the stack number: M—1000, at the bottom—the number of a shelf. Since we don't have a 100 stack, but rather a 50, so we have 1000 and 50... Further—Rynok Square, 23 ... This is a quote from the Bible «TURRIS FORTISSIMA NOMEN DOMINI» and the number "PROVERBIA 18," that is, "the name of the Lord is a strong tower. Proverbs 18;" just the line isn't specified. But it's easy to find.

78 I've opted for the literal meaning in English of the name Guzdralsky.

Let's look at the Bible... so... here's the quote... the tenth line. We write down: 18 and 10. You see how simple and clever? Further. Rynok Square, 36. "HIS DIE 1 MA IULY" and "MARIA ANNO DOMINI 1730." In other words, "Jesus the day of July 1" and "Maria, AD 1730." We write down 1730 and 1.

"How about the months?" I asked. "They also have their numerical counterparts."

"They do. But we don't need them. Throughout there should be two numbers, the ones that are bigger indicate the number of the stack, and the smaller the shelf. I'll be a lunkhead if that's not it. You don't take me for a lunkhead, do you?

"God forbid. I'm just stunned by your profound knowledge."

"Eh-eh, at one time I learned... what isn't taught nowadays...

"But how certain are you that the larger number is the number of the stack?

"Can you imagine shelf number 1730? No? Neither can I, because our library isn't a skyscraper. Though we have lots and lots of stacks! So, what do we have? Stack number 1739, shelf 28. Stack number 1000, shelf 50. Stack number 18, shelf 10. And stack number 1730, shelf 1."

She wrote out all the numbers on a piece of paper, and handing it to me, said:

"Now go on an exciting journey along the unknown paths of our library. And not in that wing that you've been going to, but in the opposite one."

"Which wing is that?"

"The one with a skull and bones painted on the doors."

"Lord! But it's written there 'Entrance strictly forbidden!'"

"Yes, that's right. There you'll find the closed archives. You can enter it only with a special pass, which only Mr. Director, who unfortunately is deceased, can give you along with me. For this is the holy of holies, a protected zone, an unbelievable land... More than one person has gone and not returned... but it won't happen to you. I believe in you. You'll return victorious."

"Over whom?"

"Over yourself. Over your fears." She uttered this as if she were sending me off to battle, and the more she spoke, the less I felt the desire to go to those uncharted lands.

"And what should I look for there?" I asked.

"I don't know. Check the entire shelf, book by book, turn every page ... Though wait a minute... We let slip from our attention the numbers of the buildings on Rynok Square—2, 4, 23, and 36. They may tell us more precisely the location of what we're looking for."

"What are we looking for?"

"If you ask me one more time about it, I'll turn you into a geranium. I don't have a clue. Maybe it's some kind of a sign—in a book or on the same shelf, maybe a little piece of paper placed in a book. So—on the 28th shelf of stack number 1739, you'll first examine the second book from the left. If there's nothing, then look at the second book on the right. If this is a blind alley, then examine all the books on this shelf. You'll find something there for sure. So, wander around in that manner from stack to stack. The number of the building on Rynok Square must correspond to the position of the book at one end or the other. Verstehen? [Understand?]

"Yes, seems so. Right in the order that you wrote?"

"What would you like?"

"Well, you see, first I have to shuffle over to stack number 1739, then turn to number 1000, then continue to go back to number 18, and then again surge over to 1730. Wouldn't it be easier if I started with number 18 and so forth?

Mrs. Konopelka straightened her glasses and looked at me so intently as she never had before.

"Young lad," she said, "you've gotten under my skin. Go any way you want, just bring me something. Ah... here's the document for you. Keep it with you. This is your access to private archives. And take this...," she rummaged in a drawer, pulled out a little piece of paper folded over four times and handed it me: "This is for when you want to have something to eat or drink... Unfold it. Don't take a look at it right now, but keep it, because if you lose it... I don't know who can help you then...."

"Eat or drink? But I'm not going for that long," I was surprised.

"What? Not for long? Where do you imagine that 1730th stack is? If you think you'll manage to do this fast, you're sorely mistaken. In the closed archives the stacks are marked not only with numbers but also letters, that is, after №1 it's №1a, №1b, №1c, №1d and the devil only knows how long it goes on this way. But you pay attention only to the shelves without letters. Got that? Oh, I nearly forgot—mattresses and bedding are located every hundred stacks. As you can see, the administration has taken care of everything.

"But, excuse me, what if I need to go to the bathroom?"

"There are many planters by the walls... various ficuses, shmikuses, rhododendrons, shmarodendrons... They haven't been watered for a long time...."

"And if I need to...."

"They haven't been fertilized either... God be with you...."

"Then I ask you kindly to tell my mom..."

"Sure, sure, don't worry. I'll send someone over to her right away."

And so I set off into the unknown, but not without trepidation, before approaching the doors with the skull and crossbones, and the words "Wejście zabronione" ["Entry Prohibited" in Polish], which repeatedly drew my attention, but I didn't have the courage to approach them. So I timidly knocked and opened the little window. Some bearded mug, one eye shining, carefully studied me, mumbling something unintelligible under his breath. I presented the document, and the mug coughed out some sounds, groaned, sighed, and opened the door. I saw a small hunchbacked man on thin legs with a large shaggy head. In order to reach the little window, he had to push over a footstool. He flicked his hand, signaling to me now that I can go wherever I want, and he shut the door without saying a word, just grunting and moaning as if he were moving some really heavy weight, then settled down in an old creaky armchair, covered himself with a checkered blanket up to his neck and fell asleep, loudly sucking in air.

My nostrils were struck by the scent not only of old folios, mold and leather, wooden stacks gnawed by some woodworms, but also some strange and incomprehensible, at least for this place, fantastic aroma of smoked meat. This odor was so clear and unmistakable that I was at first taken aback, thinking where the hell have I ended up. And I started to look around in every direction to find the odor's source. I eventually concluded that it was wafting from somewhere above, but the stacks rose like sheer cliffs, the top shelves were lost in a fog, a real bluish-gray fog that smelled of kielbasa and ham. Outside it was drizzling. It was overcast and unfriendly. Very little light penetrated into the library; for safety's sake there was no electric current, no light bulbs and no candles either. There remained just one thing—to allow your eyes to get used to it. I found stack number 18 quickly, as I anticipated, set up the ladder, and reaching up to the tenth shelf, took the twenty-third book from the left side. It was *De Historia Plantarum* by Theophrastus,[79] published in 1620. The book is rather thick and heavy; flipping through its pages on the ladder was awkward. I stepped down the ladder and sat on the windowsill and quickly began to look through page by page. I finished this extremely serious work but didn't find any piece of paper or inscription slipped inside it, and already planned to climb up for the book from the right side of the shelf when my attention was drawn to the back cover. It was slightly thicker than the front. From my pocket I took out a pen knife, which was always with me, and carefully lifted up the lining glued on the inside. I was not mistaken. A sheet of paper folded in half was pressed inside there. After pulling it out, I saw Latin text and images of plants with labels and Latin inscriptions. I put the sheet in my pocket, put the book back in place, and made my way to the 1000th stack. The rain outside turned into a downpour. With particular zeal it hammered on the tin roof so hard that my ears buzzed, and the rumble and noise deafened my footsteps. Dusk slowly began to fall, and

79 The philosophical successor to Aristotle (ca. 371—ca. 287 BC). *Historia Platarum* is one of his two extant botanical works.

fog from the upper book stacks descended lower and lower. I kept walking, glancing at the number of the stacks and sensed I was starting to lose my good mood, because the stacks really began to multiply before my eyes. Sometimes I stumbled on a book or a package of books; that's why my initial intention not to walk, but to run, turned out to be not so simple, especially after I fell a few times and painfully banged my head. So I didn't walk, but dragged myself, and reached the thousandth stack by evening. The second sheet was hidden in *Medicina Herbaria*[80] by Agricola; the book was bound in olive green goatskin with relief ornamentation and had countless color illustrations. I couldn't restrain myself from leafing through it but regretfully put it back on the shelf, because I needed to settle myself somewhere for the night, when suddenly I heard rustling. It seemed like someone was flipping through a book, spitting on their fingers to page through it so rapidly. I grew stock still and listened, and then began to sneak toward the sound as cautiously as possible, although it was superfluous because of the rumbling of the downpour. Finally, I stumbled upon a girl, whom I recognized as Milya, the one who had recently been raped by some unknown stranger. Surprised, she abruptly snapped the book shut and hid it behind her.

"What are you doing here?" she stammered nervously.

"I'm doing a job for Mrs. Konopelka."

"Can I ask what that is?"

I noticed her eyes shining and replied:

"No."

"That's what I thought," she sighed. "Are you hungry?"

"I am. It's good you mentioned that. Mrs. Konopelka

---

80 Published in 1539 by Julius Agricola.

gave me some kind of piece of paper for me to open it up when I'm hungry. Here it is."

"Yes, I know," the girl said, looking at the paper. "It's marked on which stacks and shelves there are flasks with water and something to eat. And I know where the wine is here."

"Why does a library have wine?"

"Wines have been stored here since Austrian times. Mr. Director brought them here from the wine cellars of Count Sapieha and arranged them on different shelves, and he's the only one who has a map of these wines. And there's not only wine. Right under the ceiling here and there hang hams, sausages, and briskets, all aged... When you came here, you probably smelled smoked meat?"

"I smelled it... But how is it that they age? Smoked meats need to be prepared in smoke."

"Yes, and it's prepared for months, years... but not in smoke, in fog, in this bluish gloom that swirls under the ceiling. You can't see it from here, so don't try. But I know where it is. Mr. Director gave up that secret as a compensation for my lost virginity. Which I still, hee-hee, have."

"How?" I was stunned. "So, you weren't raped?"

"No."

"What about the blood stains on the *Mr. Tadeusz* volume, and the sperm stain on *The Eneida*?"

"The blood was from my little finger, and for the semen... I mixed a little sour cream with starch and decorated the book with a tiny bit of it. I smeared the rest on the floor."

"Why did you stage that show?"

"It wasn't a show. I acted according to my plan. Everything was done in order to get into the closed archives. You have access, don't you?"

"Yes, Mrs. Konopelka gave it to me."

"Exactly. And I persuaded Mr. Director that I must also have it to find my rapist who must be hiding in the closed archives. Do you understand? Now go to this stack and on the 48th shelf behind *De Occulta Philisophia* by Cornelius Agrippa get a bottle of Barbera D'Asti 1889. Then climb a little higher and remove a kielbasa."

I was pretty stunned when I heard that, but dutifully climbed the ladder and really did find a bottle of wine, and climbed a few more steps, and my head hit a kielbasa that smelled so intoxicatingly that I barely restrained myself from biting it. We settled ourselves on boxes of books. I uncorked the bottle with my pen knife and after the first sips I felt a pleasant bliss and gratitude to the girl for brightening up my journey. We drank and ate the delicious kielbasa, its flavor enhanced by all those pundits and philosophers, heretics and charlatans, Gnostics and prognosticators, historians and literati, and poets and playwrights who were squeezed into the shelves without even knowing that someday, in hundreds of years, their old tomes would emit not only the smell of old paper, leather and paint, but even the smell of burnt wood, pine needles, dry leaves....

"So, you've grasped how valuable an asset I am for you," Miss Milya asked, playfully smiling and jabbing me with her elbow. However, I didn't catch the hint and just nodded. The wine already had made its way to my head and began to swirl slightly through the nooks and crannies of my brain. I felt good and wasn't rushing anywhere anymore. "We'll continue to travel together," she added, and just then I understood what she was getting at, but didn't express my surprise and just asked:

"Are you planning to go far away? What are you looking for?"

"I won't tell you. Although what I am seeking may be closely related to what you are looking for, but I'm not sure."

She looked at me coquettishly, as if expecting that I'd tell her the aim of my search, but I just shrugged my shoulders and said:

"Candor for candor: for the time being I have no reason to think that we're traveling with the same aim. But your lips...," she opened them in such a surprised way, as if she were going to say "Oh!" But she didn't say it because I covered them with mine, but in the meantime my hand hit upon a book which she had stuffed between the boxes on the floor. I carefully moved it to one of the shelves. At the same time her left hand gently stroked my pockets and chest, and when I tried to lower it below my waist, she took it back without fail and continued her examination that came to naught, because while I was climbing up for the wine and sausage I hid those sheets that I had extracted from the folio into my sock. In that entire time our lips never parted, but when I tried to stroke her breasts, she abruptly jerked back.

"What do you think you're doing? I told you I'm a virgin."

"But stroking your breasts while kissing isn't losing your virginity. It's really pleasant."

"I imagine. But you're not my fiancé, and I've decided to give myself only to my fiancé."

"He could turn out to be a boor and take you like a bear. Crudely and improperly. It's never worth giving yourself to a fiancé."

"How do you know that?"

"From life. It's better to pretend to lose your virginity to your husband. Especially since you've already being doing this like a pro."

"Please don't insult me. I explained to you the true reason I did it."

Here she suspected something and slipping her hand behind her back without feeling the book she had hidden from me, finally stopped being capricious and began to look around for it expressively until she guessed that something was not right, and cast a glance at me:

"Oh, you are a scoundrel! Have you taken advantage of my weakness? Where is my book? Where would you hide it?"

She suddenly rose up from her spot and began to scour the closest shelves, but already a dense fog was swirling around us and she could see no further beyond the reach of her arm's length. She was in despair.

"Why did you do it? It's not what you think! Where is my book?"

"I'll give it to you if you explain what you're looking for."

She sat on the box, grabbed the bottle and took another sip, then sighed and said:

"I have a task given by a representative of the Habsburg court. I need to find a certain treatise."

"By Johan Kalkbrenner?"

As I expected, she made a show of being surprised, which I didn't believe for a second.

"How do you know about it? Are you also...?

"What do you mean—also?"

"It's nothing, never mind...," she took up the bottle again and sighed. "Maybe I've messed up everything. So, we're looking for the same thing."

"Honestly, I don't know very well what I'm looking for. So far, eight different sheets have been found. Four are missing. Mrs. Konopelka sent me to find them."

"Hold on... you mean to say that eight sheets of Kalkbrenner's treatise have already been found?" I nodded and took the bottle from her. "You've beaten us to them?"

"Quite by accident. Tell me, are you doing this for money?"

"Of course. You think I'm doing it for some kind of fantasy?"

"Because I'm doing it because of my work responsibilities."

"Just because Mrs. Konopelka ordered you?"

"Yes. Although my friends have also taken an interest in this treatise and I guess they'll have a pleasant surprise when I find the rest of the pages."

"A pleasant surprise!" She mocked me. "You can't imagine what kind of money you can get for it! You'll become a rich man! A magnate! Help me and you won't regret it. Where are those eight sheets?"

"Mrs. Konopelka has the originals, and my friends have copies."

"And those missing four?"

"I'm actually looking for them. What's in this book you found and hid from me?"

She sighed sadly:

"Oh, well... you've beaten me to it anyway. It's *Beschreibung allerfürnemisten Mineralischen Ertzt* by Ercker, who, referring to Kalkbrenner, gives certain information. I thought that it would lead me where I need to go."

I bent down and pulled out the book that I had hidden before. It really was Ercker's work, bound in pigskin and illustrated with beautiful engravings. Milya took it and opened it at the very end.

"You see? Here's a reference to Kalkbrenner. But it's not indicated on which page he quotes the treatise. I had to flip through the whole book. That's what you found me doing. But it's already evening; moving further would be dangerous. I suggest we sleep here. Over there," she pointed to the blank wall opposite the windows, "there's a trunk, pull out a mattress and bedding from it."

I obeyed and soon returned with the mattress, sheets, a big blanket, and two pillows. Milya quickly made the bed and ordered me to turn away. I turned to the side and found a dried-up cactus that apparently needed watering. I watered it amply and then returned. The girl was already lying under the blanket. I undressed quickly and lay down beside her, but when I tried to press closer, she recoiled:

"Forget about it! I will never be deflowered in these unaesthetic circumstances!"

"Okay then... Don't worry. It was only out of politeness."

"Oh, you're also a jerk!"

"Why did you say that it was dangerous to move further? What could be dangerous in the depths of the library?"

She stretched lazily, then threw both hands behind her head and said:

"Have you ever heard anything about a ghost train?"

"What's a ghost train have to do with this?"

"It appears on a track that goes to Vynnyky most often, but it has happened that it's even ridden on the tram tracks. The train heavily coughs out clouds of steam, and in the dim windows you can see passengers dressed in the Austrian fashion. Some read newspapers, others play cards, others dine. The faces are calm, smiling, even joyful. But when the train stops for a moment near the old railway watchman's booth, the passengers, like a team, jump up from where they're sitting, desperately scream and press their faces, twisted in terror, to the windows, raking the window panes with their fingernails as if they were stripping some kind of invisible film off them. You can't hear their screams, but you can imagine it from the expression on their faces, their bulging eyes and distorted lips. During a stop the car doors open, and conductors in black cloaks appear in them, and from under the cap you can see only a dark aperture without a face. You can hear someone rushing to the exit, but all his efforts are in vain. This goes on for a minute or two, and then the train moves away. The passengers calm down and again take their seats. They continue to do what they were doing before, as if this awful stop never happened, as though they do not suspect that they, the train, and the tracks haven't existed for a long time. Time stopped for them. There have been instances when someone managed to jump into the train at the stop. From that moment he or she was never seen again.

"Why are you telling me this?"

"Once... It was in Znesinnya... I was going back in the evening from the hospital where I was visiting my sick mother... I heard a noise. Clouds of steam enveloped me. I looked up and saw that a train had stopped next to me. In the windows people were sitting and smiling at me; someone even gave me a friendly nod. And one beauty, who was holding a white doggie with a pink bow in her arms, beckoned me with her finger... Some irresistible force was pulling me inside... I had already grabbed the railing with my hand and raised my leg, when suddenly I noticed a familiar face in the window—it was my grandmother... Her face was contorted with terror, she shouted something to me, but I didn't hear anything, but recoiled from the train and ran away... Behind me I heard a rumble and the hiss of steam....

"And what is the secret link to the library?"

"You see, my late grandmother and Mrs. Konopelka look like two peas in a pod. When I got here first and saw her, I almost threw myself around her neck, but I came to my senses because my grandmother had died long ago. And then, when I heard her voice, my heart clenched. But I never gave myself away. And that's not all. Mrs. Konopelka's fiancé went missing without a trace somewhere in these closed archives. My grandfather disappeared in the same way. The only thing we know about him is he apparently got on the ghost train. Sometimes it seems that the ghost train is this library: the shelves are the train cars carrying countless long dead authors... They are numbered like train cars, and each shelf is a separate compartment. So, stay alert. There—do you hear that?"

I listened. Somewhere in the distance, from the darkest recesses a quiet splash could be heard, like waves coming to the shore and rolling away, one after another, rhythmically, soothingly, far-far away, barely audible ... And we fell asleep.

13

Not forsaking his daily habit, Joseph Milker set off the next morning for the Krakow Market in search of the familiar saleswoman who sold milk products and greeted her with such warmth as if she were the person nearest and dearest to him. If you think about it, that is really the way it was, because she was a person with whom he spoke twice a week with unwavering regularity.

"How do you do, Mr. Josef?" The woman smiled at him. She looked like she could be in an advertisement for milk right then and there. She had round rosy cheeks, and her large full breasts dangled over the counter.

"Oy, Mrs. Slavtsya, like a cow who just calved," the old man joked. "But thanks to you I'm still alive and kicking."

"Ay-ay-ay, what are you saying? Why thanks to me? Surely, you've warmed up some young sweetheart near you, no?"

"Oy-oy, if I tried to warm her up, I'd end up freezing her."

The other saleswomen burst into laughter. Milker always livened them up. Each of them thought: So, it wouldn't be too bad at ninety to be gadding about the markets like that!

"No-no," the old man shook his head, "it's still thanks to you. Healthy food—that's not a joke. Now I'll go buy some more tomatoes, eggplant, peppers, and squash, and I'll make a dish my mother used to make."

"Well come on, tell us about it," the saleswomen took an interest in it.

"It's very simple. Braise it all in oil with onions and herbs and it's fertig.[81] It doesn't take a genius.

"What do you eat it with?" Slavtsya asked.

---

81 German for "done."

"With bread."

"Without meat?"

"I eat meat only in the winter and not very often. I advise you not to overdo it."

"Uh uh," said Slavtsya, while she was packing up cheese, butter and cream for him. "Now we know the secret of longevity. And my husband screams that I'm starving him to death if there's no meat on the table. Hey, I wish I had such a treasure as Mr. Josef!"

Here her neighbor jabbed her in the side, chuckling:

"Hey, Slavtsya, it's still not too late! Look, what a guy—built like a wall! He even cooks. What do you say, Mr. Josef, will you take our Slavtsya?"

But it was not so easy to crack jokes with old Milker:

"And why's wouldn't I? But first Mrs. Slavtsya needs to go on a diet because my antique bed won't survive both of us."

The women laughed so much they clutched their sides, and Slavtsya also got such a bad case of the hiccups that she had to drink some milk. The old man politely said goodbye to everyone and went to the rows of tables with vegetables. He didn't have any friends there, so with an experienced eye followed closely how they weighed and what they were weighing. He couldn't help but say:

"Here you've tossed me a really rotten tomato on the sly and thought I wouldn't notice. I'm telling you, you're not doing something bad to me, but to yourself."

"And how's that?" The saleswoman was surprised, obediently exchanging an overly rotten tomato for a ripe one.

"It's like this," Milker continued. "When a customer comes home and finds you slipped a nasty trick past him, it invariably leads him to utter certain bad words directed at you. Maybe even some sort of curse. From those words and that curse, so you know, no good will come of it, and it will affect your health."

"Oh pshaw!" The saleswoman didn't believe him and glanced at her neighbors for support, but they were silent with looks of surprise. It was evident that Milker's words stung them, and each one was thinking over some inappropriate incidents that occurred in their lives.

"Yes-yes," he shook his head. "Words have great power. In the Bible, it is written that God created the world with a word. The word raises some people up to heaven, and nails others down to the earth. Beware of evil words spoken about you."

The saleswoman helped him pack up the vegetables, and he set off. The women followed him with thoughtful gazes. There was something in this man that compelled them to listen. Whether that would last for a long time—who knows.

After he already had stepped out onto Kleparivska Street, the old man heard someone shout from behind him: "Mr. Milker!" He looked back and saw a short wiry man with squinting eyes. This squinting gaze immediately stirred up associations with the immediate post-war years, when sitting in front of the Chekists,[82] who squinted while interrogating him as they listened to all his answers to their questions, as if letting him know that they didn't believe a single word.

"Sorry," the man said, pulling out of his pocket the ID card of a lieutenant colonel of the National Security Service

82 Chekists were employees of the Cheka (an acronym for the Extraordinary Committee), a Soviet predecessor of the KGB (from 1917-22).

of Ukraine. Milker wasn't able to read his name, but that didn't interest him. "Sorry that I'm holding you up, but I'd like to have a few words with you. Can we sit here on a bench somewhere?"

Milker recently had so little communication with others that he didn't object. They retreated to the side and sat down on a bench. The old man set down his groceries and straightened out his legs.

"This is probably not the best place to talk," the lieutenant colonel said. But, you see, we didn't want to bother you with summonses...."

"Sure," Milker laughed. "You didn't want to bother me so as not to trigger any unpleasant memories? My, you've become so considerate now!"

"Well, right now we're concerned about the security of Ukraine. I read your case. You had to endure a lot. But we're now interested in just one thing... when you were in the concentration camp you performed 'Tango of Death....'

M

The loud chirping of birds announced morning to my ears; the girl next to me was gone. I raised myself up on my elbows and looked around, then grabbed at my sock—the sheets were in place. In a moment Milya appeared:

"Good morning, sleepyhead! Come out of there—a spring is gushing from under the willow."

I obeyed and actually saw a weeping willow in a large flowerpot, out of which water was gushing and disappearing in the ground. It was cool, and I gladly washed up and then took a cautious sip—the water was delicious. I wanted to drink and drink, though it made my teeth hurt.

Milya folded the sheets. I took them back where they were, then we had breakfast and set off on the road. The fog lifted and was swirling just under the ceiling, rays of sunlight glimmered and dappled the backs of books. We moved on, cheerfully chatting, when suddenly something darted behind the stack and ran off.

"What could it have been?" I was surprised.

"Something that didn't expect us."

"It seems it was something wet."

"And hideous."

The stacks looked like cliffs, onto which you could lean and hang over a precipice, but we preferred to avoid them, although it was sometimes not so easy, because the further we went, they no longer formed into neat rows as in the beginning, but often stood diagonally, across from or against each other. Sometimes they tilted, looking like the Leaning Tower of Pisa, and then we passed them, lifting up our heads, frightened that they would collapse on us and bury us under the rubble of their wisdom. From time to time, some book would fly out from the stacks and, desperately fluttering its wings of pages, fall at our feet as if begging to come to our hands, but we just slid our eyes along the titles and went on. We were not sure if anyone was watching us, because our ears caught rustling and scratching, a slight hissing, a squeaking and sometimes a splashing and sloshing, which was absolutely incredible to hear inside a library. I had begun to think we were in some incredible apertures of the universe where the scents and sounds do not correspond to those to which we are accustomed, with which we live, which echo in our souls. We obviously are foreign here. All these stacks and books and vases perceive us as strangers encroaching on their territories. Hundreds of hostile eyes clawed at our backs, and when we inadvertently struck the book stacks with our legs or shoulders, from above tiny snowflakes or some yellowed leaves, rolled up and covered with red spots, scattered. When I caught a few snowflakes, I saw that they were not in the form of stars, but in the form of various characters and punctuation marks. They were not only in Cyrillic and Latin, but also in Arabic and Hebrew, and even in some God-knows-what kind of hieroglyphs. Unfortunately, they were melting so fast I wasn't able to figure out the message that was coming down to me from the library heavens.

The old floor creaked underfoot, and the sharp scent of the sea and seaweed wafted up from below. It seemed to rise from cracks in the floor. I couldn't resist kneeling down and looking into one such crack, it was dark there, but it smelled of the sea even more distinctly. In that black thicket in the shaggy silence, barely audibly, waves lapped slowly and sleepily onto a shore, as if the sea had not yet awakened, everything still resting in a self-absorbed slumber and rocking in a slow rhythm. The waves rolled out smoothly and gently, like a little blanket for an infant. I couldn't see anything, just sparks twinkled here and there, looking like the glow of plankton, and when they flashed, you could see some kind of black shiny humps that dove and disappeared in the waves. It would be futile to guess if it was clumps of stone or the backs of sea monsters that still were dozing, basking in a warm bed.

"Maybe I'm dreaming," I mumbled. "But there's something like the sea there."

"No, you're not dreaming," Milya uttered. "The sea was once here, and then it went under the earth and continued to live there. From time to time it rises up onto the surface, approaching the foundations of buildings, and then recedes again, leaving behind entire gulfs... Unknown beings live in that sea—neither fish nor people; they sometimes come out from the depths, and one can run into them on the street. But only late at night. They dress like us, but they have large green eyes and walk barefoot because their flipper-like feet won't fit in any shoes. It's possible they make their way even to the library."

"It explains these wet footprints... algae and jellyfish...," I said while getting up. "Well, let's keep going."

Suddenly we came upon a space that no longer oppressed us with cliffs of book stacks. We saw before us carved and inlaid cabinets, credenzas, couches, tables, writing desks, chairs—all in different vintage styles, at which one could marvel. Milya even clapped her hands: "What beauty!" We stayed a little while just to admire those treasures. Milya preened herself in front of the mirror. I looked through the cabinets and desks, thinking I might come upon something interesting there, but didn't find anything, and we again went off into the depths of the library. As soon as we found ourselves among the book stacks, some doors slammed loudly behind our backs. I shuddered:

"I closed all the doors."

"Maybe it was a draft?"

"I have a feeling someone is following us. Sometimes I hear steps, sometimes whispering, some kind of scratching."

"I also hear all this, but in such large quarters it's normal. Cold and warm air are in constant motion, and adding to that there's this fog... It's normal for the old wood on the floor and book stacks to crack...."

Suddenly, something flew across our eyes and landed on a short rhododendron, from which countless brown vines hung. It was a thin, little book with a colorful cover and resembled a butterfly that fussily crossed one leg over the other. When I tried to get closer, the little book fluttered away and disappeared. Instead, a second book jumped from the book stack and also flew off, fluttering its pages and having made a circle slammed onto the wall and spread out as if stuck. In a moment from somewhere else a third one darted and crossed the room, landed on top of the other, the way bugs do when they're mating. A rustling near our feet forced us to jump to the side. Several books crawled out of the book stacks and hobbled somewhere into the darkness, resembling turtles; and they squeaked and crunched as if they were angry at us. Before I could express my surprise, the floor beneath us began to sway, cracked, and boards parted and started to rise up. We jumped back and watched with horror as some kind of black, glossy spine began to emerge from between the boards. It was wet and slippery, with shells and algae attached, it rose up very slowly, pushing apart the boards more and more, invading more and more space. A little more—and the book stacks would fall over like houses during an earthquake. It lasted maybe a few seconds, and then the spine suddenly fell down, plopping into the water; the boards came together, and only a large wet stain remained as the mute witness of this strange manifestation. I was terrified, but I didn't want to show my cowardice to Milya, especially because she was scared even more than I was. I put my arms around her and dragged her on further.

"I didn't think it would be so terrifying," she said. "They behaved quite peacefully, it seemed they were so deeply asleep that they'd wake up only in a million years, but now some kind of force aroused them. This is probably bad. Mrs. Konopelka said that the last time she observed something like this here was just before the war. What do you think? Could there be a war?"

"Someone definitely will start one. Either Hitler or Stalin. And we'll again be ground to dust."

"I'm tired and hungry, and as the man you are simply obligated to get food," she pulled out a map out of her handbag and explained above which book stack meat was hanging and where to find a block of cheese and wine. In a minute we already had settled on piles of books near a ficus tree and were having our lunch. I looked at the book stacks. It wasn't very far any longer to №1730 because we were sitting next to №1688 F. The letters rarely reached K or L, so there was hope that later that day I would get the rest of the pages.

We had already decided to go farther, when suddenly from behind the book stacks a bony little man appeared with a crooked-nose and small narrow eyes, dressed in some kind of old-world rags, well-worn and soiled.

"Yes, I knew it! She's sent off the expedition to find me again!" He cried out. Casting his eye on a chunk of kielbasa, he grabbed it and in three seconds gobbled it up, then grabbed the wine from me and drank it with gusto. "Tell her that I'll never go back to her world. Never!" Then he also stamped his foot.

"Tell whom?" I asked with interest.

"Just don't say that it wasn't Konopelka who sent you! So, pass this along to her."

"Aha, so you're the fiancé for whom she's been waiting in vain for so many years?"

"I'm no longer her fiancé. I left her to devote myself to the study of the seabed. I live there," he pointed his finger at the floor. "There's my world. The finest girls of the sea attend to me there. I sleep on a bed of dried seaweed, cover myself with a blanket made of seagull down and eat fish and shellfish." On seeing our surprised looks, he added: "Today I had a creative day, I didn't go hunting. That's why I'm hungry. But I discovered an unknown genus of Asturia Mitylenska,[83] that is kindred to Rodelia Tsurymska, which became extinct before the birth of Christ. But here ... here it blooms and intoxicates with its fragrance. But why? Because under the influence of the sea, the books create a special microclimate, and even come to life themselves. Last month several books, huddling in a predatory flock, literally chewed up a famous scholar who wandered here in search

83 A flower that grew on the oceanside cliffs of Arcanum.

of Albrecht von Wallenstein's memoirs and his letters to Gustav-Adolf. The library is becoming dangerous. It lives its own life. Yes-yes, don't be surprised. Even these book stacks," he tapped his finger on the wood, "even they aren't as completely dim as you think. And not entirely immobile. Sometimes they travel. They change places. And right now they're listening to our every word. Oh, here, see for yourself!" The old man put his ear to the dull surface of the book stack and listened. "To someone it might seem like it's woodworms lisping and murmuring, but I can tell you that it's not. They're whispering among themselves in their rustling language. Just between us: did you really believe you could find me?"

"You will probably be surprised and disappointed," Milya put her two cents in, "when I tell you we're not looking for you. Mrs. Konopelka really sent one of us, but with an entirely different purpose, and we still have much ground to cover to achieve it.

"What's this, did the old mushroom already forget about me?" The little man uttered with deep sadness.

"No, no," I said. "She hasn't forgotten you, she's waiting for you. Moreover—she's keeping her chastity and says she can't die before she loses it to you. But we've really come here for another purpose.

"May I ask which?" Sparks flared in the little man's eyes.

"No. This has nothing to do with your business."

"Hmm. So, you're not looking for maps of the bottom of the Carpathian Sea?"

"No. And you?"

"I'm actually looking for one. The twenty-eighth map of Claudius Ptolemy. Pausanias mentioned it. I know it's somewhere here. But I need to warn you—the old books have already really gone wild. If you don't watch out, they might bite off a finger. You know there are meat-eating plants, right? These old tomes here eagerly devour everything they come across—flies, mosquitoes, night moths, moths, mice... I've already stumbled upon gnawed human skeletons twice. I won't get in your way. Godspeed."

We said goodbye and walked on in silence for a while. Then Milya worriedly spoke up:

"Who knows what awaits us...."

As if to confirm her words suddenly books fell down right in front of our noses. Among them were thick tomes that might have harmed us really badly if they fell on our heads. We couldn't help pressing ourselves against the wall and moved on farther alongside it.

By evening we reached book stack number 1730. I climbed the ladder to the top shelf and pulled out a book with metal latches, *Occulta Occultum Occulta* by Paul Skalich.[84] I couldn't open the book—it was locked, but the key was nowhere to be found. I had to take the book and stuff it in my backpack. I was already about to go down when the book stack suddenly leaned in my direction. The ladder jumped back and leaned on the second book stack, and books again were strewn on top of me. The pages of many of them flew in every direction, fell up to my face and stuck on it. With one hand I swatted them away like birds of prey, and with my other hand held on to the ladder, which shook and ominously cracked. Frightened Milya shouted for me to hurry, but I couldn't fight off the countless pages and the

84 An alchemist, writer of one of the earliest encyclopedias, and adventurer (1534-1573) born in Zagreb, Croatia. He is also known as Stanislav Pavao Skali⊠ and Paulus Scalichius de Lika.

books that pinched and bit me. In the meantime, the book stack behind me cracked and bent. Then I blindly began to step down the ladder, pulling my head in between my shoulders, and covering myself with one hand, though I could see nothing below me, but Milya shouted out: "Jump! You're already low!" I jumped and bounced to the side, and it was just in time because the book stacks, between which I found myself, lay down on top of each other. If I had delayed, I would have been crushed. The books stopped falling down, and near the ceiling something cried out and began to snort.

We retreated to a safe distance and in an hour reached book stack №1739. The fourth and final sheet was in the folio called *Labyrinthus Mundi* by the legendary Hermes Trismegistus[85] and had the bookplate of Anton Schwarz von Steiner, Viennese bibliophile. Meanwhile it was getting dark, and again we encamped for the night. Weariness did its job. After having supper and drinking a bottle of wine, I slept like a baby and woke up in the morning at the light of dawn. Again, I didn't see the girl next to me. Thinking that she was washing up and smartening herself up somewhere, I didn't immediately feel worried, but after some time without noticing any signs of her presence, I felt around in search of the pages. When I couldn't find any, I wasn't surprised that the folio was gone as well. The one and only angel that hides in a woman can justify the hundred devils that abide in her, but Milya was the exception. Shouting "You bitch!" I ran at full speed in pursuit, and so my footsteps wouldn't be heard, I took off my shoes and threw them into my backpack. I ran, avoiding obstacles and listening

85 The legendary Greek author of *Hermetic Corpus*, which were sacred texts that formed the basis of Hermeticism.

attentively, but I didn't hear anything comforting. Silence reigned everywhere, only a slight breeze casually sifted the leaves of bushes and trees. From time to time a book would fly through the air frighteningly. The pages would be strewn and sway in the air. Already entirely soaked in sweat, in about three hours, I switched to a quick pace, upset over just one thing: that bitch could be hiding somewhere and waiting until I passed by. She couldn't escape too far, because yesterday she was just as exhausted as I was and had to get some sleep, so got a head start on me maybe by about two hours, not more, not to mention the fact that she can't run as quickly as I can without a rest. She had to catch her breath somewhere. It was already afternoon when I heard a fuss. Someone was struggling with someone else. A male voice cursed and grumbled, and the female voice desperately squealed; it seemed like someone raping someone else. A moment later I saw between the book stacks a couple desperately wrestling, and I easily recognized the fiancé of Mrs. Konopelka and Milya. The folio of Paul Skalich lay nearby. The fight was over the sheets that Milya had apparently hidden in her bosom. Her blouse already was torn. The sheets peeked out of her bra, but the old man couldn't reach them because Milya fought back with her hands and feet, and sometimes even snapped her teeth, so the old guy was already all scratched and bitten, and his nose was bleeding. I had nothing better to do than take a look and hastily to grab the sheets, and picking up the folio, to hide them in my backpack. The embattled pair instantly ended their struggle and, panting heavily, stared at me. Despair and rage consumed them, but I was in a quite friendly mood. That's why I waved to them amicably and started off on the road. Milya screamed after me:

"You are a fool! This is big money! Come to your senses! I'm ready to go with you to the end of the world!"

But her voice was as cold as the soup at a roadside tavern. And the old man snorted, coughing,

"Don't believe a woman, wine or the light of the moon!"

At noon the next day I returned to my work station and handed the sheets and folio to Mrs. Konopelka. She listened carefully to all my adventures and expressed indignation at her fiancé's behavior.

"If he is such a cad, then I have no more reason to keep my virginity. What do you think?" She squinted at me. "If I doll myself up like a slut, put on a garish dress and wig, then stand by the Viennese Café, will someone give me thirty zlotys for the night?"

"Maybe. I just advise you to take the money up front and slip out of bed before dawn. Otherwise you'll return to the library with a black eye."

The old woman laughed and said that I could have the day off today, but I drew her attention to the folio of Skalich, for which I couldn't find the key. Mrs. Konopelka pondered for a moment, but then slapped herself on the head and pulled out from her bosom a small gold chain on which a golden key was hanging. It fit the lock perfectly. She opened the book and extracted one more sheet. I requested permission to take pictures. She was not opposed to that and even gave me her camera. I photographed each sheet in parts, so as not to have to pore over the photographs. From the library I headed with the camera to Yosko's. He developed the negatives and began to study the sheets. During the time I was wandering through the closed archives, he already had figured some things. It turned out that some of the notes replaced letters and individual letters took the place of notes.

"Well, look here," Yosko explained. "In modern practice the following names of notes are accepted: do, re, mi, fa, sol, la, si. They all come from Deacon Paul's hymn in honor of John the Baptist. The first syllables of the lines of the hymn that were sung in the ascending octave were taken for the names. Guido d'Arezzo introduced the names of the six notes. Although, he called the note DO UT, and the first line was sung as follows: "UT queant laxis." But later UT was replaced by DO. In 1574 the note of CI was added. Thus, the first verse of the hymn looked like this:

DOminus, Lord
REsonare fibris
MIra gestorum
FAmuli tuorum,
SOLve polluti
LAbii reatum,
Sancte Ioannes.

"And what does this mean?"

"The fact that some of the notes have dots above them which appeared visible only now in the photographs. And these notes with dots are not notes, but letters. When performing the music, you need to skip these notes. One dot means the first letter that follows the name of the note. If it's SOL, then the first letter after the name of this note in a line of the song will be "v." If it's LA, then—"b." Two dots are the second letter and so on. The work is tedious, but I'm absorbed by it."

How Yosko's work on the manuscript pages moved along further, I don't know. Soon certain events occurred that knocked us all off track. It's true, Yosko even requested that I write words to the chorus of the tango, which he began to play at the Bristol Restaurant. The tango was quite famous, and it had already been performed for several years, but Yosko said that his was unique, because he inserted the deciphered notes into it, and now he wanted to introduce changes into the text. He sang the melody for me. I entered into my usual poetic trance and created the following:

And when I am no longer with you,
and sands will cover our bodies,
we will meet where the poppies flow like a river,
there where their shadow fell.

Yosko read it once more, and was very surprised:

"Why is it that poppies came to your mind?"

"I don't know. It just came to me."

"That's really strange. Because I found a mention of poppies and their shadow in those pages of Kalkbrenner but couldn't figure out why they were there. I never said anything to you about those poppies. And suddenly... it's a strange coincidence. But I like the words. Meeting after death... in the shadow of poppies... Is this precisely what you wanted to express?"

I puffed myself up like a turkey and answered:

"My dear Yosko! A true poet can never explain a single one of his images or metaphors. Only a graphomaniac is capable of that. So, let's assume it's all in the subconscious." And I tapped my finger on my forehead.

None of us could imagine even for a moment that the words of my refrain would become prophetic.

14

Yarosh was incredibly comforted by an amazing coincidence—he was invited to Istanbul to a conference on the literature of dead languages. It was quite natural to hold it there because the territory of Turkey included the states of Lydia, Lycia, Urartu, the Hittite, and Arcanum. On the plane flying from Kyiv, Yarosh unexpectedly caught sight of Andrei Kurkov and couldn't restrain himself from introducing himself. The writer was on the book tour for his novel *Picnic on Ice*, which Yarosh had already read. The sad, pensive penguin who lived with the main protagonist was especially etched into his memory. He and Kurkov chatted extensively on the flight, and the Turkish wine served by the stewardesses in 100-gram bottles was very tasty. When Yarosh told him what he was working on, Andrei showed a lively interest in it, divulging the fact that he hoped to write a mystery novel, the events of which would revolve around an ancient manuscript that travels from century to century, but brings its new owners only suffering, pain and death. He even mused about which culture the manuscript should belong to—the Egyptian or to the age of antiquity. When Yarosh related what he knew about Arcanum and its marvelous literature, which writers and historians produced not only on clay tablets, but also on papyrus, Kurkov took an interest and began to ask for more details. Yarosh spoke in general terms, promising to send him his history of Arcanumian literature along with an anthology.

"According to my conception of the book, the death of anyone who takes possession of this manuscript would be encrypted in the text itself," the writer said. "That is, the key to this cipher is found only at the end. That's why it would be important for me to become familiar with these texts, although I would be forced to modify some things, with your permission,...."

"In a work of art that's permitted. It is we, scholars, who are bound by certain conditions and are forced to rely on solid evidence. I can even tell you the manuscript it should revolve around—the Arcanumian Book of Baal. Baal was a dark spirit, something like the devil. It's a strange and mysterious book. According to legend, Baal wrote it himself in a single night. More precisely, it wasn't him, but a hermit whom he possessed. The book is full of mysticism and incomprehensible phrases. When you read it, you feel anxiety and incomprehensible fear creeping into your soul. It's enough to skim through a dozen pages before you toss away the book in a panic, although for some time it will remain in your memory, and you'll even dream about it."

"That's strange. I heard that in Prague there's also a book written by the devil. It also was written in a single night."

"Yes, I know about it. It's the so-called *Devil's Bible*, which helped a monk rewrite the Scriptures and other works. It has nothing to do with the *Book of Baal*, which after reading, enables you to attain fame and wealth, but the payoff at the end of life will be horrific."

"Nowadays, few people would be scared off by that."

"Of course," Yarosh concurred. "But here's what's interesting... In Istanbul, there's a manuscript written by Iblis kept in a scholarly library. It was also written in a single night. I'd be very interested in whether or not it has some parallels to the *Book of Baal*."

"Oh, you have a wonderful opportunity to determine that."

"I don't know. They may not show me such an old book. And who knows whether reading the book is safe."

"But you'd like to read it anyway?"

"There's an ancient method for doing that. It's the same method I used to examine the *Book of Baal*, which is kept in London." Yarosh took out of his bag and showed to Kurkov a head of a poppy flower and an old wooden knife, which you use to cut pages in magazines. "If you flip through each page with the knife, which has been blessed twelve times, and sprinkle it with the blessed poppy seeds, then the evil forces that live in the book will not harm you."

Andrei smiled in disbelief: "Doesn't this seem a bit comical to you?"

"It might appear so. But only superficially. I spoke with a certain old priest in Lviv, who practices exorcisms of the devil. I told him about these books, and it was his idea to bless the knife and poppy seeds. Why shouldn't I believe a priest, who for many years has been battling with evil spirits?"

"Then I concede. Because I thought it might have been some kind of sorceress who whispered this advice to you. You know, maybe I can help you. I have a writer friend at the National Library in Istanbul. I'm also really eager to look at that book."

On the first day of their stay in Istanbul nothing interesting happened. The two of them had taken up residence in different hotels. Yarosh and Kurkov met after dusk and went for a walk along the evening streets, "leading a goat to water" (as they say in Lviv) to the various taverns there. It turned out not to be so easy to find a snack bar that served wine. They finally came across a bar that was filled with young people and buzzed like a beehive. It was a European-style tavern, and the young people were no different from what you'd see anywhere elsewhere in the world. The next day after lunch when both were free from their affairs they met in a coffee shop with one of Kurkov's acquaintances Orhan Nadim, who was fluent in English. Upon hearing what Yarosh and Kurkov desired, the latter was surprised:

"How do you know about this book? Because there's no mention of it in any catalogs."

"The Austrian scholar Kalkbrenner refers to it. He examined it in Istanbul with the permission of Sultan Murad IV himself. The book is kept in his library."

"Yes, but Murad's library still hasn't been fully processed. I can take you there, but I don't know whether you'll be able to see the book. Mr. Baykurt, who works there, is a relative of mine and he'll do everything possible to help."

Orhan led them to a branch of the national library, located in an age-old annex laced with large tracery windows. Murad's library books were kept there. In the small cozy reading room silence prevailed. At the tables there were only three readers working, who paid no attention to the newcomers. Two of them were taking notes because it was forbidden to make copies of old publications, and the third, armed with a magnifying glass and with his bald head shining from the light from the chandeliers, was thoroughly engrossed in some large-scale maps. Orhan registered the guests in the visitor's book and took them to an old librarian, who was sitting in the corner at a table laden with card catalog drawers. They exchanged a few words, from which Yarosh understood that Orhan was introducing them to the librarian, and then in a whisper explained the reason for the visit. But from the way the librarian's face grew long, and the way he suddenly began to wipe his eyeglasses nervously with a handkerchief, it was evident that it would not be so easy to grant their request. At first, he even decisively shook his head, then stroked his beard with his hand and spoke in Turkish while Orhan interpreted:

"The great Sufi poet, Jalal ad-Din Muhammad Rumi, the classic of Persian and Turkish literature, wrote the Book of Iblis."

"And did he write it with Iblis?"

"No. The title is fake; it's exclusively meant for deception. According to the Sufi sect, to which Rumi belonged, the name needed to frighten away random people from this book. In fact, he wrote it from the words of al-Khidr, who was a teacher of Moses. Al-Khidr, or al-Khizr, is endowed with eternal life as the legends say. Even before that, he was in the service of Alexander the Great, and went with him to the Land of Darkness at the edge of the world in search of the Water of Life. Alexander endeavored above all else to find this water but failed. On the other hand, al-Khidr, who was less interested in the Water and who did not think about it as much as Alexander, found it. "In searching, Alexander did not find what he sought, but al-Khidr not searching, found it." Since then, al-Khidr lives forever; from time to time he appears to chosen individuals and tells them certain higher truths, tells them about his journeys, and shares his knowledge. All who have managed to see him describe him as not yet an old man, although he has a long white beard, and he's very lively and strong-minded. Each year, al-Khidr comes to Jerusalem for Ramadan and meets there with the prophet Elijah."

“So that book is not cursed?” Yarosh queried.

“My friend brought special amulets that are supposed to protect him from any bad influence of the book,” Kurkov said, smiling.

“No, no, this is not necessary,” Mr. Baykurt shook his head. “Al-Khidr appeared before Rumi in the form of the itinerant Sufi preacher Shams al-Din Tabriz. The sermons of the dervish had a tremendous impact on Rumi’s mind. They became fast friends and were inseparable for several years, but the mysterious disappearance of the dervish in 1247 shocked Rumi the most. For Al-Khidr unexpected appearances and disappearances are quite normal. From that time on Rumi signed many of his works Shams Tabriz.

“So is this book something like the long poem “Masnavi,” which Rumi, and after him Jami, called *The Persian Quran*?” Yarosh asked.

“At first glance it really does resemble “Masnavi” and the long poem “The Garden of Truths” by Sana’a, the forefather of Sufi poetry. There are many parables, teachings, and legends, but...,” here he raised his index finger, “... also much mysticism. What in fact interests you?” He turned to Yarosh.

“In general, I do research on Arcanumian literature, and in particular the Book of Death. I wonder if I’ll find some analogies in the Book of Iblis.”

“Oh, yes-yes... It has something about what we now call reincarnation. As one of the Sufis wrote, “our souls were intoxicated with the wine of immortality even before gardens, vines, and grapes appeared in the world.” However, first, before you examine this book, I want to explain something to you. Views on the nature of death outlined in the Koran are closely related to two other issues: the relationship between sleep and death and the existence of the soul. Indeed, in the Koran there are ancient notions where death is identified with sleep, and the resurrection from the dead with awakening: 'The Lord made the night for you as a cover, and sleep as rest, and created the day for awakening (nushur).' So, the night is a veil that covers the sleeper; the dream is a prototype of death, and a star—the symbol of resurrection (nushur)... Ancient Islamic notions of death were inextricably linked to the idea of reincarnation: he who is asleep invariably is bound to wake up! Theologians, of course, have argued about whether this awakening can be considered a final resurrection and whether it will come to be in the cycle of births and deaths. But the question of existence after death has occupied an important place in early Islamic philosophy. Representatives of mystical Islamic sects, especially Sufis, always treated death as the beginning of a new life and interpreted the word *nushur* as the awakening of the soul, which settles into a new body. In Islamic writings reincarnation is indicated by the word *tanasukh.* Islamic advocates of reincarnation argue that the Koran supports the doctrine of reincarnation: "He who has angered Allah is the worst of all and has incurred His damnation. Allah shall turn him into a monkey or a pig. Allah gives you life from the earth, then swaddles you in the earth again, and He again will give you life."

Besides Rumi, other famous Sufi poets such as Saadi and Hafez have investigated the secret meaning of these and other verses of the Qur'an. Mansour al-Hallay, who lived in the tenth century, left for posterity many lyrical works, the theme of which was the transmigration of the soul:

Hundreds of times I grew like the grass

On the banks of swift rivers.

For hundreds of thousands of years I kept being born and lived

In all the bodies that are on Earth.

For several centuries, prominent followers of Muhammad, accepting the doctrine of reincarnation, hid it from a wide circle of the faithful. Now it is discussed and interpreted only in conjunction with the Sufi tradition, although many modern Muslims are ready, at least in theory, to allow for the existence of these forms of reincarnation that mystics mention... Orhan told me you learned about the book from the work of some Austrian. What did he write?"

"Johan Kalkbrenner wrote that in the Book of Iblis certain rituals are described to help you learn who you were in previous lives. Moreover, you can also learn all the knowledge that was gained in those previous existences.

"Of course. There's just one problem...," the librarian shifted to a whisper. "This book is quite ancient, and it's not permitted to be given to researchers. You need permission from the director for this. But Orhan really asked... Let's do it this way: you go with me to the repository. I'll bring out the book to you and you can examine it there."

In the repository it was dark and uninviting. Longish narrow windows rose high near the ceiling, but the book stacks overshadowed them halfway. Mr. Baykurt disappeared, and in a moment he returned with a cardboard box and laid it on the table, saying:

"I'll go back to the reading room. And if one of the administrators should drop in, I'll call Orhan's cellphone. But, Orhan, you turn off the sound. When I call, move back to the very end and wait for another call. But I ask you not to stay here for too long. And one more thing... Sufi works are special and unique, their true meaning reveals itself only to those who possess the key to the cipher, while the uninitiated understand everything literally or nothing at all. Do not try to delve deeper into the boundless."

The Book of Iblis was half a meter in length and rather thick, but that was due to the thickness of the parchment pages. Illustrations were almost on every page, sometimes very small ones, sometimes a half page. The book was written in Persian, which Yarosh did not know, but, fortunately, Orhan was fluent in it and translated those passages that interested Yarosh.

"Here," said Orhan, flipping through the pages, "it explains how in becoming a follower of Sufi teachings, you can read minds from a distance... Here—how instantly you can be transported from one place to another... Here, how to communicate with the other world... How to cure a person with just a single glance...."

One of the pictures depicted a dervish who was walking on water, and another—a person who was growing out of a flower. Yarosh asked for a translation and heard what he wanted to hear:

"I died as a man and became a plant. I also died as a plant and became an animal. I died as an animal and became man. Why should I fear losing my human qualities? I will die as a man to be resurrected as an angel... And the path to our origins, to our sources will be illuminated by beacons, which we need to recognize in order to meet under the shadow of the hashhash blossoms."

"Hashhash?" Yarosh asked. "What is that?"

"A kind of flower...," Orhan thought. "I don't know how to translate it... a wild flower ... but it's grown for getting opium...."

"Hashish!" Kurkov guessed. "So, is it a poppy?"

"Yes," Orhan nodded happily—hashish comes from "hashhash."

"Rumi says that a reincarnated man striving to gain knowledge of all his former lives should recognize the beacons... that is, the signs...," Yarosh said. "Jewish mystics have spoken about the same thing. But the shadow of poppies... There's something strange... They're not trees...."

"Among the Sufis much was said with a subtext," Orhan explained. "And Baykurt warned us not to interpret everything literally."

"Yes, but that very phrase about the shadow of poppies appears in the Arcanumian Book of Death...."

"There's one more thing...," Orhan said. "In all this the most important thing is that a person right before death needs to undergo enlightenment... Just before death he must take part in the dance of the dervishes, or to hear this dance...."

"Is 'hear' and not 'see' written there?" Yarosh was surprised and even leaned over the book, although he couldn't comprehend anything in it.

"Yes, 'hear,'" Orhan confirmed. "It's about the melody."

"And what is that dance of the dervishes?"

"This is the dance of the followers of Rumi, whose order was based in central Turkey in the city of Konya. The so-called whirling dervishes perform it. Continuing to today, the festival commemorating Rumi takes place in December. During the religious ceremony, dervishes, clothed in white, flowing garments, and in conical hats, twirl to the rhythm of drums and sounds of mystical music. Music here plays a huge role, it purifies and frees the soul, allows a person to look deeply into himself and to make sure that Allah is nearby."

"Could I possibly hear the dance of the dervishes?"

"Why not? You can hear it this evening."

Kurkov was unable to go with them. Orhan drove Yarosh to the outskirts of Istanbul and accompanied him to some building with carved pediments and blue mosaics. At its entrance they were stopped by a stern, powerful man. After conferring with Orhan, he checked the pockets of both guests and only then allowed them into the spacious hall in which there were no chairs or tables. Along the walls men of all ages were sitting; hookahs were being smoked and coffee pots were steaming in front of many of them. A quiet murmur spread through the hall, and no one paid attention to the new arrivals. Orhan and Yarosh occupied empty places by the wall and waited. Quiet calm music began to build from somewhere out of the depths—either from the ceiling or from the floor. Those present stopped chatting, put down their hookahs and cups and prepared themselves for something that was well known to them.

"What you will see and hear now is impossible to see and hear anywhere else," Orhan whispered. "The dancing of dervishes for tourists—it's not the same thing."

The music enveloped, shrouded, and rocked them. Yarosh sat cross-legged Turkish style, put his hand on his leg above the ankle, and inconspicuously pressed something with his finger. The music kept growing more and more intense, until in the middle of the room twelve young men in white robes appeared. When they raised their hands up, the drums and flutes started. The dervishes circled slowly at first, then faster and faster until the hems of their garments soared up and they began to look like tops. Their whirling seemed like something phantasmagoric. You couldn't believe that people were capable of such things. Then the dervishes closed their eyes and went into a trance, already tuning out the world around them, focusing only on their dance and contact with heaven. Yarosh saw all those present sway to the beat of the music and also shut their eyes. After some time without noticing it he also closed his eyes, feeling that some force was tearing him from the ground and lifting him up. Here he was swinging in the air, the ceiling was disappearing, and azure blue space was drawing him upward. He became afraid. It seemed he would never be able to come back, but he didn't have the strength to open his eyes. Even though it was impossible to call what rose up before his closed eyes darkness—around him stars twinkled, some bright lights flashed and shot off, blossoming in colorful sprouts, and soon he realized that he himself was circling in a dance, but not on the earth but in space, and lights danced around him, and among those lights faces floated out, in which he recognized one but not another, although those whom he recognized he could not remember by name, he just was certain he knew who it was. Someone's arms stretched to him, he felt their touches, a warm hand stroked his face, it was a very pleasant feeling, and he was about to hold it, touch it with his lips and kiss it, but the hand disappeared, and near his ears a whisper resounded, "under the shadow where the hashhash blossoms." Panic gripped him. With all his strength he wanted to shake off this dream. He twitched, flung himself. With all his might he wanted to make his way to the ground, to open his eyes, and to break free from the shackles of this music. But the music did not let him go. It peeled him from the inside. It turned him inside out like a glove. He no longer recognized himself. It seemed as if someone else had taken root inside him, but not someone unfamiliar, someone close though not yet recognized, whom he desired to hug. But it didn't last long, because then that unknown person abandoned him, and this loss seemed so incredibly horrible that Yarosh opened his mouth and began to scream. He screamed for that unknown person not to abandon him, to remain close to him, but no one, including himself, heard his scream, because he screamed in silence, unheard and mute, and in a moment he felt he was beginning to fall slowly like the petal of an apple tree picked up by the wind. The music grew quiet, decreased, then ceased, and when he finally managed to open his eyes, he saw he was in the hall by himself. There was not a single living soul. The hookahs and coffee pots had disappeared; athletic training machines, black mats, weights, barbells, and twisted ropes were standing in their place on the floor....

Yarosh touched his leg above his ankle. His voice recorder was in place. He turned it off and put it away in his pocket, then he tottered as if he were drunk, got up, and walked to the exit. In the hallway some old woman in a gray hijab was sitting at a table; she smiled at him and warmly nodded her head. On the street he saw a taxi with the door open; the driver crawled out of it and asked him in English:

"The Golden Horn?"

"How did he know which hotel I need to go to?" Yarosh was surprised. He got in and spent the entire ride to the hotel in a semi-somnambulic state. When he tried to pay, the driver said that everything had been paid for.

N

I courteously worked in the library until I got myself into such an adventure that I barely made it out of there alive. Our Uncle Lodzio, who was a member of the OUN (Organization of Ukrainian Nationalists) and bravely fought in the deeply embedded underground against the Polish occupation of Galicia, summoned me one day to talk and reminded me that every conscientious Ukrainian in his life must plant a tree, have five children, and kill the enemy. I replied that maybe it would be a good idea for me to start with a chicken, because killing a person is not so easy, given the only practice I had so far was on flies and mosquitoes. But Uncle explained that a specially trained fighter would kill the enemy, and I just have to assist because a political attempt on someone's life—that is a very serious matter, on which a large group of people always works. So, that evening I needed to go to Fiyalkova Street, house №5 and knock, and when they open the door, I was to ask: "Have you come to poison the rats?" The answer would be: "And the mice too." Then I had to repeat the two phrases several times to Uncle so as not to make a mistake. But in the evening as I started off for Fiyalkova Street, I couldn't remember who I was to poison first—the rats or the mice, so the entire way over I played with both phrasings in my head, and in the end decided that, so as not to make a mistake, to ask both about the mice and the rats to be on the safe side.

Fiyalkova is a small street, ideal for the arrangement of clandestine meetings because it was completely deserted. I knocked, and when the doors opened, I rattled out "Poison rats-mice, mice-rats...." A large hand grabbed me by the collar, pulled me into the house and slammed the door. The hand belonged to Uncle.

"What a cretin you are! Can't you be entrusted with an important matter?"

"You shouldn't have invented such silly catchwords," I muttered. "It'd be better to replace rats with beavers or badgers, then I'd never confuse them with mice.

Uncle stared at me as though I was a crazy guy and his mustache angrily twitched; now he himself looked like a badger. Suddenly he grew serious and said:

"No real names! Understand? Just code names. What's yours?"

"Mine? But I haven't chosen one for myself. I didn't know I had to think up a code name."

"Code name!" Uncle snapped back and knit his eyebrows.

"Good, let it be 'Horesradish.'"[86]

We already have "Horseradish." And "Thunder" and "Oak" and "Eagle...."

"Then 'Carrot.'"

"Have you gone crazy? What my ass 'Carrot'?"

"Well, if I can't have 'Horseradish,' then let it be 'Carrot.' Or 'Beet,' 'Cabbage,' 'Pea,' 'Bean,' 'Turnip-Cabbage,' 'Strawberry...,'" Uncle gasped and began to gnash his teeth. But I boldly continued: 'Parsnip,' 'Pumpkin....'"

"Whoa!" Uncle stopped me. "Screw it—you'll be 'Pumpkin.'"

We went to a room where some two dozen boys and girls had gathered. Uncle said: "This is 'Pumpkin,'" and those

86 The word "khrin" used euphemistically in slang means something like "bugger."

present almost answered in chorus: "Greetings, Pumpkin!" Uncle then unfolded a large sheet of paper on the table on which a plan for the assassination was drawn. The entire time he was explaining to each person his or her role, he never named the target who was to be killed. I won't say it particularly interested me, but I don't like surprises, because if it's someone I know, it would be my complete relief that I won't be doing the shooting, that my participation was limited only to signaling the appearance of the one doomed to death. When he passes me, all I'll do is take off my cap and wipe my forehead with a handkerchief. What could be simpler? But how would I recognize him? And right here at the very end of the meeting Uncle took out of his pocket a couple of pictures of a man in different poses and ordered me to remember him well. With that he angrily looked at me, obviously alluding with that gaze to my flightiness. The man in the photo was middle-aged, tall, lean and with a square chin; his gaze portended determination and energy.

"This is Mr. police inspector Lukomsky," Uncle said. "He's a terrible sadist who personally participates in interrogations. Once he even studied medicine, so he's versed in anatomy and psychology; he knows where to find the most raw spots. He can easily drive anyone to madness. His colleague, Commissar Mikhal Kaidan is considerably dumber and more straightforward. The latter grabs a stool or a stick and bangs at whatever he sees, in special moments of inspiration he beats at heels with a baton, pushes needles under fingernails, pumps water into the nose. It was he who in 1924 tortured Olha Basarab to death. Incidentally, this degenerate is by birth a Ukrainian, who renounced his faith. Lukomsky, quite to the contrary, prefers refined methods, for example, electric shocks. He could throw a live rat into the bosom of a girl tied to a chair. They say he studied treatises about the various methods of torture of the Inquisition. He isn't called Satan for nothing. But at the same time in the company of officials or the Polish gentry he is a very nice, polite man. Ladies love to swarm around him at balls and listen to his funny stories; his wife and three children adore him. One of our young ladies, who is present today, visited several winter balls in the Officers' and Municipal Clubs and was even among the ladies who listened to his stories. She told me that if she didn't know the truth about him, she would never have guessed that he was a ferocious animal. As you know, for two weeks we've been regularly monitoring his way home from work and from home to work. He lives like most of the high officials in the city's Stryisky neighborhood. Our people will be standing the entire length of the road from Batory Street to Stryisky. Usually, he returns home by tram from work. He gets on at Bernardine Square, gets off at St. Sophia Square, and then minces through Stryisky Park. Anyone encountering the man will make some kind of special movement, "Violet" will fix her stocking, "Potato" will tie his laces, "Camellia" will take off her shawl, "Hollyhock" will light a cigarette, and a couple will start kissing...." With these words you could sense excitement; obviously everyone desired to be part of the couple. "It will be "Jasmine" and "Oak." Keep in mind that none of you should pay the slightest attention to him, you shouldn't even look at him. Lukomsky is cunning and crafty and never parts with his revolver. You must be cautious and careful. We're planning the assassination for tomorrow, August 13. If we're lucky enough and Lukomsky leaves from work late just as he often does, the assassination will take place in the dark. But if not—we'll have to shoot in daylight. After the subject passes by you and you've performed your task, you need to disappear right away. There's no reason to lollygag. And one more thing. Remember, if someone gets caught and is arrested, at the interrogation do not at any cost answer in Polish. Just in Ukrainian! Because as you're being slapped, tormented, and tortured—nary a word in the language of the occupiers! Repeat that!

They all repeated in unison:

"Nary a word in the language of the occupiers!"

Uncle nodded, and when we were leaving one by one, he, letting me out last, held me back, and said:

"You won't mix up anything? You watch it!"

It was already dark and after stepping out of the house, I didn't immediately notice one of the girls who was at the meeting on the street. She stretched out her hand and said:

"Greetings, Pumpkin! I'm Cornflower. I see you've joined us for the first time. Are you scared?"

"No," I said, because Cornflower was attractive and had large cherry-red lips. Looking at them it was impossible to deny anything, especially to admit fear. We walked off together. I casually shrugged my shoulders: "Why should I be scared? I'm not going to be the assassin."

"Well, yes, your task is quite simple—take a spot next to the park. I will also be nearby."

"We've lucked out, we'll see everything!" I was happy that I'd at least get something out of it.

"Probably. But I wouldn't be so happy, because we've got to get out of there as soon as possible. In these kinds of cases there will always be witnesses who could remember us.

"Really? But why if I'm only taking off my cap? You can see such a thing anytime and anywhere."

"It seems like that to you, but Kaidan may look at it differently."

"Seriously? But Unk...," here I stopped myself, remembering that using the word "Unk" was inappropriate and corrected myself: "...Mr. leader didn't say any such thing and didn't warn me."

"Well, it goes without saying, you shouldn't wait for the assassination attempt, and should disappear immediately. I live nearby on Kryvchytsi Street. Will you escort me home?"

She took me by the arm, and I felt her supple breast, which she pressed up to me, then we talked about some cheerful things that had nothing to do with tomorrow's event. When we stopped at her house, Cornflower said:

"To be honest... tomorrow's event is making me anxious... I'm terribly nervous... I have to have a drink... Can I invite you in for some wine?"

It wasn't late yet, but returning home by Lychakivska Street after dark is too risky. Hoodlums might beat me up. I thought that I'd drop in for half an hour and then leave while the trams were still running, but it turned out a little differently. Not just a little, actually, it was quite different. Cornflower lived in a separate house all by herself except for a dog and cat. Having a large garden, she made various wines, which she served me, so there was no escape. I had to try this and that one, and she also baked such a tasty torte, yum-yum-yum, I couldn't tear myself away, and there were also different preserves... In short, I stayed with her until late. My head was spinning, and love birds were singing. Cornflower also got tipsy. For a while, we sat opposite each other, but somehow she unnoticeably moved next to me on the couch, which was the moment I was waiting for. We drank and kissed, but our kiss lasted for a long-long time, and by the time my left hand wrapped around her back, the right couldn't avoid those luxurious breasts that begged to be touched, and when I stroked them, I heard Cornflower sigh. It's possible the reason for this deep sigh was the fact that she gave up expecting me to make any kind of move, and when it happened, she was relieved. But I'm saying—my head was spinning, but until now I had not experienced the tenderness of love. I loved Leah, but she was completely into her music; for her nothing else existed besides singing. Indeed in childhood she was different, and I could not forget that beautiful spot between her legs. Meanwhile Cornflower had taken off her dress, and I took it all in with my eyes gaping from delight, because she didn't stop and removed all her other clothes. Then I started to undress. My head was pounding, I thought to myself, now what I've dreamt about so much is finally happening. But it's one thing to dream, and another to make it a reality. I was quivering with excitement, and when the two of us nakedly entwined into one, I was grateful to Cornflower who directed me into herself, but it didn't last long, just a few seconds. Having spent myself, I saw that I didn't satisfy her. But I sprang on top of her, and I lay there snugly, curled up like a snail, clinging to her breasts, and grew still. I don't know how long this lasted in dead silence. I was embarrassed, but I didn't explain anything. But soon her hand slid over to me, and I felt her playful little fingers. Trembling but skillful, they revived me, and again I penetrated her, and this time it lasted longer, much longer, and I came only when

I heard her moans of delight and pleasure. Then I poured some currant wine for her and myself, we drank it up, and as she lay before me in all her splendid nakedness, she said in an absent otherworldly voice, directed not to me, but to some point on the ceiling:

"I am the one who'll be shooting."

I opened my mouth but didn't say a word. It seemed to me that all words would be superfluous. I suddenly sensed my smallness, baseness and insignificance, for who am I, I'm nothing, and she's a hero, she's dared to do an assassination, she's perhaps going to her death, and I, a man, am just going to give an agreed-upon sign. How did this happen that they ordered her in this matter and not someone of the guys?

"You're probably thinking, why me?" She said, but she didn't need an answer because immediately after she continued: "It's very simple. I'm a good shot. I've been a member of Plast[87] since childhood, I shot with a bow, with a crossbow, and then with a revolver. But that's not the main thing... Rather the fact is that I've carried out verdicts twice. But it's always a great amount of distress for me. It's hard to shoot a man... Maybe at the front it's not like that... On the front I could be like Sophia Halyechko, stabbing with a saber and shooting at the enemy... but when you aim at someone who's not expecting it... who's walking along, not thinking anything bad... it's not that simple... The day before I'm always in a terrible state, but lovemaking and wine help get me through all of it...."

87 The largest Ukrainian scouting organization founded in Galicia in 1911 that was banned from 1930-1944 in the USSR. It flourished in Displaced Persons camps during and after WWII as well as in the post-war diaspora.

Here a quiet suspicion crept into me that I had been used, that I had played the role of some cooling compress, but I didn't resent it, because eventually someday it had to finally happen, so why not right now and this way. I embraced her supple body, and we lay in thought until we fell asleep. But before that she said:

"Pumpkin... What's that for a code name? How did you get to be Pumpkin?"

"I wanted to be 'Horseradish,' but that didn't work out."

"Well, yes, there's already a 'Horseradish.' And I'm Lucia."

She said it in such a way that she seemed to be saying goodbye to life. Then I also gave her my name, and I thought that the two of us were like gladiators before entering the arena. In the morning I was awakened by a sound as if something had banged, but Lucia was not nearby. I found a note that explained that she had to take care of certain matters, breakfast was in the kitchen, and I was supposed to leave the key in the rain gutter. Eggs, bread, butter, freshly-boiled coffee and milk were waiting for me in the kitchen, and several jars of preserves, with a note next to them in Lucia's handwriting: "I made all these. You have to try everything. I'm going to check." I don't like preserves, but to please Lucia, I tasted half a spoonful from each jar. I wonder where she's off to in such a hurry? The assassination was planned for the evening. I ate breakfast slowly; some force was holding me on the spot. I was comfortable in the house and wanted to stay there as long as possible, because I didn't know whether I'd ever end up here again after the assassination attempt. Through the window I saw an apple tree and a magpie that was weaving a nest. She disappeared somewhere for a moment and upon returning, deftly with her beak laid out a soft bed on skillfully interwoven branches. Perhaps, she was some crazy magpie, for she was weaving her nest in the middle of the summer, but that's not so strange: if there are madmen among people, then why not among birds... I looked out the window, and I wanted it never to end, this morning and breakfast, and a kind of unquenchable sadness crept into my soul, I suddenly felt that I don't want to go anywhere for any reason, I want to remain here in this house, in this building, and wait it all out. But something stronger than I lifted me up and led me out.

While walking to work to the Ossolineum and passing Batory Street, I couldn't restrain myself from looking in the direction of the police station building. I was pleasantly amused by the feeling that I knew something that thousands of people in Lviv do not know, not even the police, not even my mother. I became agitated when I recalled my mother because I didn't let her know that I would not be sleeping at home. You can only imagine her condition, taking into consideration her exalted character, also her fussing, her running all over to friends, a sleepless night, and a bustling morning. Indeed, I wasn't mistaken, because she was already waiting for me at Mrs. Konopelka's.

"Ahh!" She screamed. "Finally! Where have you been dragging yourself, ya dang scatterbrain? Huh? I didn't shut my eyes, I thought maybe I should smack you till you're silly, which slammer did they take you to! What are you doin' to yer mother? Was it for this I gave birth to you, hugged you, cherished you, for you to disgrace me like this in me old age? At least if a duck kicked you [for good luck]! Tell me: Where's were you?"

But I couldn't tell my mom about my adventure in front of Mrs. Konopelka. I calmed her down as best I could and promised that I'd tell her everything in the evening as I accompanied her out of the office. Mrs. Konopelka wagged her head.

"Yes-yes, you shouldn't make your mom nervous. She's been sitting for an hour here on pins and needles... although I do understand... at your age... and on such a day...."

I looked at her in amazement: what day was she talking about?" But she lowered her head to her papers, with only the hint of a smile on her dry lips. By evening, she looked at me carefully and said:

"Seems to me, it's time to go, no?"

"There are still fifteen minutes before seven."

"Who is in these moments cares about minutes? Go. And don't forget your cap."

I was stunned, suddenly realizing that in fact I didn't have a cap, because in the summer I don't wear one. At seven twenty I was already supposed to be on Stryisky Street. If I hurried to Kleparivska Street I wouldn't have enough time, I won't be able to buy a new one, because I had just a few coins in my pocket. At the same time, Mrs. Konopelka's words made me uneasy: how would she know anything about the cap? In an instant she stunned me even more when she pulled out of the drawer a plain, checkered cap and handed it to me with a smile. I didn't know what to say, thanked her, and moved backward toward the door. When Mrs. Konopelka looked at me with warm eyes and gave me a sign of the cross, tears trickled out of my eyes. I flew hastily from the library and marched toward Stryiska Street. Mrs. Konopelka's behavior remained a mystery, and I couldn't even guess for how long.

Climbing up Stryska Street, I passed the girls and boys whom I had seen on Fiyalkova Street, and only glanced at them. We didn't greet or pay any attention to each other. The scent of blooming linden trees wafted from the park , they actually had already bloomed, and in these last days of their flowering poured out all of their bouquet with some sense of self-satisfied doom, like their last words before death... There were very few passersby around, just one or two were hanging around the wooden kiosks with lemonade. Making my way right up to the entrance to the cemetery, I stopped. There was my observation post. There further up I saw Lucia near the lemonade kiosk. She was rummaging in her handbag, looking for change. She had on a white dress with flowers, low-heeled shoes, which obviously made it easier for her to flee, and she put up her hair up in a beret. I didn't smoke, but I bought a pack of the cheapest cigarettes and put one to my lips. Even though I didn't light it up, it seemed I looked more natural like this—hanging out in one place. At least I looked more like a hooligan than someone participating in an assassination. I felt the pounding of my heart. It was pounding even more when I saw a girl at the bottom of the street bend over and latch the buckle on her sandals. In the meantime, a man with a folder under his arm passed her; he even turned around to look at the girl who was bending over in such a way to show off all her enticements and smiled. I struck a match and lit up a cigarette, but I didn't inhale, then looked in Lucia's direction. She was slowly drinking a lemonade and admiring the blossoming linden trees. Two elderly women in black came out of the cemetery; they were wearing hats with black veils that reached all the way to their mouths. Walking arm in arm, they turned right and went up the street. If they hobble along as slowly as this, they certainly would witness the assassination attempt. I thought it was necessary to delay them, especially, because the inspector already passed me. I took off my cap and wiped my forehead, then overtook the two grannies and spoke to them in Polish, because I heard them speaking in Polish. I asked them if they had seen anything suspicious in the cemetery, because I'm a secret agent of the police, and we're now investigating a dangerous maniac who attacks elderly people and robs them. The two grannies suddenly stopped and became very still. They first asked each other if the other had happened to notice anything. They later assured me that everything in the cemetery was peaceful, though...."

"Yes-yes...," one of the grannies shifted to a whisper. "Something seemed to me... there in the bushes... oh, do you see?... there in those box-tree bushes... near that white cross... something was rustling there... I thought it was the wind, isn't that right, Adela, I even told you: it's the wind... but do you think it could be him?... How good it is that you're taking care of us and watching over us... we'll feel more secure... so tell us, will you be here tomorrow too, because we'll be coming here in the afternoon... our husbands are buried here, they're veterans, Sunday the orchestra will play here, we need to put their graves in order..."

I didn't have time to answer because I saw Lucia place her unfinished glass of lemonade on the counter, then calmly take out a revolver from her handbag, and with three shots she took the policeman down. He still tries to reach for his weapon but has no strength and dies. Lucia immediately runs across the road and disappears in the park. The grannies squeal like stuck pigs, shouting something to me as though to a policeman, but I'm already not listening to them, and I'm also running into the park as if in pursuit of a killer. Behind my back I heard: "Faster, mister! Faster!"

15

Yarosh took off from Istanbul earlier than Andrei Kurkov but with him managed to visit Istanbul's famous covered bazaar, which stunned him with its immensity. When Kurkov, who had been invited to Ankara, was returning home on the plane, a short guy sat next to him squinting the whole time, as if someone were shining something in his eyes. In any case, the writer didn't like something about his appearance, and he didn't pull out his laptop from its carrying case as he usually does, to work on his next novel. He imagined those squinting eyes next to him. After the plane took off, gained altitude, and the flight attendants appeared with a cart, offering dinner and drinks, the stranger asked Andrei whether he'd be drinking something. Kurkov, who was distinguished by a kind disposition and was accustomed to converse politely with anyone, and would even listen to an alcoholic, immediately felt a strange aversion to the man. He didn't want to enter into conversation with him, and shook his head no; The stranger, apparently, was glad to hear it, because he immediately asked Andrei to take a whiskey, as though for himself, because today he, had too many emotions and needed to relax. After receiving two glasses of whiskey, the man gulped them down in one fell swoop and scarfed down his salad. "Now whenever the stewardess passes out the drinks from the cart, he'll ask me to take one more glass," Andrei thought. He had the brilliant idea to sleep a bit, because he thought the man would not wake him. Just as the writer settled himself more comfortably in the seat, the stranger, who had finished his chomping and slurping, said, "I recognize you. You're Andrei Kurkov, right?" Without waiting for an affirmative answer, continued:

"No, I won't say I've read you, but I follow the newspapers. Pleased to meet you: Lieutenant Colonel of the SBU Knysh." He had to shake his hand and mumble the customary words in such situations. The flight attendants appeared again; this time they took away the trash and food scraps and poured drinks, and Kurkov again had to provide his neighbor with a second drink, in his mind deciding that this would be the last time. But he was mistaken, because guzzling down one glass and starting the second, the guy said:

"You see, I was on a business trip... my work... I won't beat around the bush... I have a few questions for you regarding a person... uh, how shall I say it... close to us...."

"What do you have in mind? I never served in the KGB."

"You were supposed to serve in the KGB but got yourself out of that. This we know. But you worked in the penitentiary...as a prison guard. So, you're one of us."

"I won't order any more whiskey for you, because you're starting to spout nonsense."

"Well, sorry if I spoke inappropriately. The whisky certainly has done its job. But I still have hope that you'll help us. Now we're on the same side of the barricades."

"Which barricades? I don't see any." Well, I've read one of your interviews where you said that you consider yourself a patriot of Ukraine and you don't feel any sympathy for Russia. That's why I'm appealing to you exclusively, as a patriot of Ukraine. Because I'm a patriot."

"And when you served in the KGB, were you also a patriot of Ukraine?"

"I appreciate your humor. But let's get to the heart of the matter. We are interested in Professor Yarosh. In particular his research about Arcanum and a certain book piques our interest. I don't know if you noticed in the reading room of the National Library an unassuming man with a magnifying glass...."

Kurkov with surprise looked at his traveling companion; apparently, he was one of the three readers who was examining certain old publications.

"That was you?"

"Yes," Knysh said, coyly lowering his eyes. "I was looking through the Turkish atlas of Ukraine by Evliya Çelebi. A very interesting traveler. It's been partially translated. But of course, I was not interested in the atlas, and what was being said behind me. I don't understand diddlysquat' in Turkish. As for English, you know, like all graduates of Soviet schools, I'm also not on the best of terms with it. I'm like a doggie, I understand everything, but I can't speak at all. That is, in everyday conversation—no problem... as they say, howmatch, howduyudu, mayaispeek, senkyuverymatch, and so on. So, what you said in the hall, I grasped. But I'm interested in what was said in the repository ...."

"How I understand you," Kurkov smiled. "Even more so—I sympathize. But I want to get some sleep." After those words he straightened out his legs as much as possible, folded his arms, and throwing his head back, shut his eyes. Constant flying instilled in him the enviable ability to feel at home on a plane. With a kind of self-satisfaction before falling asleep, he listened to another rattling of the cart and the bubbling of drinks.

O

It wasn't even seven in the morning when a merciless din at the door awakened me; then I heard the frightened scream of my mother as three policemen tore into my bedroom, ordering us immediately to get dressed and go with them. Mom tried to argue something with them, to convince them, but they didn't pay any attention to mom's screams. Then mom instantly got control over herself, rushed through the house and quickly put into a bag everything I might need where they were taking me to. As we were walking out of the house, mom's curses echoed after us along with the promise to contact Mr. Minister, whom she knows personally, and then the police would learn with whom they are dealing. However, mom discreetly didn't give the name of the minister. All of her howling made no impression on the police, and after a quarter hour I was in Brygidky[88] Prison on Casimir Street before the lucid eyes of Commissar Kaidan, the monster known to all Lviv's populace. In the interrogation room they sat me on a small stool, and near the walls were lying ropes, cudgels, tongs, and other apparati. My eyes grew dim just looking at them.

"What a name the Lord's endowed that man with!" And then I looked at his face and thought: "And what a mug He also gave him!" With this my thoughts ended as the commissar approached and smacked me in the face so hard that I fell backward and flew off the stool. I hurt so much that I almost fainted, not from his punch but from banging my

88 Brygidky is a prison in the building of a former Bridgettine nunnery in Lviv, Ukraine. Thanks to Olha Tytarenko for pointing this out.

head hard against the stone floor. I felt blood on my lips but decided not to wipe it off, let him think that he beat my face black and blue.

"Get up, you pig," Kaidan said quite gently, "get up and tell me who the gunman was."

Aha, so this is in regard to the assassination attempt? But what can I tell them that would be useful? I got up, lifted up the stool, and sat down on it, saying in Ukrainian:

"Please, sir, I work in the library... In the Ossolineum... I don't know anyone who knows how to shoot. I don't even know at whom they were shooting."

The next blow struck me right in the ear, and again I fell to the floor, with my feet in the air, and above me hung Kaidan's red mug:

"What language are you speaking, you son of a whore? Eh? Where are you living? In Poland? Then speak Polish, otherwise I'll break your head! You want your Ukraine? Do you know where Ukraine is? Beneath the grove is a valley—Ukraine is there in the arse! Weren't you on Stryska Street last night?"

Remembering my uncle's guidance "nary a word in the language of the occupier!" I silently wagged my head, hoping not to get another whack.

"And till what time were you in the library, pig?" The commissar asked, grabbing me by the lapels and pulling me up on my feet.

I moaned something unintelligible, as if I were choking on my blood, and showed him eight fingers. The commissar looked at me, screwing up his eyes, the way a butcher looks at a calf, then grabbed some blotting paper from the table, wiped my mouth with sharp movements, threw the blotting paper into a basket, and then shouted at the door:

"Bring in those old bats!"

In a minute the two older ladies whom I met near the cemetery entered the room. They were no longer dressed in black and had a much more festive look, as if they were awaiting a visit with the Burgermeister [Mayor]. Both were wearing colorful dresses, and their hats were decorated with ornamental flowers and leaves, with the only difference being that on one of them red strawberries peeked out from among the flowers and leaves.

"Is that him?" Kaidan asked without any delay, pointing at me.

"Ah yes-yes, sir," both grannies hastily clucked, incredibly happy that they were so honored to be witnesses, and the one whom her friend yesterday called Adela, excitedly jabbered: "This is the boy who informed us that he was an undercover police officer investigating a dangerous maniac. And he asked us to be vigilant. We're really grateful to him for that. And then he courageously threw himself in pursuit of the woman... the one who was shooting... We shouted to him, 'Faster! Faster!' And waved our umbrellas...."

"Adela honey!" Granny-Strawberry interrupted. "You're always confused, I waved the umbrella, and you whooped 'Faster! Faster!' because you didn't have an umbrella...."

"How is it I didn't have an umbrella!" Adela was outraged. "I haven't been without it since Mr. Dr. Cybulski ordered me to stay in the shade!"

"But you didn't have it then, because with your left hand you were holding me under my arm, and in your right hand you were carrying a handbag."

"Lord! And you're telling me this now? Then it turns out I forgot my umbrella in the cemetery?

I would have loved to listen to those good and pleasant grannies for longer, but Mr. Commissar had a different opinion and snorted so fiercely that both ladies suddenly grew silent, and he said:

"Now, please go to the office and sign a deposition. Thank you for your civic consciousness."

The grannies disappeared, and Kaidan smiled at me and continued:

"And what? Are you going to keep yanking my chain?" After this, as deftly as a soccer player, he kicked out the stool from under me, and I slammed onto the floor again. This time I hit my elbow badly, but not as painfully as I pretended because in the end Uncle said nothing about whether or not I should produce a sound when they're beating me. It's easy for them to say "endure," but unlike those who squeezed their hands in doors and even poked needles under their fingernails in order to get used to torture, I didn't prepare to carry out assassination attempts. Meanwhile, as the Commissar was intending to kick me in the ribs, the phone rang. He picked it up, sighed and said:

"Let her come in." Then he shoved blotting paper into my hands: "Stand up, wipe off your ugly mug, and sit down!"

I barely managed to fulfill his instructions as the door opened and Mrs. Konopelka entered accompanied by a young policeman.

"This lady says," the policeman nodded at her, "that he was in the library all evening."

"Is that so?" Kaidan smiled. "And till what time was that exactly?"

I grew numb. Now she'll say some other hour, and then everything will be truly over for me.

"On that day we received a package of books and magazines from Prague," Mrs. Konopelka began completely calmly. "So, we were somewhat delayed at work. We all had to catalog and write out the numbers on individual file cards. Usually the bibliography department deals with this, but when it comes to Czech publications, I can't trust them to anyone else since Mr. Barbaryka has considerable experience working with the Czechs. So, Mr. Barbaryka was next to me till half past seven, then I let him go, but asked him to take those cards to the person who manages the General Catalog, so that the next day she could distribute them to the branch catalogs. And since that person is young and attractive, you can understand, they weren't in a rush. In a word, I don't know when he left because I sat in my office for quite a long time."

Kaidan snorted as if he were about to fly up to the ceiling, his fingers frantically clenched into fists, and I was worried for Mrs. Konopelka, but she courageously maintained her composure and boldly stared into the eyes of the Commissar.

"Will you give this evidence under oath?" Kaidan queried.

"I will give it under oath in court," Mrs. Konopelka did not let herself be led astray. "And I'll sign the interrogation protocol right now."

"Fine. And that person?"

"She also came," said the policeman, who was still standing silently. "Should I bring her in?"

The Commissar nodded. Imagine my surprise when Milya appeared. She was dressed in a cotton dress with bare shoulders, and on her charming lips a charming smile bloomed. On seeing me, she threw herself into my embrace so passionately, as if the incredible power of love united us, that the Commissar was stunned and didn't stop her immediately, before she finished kissing me all over. In the end with the help of the other policeman he tore her away from me.

"Well, you're not at a railway station, and he hasn't gotten off the train!" Kaidan barked. "When was the last time you saw him yesterday?"

"Lord! Why the last time? What are you alluding to? Orest honey!

Sweetie!" Here she wringed her hands in despair and began to sob so theatrically that I nearly started to weep.

"Stop immediately!" The commissar barked. "Answer the question!"

"We left the library five after eight and parted."

"Who saw you leaving?"

"No one, because we came out last."

"And you're such a loving couple, you didn't go for a coffee and parted right away?"

"I didn't feel all that well," and squinting at Kaidan, added with a smile: "You know how it is with women...."

This time the Commissar snorted like the bellows of a forge. Milya replied quite wisely, because if she had said that we were having coffee, the waiters would be questioned. Kaidan swayed for a moment on his bootheels, biting his thick lips, and said to the policeman:

"Call in those... those old toads...."

Both the old bats reappeared before us and their good smiling faces shone with inexpressible joy; kindness just poured out of their eyes, with which they almost swallowed

Mr. Commissar, prepared for anything for the sake of their good deed.

"Ladies," Kaidan addressed them. "I do not know who to believe. That lady and that young miss are trying to convince me that this... this... guest could not have been on Stryisky Street yesterday because he was working in the Ossolineum until eight in the evening, and the assassination attempt took place at half past seven. And you say it was he you saw."

"The Ossolineum!" Mrs. Strawberry smacked her lips. "Lord, I spent the best years of my life there. I worked in the department... in the department of...."

"Of course," Mrs. Konopelka responded. "I remember you well. You worked in the staffing department. We rarely ran across each other because I worked one floor above you. But once I awarded you a letter from the president himself for your conscientious work...."

"Oh, yes-yes!" Mrs. Strawberry clapped her hands. "You even called me "flower." I was young and beautiful! Did you really recognize me?" She sweetly adjusted her hat. "So many years! But you... you haven't changed...."

"Enough," Kaidan interrupted. "Do you insist that you saw this boy on Stryisky Street at half past seven?"

The grannies looked at each other and blushed, then both took a look at me and at Mrs. Konopelka, then shrugged:

"He's similar!" Mrs. Adela said.

"Very similar!" Mrs. Strawberry nodded her head.

"Maybe if he said something to us... maybe it would become clear for us...."

"Yes," Kaidan addressed me. "Well then say: "Jestem agent policyjny. Tropimy maniaka."

I repeated it word for word, but in Ukrainian: "I am an agent of the police. I'm investigating a maniac." Kaidan snorted again, flashed his eyes, clenched his fists, but restrained himself from decisive action. Instead, he dryly said:

"Please say the same thing in Polish."

Mrs. Konopelka intervened:

"Mr. Commissar, according to the law only government employees are required not only to be fluent in Polish, but also to be Poles...."

"There is no such law."

"But you know how it is in reality. Ukrainians and Jews are not taken for government work until they convert to Catholicism."

The Commissar shook his head with dissatisfaction.

"We are not here at debates in the Sejm. Are you saying that he is not conversant in Polish?"

"I've known him for a long time. He can say something in Polish, but it will be so awful that I feel pity for the great language of our Prophet."

"Let him say it any way he can."

I thought that Uncle would not be offended if I mangled Polish, so I blurted out:

"I am agent poleece. We maniac corpsing."

Kaidan contorted his face as if vomit had come out of my mouth instead of Polish. The grannies looked at each other again and almost in a chorus rattled out:

"No-no," that one spoke differently... and his voice was not like this... it was more sonorous...."

For sure! So much blood and saliva had accumulated in my chops that I didn't utter that phrase as much as mumble it.

You know Adela honey," Mrs. Strawberry said. "That boy had lighter hair... Don't you think?"

"Yes, he did," Mrs. Adela nodded. And it was wavy, and his ears were closer to his head."

"And that one was taller... not too much, but taller...."

Now the Commissar became seriously irate, and barely holding back his rage, said hoarsely:

"Everyone's free to go!" And said to the policeman: "Write up the protocol."

Already on the street I asked Milya and Mrs. Konopelka:

"How did you know which hour to tell them?"

"That was easy!" Milya laughed. "The library is closed at eight, you could name any time from seven-thirty. We assumed you wouldn't say something like seven forty-two or seven fifty-seven."

"And that lady... what a blessing that you recognized her after so many years... she was a girl then...."

"I never recognized her! I'm seeing her for the first time," Mrs. Konopelka waved her hand.

"What do you mean? You handed a presidential letter of commendation to her!"

"So, what of it? We present those letters every year on several holidays. If she worked with us, sooner or later she would get it."

"And what if... if she hadn't received one? If she only had worked there for a year or two?"

"Well, what then," Mrs. Konopelka shrugged her shoulders. "Sometimes it's worth taking a risk."

"I don't know how to thank you. Because I...."

"We know where you were and what you did," Mrs. Konopelka smiled and with a mysterious expression, right before looking all around, whispered: “Have you come to poison the rats?”

“And the mice too!” Milya burst into laughter, and while saying farewell tossed out “Ciao, Pumpkin!” She took Mrs. Konopelka under her arm, and the two minced their way toward the center of the city. I scratched my head and went to comfort my mother, and on the way washed up at a pump, so she wouldn’t be frightened.

16

Josef Milker's lessons became a kind of sacred activity for Yarka. She suddenly became aware that going to the old man, she was adjusting herself to a certain mood, she would even talk with him in her imagination, hearing his remarks. She truly was imbued with music more than anything else that surrounded her. Milker truly became a guru to her. She was ready to fulfill his every desire, and if the teacher had ordered her to jump out the window in a particularly inspired moment while she was playing the violin, she would have jumped. She also knew this, and now, in addition to an unrestrained desire for the lessons, fear nestled inside her, but it did not interfere, it just tickled her nerves, excited and encouraged her. The music lessons that Milker gave to Yarka were totally different from all those that she had taken until then. When any other new teacher began to instruct her, it seemed at the beginning as if the most important thing to them was to erase from her memory all previous knowledge and skills. Milker took another path:

"Extracting sound—that's something you have to work on the most. The violin should have a beautiful sound, and the bow should literally suck the string. God gave you a fair share of musicality, so I'll teach you the ability to convey to the violin what sounds in your soul!"

At first the lessons were held at the old man's house which Yarka liked very much. Everything in his abode served to create a particular mood, the old furniture smelled a special way, conjuring something long forgotten memory in her, something that smelled like childhood. The spines of books both hypnotized and fascinated; the girl noticed that while playing she was even looking at the spines of books as if at musical notes. But soon everything changed when Milker suggested she play in the street. Yarka was surprised. She could not understand why he'd conduct such an experiment, how could one take lessons on the street where strangers scurry in front of you, and some stop and stare? But the teacher insisted:

"You are bound, you are like a snail in a shell, and you need to break free. Your soul must fly out of you when you play, and soar into the sky. I noticed how you glance over at the books; it should not be like that."

"But then I'll end up glancing at the passersby...."

"No. They'll disturb you, so you will stop paying attention to them. You will ignore them and not notice. This will force you to focus and not associate yourself with the place where you are."

Yarka had no choice left but to agree, but the final straw was when Milker, right as they chose a place to play at Rynok Square, took his hat off his head and set it down at her feet. The girl was so anxious, she couldn't catch her breath. She desperately shook her head and whispered: "No way... I will not... what you are thinking?" Milker patiently listened to her and waited, sensing that she was slowly losing her desire to resist, and then said:

"Start playing, and the music will lift you above the city, you should not see anything or anyone, you should not hear anyone but me. The wave of music will pick you up and carry you off."

And Yarka obeyed. From then on, each lesson took place in a different part of Lviv: in Strisky Park, on High Castle Mountain, in the Kaiserwald, at Lychakiv Cemetery, on Kortumov Mountain....

Yarka didn't know that a few days before Yarosh had come to Milker and asked how one could hear the real "Tango of Death." The old man just shook his head sadly:

"Unfortunately, for the time being, it's impossible. I can't perform it with one hand. And even if I could, I don't have the notes. Those twelve notes. There was no need, I used to know the melody by heart, I could even play it in the middle of the night. But I recently had a stroke and my memory is pretty ragged; only then did I regret not recording the music. Though I hope I'll still remember."

"Maybe you'll be able to reconstruct the melody. A few days ago, I decrypted it from the Arcanumian *Book of Death*. The Arcanumians marked the notes with letters. The melody, which they performed during the rite of death, consisted of twelve notes. Here they are... Perhaps this CD will also help you. This is a recording of the dance of the dervishes."

"The dance of the dervishes... yes-yes... I've heard about it. Twelve unique music notes are also included in that dance. All the others play no role, all the rest are just background. Like in our tango," the old man twirled the disk in his fingers, and then became absorbed in the notes that the professor had decoded.

"I must say that when I was present during the performance of the dance of the dervishes, strange things happened to me. It was as if I had abandoned my body and rose above the earth. And then, perhaps, I went completely unconscious. I didn't listen to it after that. I was terrified. Perhaps these are the same feelings a person has when he's dying.

Milker stared at him with a pensive look.

"I think we are close to the truth. But... there are certain problems. Let's say I manage to recreate the notes. But who will perform them? The fact of the matter is that there are some nuances, and if you don't hold to them, the effect of this melody will be the same as that of any tango. The human ear is unable to distinguish these nuances but is still able to respond to them. If you do not know the secret of the performance, then even if you give these notes to the greatest virtuoso the consequences will be fruitless."

"How did you succeed?"

"Kalkbrenner encrypted the notes. But I managed to decipher them. Following his instructions, I was able to perform this tango...," Milker again looked at the notes, and the paper trembled in his hand. "It seems... it seems," he whispered with agitation. "It's similar to... to the notes of 'Tango of Death'... but I have to make sure. It will take a little time. And also...," he anxiously looked at Yarosh. "All this time I've been looking for an apprentice... a person whom I could teach the tango in the way we used to perform it... But each time I've experienced defeat... Though hope doesn't abandon me...."

P

Soon after I escaped from prison, I was drafted into the army. My mother immediately said that she would not give away her beloved son, that she'd rouse all her friends just to save me from conscription, but I calmed her down, saying that I could extricate myself from that problem and, pretending I was deaf, boldly went to the medical board. Well, not entirely, but in one ear. The doctors had to shout at me as though we were in a mountain valley, and I answered them just as loudly. Then they ordered me to wait in the next room, where a good dozen of similar deaf and hard of hearing had gathered. Some of them thinking that it was safe, didn't play the fool, but not me, because I was not sure whether agents of the Commission were among them or whether anyone was spying on us. Then they called us, we went back in and stood in front of the doctors. They ordered us to stand in a single row. And then one of the doctors leaned to another and said softly but clearly:

"Mr. Mixovski, maybe let's check their vestibular apparatus?"

"Of course, Mr. Zhmixovski," He responds just as quietly. "We'll command them to stand on one leg."

"Great idea! None of the deaf will be able to do that because their vestibular system won't allow it." And then he loudly said: "I ask everyone to raise your left foot and stand on your right foot for five seconds."

As one would expect, all the deaf guys crashed onto the floor, and only I, as a stork, was left to stand because my vestibular apparatus did not succumb to the provocation. I would have continued to stand if the doctors hadn't already begun to scream like madmen and wave their hands. So, they transferred me to the reserves. My deepest gratitude goes to my uncle for my success, because he used the same trick twenty years before.

Although I avoided the army, Lviv wasn't saved from the war. One night when my friends and I were returning on foot from upper Lychakivska Street, where we really tied one on at the Under the Squirrel Tavern, we suddenly caught sight of a strange procession. Several dozen squat types in long raincoats and green helmets were mincing toward us. For some reason, instead of looking ahead, they were looking at the pavement. When they approached, we saw that their raincoats were wet, and that underneath them instead of shoes or boots there were fins, which stank of rotten seaweed and iodine. They shuffled along clumsily and awkwardly, paying no attention to us. Only their eyes shone with a green light, in which there was nothing living because even that light was dead. None of us said a word, not yet fully comprehending whether we were seeing this in reality or dreaming it. We followed them with our gaze, watching them disappear in the mist that suddenly descended from above. Then we looked at each other and went our way, still stunned and confused, and that was the last night of August 1939.

The day of September 1 was sunny, many residents of Lviv were still on vacation in the Carpathians. Lviv was not as crowded as usual, and when I heard explosions, I didn't immediately comprehend what it was. I thought maybe it was artillery training, but the explosions didn't subside, but instead advanced from the west and sounded like thunder. Then that thunder turned into a din, and German planes appeared in the skies. Bomb explosions shook the city, fires ignited, sirens wailed. A week before the same sirens wailed, announcing the enemy aircraft's attack on the city, but that was just a training alarm, although it scared a lot of people when in the middle of the night during the sirens' drone the watchman banged on all the doors and shouted for everyone to hide in the cellars immediately. During the day at every step Lviv's inhabitants were alerted by multicolored posters, informing them of sales of gas masks on the streets. More and more people shuffled along the streets with gas masks in gray-green cases attached to their belts. Some even wore them on their faces, resembling monsters. Planes dropped leaflets with instructions on how one should behave in the event of a gas attack. The newspapers advised people to stock up on potash. They didn't write anything about flour, sugar and grains, but the people themselves knew that it was also worthwhile to buy all that—it wouldn't go to waste even if there was no war.

The radio repeatedly interrupted the music and you could hear the familiar voice of the Warsaw announcer: "N. O. 28. Ryba. Nadchodzi," and again: "N. O. 28. Ryba. Nadchodzi." Its tone sounded different than before; you could sense anxiety in the voice, and the incomprehensible text evoked even more anxiety and fear in the listeners. Even when music began to play again afterwards, those words continued to echo in your ears, eat their way into your brain, and involuntarily you wanted to repeat them yourself like some kind of incantation that could rescue us all from calamity. But it didn't save us. With every day Lviv swelled with more new people. They were traveling by car and on carts, they were walking, laden with suitcases and bags, and then they scattered to close and distant family, plunged into villages, or went farther on to Ternopil or Stanislav, and from there to the Romanian border. Later it became clear that those who went to Romania were the wisest. They all managed to save themselves and survive the war, but then, at the beginning of September, nobody knew what awaited them. "Uwaga, uwaga! 125, przerzedł," a female announcer from Warsaw kept repeating over and over, and later marches played, but those anxious words were not forgotten and continued to be vexing, and the marches no longer sounded cheerful, but seemed like tolling funeral bells....

Leah hunched over on the couch with her feet tucked under her, looked at me with frightened eyes and asked:

"Why, why are they saying that? I don't understand anything. This is making me terrified."

"They're transmitting information for the army," I said. "They're reporting the Germans' movement.

"What do you think? Are they close?"

"Maybe. But we'll defend ourselves."

"We? You're going to defend Lviv alongside the Poles?"

"This is my Lviv too."

I went outside for a newspaper. It was completely covered in large headlines and joyfully reported that the brave Polish army was heroically resisting "the impudent Hun, the barbarian of the 20th century" on the entire front line. However, those who came to the city from the west, were saying something different. The Germans were already near Czestochowa.

On Horodotska Street bombs were dropped and two large buildings were destroyed. Aircraft buzzed over the city, people scattered in a run, a boy was running in front of the window and blowing a whistle: alarm!—Planes buzzed, and that buzz triggered horror and the desire to hide in some little burrow. Then there was a bang, the street shuddered, the earth vibrated underfoot, windowpanes quivered, a human cry cut the air, and then suddenly there was silence. There was only smoke and dust rising up and enveloping everything. It obstructed breathing, triggering a desire to spit out something unpleasant that scratched your throat, it grated on your teeth and wouldn't let you breath. Smoke that was dark brown at the bottom and yellow on top could be seen from the main door, it swirled and swayed like crowns of trees in the wind, each time changing its color, first darkening and becoming thick, then becoming lighter with flashes of pulsating red tongues that tore out of the station warehouses. The watchman went from home to home and told everyone to fill up their bathtub and washtub, as well as washing machine basins and pots with water in case of fire, and generally to safeguard water, because the water would be cut off, and the only water left would be in street pumps.

17

"Every great man has his disciples, but it's always a Judas who writes his biography," Yarosh stated, finishing his lecture on Arcanumian literature. "This is what happened with Lucilius.[89] Alceste became his biographer. Early in his life he hated Lucilius with his entire soul; he was jealous and strove to eclipse his talent. When Lucilius died, Alceste calmed down and suddenly began to write exceptionally well about him, as if he had been his closest friend, and as if having privatized all reminiscences and research. And whenever anyone else dared to write something about his "idol," Alceste attacked him like a hawk. Thus, for us the life and work of Lucilius are obscured by the haze of imagination; we can only suspect what it was in reality, because no other information has survived for the sake of a balanced view. And this is the mystery of Lucilius. For what do we have? On the one hand—the biography in which he mythologized himself, and on the other hand—the biography in which Alceste mythologized him. Where, then, is the truth? We do not know the truth. We are like Buridan's ass, caught between two haystacks and unable to decide from which stack to grab a tuft. As you know, Buridan's ass died of hunger in the end. But we are thinking beings. We must without assistance figure out our own truth. And how exactly we will do that, I'll explain at the next lecture."

This was the last lecture of the day and Yarosh was already preparing to head to the library when Danka approached him and asked if he had ever gone to Devil's Cliff.[90] He was surprised:

---

89 Gaius Ennius Lucilius (ca. 180-103/2 BC), the Roman satirist.
90 A rock outcropping and the highest point in a forest in Lviv oblast outside of the city west of the village of Vynnyky, where Yuri Vynnychuk lives. Today it's a popular spot for nature lovers and especially rock climbers.

"No, I've never been there. Why are you asking?"

"Because I haven't been there either," she laughed as she said that and shot him a playful look over her big glasses as she was spinning her purse in her hands. "My mom baked a sheet cake and said that I definitely should treat you. So, I thought it would be nice to take a hike... While the weather's still sunny."

"Hmm...," Yarosh smiled. "That's a tempting proposition. But we could eat the cake in the park."

"The cake isn't important. The main thing is something else. I want to read you my translations of Lucilius's poems from the Devil's Cliff."

"Oh-oh, you should have started with that! Then let's hurry up and go. But... probably it would be smart if we leave the university separately. Okay? Let's meet at the bus stop across from the monument to King Danylo."

He also wanted to ask her about her glasses that made her look somewhat older and like a teacher, because he hadn't yet seen her wearing glasses, but wasn't able to

because she turned on her heels and disappeared. On his way to the bus stop Yarosh bought wine, water and cheese. Danka was already waiting for him. They pushed their way into a crowded bus heading to Vynnyky and got off by the lake, setting off up through the forest. You could walk to Devil's Cliff on a flat serpentine path, but they decided to clamber straight up, and after a half hour made their way to where the mighty Devil's Cliff towers, plowed with cracks and caves. It stuck around in the forest like a cataract on an eye. Yarosh and Danka climbed onto the cliff and, setting out napkins, arranged their refreshments. There was not a soul all around—during weekdays hardly anyone hiked there.

"By the way," Yarosh said, "where we're sitting, Josefa Kuhn, Mother Superior of the Convent of the Benedictine Sisters, built a gazebo with a sharp-pitched roof and veranda, called "The Shrine of Apollo." In 1834, she published a collection of poems *Lembergs schone Umgebungen—Beautiful Lviv Neighborhoods*, in which she described the Devil's Cliff, because it was a really popular place of relaxation for the local inhabitants of Lviv."

Here he noticed that Danka placed her ear to the cliff and listened.

"What are you doing?"

"I'm listening to check if I hear a rooster crowing." Noticing that Yarosh's surprise, she explained: "Haven't you read about it? Devils carried this cliff to drop it on St. George's Cathedral, but they dropped it to the ground here upon hearing a rooster's crow. The evening before, a drunkard sleeping in the field overheard the devils' council. He lay in wait for them with a rooster. But the cliff fell on him. And now sometimes, placing your ear to the cliff, you can hear the rooster squawking."

"The rooster began to crow in the middle of the night?"

"Eh, that drunkard wasn't stupid. He put a hat on the rooster's head to cover his eyes, and when the devils flew up, he lit a lantern and abruptly took off that hat. The light flashed before the eyes of the rooster, and he began to crow. By the way, that's been confirmed. Once, when I was in the village, I conducted a scientific experiment. I caught a rooster, brought him to the root cellar, where it was dark, and covered him with a washtub. And in an hour, I lit a candle in front of the washtub and lifted it up. The rooster joyfully began to crow."

"And from that time on your attraction to science was awakened?"

"I have a special kind of attraction to science. I like diving into it, but don't feel like drawing any conclusions."

The sheet cake was crumbly with nuts and sweets, but without fatty cream. This was just how Yarosh liked them; he hated greasy tortes.

"This is delicious, pass along my deep gratitude to your mother," he said as he was pouring out some wine. "Do you do any baking yourself?"

"No, I haven't had the chance. Mom doesn't let me into the kitchen. She believes that I am completely worthless as a future lady of the house. I don't know how to cook or bake. Every time I put things in a different spot and then have to look for them for a long time. I'm a hopeless scatterbrain and dawdler."

"Wow, you have so many great features! All the signs of a creative person. You haven't put on shoes from different pairs? Or mistaken a colander for a hat?"

"Well, don't mock me. I am not that brilliant."

"Once I left the house in slippers, but fortunately caught myself on the street. So, I'm not hopeless. Another time instead of my mobile phone, I put a voice recorder in my pocket, and then wondered why nobody called me all day. Your glasses have especially piqued my interest. I've never seen you in them. Are you nearsighted or farsighted?"

"Neither," Danka laughed. "These are clear lenses. I wear them for fun. Most guys treat girls in eyeglasses with caution, suspecting that they're dealing with a smarty-pants, with whom it's not worth it to start up anything. So, I wear them on my first date. Then I get a kick out of it when a guy begins to blush, especially when I pretend I'm nearsighted and ask: what's that rag there hanging onto the tree? He then says: 'it's a crow!' After that you only need to ask a few more analogous questions, and it becomes clear with whom you're dealing. A classic test on 'How to reckon with a bumpkin."

"So that's what it is. And why did you put them on today?"

"Because I'm a mysterious girl. You'll never guess, so don't even try. Well, come on down now and listen to me read the poetry of Lucilius. If you see any strangers, give me a warning."

"You've translated these verses again from my English interlinears?"

"No. This time I dug into the original, like a woodworm into a bookcase. Though, of course, I did look at your interlinears."

Yarosh shook his head, marveling at the courage of this young woman who not only mastered the Arcanumian language incredibly quickly, but also plucked up the courage to translate relatively complex and intricate poetry of the greatest Arcanumian poet Lucilius, who was in love with a certain mysterious Ilayali, to whom he dedicated many poems. Having made his way down to the foot of the cliff, he settled himself on a fallen trunk and prepared himself to listen. Danka meanwhile was at the very top with papers in her hands, and a slight breeze gently shook her skirt.

"'Spring Letters to Ilayali," she announced, as if on stage, and began to recite in a soft deep voice, noting each verse with a number.

1

In the constellation of your hair my kisses have roamed,
like sylvan demons[91] they wink and howl...
Oh kisses, which in vain I released to freedom from their cage—
no one will pity you or give you a name,
nor will stretch out hands, so you fall into them,
like honey falling from a honey cloud into a flower.
Night with a basket full of dreams
goes from house to house,
leaves everyone on their windowsill a fragrant tuft.
Maybe it will leave me
a dream about a girl-river,
that completely flowed out to the last drop,
flowed out from my eye—
and I became like a seashell,
in which nonexistent waves on a nonexistent shore
lap stubbornly.

2

All of you has remained in me, though you've long gone away.
Here are the traces of your white knees on my hands.
Your entire body leaves an imprint on mine, like on sand.
All that I want to touch—I touch.
Don't look for your shadow in vain,
because it walks by my side, holding my shadow by the hand.

---

91 The *potercha* is a demon in Ukrainian mythology that comes from the soul of an unbaptized child.

I have deprived you of your beauty.
You have become so ordinary and uninteresting,
so pay no attention to those who look back at you.
They are joking. They're mocking you.
I robbed you entirely—
your voice, your scent, the shine of your eyes and lips,
the silk of your stomach and the melted honey of your thighs.
You are almost gone.
All your past—is just my memory.
All the present—on the tip of my tongue.
All the future—is a slight sliding of a feather on a cherry tree leaf.
I plant your hair on the windowsill and already see the slimmest golden sprouts
that quiver in fright from my breath.
I glue your lips to the windowpane—right onto the sun.
Now let them rise together each morning.
I am giving your voice to the birds, the dew, and the streams.
My garden—is your nocturnal whisper.
Bees collect your saliva from flowers and carry them to their hives.
Your stomach in the well—I submerge my fingers in it and feel
the water seething around my fingers,
warmth along my arm rises to my chest and drowns me in thirst.
I kiss your fingers and put out the fire burning in them,
and hot honey drips onto my lips and sets them uncontrollably on fire.
I dive into that well and swim,

I bathe in it and drown,
choking and feverishly gulping air.
Oh, Ilayali!
When you finally return—I'll gather all of you piece by piece
and give back all that I have stolen.

3

Spiders weave an invisible lace,
catch the sun's rays, catch the silvery mist...
catch large butterflies of the night and subdue them...
catch dark rivers and spool translucent balls...
And then She comes, whom they don't expect,
and collects all this into a basket, giving dreams to the lovers...
She puts them at the head of a bed with a tuft of mist...
Oh, give me the mist, too, my Ilayali!
Give me a rose-colored dream with golden edges,
I will wrap myself with it right up to my eyes,
for this world is like a knife blade, sailing past the throat,
and shines in the glow of the moon.
Here I touch it with my hand—
it so gently evades me,
as if this is not a blade, but a fish or woman who lost her eyes...
"Why do you need this mist?
Your eyes are all mist, your heart is in a cold fog."
Then she whispers something mysterious and dear to me,
and I can't help being surprised at it—
for no one is eavesdropping on us.
Yet she shyly keeps whispering.

And the wind soothes the rustling of the leaves,
and the sky falls asleep,
and no longer flows above us.

4

I want to lock up my own self,
to rustle as rain, grass and butterflies and groves,
but your face, blossoming in the dark, still chastises my memory.
With your hair you've veiled the world that surrounds me
and the light of the moon cannot penetrate through.
How do I open these thickets full of unexpected mysteries
that just breathe into the heart with the lava of thirst and the pungent scent of night?
Every step of mine frightens colorful flocks of lizards,
countless crows tear upward and lock the sky in black rings.
Wolves and foxes with their eyes signal: do not approach - do not approach.
And I shut my eyes in vain—
your voice tears me out from my spring
and in empty rooms,
before you've changed beyond recognition, I look for you.
I open up all packages and boxes,
I nervously leaf through the surprised pages of dead books.
I am looking for you everywhere—even in the ashes of burnt poems.
Until everything in me falls apart, pleading for your appearance,
I do not find you.
Where were you that night when...

But you remember nothing,
though you were next to me, around me, in my very self.
And we exchanged dreams like birds exchange nests.
But when you departed, autumn was burning out in the pleats of your dress.
A daring leaf latched onto my sleeve—the only evidence that you were here.
My hands fly in pursuit of you,
From time to time they let me sense the warmth of your body.
I am sated by their touches to your hips.
I examine traces of distant kisses.
I dissolve them in water.
And drink every morning.

Danka read, going into some kind of uncontrollable trance, cutting herself off from everything that was around her, and her body swayed back and forth to the rhythm of the poetry, and a barely perceptible trembling ran through her thin, small fingers, whitened from emotion. Her voice sometimes cracked; she was swallowing saliva or air but kept reading without stopping and did not even glance at Yarosh. She was entirely immersed in the text from head to toe. Yarosh could not tear his eyes from her and felt like his body was being subdued by the rhythm of the poems that he knew well and was planning to translate. It would be a different translation, obviously drier, not as sensitive and penetrating; it seemed she was not reading a translation, but a text that she wrote herself, and she was addressing someone very specific, someone who was both far away and near, within hand's reach or in a distant dream. When she finished the reading, her voice went hoarse, she couldn't get enough air, and she already was whispering the last words, and then sighed. She didn't dare to look down at the professor, expecting his sharp criticism. Instead, she heard something quite different:

"Unbelievable! You've really boldly approached the translation," Yarosh said, climbing back onto the cliff. "In the original you cannot catch they rhythm, most likely there was none. And these pauses... these pauses are missing in the original too, but you somehow sensed them. I swear, I would have translated it as a continuous text. Just like any *Gilgamesh* or *Enkidu*. Lucilius from worlds beyond sends you his congratulations.

"Through you?" Danka laughed, shaking off from herself the petals of anxiety and fear.

"Assume it's through me," he was even short of breath because he had climbed up too quickly. "By the way, there is a certain mystical connection between translators and their dead authors. I repeatedly dreamed of Arcanumian poets, and sometimes they physically affected me. Especially Lucilius.

"Lucilius? But he's such a gentle creature...."

"However, I often felt his presence."

"Physically? How is that?"

"Well, first I'm translating, translating... then and I'll start doing something else. If it's just a few days, it's not a problem, but if it's more than a week—it starts getting to me, I'm afflicted with some kind of sores. Just as I undertake the translation—the sores suddenly disappear."

"You're kidding!"

"No! I've even quarreled with them. In all seriousness. I

stepped out on the balcony, turned up my head to the night sky and shouted out to them: "Leave me in peace already! I need to earn a living after all! I can't just work on you! "

"What did they say?"

"They solved it in their own way. Suddenly I got an honorarium for a certain article that was translated in the West. Or for a new edition of my textbook. And it's when there was no talk of this new edition earlier."

"Great! I'm happy for you. Maybe I'll be so lucky too. Hey Lucilius!" "She shouted toward the sky, bursting into laughter. "If you want me to translate you, make me an offer I can't refuse!"

Now they were both laughing and happy like little children, and yet on their way from Devil's Cliff back to the city, sorrow along with dusk began unnoticeably to envelop them from all sides, plunging them deep into thought and few words; they even were wary of looking each other in the eye. Danka for some reason put her glasses away in her handbag. Maintaining the conversation, Yarosh looked just at her lips, as if along with her eyeglasses she had removed her eyes. Besides, Danka herself gazed away to the side while a mass of unspoken words flew between them, their presence betrayed only by the fact that their lips repeatedly quietly trembled.

Q

September 2. Yosko, Wolff and I volunteered for the army. Yasko, who had the title of corporal and managed to undergo military training earlier, was taken to the front the day before. They reacted to Wolff with disbelief, but they signed us up and assigned us all to a detachment of the militia. For days they drilled us and taught us to shoot, but Yosko and I were awful marksmen; though Wolff could brag about shooting well. In the evening we returned home tired and hurriedly read the newspapers.

The daily newspapers continued to be published and kept up the illusion of a normal life, publishing sensational stories, and even all twenty-seven cinemas cheerfully advertised their repertoire. On September 8, Leah and I even went to the premiere of the English comedy *Old Wine* at the Opera House. Children were getting ready for the new school year, which now fell on Monday, September 11.

Every morning, from the first day of the war, a reconnaissance plane appeared over the city, circling at high altitude. It was the herald of another air raid. After a certain amount of time you could hear the roar of engines, and bombers dropped their load. The antiaircraft defense did all it could, several planes were shot down.

In all parts of the city ruins were smoking. Lychakiv Cemetery was strewn with bombs, especially at the pantheon of the Defenders of Lviv. The Germans persistently attacked districts with hospitals, looking for railway stations, industrial facilities and cafes, but the bombs did not always hit the target. Those meant for the railway station fell on Horodotska Street, destroying the St. Elzhbeta Polish Catholic Church and several buildings. Those meant to hit the Citadel destroyed a church on Copernicus St. and other buildings. In the ruins many women and children were killed. Fires blazed up, which initially the citizens of Lviv enthusiastically tried to put out, but then they gave up when there was nothing to put them out with. Black smoke crept all over the city, and the wind carried the unpleasant stench of something burnt badly.

September 9. There were long lines for bread and oil, flour and grains in grocery stores. The countryside was quiet at that time, markets were empty, the city was devoid of milk and vegetables.

September 10. The newspaper *Wiek Nowy*, notifying us of the surrender of Westerplatte, wrote that "this war is a fight for two very different concepts of Europe, the democratic and the imperialist, the latter of which came as a product of totalitarianism... The soldier-Pole stood shoulder to shoulder with the solder-Jew, and next to him the soldier-Ukrainian. All of them are united by the same idea and the same feeling: to defeat a common enemy."

Meanwhile, the Germans could arrive in Lviv any day. One thing then became clear: we must defend Lviv. The commanders who had ended up here by chance and had never worked in the headquarters, along with those who survived, reservists and police, had to defend it as well as we the militia who didn't have the slightest experience in soldiering. But Colonel Bolesław Fiałkowski quickly went to work, taking under his command two battalions of infantry, an air defense company and a battery of fifteen anti-tank guns. With these forces at the approaches to the city he was to build barricades and anti-tank trenches with the help of local people, and within the city, divided into separate sectors, not only did he have to build barricades but also to prepare stockpiles of ammunition, food and medicine.

September 11. Each sector received a sapper detachment and equipment. Yosko, Wolff and I were at the end of the Horodotska Street all night digging trenches and collecting everything that could be used for barricades. The mood was depressing, that day Lviv radio fell silent. After reading announcements about the end of the broadcasts, the announcer Celina Nahlik broke into spasmodic wailing, and now her wailing lingered in our ears.

Weary and sleepless, we sat in the trenches. It's good that our mothers didn't forget us and brought us food because the regular army didn't share their food with us, and thus many of those who volunteered to build barricades took to their heels. They were ordinary townspeople. On the other hand, the hoodlums didn't let us down. They came from Zamarstyniv, from Klepariv, Lychakiv, Levandivka and brought shovels and pickaxes, and demonstrated the wonders of ingenuity when it was necessary to get some piece of iron, which later they used along with wire to construct and arrange hedgehog barricades[92] on the road. For them everything seemed romantic, in the evenings they visited gardens, bringing back potatoes, cabbage, and sometimes even chickens, singing loudly as they prepared dinner.

The only joy that day was that Yas appeared and joined us. He had black eyes and a torn sleeve; fortunately, a bullet just grazed him. His regiment had been defeated.

"How can it be," Yosko shakes his head, "we heard the Polish army was invincible... We've heard cheerful songs

92 Defensive fortifications against tanks and infantry, which are also called double apron fences.

about it... And suddenly we learn that it's not ready to take a stand against the Germans...."

"No, no," Yas raised an objection. "In spirit and heart, it's ready, I can talk for hours about instances of heroism... But our weapons and equipment are obsolete... Go on attack on horseback? Is that heroism or folly? I think both at the same time. It wasn't nonsense for those who attacked. But it was nonsense for those who gave such an order. And now... Now, in truth, the defense of Lviv is useless."

"Why do you think so?," we are surprised.

"General Schilling's army retreated from Krakow to the northeast. General Sosnkowski's[93] troop no longer exists. The defense, which they tried to organize on the Dniester River, has been liquidated. Lviv is left alone with the enemy.

He was saying this so quietly so that no one else could heard, but one of the hooligans, apparently, caught the last phrase and shouted:

"What kind of jawing is that? How is it we're on our own? Are you knocked in your noggin? The Polish army on bicycles is still powerful as hell! And we'll give them Germans such a whacking they'll shit in their pants!" Right, guys?"

"For sure! Be good with us and don't worry 'bout nothin'!" His pals shout but don't bother us anymore.

In the afternoon we heard the roar of engines, everyone grew tense, even the hoodlums jumped up on their feet, only to hear:

"Lookout, Misko! God damn it, it's coming!"

"Why are you such chickens? Don't pay no attention!"

93 General Kazimierz Sosnkowski (1885-1969), who was also an intellectual and diplomat.

"Don't be such a nervous Nelly!" Hold 'er steady!"

"Gimme some swagger, you snot-nose! Watch out—don't shit in your pants!"

This is the way they cheered themselves up, but the roar in the meantime continues to grow. The Germans are approaching. We lie down behind the barricades, and right from around the bend two motorcycles suddenly jump out, and behind them next is an armored car. Just when they reached one of the barricades, the command echoes out "Fire!"—once, then a second, then a third time. I don't know if my or Yosko's rifle hit the mark, but a motorcycle got tossed up all the way onto the barricade. On the road two motorcycles and a smashed armored car were left, and when in a minute a tank crawled out, it was aimed at so neatly that it blocked the road with its helpless body.

"Mommie dearest! God damn it, what a big whiner!" A hooligan smacked his lips, nodding toward the tank.

"Now do you see, you dunderhead, this ain't no game? You's wanted something new! You got it!"

"And where's did I think they'd be shootin' at people like this? I thought they'd be nice guys! I'll's give it to 'em—then they's give it back to me, I'll stick 'em first with a shank—then he sticks me with a shank, then it's over. Likes decent people. Right? And he, look at him, went completely bonkers! May his knickers get tied up in a knot!"

But this was only the beginning. Armored vehicles drive up one after another, the infantry jumps out, scatters and hides between walls in order to move forward again from house to house, circling around dangerous places, disappearing in gardens and gates and hitting our guns with their heavy weapons.

"Watch out from the corner!" Indeed, from around the corner an automatic round pierces our barricade. Poor Lieutenant Panek sends shot after shot with his two cannons, but one cannoneer falls, then the other. Within an hour the majority of the cannon gun squad was wiped out, the cannons grow silent, but just for a minute, because others stand up to take the place of the dead. Yosko and I rush to lift up shells. Wolff and Yas shoot their carbines, nestled in a narrow gap in the barricade, from which they can clearly see the attackers, but themselves are safe.

Later on, they'll say that we stood at the fork on Horodotska Street to the death. Although there were no reinforcements, the Germans couldn't break through this thin defensive line because they didn't expect to encounter such fierce resistance on the outskirts of the city; that was what forced them to begin the siege. I don't know if we could hold out for at least another hour if not for the fact that reserve units of the Government Police and Polish infantry units arrived toward evening. The Germans were forced to retreat. But only from here on Horodotska Street, because at that time they surrounded the city from the north and south, as if they depended on taking Lviv as soon as possible.

At night the battle quieted down. Although the machine guns still rattled, we managed to doze for a few hours.

September 13. The enemy struck with renewed strength—from November 29 Street and from Stryisky Street, vigorous battles heated up for Kortum Hill in the northwest of the city. The Germans took the mountain that morning.

Meanwhile, Lviv's inhabitants rushed with a certain doomed despair and uncommon zeal in their eyes to barricade off all the streets without any plan, guided only by the desire to protect the city at any cost. Finally, the city government had to intervene in this patriotic chaos and through the press request people restrain themselves, because such things are not done amateurishly, but only under the supervision of professional military engineers. But that didn't stop anyone. The citizens dragged old cars, broken tables, tubs and bathtubs with holes in them, ladders, beams, doors; they even dragged out their own furniture from their homes, felled trees, pushed heavy carts in front of them, on which there were bags with sand and crushed stone. They took off sewer manholes and hid them, and they camouflaged the sewer vaults so the enemy would fall in them. Even Mr. Knoflyk drove in on a large ladderlike cart and donated four coffins, into which he advised that cobblestones be taken up from the street and placed one on top of another. He looked cheerful and fresh, but I didn't have the time to ask him how he was doing. Meanwhile the entire city was constantly bombarded both by air and by artillery. Hydraulic pumps and the electric station were damaged, and fires burst out. Not only military personnel but civilians were also killed.

September 16. There are many veterans and reservists ready to defend Lviv, but there's not enough ammunition. Wolff and Yas managed to break through at night with several trucks to Holosko to warehouses and brought back weapons. In the Zhovkva suburb an entire squad of delinquents was killed defending the fork in the road; another group of hoodlums found an old Austrian cannon somewhere and fired it until it exploded and crippled them. The entire Zhovkva district gathered for the funeral and made a common grave for them.

Who knows whether that zeal to defend would have been maintained if it had not been strengthened by the newspapers, which though limited in size to two pages, nevertheless spread illusory hopes, either heard from someone, or invented. All the same, the inhabitants greedily gobbled up the cheerful news and passed it along by word of mouth.

"What is this nonsense?" Yas wondered. "It's a complete lie. 'French troops are occupying key strategic positions on the German side, and are even bombarding Berlin,'" he quoted, still cursing. "French and British pilots destroy the German military industry... The French army is constantly moving forward. According to an announcement from the French headquarters, their army has penetrated deep into German territory. Yesterday a series of new points were occupied where fortifications were immediately established. The French press in its comments stresses that the steps taken so far do not yet have an offensive character, but more definitely are intelligence-gathering. The command of the French army is striving to become acquainted with the terrain and methods of the German army, after which the real attack of combined French and British forces will come."

"Do you think all this is a lie?" Yosko asked with concern in his voice.

"My mom listens to London," Yas switched to a whisper, because he knew that everyone was supposed to turn in their radio, and there were rumors that some people were shot for having a receiver in their possession. "On the western front nothing is happening. We are doomed. The French and the British are waiting it out. And look what they're writing here... It's as if the Germans have evacuated the population of their cities before the attack of the allies. They describe dramatic scenes of evacuation: 'Residents are not allowed even to bring suitcases. The army is driving them forward in a brutal way. Among the refugees, hunger and disease abound... This caused anti-Hitler demonstrations.' You really want to go back and smash that editor's face."

"But maybe this is a tactic," Wolff shrugged his shoulders. "To encourage us. So that we don't lose heart."

"And so that everyone lies down here, screw it," I sighed.

"If they thought about what to do to keep from spreading panic, they would not have passed out gas masks to the soldiers. Not a single gas bomb fell yet, but they are walking through the city with masks tied to their belts, and everyone sees it. Civilians don't have gas masks. Is this normal?"

Every day the German radio calls for surrender. A German plane scatters leaflets: "Soldiers! Stop your aimless struggle! Don't waste your blood and your sacrifices for the British capitalists! You are surrounded on all sides! Surrender! This is your only salvation! Put down your weapons!"

18

Yarosh recalled that he had already read about the heroic defense of Lviv against German troops, and that the Germans were unable to capture it. A ten-day defense of the city is not that long, but this period of time was entirely enough for whole countries to fall. It took Germans five days to capture Holland, and another five to capture Belgium and France, and seven days to break the resistance in Yugoslavia. In four days the Germans reached the Polish-Soviet border in northern Poland. In ten days in the summer of 1941, they took all of Western Ukraine, and in another ten—reached the banks of the Dnipro River.

But they failed to capture Lviv in ten days. Lviv stubbornly defended itself and would have continued to defend itself, if not for the unexpected allies who came from the East to help the Germans.

R

September 17. In the morning, we learned about the arrival of Soviet troops in the eastern part of Poland. General Langner[94] received an order from the Chief Commander to fight only against the Germans, and to open fire against the Red Army only in cases of clear self-defense. Now despair was creeping into my soul, despair and uncertainty.

September 18. Newspapers reported the arrival of the Red Army in Poland. There was no sensation, because yesterday radio news from Moscow heralded it. Newspapers continue to maintain calm, assuring us that this fact should not give cause for concern. The *Dziennik Polski* newspaper responded to German flyers that were addressed to Ukrainians with their own desperate appeal: "The Germans are spending much effort trying to bring two fraternal nations into battle with each other—the Ukrainians and Poles. We caution you Ukrainians before the new machinations of the Teutons, the eternal enemies of the Slavic tribe.

Every day along with the bombs that sow death and ruin, they scatter leaflets with which they incite you against the Polish army. Ukrainians! Germans are bombing and robbing our and your villages, farms and estates. They are killing our and your women and children, destroying Polish Catholic churches and your churches. Let us take revenge together for common injustices, let us fight side by side."

While the Russians are still far away, the Germans try to take the city at all costs by using appeals and threats. In

94 Polish general Władysław Langner (June 18, 1896 - September 28, 1972).

their last ultimatum they state that if by noon of the 19th Lviv does not surrender, it will be stormed and destroyed. But our people paid no attention and attacked Tsetneriv-ka and Pohulyanka with two battalions and beat back the Germans to Sykhiv and dislodged them from the village of Zboiska.

September 19. Bolshevik planes also dropped a leaflet:

"Soldiers! In recent days, the Polish army has been completely vanquished. Soldiers of the cities of Ternopil, Halych, Rivne, and Dubno numbering more than six thousand have voluntarily switched to our side. Soldiers, why and with whom are you fighting? Why risk your life? Your resistance is useless. The officers are herding you to senseless carnage. They hate you and your families. They were the ones who executed the representatives you sent with a proposal to surrender. Do not believe your officers. Officers and generals are your enemies. They want you to die!

Soldiers! Kill your officers and generals! Do not listen to the orders of your officers. Chase them out of your land. Come boldly to us, your brothers, to the Red Army. Here you will find sympathy and care.

Remember, only the Red Army will deliver the Polish people from this unfortunate war, and you will have the opportunity to start a new life.

Commander S. Tymoshenko. Ukrainian front."

"Oh, rejoice," Yas laughs to me. "Your Ukrainian army is approaching."

"It's as much mine as it's yours," I snap back.

The *Dziennik Polski* newspaper describes the French press's indignation about Soviet aggression and the indefatigable newspaper *Wiek Nowy* tossed in another sedative pill:

"The Polish army goes on the offensive... Italy, Yugoslavia, Hungary, and Romania have declared war on Germany." The city greedily swallows any encouraging information. The Lviv newspapers resemble the legendary orchestra that never stopped playing cheerful tunes to the last seconds on the Titanic.

Overnight from September 18-19, advance units of the Soviet motorized army and tanks approached the Lychakiv fork from the direction of Vynnyky. Lviv was ready to go to war on both fronts. The eastern border of the city was feverishly strengthened to counter any Soviet attempt to break into the city. Meanwhile the Germans approached from the south toward Vynnyky. After some time both armies stop, as if gathering strength before a raging strike. Anxiety and uncertainty grow in the air.

Yas reported another disappointing bit of news: General Langner, assuming that Lviv soon would be tightly encircled, said all that was left for the army to do would be to make its way to Hungary.

"But how can that be arranged?" Yas lamented. "We can't do this in a day, we need to prepare everything, and then the next night we can break through."

"For you," Wolff said. "But how about us?"

"Just disperse to your homes. There's no threat to civilians."

"Why don't you do the same thing?" Yosko asked, washing away black oil and gasoline from his long fingers.

"I'm not a deserter. I'll go with everyone."

"You won't get very far," I said. "You're all on foot, and they have tons of vehicles and aircraft. Even today, the Soviets are flying over the city."

September 19. In the morning Yas announced to us that Bolshevik officers arrived at the Lychakivska Street junction and offered to negotiate with the leaders of the Polish army, and he was supposed to drive the car, in which General Langner, Colonels Rakowski and Ryzinski, whom we call Lynx, would go.

"We're driving to Vynnyky," Yas told us later. "We pass countless armored vehicles and an awful mass of Russian soldiers. They look at us like wolves. Fuming evil eyes and angular jaws, as if hewn from a block. Outside of Vynnyky we meet a group of their officers. A pot-bellied guy in a tank driver's helmet meets us. Colonel Ivanov. And Colonel Rakowski asks him: "Why did you come?" He was stunned: "What—don't you read the newspapers?"—"No, we haven't read the newspapers because the city is surrounded, and they don't get to us."—"So maybe you've listened to the radio?" He's been hinting in such a roundabout way at Molotov's speech that we, of course, heard and read their leaflets about a liberation campaign, but our guys answered, "No, the radio isn't working because German bombs smashed the electric station. We know nothin'. So why did you come?" And here Colonel Ivanov says—you won't believe it: "We came here to beat back the Germans. We'll be fighting against them with you." To this Colonel Rakowski said: "Super! Now we'll show you a map of the locations of the Germans and how best it would be to hit them."—"But we would like to enter the city."—"That's impossible. We are not authorized to approve that. After all, this is needless. There's no room in the city to house such a quantity of people and technology. Throughout there are barricades, there's no water. And the Germans are all around. They're not in the city." In short, the conversation ended here.

Then a strange game began with both armies trying to get into the city. Both sides are shooting. The German bombs fall in the city center, and the Soviet anti-aircraft guns fire on German aircraft.

September 20. Late in the evening two Soviet tanks suddenly strike the barricades on Lychakivska Street and began to shoot at buildings. Window panes began quivering, screams reverberated, then they moved at the barricades and crushed them like nuts, turned around and went back. This greatly disturbed us, because it turned out that our hastily erected barricades were worthless, but the purpose of that demonstration was unknown.

And that evening, the *Ilustrowany Goniec Wieczorny* did not bring us any joyful news of a Franco-British offensive on the Western Front or that America had sent an ultimatum to Germany, nothing of the sort, just the wish: "May disappointment and despair not clip your wings."

September 21. On Thursday, the last issues of the Lviv newspapers appeared. "The army has decided to continue to defend Lviv," they wrote. At five in the afternoon during negotiations with Langner the Bolsheviks promised to allow the Polish army safe passage to Romania, provided that the general would sign the surrender order, and the army would come out with their weapons and discard them at an appointed place. But the general, stressing that he was surrendering the city to the Russians only because they are Slavs, would not agree:

"No, the army will not discard its weapons at your feet but will leave them where they are. I will come here without weapons."

It's true, the army will be divided—senior officers will leave by car, junior officers will walk along Lychakivska

Street and will then turn toward Sykhiv to go to Romania, and enlisted men—another way. The Russians are in a hurry and quickly agree to the proposals of the Polish command.

September 22. It was a black day for the city. The Bolsheviks entered the city in the afternoon. After the regular troops entered, the gallant boys of the NKVD followed behind them.

19

The next day he received a phone call from the SBU Ukrainian Security Service. He was incredibly surprised because the KGB used to call him in to see them by phone. They never sent him any announcements or left any traces of their presence. Even when he didn't have a phone, the military commissariat used to call him in with a hand-delivered notice. This time, too, they called and suggested a meeting, but he said he no longer accepts invitations over the phone, so let them invite him in writing. The male voice at the other end of the line was at first surprised and then chided him for being capricious this time when earlier he would come when called by phone.

"When before?" Yarosh asked. "When the KGB called? So, have you adopted their methods?"

He hung up. The call coincided with the fact that a few days before Kurkov had called and announced he would be in Lviv because he was writing a novel about the city and would like to meet up with him, and during their meeting reported on his conversation with the secret service agent on the plane. Yarosh was already prepared for what awaited him and decided not to give in—he would have no informal meetings. But several days later he was summoned by the chair of his department who began to explain the difficult situation, because he was getting pressure from above. While saying those words, he reverently looked up at the ceiling. The SBU has influence when they want something, in the end we're talking about an ordinary conversation, perhaps even a consultation, confidential, a notice here would only get in the way. The department Chair held out a paper to Yarosh, the room number was written, the date and time when he should... no-no, in no case he should... when they ask him to come ... Yarosh took the piece of paper, put it away in his pocket, and he fumed from impotent rage. The department Chair's face was frightened and imploring, his little eyes darted, his fingers trembled. It was evident he was above all fearful of rejection or of any rash action such as, say, ripping up the paper and throwing it into the trash.

Yarosh acquiesced and the next day at the appointed time went to a small classroom where training workshops were held and there were no lectures. From behind the desk a small lively man of Yarosh's age rose up. As all people of diminutive stature, he made rapid movements, leaning his entire body, and held out his hand for a handshake, calling himself Lieutenant Colonel Knysh. Yarosh could hardly resist asking whether in the era of the KGB, was he still Knysh or was it Knyshov? Something in the appearance of the SBU guy made him feel wary. He had seen him somewhere, but he couldn't remember where. Besides, he also looked at Yarosh as if expecting something like "Well, hello there! Long time no see!" They sat on either side of the desk, and the lieutenant colonel began to ask familiar questions about his life, about his scholarly achievements, and his future plans. Yarosh was one tough customer and immediately cut off this prelude, asking him to get the point. Knysh frowned and became serious, as if he were about to tell Yarosh about the death of someone from his family:

"Well, okay ... We're interested in your studies of Arcanum. We believe you've already done a lot on the subject: a textbook, a dictionary, you're preparing an anthology of literature... but your digging deeply into the Arcanumian so-called *Book of Death* will not add anything either to scholarship or literature. But for us... for the SBU security services, it may have value... So, I would like to offer you a stipend, which we will give you during the duration of your study on the subject.

"I don't understand," Yarosh reacted in surprise. "I work on this even without a stipend."

"Of course. But other things distract you. You don't completely devote yourself to the "BoD." Can I call it that—'BoD'?"

"You can call it whatever you like."

"Great. We'd like to help you and monitor all your research. That is, in simple terms, to guard it. Since it's a strategic issue. You know, we wouldn't want such a discovery... in fact, I have in mind immortality... such a discovery to fall into the hands of our enemies.... After all, you do realize that sooner or later other intelligence agencies will take an interest in you. We want to protect you from any unforeseen excesses. On our part we are ready to help you too. In particular, we can introduce Kalkbrenner's treatise to you. You've probably heard of it? Yes-yes, don't be surprised, we have it... While I understand this is not the original source on which you are currently working, but still...."

"You see, I'm examining the literature and looking at the *Book of Death*...."

"Pardon me, but would you please call it 'BoD'?" The SBU guy began to fuss. "Do me a favor."

"It's like this, I look at the *Book* only as a literary work. I'm not interested in how to apply it in practice."

"And you are right. The practical side of the matter lies with us. But in light of this, I would like to ask you, how do you explain the phrase from "BoD" that different signs are given to us.... And this has gone on for centuries... from the beginning of creation... However, we do not accept these signs, we don't notice them, don't react to them... And then, I copied out: 'We sometimes speak with the animals who live with us, but never talk to birds, fish, snakes, bees, butterflies, flowers, trees... Yet the gods send us their messages through all that is living and all that is inanimate, through the mediation of water, fire and stones; they give us signals through the stars and clouds, the rain and wind, the thunder and lightning... Open your eyes and look closely, open your ears and listen attentively, open your heart and absorb it, open your souls and exalt. Everywhere you look, I tell you, everywhere, are the messages of our gods.' "That's the way it is in Kalkbrenner. How is it in the original... in 'BoD'?"

"Right after the sentence that we do not speak with other animals are the words: "Learn to love them the same way as those around you, then they will reveal their secrets and will illuminate you and show you the way. Let us be prepared for their signs so we can meet under the shadow where poppies bloom."

"Ah, yes-yes... It's true, though not entirely. Excuse me, I have been cunning here and intentionally skipped these lines... in Kalkbrenner it's a little different: 'in the shadow of poppies.' What does that all mean? How do you interpret this... ummm... advice? About which signs? And how you can meet in the shadow of poppies?"

"It seems to me it's similar to a charm. In general, in charms there are many poetic metaphors and symbols. As for the poppies, they are a symbol of dreams. We don't know what kind of poppies grew in Arcanum—maybe even giant ones. But the mention of poppies is quite natural; sleep and death always have been closely intertwined in folklore."

At that moment Yarosh remembered the poppies that he saw at Milker's, the poppies with which Milker spoke... the poppies, which cast a shadow... and the poppies—hash-hash—in the Book of Iblis... Is there a connection here? Knysh interrupted his thoughts:

"But here we're talking about signs, that upon recognition enable a person to acquire the ability to gain knowledge from previous lives and the confidence that he can live more than just one life. We are just not given that ability to read these signs, because as it is written in Kalkbrenner, "your eyes are closed, and hearts are closed." Therefore, you know that the Austrian created his music with that aim of facilitating the recognition of those signs. Those who work for us already deciphered these notes and even staged a small concert for the insane in the Kulpark. We decided to experiment on patients in the hope that they would become sane again, after remembering previous lives,... However, the results were deficient. More precisely, there were none. It's true, a woman suddenly began speaking Spanish, in an Asturian dialect in fact. It lasted only a few minutes. We managed to record it on tape to listen to later. Here, I'll turn it on for you."

The lieutenant colonel pressed the button on the recorder. At first the sounds of the tango echoed and went on for three or so minutes. Then you could hear a short scream and someone sobbing. It grew, becoming louder until it turned into a woman's hysterical scream, in which one could perceive fear and despair. The woman screamed frantically like a wounded animal. Something fell, banged against the floor, began to clap, to stamp; words broke through the unintelligible sounds of desperate sobbing. There were few of them, but they were repeated over and over: 'amapolas en la sombra ... amapolas en la sombra ... amapolas en la sombra ...'—some twenty times until she began weeping spasmodically, then sobbing and moaning. The voice recorder turned off.

"Do you know what these words mean?" Knysh asked.

"Sombra is a shadow, from which the word "sombrero" comes...."

"Great. And together it will be 'in the shadow of poppies'!!!" Knysh could not conceal his joy from the fact that his words triggered surprise in the professor. "So, you see, we've actually made one step. However, it has not led anywhere. Kalkbrenner writes that when a person has not heard this melody right before his death, it never will affect him in his next life. Maybe just that woman had heard it... most likely not quite in its entirety... but the poppies... poppies... How else would she know about the poppies' shadow?... One more thing. The music that we deciphered is incredibly similar to a certain tango." Here he looked into Yarosh's eyes, expecting to catch some of his reaction, but the professor was lost in his own thoughts. A shadow of discontent flashed across Knysh's face, but only for a moment. "You probably also have recognized the melody... The so-called 'Tango of Death.' It was played in the Yaniv concentration camp when prisoners were being taken to be executed by firing squad. There are several variants of the lyrics... In one of them, interestingly, there is this strophe:

And if when I am no longer with you,
sands will cover bodies,
we will meet where the poppies flow

like a river, where their shadow has lain down.

So as not to betray his surprise once again, Yarosh took off his eyeglasses and began to wipe them with a handkerchief, pretending that this was of little interest to him. Knysh squinted at him and waited. He knew how to wait like a fox hiding in the bushes. His eyes, ears and nostrils were ready. It seemed as if he were even listening to Yarosh's pulse, his heartbeat and his blood flow.

"The mention of the sands, by the way, is not accidental, because the prisoners were shot right in the village of Pisky[95] in Lysynetsky Forest. So, between you and me...," Knysh mumbled while lighting a cigarette, "... it was a coincidence that I was in Istanbul the same time as you." Yarosh smiled, how trite and uninteresting all this was. "In the very same library. Well, and I overheard something... I am wondering what you found out when you examined the Book of Iblis."

"Nothing new."

"You can't imagine how sad I am. I'm not kidding. I'm immensely sad. It seems like all the sorrows of the world have collapsed on me. I'm just stifled by them. I fall down under their burden. And here's what's strange—no one wants to help me." Suddenly he stood up and said while extending his hand: "Well, okay. For the time being our conversation is over. Here are my phone numbers. When you finish your work on "BoD," I ask that you let me know. I do not recommend publishing the translation without our consent. Are we agreed on that?" Yarosh nodded. "That's good. We may still have questions, so don't be angry. And if you manage to clarify something about these poppies, give me a call. May-

95 A village outside of Lviv whose name means "sands."

be all of this is just some fantasy, a fairytale for fools, but maybe not. Good luck."

And when Yarosh had begun moving to the door, Knysh suddenly blurted out:

"Did you really not recognize me?"

Yarosh shrugged his shoulders in surprise. Something about Knysh was familiar, but it was lost to him.

"Well, never mind," Knysh nodded his head. "That's our kind of work—to remember every face." Then he suddenly blurted out: "How is our sweet Nadya doing?"

Yarosh was stunned, turned around, and only then recognized Knysh as the male friend, who seduced Nadya at Rusya's birthday.

"They say she's a well-known writer now?" Knysh grinned, suddenly softening and throwing off the mask of a tough law enforcement guy. "I really haven't read her works, but wanted to ask you had come across a modest SBU[96] agent among any of her characters?"

Yarosh laughed:

"That's what worries you? That's really pleasant. Then someday you could show your grandchildren—here, look what's been written about your grandpop."

"Heh-heh, well, you know... Since then I've climbed up the career ladder a bit... I wouldn't want my superiors find out."

"What exactly?" Yarosh pretended that he doesn't understand anything.

"Well, how can I... We ah... What do you mean, you don't know anything about it?"

"What am I supposed to know?"

96 The Security Service of Ukraine.

Knysh rocked on his heels, scratched his nose and said:

"Well no, nothing special. Simply, if you have contact with her, I'd ask... how shall I say it... They say, she is too candid in her works... Although she doesn't mention real names... but you can figure it out... Do you understand? Among us some people do read books. Of course. That is, I wanted to say, it's job-related... Such is our work... They read, take notes, catalog, slice and dice... It's impossible that you don't know what happened then... At Rusya's birthday... I'd like to apologize to you if I've caused you any unpleasantness, but circumstances have been such ... Do you want me to be totally honest with you?"

"Well, try."

"Right now, we're resolving something way more important. That's why I have to explain that we had a mission back then. At any cost to break up your relationship."

"I don't understand. Why?"

"I was small fry back then. They ordered—I complied. Thus, we've also involuntarily become 'milk brothers.'"

Yarosh flinched from the phrase. There's no way that they could be "brothers in milk!" That's what they say when the same girl performs oral sex on different men, but to become "a milk brother" with a KGB guy?

"Are you saying that Rusya wasn't the one who planned it all?"

"No. It was our job. As you know, Nadya was planning on going to Germany to work. And if everything worked out between you and her, she might not have gone. Right?... But we really needed her there. But what function she performed there, I don't know. I was like the Moor, I just did my job... By the way, didn't you recognize the voice of the woman who shouted out in Spanish?"

"Why, was I supposed to recognize her?"

"You know her well. It was Rusya."

Yarosh wiped the cold sweat from his forehead. Everything fit into some wild phantasmagoric picture.

"What happened to her?"

"Another unhappy love affair. A new attempt at suicide. She swallowed some pills. But this time with irreversible consequences."

"Wait... My colleague who used to date her and who convinced me to come to her birthday... That's your colleague?"

"Everything in the world is closely intertwined. He was also completing his mission."

"And it's because of him Rusya poisoned herself?"

"You have to agree, it could have been anyone in his place. Some people are doomed to suicide. Do you know the statistics? Today a third of suicides have already had a dress rehearsal and are on the eve of their premiere. But let's not talk about sad things. Goodbye.

S

The stunned warriors put down their weapons, despair clenches their throats, some can't stand it and wipe away their tears, and some have tears streaming down their faces. We are no exception. Hugging Yas, we cry, and our mothers, saying goodbye to him, loudly cry and bless him with a sign of the cross. Then as part of a long column of officers, he slowly moves along Lychakivska Street. On both sides, there are throngs of foreign soldiers—pushing the officers, taking away their weapons and swearing. And somewhere far off shots and bursts of individual cannon salvoes rattle off because not everyone has agreed to surrender. Separate groups of dedicated fighters keep defending themselves, preferring to die here than who knows where.

Soon we receive news that the convoy officers at the barriers on Lychakivska Street were surrounded by NKVD agents and escorted away as prisoners and not allowed to go off to Romania as had been agreed upon. What can that mean? When the news comes from the head of the column that they are being taken to Vynnyky, individual soldiers try to escape and mix in among the crowds of people standing on the sidewalks, who with sadness were watching their retreat.

The Bolsheviks entered Lviv on the right-hand side of the sidewalk. They looked really wild, as if they had come out of an underground cave in their dun-colored long overcoats, tunics down to their knees and really wide breeches that swept back and forth as they walked, tarpaulin boots from which dirty gray footcloths peered out and rifles on ropes.

Pointy "Budenovka hats"[97] with red stars would have made these men into a caricature of an army except for their military equipment, their tanks and cannons, of which the Polish army could not boast. What surprised the Lviv residents the most were the liberators' faces: very few of them were European. The majority had high-cheekboned, wind-worn, emaciated, and evil miens; caution and distrust shone in their eyes. At first, they even twitched and exhibited hostility, setting out their bayonets in front of them when ecstatic Jewish youths rushed toward them with flowers, trying to shake hands and kiss them. Some kissed the tanks and happily shouted: "Long live Stalin," "Long live the Soviet Union," "Long live Soviet Ukraine!" Although a few days before that, on September 5, they were shouting "Long live England!" in front of the British Consulate on Niedzialkowska Street. Mr. consul even went to the balcony and wanted to make an announcement, but suddenly German planes began to roar, and everyone fled. Elderly Jews also joined the young people and also screamed, waved their hats and handkerchiefs, not even suspecting that for one joyful meeting with their liberators, they would be mercilessly beaten on the streets of Lviv, accused of all manner of mortal sins and of this one too.

The disarmed Polish army left the city along the left sidewalk. Waving yellowish handkerchiefs, single soldiers and small groups streamed out of alleys and gates and joined this dismal procession.

Having learned that they had led the officers toward Vynnyky, we quickly gathered up civilian clothes for Yasko

---

97 Pointed caps worn by members of the Red Army. For a picture of one see: https://en.wikipedia.org/wiki/Budenovka.

and started to run along Lychakivska Street. Up the street we caught up with Lucia, who was rushing somewhere with a package under her arm.

"Hello, guys! Where are you rushing so fast?"

"We're looking for Yasko. He must be somewhere in the column."

"Come with me, maybe he's in the Polish church!" She pointed at the Basilica of Our Lady of Mercy with its high spire. "The officers are changing into civilian clothing there. You see—I'm also carrying things for them that I gathered up from neighbors. Have you heard? In Sykhiv the Russians surrounded the police officers from Lviv who were trying to get out to Romania and shot everyone on the spot. They're arresting all civil servants, and the police are shot immediately. Nothing good is waiting for the officers either."

In the Polish church we saw a crowd of soldiers who had hastily changed into what their wives and children had brought. Monks quickly raked up the uniforms, belts and boots off the floor and carried them off somewhere, urging the soldiers to finish changing their clothes quickly and to leave the building.

"Who else needs a suit! Who needs a suit!" Lucia shouted, and hands from every direction stretched out to her and instantly snapped up everything that she had brought.

"Has anyone seen Yasko Bilyevich?" We asked, pushing through the throng, but no one could tell us anything except for the fact that the tail of the officers' column could be seen on upper Lychakivska Street a few minutes ago. Finally, Lucia dragged over a man by the hand who said he had been with Yasko in the column of officers.

"When we learned that the column was not allowed to pass to Sykhiv but instead was being led to the east, some people began to take off. Five of us also agreed to run. After we passed the School of St. Anthony, we rushed to the gate all together, but the guard noticed and shot his gun. I heard Yasko call out; they probably wounded him. However, I didn't see him after that."

"Where are they taking them?"

"I heard they were taken to Ternopil. They're supposed to release everyone there, but that's unlikely. They'll stop overnight in the lowlands outside of Vynnyky. We should be able to sneak up to them there."

We said goodbye to Lucia and rushed to Vynnyky. We went off the road into the woods so the Red Army guys, who were moving in a really long column, wouldn't catch sight of us; we could even run along the well-trampled paths that sportsmen have been using for a long time. Suddenly the tapping of rapid fire reached our ears; it was somewhere ahead of us. It was far enough away and didn't last long. No one was surprised by the shooting. Shots were heard all the time both in the city and outside of it, so we continued to run without stopping. The road was still jammed up by the Bolsheviks and their military equipment; it seemed there would be no end to them. Then suddenly we heard moaning and the sharp scent of fresh blood, a scent that only recently permeated the air and has not had time to putrefy and turn into a stench; right now it was striking and could not be overcome. We looked around but didn't see anything; the forest surrounded us. There were fresh traces of bullets on the trees and the grass was covered in white chips of wood.

"Look—over there!" Yosko shouted and pointed toward a clearing where hikers often had picnics before climbing the Devil's Mountain. There was something there, the scent of blood and moaning came from there. We rushed in that direction and saw a mountain of corpses carelessly covered over with branches. The executed Lviv police lay there in their garnet-colored uniforms but without weapons along with teenage boys and adult men, and moaning could be heard from under this mountain of corpses. We ran up to the pile, pulled off several bodies and freed a boy, still too young to grow a mustache, who had been shot in the shoulder. Wolff checked him out and said,

"It didn't strike the bones, it shot through. The wound isn't bleeding. Can you walk?"

"I think I can," the boy nodded, looking at us with hope. Looking him over more closely, I recognized him as the guy who took me for questioning to Kaidan and who brought in the witnesses."

"You don't recognize me?" I asked.

"No," the boy replied, but fear flashed in his eyes.

"Don't be afraid," I said, pointing to the executed police, and asked: "Is Kaidan among them?"

"No. I don't know where he disappeared. What will you do to me?"

"Nothing. Yosko, take him back when you reach Lychakivska Street, leave him in the bushes, scamper over to the church and ask the monks for civilian clothes and take them to him. Maybe you'll still find Lucia there, she'll help you. Just go through the woods so they don't see you. Wolff and I will run farther."

We caught up to the tail of the officers' procession just before Vynnyky but didn't approach it. We followed them until they led all of the prisoners out beyond the village and ordered them to set up camp in the pastures. It was already getting dark, the camp guards set themselves up around the camp at a certain distance from one another and took a smoking break. Some of them fell exhausted on the grass and began to eat. The guard was not too vigilant, and that encouraged us. The prisoners broke up into small groups and pulled out food from their bags. Villagers approached them, asked something, the guards didn't chase them away, and soon villagers began to bring the soldiers water, milk, bread, apples—whatever they happened to have.

"What do you think," I asked Wolff. "Do we look like villagers?"

Wolff laughed, stroking his face, "We're pretty stubbly."

"We can try."

We stopped an old guy who was carrying a basket of potatoes and under his armpit a ripe yellow pumpkin and offered to help him. I took the other end of the basket and Wolff took the pumpkin. We stuck Yasko's clothes under the fronts of our shirts.

"What are they gonna do with the pumpkin?" I asked.

"Don't ya know what?" The old guy was sincerely surprised. "Bake it. The same delicious taste. Ya ain't ever had it?"

"No. But I'll try it for sure."

"You aren't from here."

"Nope. We're looking for our buddy."

"You want to get clothes to him?"

"How do you know?"

"One guy comes to me that he's going to make a run for it." Then in a whisper he added: "I got old breeches and a shirt in the pumpkin."

"Really delicious," we started laughing.

The guard just took a quick glance at us and let us pass, and we immediately started asking about Yasko. The officers were quite amused by our pumpkin. Jokes and advice on what to do with it came from every direction; someone even offered to cut it in half, scrape out the inside and use as a nighttime chamber pot, but Lieutenant Hrytsiuk, who was with us on Horodotska Street, said he knows how to cook pumpkin and will not allow anyone to make fun of it, and then brought us to Yasko. On the way I told him the terrible pumpkin secret, and he whistled: "Wow! We'll have to play cards for the clothes." Yas was sitting by the fire with a bandaged left arm. On seeing us he was incredibly happy and surprised. I explained to him:

"We brought you clothes. Quickly get changed. They can't see you here behind the flames."

Wolff took a knife and ripped open Yas's uniform and freed up his arm. We helped him pull off his pants and boots, though he didn't want to leave his boots behind.

"You dummy," I said. "Do you know the saying: you can tell a bird by its flight? They'll figure out who you are quickly by your officers' boots. Put on slippers. And toss your documents into the fire."

Near the fire lay an empty bag, which probably had held potatoes. I picked it up and threw it on Yasko's wounded arm so it wouldn't be obvious that he was keeping it bent. Upon leaving the camp, I smiled to the guard, but he made a wry face and turned away. I had nothing against that, after a few steps we disappeared into the dusk. I advised Yasko against going home and took him to Lucia instead. There, surprisingly, we found Yosko and the wounded policemen whom she had bandaged and given a change of clothes. She took them to her home from the church. And this is how a good company gathered. Lucia prepared some refreshments, got some wine from the cellar, and we passed the time pleasantly. The results of those gatherings were that Yasko fell head over heels for Lucia, and she for him. Well, she finally found a true connoisseur of her preserves.

20

Stammering and shifting from foot to foot, Marko said:

"You know, Danka and I are planning to get married."

After these words, he paused, but Yarosh was silent. The news struck him, but with all his strength he tried not to show his apprehension. It seemed to him he was badly failing, but Marko did not look at him. Instead he leaned on the windowsill and marveled at a squirrel that was jumping along a walnut tree. Yarosh feverishly sought words that would support his son's choice, but words failed him. He barely choked out a brief "uh huh;" for some reason what his son told him deeply troubled him, even something like a sense of panic. In an instant he desired to be alone, to lock himself up in his office and digest the news alone, but it would have looked strange, and having approached the bar, he poured two glasses of wine and handed one to Marko.

"Well, then there's a wonderful reason to have a drink," he said in as calm a tone as possible, but it turned out somewhat theatrical and strained, his lips barely smiling.

"Isn't it true, she's the best?" Marko asked, now looking right into his eyes.

"Of those you've brought by before?" Yarosh looked away, stepped back into a corner and sat in an armchair. "Of course, of course... she's the best...."

"I get the impression you're not completely sure."

"Why? You probably know her better. I like her too. She's clever, purposeful, she knows what she wants. But... will a scholar be the perfect wife? As I understand it, you aren't planning on diving into scholarship."

"No, I decided to focus on computer programs... Theory doesn't attract me. So, we'll have harmony: she's a theorist, I'm an empirical guy."

"Maybe. Actually, I don't have any reservations... I said it for no reason...."

"Well, if so, then maybe you won't mind if next Sunday we bring her parents over?"

Here again he felt the same panicked fear and the desire to disappear, to hide in some dark quiet place and close his eyes. He rejected the very idea that the news wasn't okay with him. He tried to accept it as he should have, but for some reason it wasn't working. Incomprehensible fear and a sense of incredible loss permeated him. The loss of what? He didn't want to admit it to himself, but recently Danka became positively rooted in his consciousness. The days when they didn't see each other were filled with sorrow for him. He kept rereading her emails with the texts of her translations, reading between the lines for some kind of different meaning, absent at first glance, for certain secret signs to him, but they weren't there, not even in the hieroglyphs that she asked him to explain. The content was very far from what he would have liked to have seen. Finally, this game with words and signs seized him. In his emails, he began as if joking to toss out certain phrases that should have brought them closer together. He did this very delicately, resorting to chimerical allusions and hints. In response, he received businesslike observations or questions. However recently, in fact the last time, this businesslike character seemed to have been broken. He already began to notice on her part a playful tone and a certain ambiguity. Perhaps it only seemed that way to him, but he began to read in her letters certain special words, addressed only to him, and understood by him alone. And once that small bridge seemingly had been built between them, suddenly everything underwent ruination. After all, what was he expecting? If what he understood in her letters really existed, it would have manifested in their relationship outside the letters. How many times were they alone in his office, sitting shoulder to shoulder over manuscripts, with their knees, faces and hair often touching but their conversations were always professional, with no other gestures or words, nothing that would give him any reason to feel now what he felt. Hikes to Kortumov Hill and The Devil's Cliff turned out to be the happy exception, from which it would be premature to draw any conclusions.

"Yes, of course ...," he finally said to Marko. "Have you introduced them to your mother?"

"No, she won't make the right impression on them."

"And you think I will?" Yarosh laughed. "Who are her parents?"

"You won't believe it. Until recently her father worked at the customs office as the chief administrator, but the new government dismissed him. However, he's planning on trying to reestablish himself at the Ministry. And her mother's a homemaker. Although she has a higher education."

"Her father worked at the customs office? And as the chief administrator? It's hard to imagine that such a man would be very pleased with his daughter's choice. Money loves money."

"But their daughter isn't like that, you've seen her yourself."

"Yes... she's not like that... And where will you live?"

"Her father has several apartments and private homes.

We have a place to live. And he has several cars. In short, he's a businessman."

"That's why I'm saying that he could look down his nose at you."

"But I earn decent money. I have a reliable salary, and no one knows if they'll renew him at work. They might even send him to the slammer. Well, okay, if you don't mind, then expect us on Sunday. Danka and I will come early to cook something, and her parents will join us later. Just don't get worked up on political topics, because whether he wants to or not her father has to support the criminal regime, even though it betrayed him."

"What if he broaches the topic himself? Do I have to praise the idiotic government?"

"Of course not, nobody's asking you to do that. It'll be enough not to express the views from your interviews and articles."

"Are you sure he hasn't read anything of mine?"

"For sure! He just reads the tabloids and watches the stupid TV. He doesn't use the internet. Neither does her mother. She just reads chick lit. In fact, you won't have too many topics for conversation. The weather, soccer, cooking, medicine...."

T

The sun set without any indication it would return. From September 22 to 23, that first night of the Soviet occupation, Lviv did not sleep. Gunshots and screams echoed. Taking advantage of the disorder, robbers looted jewelry and watch stores. They feared nothing because they had weapons. Whole piles of them were lying around the city. Even the Bolsheviks were wary of intervening. The next day Lviv was awakened by entirely different, unusual sounds. You couldn't hear all the voices that formerly inhabited the city until now, because even during those ten days the city's defense did not capitulate. It tried as best as it could to convince its citizens that it really had not changed, it was living and pulsating, happy with life, as before. But now that the city was defeated, humbled and captive—a prisoner city—sadness and disappointment appeared on the faces of the inhabitants of Lviv.

When the renowned Baczewski Vodka factory caught fire from bombs, people rushed to save the priceless treasures it produced. They carried away the vodka, liqueurs, and fruit cordials in boxes, bags and burlap sacks, like ants rescuing little pillows that they had come across. A Red Army detachment saw the miracle and rushed to save the people's property too, leaving only one soldier to guard ammunition. One must say that they indeed did this heroically, because the factory was not just burning, but also exploding and shooting flames into the skies, and feet slipped on the streams of alcohol, and these streams also flashed in blue flames which sometimes gleefully licked their boots. Unlike the residents, who immediately disappeared with their rescued treasure, escaping to their homes, the soldiers of the legendary army had nowhere to carry the vodka and made a stockpile of it next to the guard of the ammunition until they realized that they had saved so much of it that they would be given credit for their feat both here and in their homeland. They sat down to drink next to the boxes, drinking straight from the bottles, fastening them with a screw so that the vodka, pouring into their throats, would swirl without gurgling and splashing. However the healing liquid splashed anyway and dripped all over their beards, chests, pants and into their boots, but they paid no attention, and drank as if it were the last day in their lives, and after about a half hour they all got so drunk that they couldn't understand anything. For some reason grabbing their bayonets, some headed to the fences on the opposite side of the street and began to shake them, and then fell into a ditch. Others lay near the ammunition and began to snore like piglets, while others wandered the streets with arms outstretched and tried to stop the people who were dragging the vodka. Then they all almost simultaneously began to vomit a colorful stinking mixture, in which one could make out bits of undigested barley, corn, red, orange and green tomato peels, watermelon seeds, chewed apples and even eggshells. And right then when they were dead drunk and lay down wherever they could, Yosko's uncle Zelman Milker came with a cart. Although he was a communist and a member of the Communist Party of Ukraine, he was still in his right mind. For when the Soviets stopped giving money to foreign Communists, many emigrated to the country of their dreams, to that Garden of Eden promised by Lenin and Stalin. Members of the Communist Party even went, but all of them were liquidated in 1937 as imperialist spies. Zelman was wise. He preferred to cultivate a Garden of Eden near his house. When the liberators came, he gathered some three-dozen people who dreamt about the communist paradise and went to greet the liberators with flowers and flags, which he cut out of a red curtain. But because the material was coarse, the flags wouldn't flap in the wind, and instead they hung like dog tails. Zelman, who had made several successful runs with his cart, upon seeing eight soldiers drunk as a skunk, could not restrain his fiery communist passion, and with the help of several volunteers loaded two soldiers onto his cart and took them to his house, and there he and his wife Rivka carried them into the living room and put them on the floor. Thus he carried the rest of the glorious Red Army soldiers along with their rifles and the vodka saved for the people to his place, and so the dream of his life came true—the long-awaited liberators, guardians of the proletariat were sleeping in his house. But Zelman couldn't fall asleep. He wanted to do something extraordinary, something that all the liberators would remember their entire life, so he went to the garden and, although his Rivka wrung her hands and bawled, because she did not share his progressive views, he plucked entire bouquets of chrysanthemums, dahlias, roses, and marigolds, and stuffing them in vases, quietly carried them to the living room. But that didn't calm him down, because he remembered he still had crocuses, immortelles, daisies, and lilies, so he plucked them and crammed them in pots and buckets, and again quietly carried them to the living room. He couldn't sleep for a long time, fantasizing about what a wonderful awakening awaited his favorite liberators who had brought on their bayonets freedom and the equality of workers. He woke up quite late, the sun already struck his eyes, and Rivka was mercilessly clanging her ladle in the wash basin, stirring the pea soup she was going to feed the guests. Zelman asked what time it was and was very surprised that the guests were still asleep, but decided that there was nothing strange in that because the liberators must have gotten pretty darn tired during their liberation campaign. He asked Rivka not to bang the pot with the ladle so loudly, to which she called him meshuganah and tapped herself on her forehead with the wet ladle, apparently hinting that Zelman had gone off his rocker with this feast and with the flowers, because now there wouldn't be anything to take to the cemetery to their dear family after he stripped all the flowerbeds. Some more time passed, and not a single sound echoed from the living room. Finally, Rivka couldn't take it, so she shoved her husband so hard that he fell face down on the couch, then she opened the door. Her nose was immediately struck by the intoxicating fragrance of autumn flowers, that entire bouquet of scents that overnight combined into a strange-smelling cocktail, so pungent that it made her head spin, but she did not lose consciousness, noticing that the glorious liberators continued to sleep, and when she coughed, they remained asleep. Rivka stepped out of the living room, staggering and holding one hand on her head and with the other trying to grope for the wall. If not for her husband, she could have fallen. It was right then that he began to suspect something was wrong, that the men were sleeping an unnatural sleep. After settling Rivka on a chair, he jumped over to the nearest soldier and touched his hand. The hand was cold, the face—cold. Horror gripped Zelman's heart. He ripped both windows wide open and began to touch soldier after soldier. They were all stiff because they were dead, though their death was beautiful, much nicer than on the battlefield, because they had been asphyxiated by autumn's finest aromas. Fleeing from the living room with mad eyes, Zelman saw Rivka's crazed eyes and muttered: "We're dead!" With a doomed look Rivka nodded in agreement, in an instant withering like an autumn flower, also realizing what kind of mess they got themselves into because you can't explain how eight Red Army soldiers perished by accident. It was obviously a terrorist act, the work of Japanese intelligence and a counter-revolutionary coup attempt. Zelman grabbed his head with his hands and frantically began thinking how to get out of this tragic situation and in his despair could think of nothing else to do but to rush to Yosko's mother. But upon hearing the news, Golda couldn't help sharing it with her girlfriends. So, good company gathered at our house—Yosko, Yas, Wolff, all our mothers and me, led by Zelman. On the table in front of us lay the papers of the eight Red Army soldiers. At first Rita, as the most principled, concluded: "Sergeant Kuzkin and his company suffered a heroic death, and if no one has asked about them, that means their superiors don't know where they disappeared."

"Oh, Rita!" Golda clapped her hands. "You are so wise! I was about to say the same thing! We don't have to worry, no one will come for them."

"Well, yes," Yas said. "But what do we do with the corpses now? It's not just one or two, but eight in all."

"They should be buried," my mother said. "And I even know how."

It wasn't even necessary for her to look expressively at me. I immediately got the picture where she was heading, but I shook my head and said that for no amount of money would I go to Mr. Knoflyk because since he went bananas, it was difficult to come to an understanding with him. But Zelman wrung his hands and looked at me so imploringly, and Mrs. Zelman promised a large stuffed carp and an onion cake if I would go, so I reluctantly agreed.

"Orko," [98] Zelman said, seeing me out the door—tell me, if I can settle accounts with horilka. Because I can't drink as much as I brought home.

Imagine my surprise when I found Mr. Knoflyk in a good mood, in ironed clothes, smoothly combed and shaved. Upon seeing me, he went immediately to meet me with outstretched arms and hugged me:

"Praise be! Holy smoke! Who do I see? Six-winged cherubim sent you to me, camerade. Please let me introduce you to my wife Lenka," and he pulled me deep into the building, where next to a coffin decorated with roses a plump blonde with ample bosoms and an equally luxurious belly was tidying up. "You see? You see?" He stroked his wife on her tummy. "Finally, I'm going to have an Irzhyk or Vlasta."

His joy was understandable, since the late Vlasta could not have children, and now it was as if Mr. Knoflyk had been reborn into the world. In his own bubble, Mr. Bouchek rustled with a wood block plane and hummed something under his breath in the back. I waved to him, but it was as useless as waving to willow trees along the roadside.

"How good that you came, I missed you," Mr. Knoflyk babbled—"your aesthetic attitude to the profession, the poetic gift with which you approached each of the deceased. You can get back to work right away. I have an exclusive

98 The diminutive form for the Ukrainian name Orest.

for you: the gorgeous, sexy, fresh corpse of an opera singer with an angelic voice, who looks like she seems about to start singing an aria from *Aida*. Why? Why does she look so wonderful? Because she was wise and prudent and didn't hang herself or drown, didn't jump, didn't poison herself with some disgusting stuff that would have distorted her delicate features, instead she carefully climbed into a warm bath at the Hotel George and precisely sliced open the veins on her hands. This is what I call a sign of the highest nobility and aesthetics! As the poet said, beauty saves the world."

I barely managed to stop the unrestrained flow of chatter of Mr. Knoflyk, informing him about those eight corpses whom we suddenly had on our hands....

"Holy smoke! Oh, my Lord, what joy!" Mr. Knoflyk slapped his hands and turned his grateful gaze at the sky. "No wonder I dreamt of eight doctor fish that I caught barehanded in my own bed! And so's you know, I have exactly eight coffins of superior quality."

"Mr. Knoflyk, these eight dead are not just any old dead," I said in a whisper. "These are our liberators."

Mr. Knoflyk immediately looked around, grabbed my hand, and dragged me to his office. Seating me beside him, he was all ears.

"These glorious liberators of ours died as heroes," I continued. "Saving the legendary Baczewski Vodka factory. They lay down their lives in a heroic death."

"Sehr gut! Yes, yes, yes," Mr. Knoflyk grew lively. "That's very interesting. We will arrange a grand triumphal funeral for them. I'll hire the choir of the girls' gymnasium. They'll wear white Greek tunics with veils and wreaths, attired like despairing brides, and will mourn the heroes, wringing their hands as the Trojan women mourned the Trojans."

"Mr. Knoflyk! Hold your horses! The heroes really died like Trojans. But the Trojan horse turned out to be vodka. It killed them. Eight of the company lay down and died."

"Wow! Vodka! That's a dark matter. A grand funeral drops out of the picture."

"They should be buried in the Jewish cemetery as Jews. Mr. Zelman Milker will pay for everything. With vodka."

"Great. Because these zloty of ours will soon become garbage. So those dead people were Jews?"

"Can anyone be a hundred percent sure that he isn't at least a little bit Jewish?"

Mr. Knoflyk shook his head in deep thought and said:

"Sure thing! Even I can't. But eight coffins going to the cemetery at the same time could attract attention. Today someone with shaggy, unkempt hair and a star on his cap came to me and said I was no longer the director, because I've oppressed the proletariat long enough. So now the director will be Comrade Bouchek, a representative of the proletariat. I had nothing against it. Comrade Bouchek is as deaf as a stump, so I nodded my head and exclaimed: 'Down with the bourgeoisie and priests!' Everything works out well. I'll have some holy peace, and Comrade Bouchek will go to gatherings, meetings, and banquets. Aha... so how do we deal with the coffins?"

"Really, it's too risky a sight. Maybe we can bury them as Jews in white sheets without coffins? Then you put all eight corpses in their catafalque and off we go.

"Yep, that's it! That's how we'll do it. Only, it would just be good if the dear family would walk behind the catafalque in mourning. So somebody's crying. And since I won't make anything on the coffins, then at least maybe on the wreaths, don't you think?" Mr. Knoflyk put on the table in front of himself a paper card and an abacus and started doing the calculation. "Two wreaths for each—sixteen wreaths with black ribbons. Plus, eight bouquets, eight candles... Paraffin candles or tallow?"

"Let them be paraffin."

"Pa-raf-fin... Yes... Eight sheets... Silk or linen?"

"Linen."

"Li-nen... Mmm... Oh! Wait—are they in uniform?

"Of course."

"You must change them into civilian clothes. What if some dipshit wants to take a look! And finally, how many graves should there be? Though what am I asking! Eight graves—that's an epidemic already! Right when they liberated us, people started to die. That's no good. But... even if I lose on this deal... we'll put them in two graves. Only someone has to go to the cemetery and negotiate."

Mr. Knoflyk wrote down the address and promised to arrive with the catafalque around evening when it would be already turning dusk. I rushed home to comfort poor Zelman with the fact that all would work out well. After hearing the news, Zelman and Golda began to ask us if we would agree to accompany the catafalque, pretending to be the family, devastated by inexpressible grief. What could we do? We agreed, then our mothers went to Zelman's to dress the liberators in civilian clothes. Fortunately, beforehand Zelman had already brought several bags of clothing from a bombed-out store, so there were no problems with that. Yosko raced off to the gravediggers at the cemetery, gave each of them three bottles of vodka, and they agreed to bury the eight dead bodies in two graves. By evening everything was ready and in place. I put on a black shirt and black pants. Yosko planted his yarmulke on my head. For him it was superfluous because he looked Jewish as he was. Yas and Wolff put on black hats from under which curlicues of red hemp stuck out instead of sidelocks. Mr. Knoflyk busily ordered the corpses to be wrapped in canvas and loaded on the catafalques. They placed four of them lengthwise and four crosswise on top, but slantwise, otherwise they wouldn't have fit. Zelman couldn't find enough shoes, so the deceased were shoeless in soldiers' footwraps. Zelman burned the soldiers' clothing, feeling bad only about the tarpaulin boots and belts from which he prudently removed metal buckles with little stars. Finally, as the funeral march began, Mr. Knoflyk sat on the coach box and made clucking sounds to the horses, and we walked behind, supporting our mothers, who bowed their heads covered by black scarves. They incessantly jabbered about everything in the world and grew silent only when they passed onlookers. Only our grandmother worked conscientiously. She was wailing into the skies in a language incomprehensible to anyone except her, but otherwise, everyone would have concluded that it was a Jewish funeral. When we arrived at the cemetery, we saw two freshly-dug graves at the bottom of which lay drunken gravediggers—two in each pit. We weren't able to pull them out right away, so we tied the breast-bands usually used to lower a coffin into the grave to their feet, and we tied the other end to the catafalque and in this way pulled them out and laid them by some bushes. After that we lowered the liberators into the graves, covered them with clay-like dirt, formed small mounds and surrounded the grave with wreaths and bouquets. Zelman lit eight candles and stuck them in the ground.

"They had a beautiful death," he said with all his communist straightforwardness, "at first they had some good drinking, and then fell asleep eternally among paradisal fragrances... Anyone would wish for that, especially in our troubled times...."

21

On Sunday, Danka came with Marko in the morning to help tidy up the house and cook for the guests. Yarosh wasn't distinguished by any particular pedantry, that's why everywhere a bigger or smaller mess reigned. Things tended to disappear from places where they were supposed to be and ended up in truly unexpected places, but the owner got used to it. But now that Danka found a place for everything, he anxiously thought about how many days in the future he'd have to search for this or that kitchen implement, a newspaper he had not quite finished reading or a pencil, index cards with jotted-down phone numbers, bills for gas and light. He'd have to search through the trash tomorrow in case something made it all the way to the garbage, because no one other than the owner is in a position to determine the value of a little piece of paper with some chicken scratches on it. At first Yarosh tracked the migration of all those little things, but because everything was happening very quickly, he finally became resigned to it, and began preparing the goose, which he had procured yesterday at the market especially for this occasion. First he braised it, then he took out all the insides, cleaned them and ground them with soaked bread, added fried onions, chopped parsley, two raw eggs, and mixed it well with his hands. Then he stuffed the goose and stitched it closed with a hooked needle that a surgeon friend had given him.

"How deftly and quickly you do that!" Danka enthusiastically exclaimed. "I would have puttered around half a day."

"You're probably accustomed to doing everything carefully, and I—any which way." Yarosh laughed. "I guarantee that it doesn't affect the taste."

"No doubt."

After the goose ended up in the broiler, Danka took out several sheets from her purse and asked Yarosh to look at her translations. She had translated several other poems by Lucilius. Yarosh proposed going over to his study. Marko waved to them, "Go, go!" And he turned on the TV. Yarosh felt like his voice was trembling, and not just his voice, but also his hands. They sat next to the desk. Yarosh, trying to hide his excitement, stared at the text. Danka translated quite adeptly, striving to select ancient words to give the text an original sound. Yarosh wanted to comment but felt that his voice might betray him. He rose up, went to the cupboard, took out a bottle of wine, poured a glass and drank it in one gulp.

"Sorry, but I'm a little nervous before the visit of your parents. Can I also pour you a glass?"

"By the way, I was about to ask you for one, because I'm also nervous.

"Why would you be? You know your parents well," he laughed, pouring her a glass.

"Precisely because I know them."

He poured himself another and they clanked their glasses. A pleasant warmth spread through his chest. It seemed to him that together with that warmth incredible courage was pouring into him. He felt he could say it right now... say.... say what?... The words curdled, bunched together in an uncontrolled herd and were stamping in one place. In truth, he couldn't say a word. He finally sat down again at the desk and picked up the sheet of paper. He remembered that this already had happened previously in his life when a girl, with whom he had danced the entire evening, was getting ready to leave and her boyfriend was waiting for her. But she didn't leave and stood next to Yarosh. However, he couldn't choke out the words that would have given them the opportunity to meet again. He let her go and she left, casting him a farewell glance full of surprise and regret. The lines of poetry were jumping before his eyes, he felt sweat on his brow, and right when he wanted to wipe it away with a handkerchief, he noticed that Danka was looking not at the text, but at him. Some force turned his head toward her. Their eyes met and whether it was true or whether it just seemed that way to him—in the corners of her eyes he noticed sparkles. Only tears could shine that way, but they didn't flow, they froze on the shore of her eyes. Yarosh forced a smile and muttered: "Your translation is really good," then looked away, but she continued silently to look at him. He felt it, though, and tried not to glance askance. His eye began twitching. He wiped the sweat from his forehead. It was becoming unbearable for him. Looking out the window, he could see an apple tree and a fidgety magpie making a nest on a branch (he needed to chase her away, as if there weren't enough magpies, especially, if they start to steal chickens from the neighbors), he took a deep breath and said: "Do you want to ask me something?" His voice reverberated as though it were coming from some mysterious depths. He didn't recognize it, it even seemed that he didn't really say anything, that it was all in his imagination: "Be fearful of the midday demon." The magpie flew from the apple trees, and in a minute returned with a tuft of wool in her beak. That's what she's weaving a nest with—a Hutsul woolen blanket that Danka had hung out on the balcony to air out. I have to chase it away or it will pick the blanket all out. That magpie is strange, making a nest in autumn? What could that mean? But the magpie diverted his attention only briefly. He turned his head to the girl and looked at her with undisguised fear. There was no longer that shine in her eyes—maybe she unnoticeably wiped the tears away. Danka bit her lower lip and very slowly shook her head, not taking away her thoughtful gaze from him. It seemed she was now somewhere far, far away in her thoughts. He nodded, licked his parched lips, and then got back into the translation. The lines swam before his eyes, colliding into one another, rose up, became blurred. But where her hand lay on the text, the lines suddenly froze and lined up. Her thin fingers trembled. She asked:

"What do you think?" Her fingers slowly closed into a fist, slightly crumpling the paper. "Am I doing everything right?"

The question was too abstract and could apply to anything—to the translation, to studying ancient languages, and to marriage... He wanted to say something about her scholarly promise, that she was very talented, but involuntarily shook his head from side to side. At that moment fear seized him. Because he gave himself away with this, betrayed something that he had kept for a long time on a leash, and perhaps she read on his face what she wanted to and said:

"I think so too."

Then she pressed her lips to his, and he felt that they were soft and compliant, hot and sweet. He embraced her, pulled her toward himself and, it seemed, no power could unlock their embrace. But common sense prevailed. They broke apart from each other just a moment before the door opened and Marko entered. Smoothing the crumpled paper with his fingers, Yarosh loudly began to recite the translation, perhaps even too loudly. Both of them blushed, but Marko interpreted it in his own way:

"Oh, you've already started drinking without me."

"We thought it would be a stressful situation. Pour yourself some."

"I won't refuse. Do you still have a lot to do? They already left. If they don't get lost, they'll be here in ten minutes.

"Well, then it's time...," Danka said and got up from her chair.

She's superbly in control of herself but you can't say that about me, Yarosh thought and felt all sweaty from worry. After they left, he changed his shirt and then stood in front of the mirror and asked his reflection: what was that? Maybe there in the looking glass his words rolled. He didn't receive a response, but he no longer felt fear or panic, or the desire to escape. Instead he felt joy. Now he was filled with happiness, but this happiness was still too vague and unknown. Who knew what it had in store for him? But it didn't worry him too much, he wanted the events to unfold with increasing speed, to unwind and carry him farther and farther. The honking of a car echoed on the street. Danka and Marko rushed to meet the guests. Yarosh ran his hand over his face, as if erasing all his previous worries, nerves and fear.

U

In the first days the liberators seized the freight wagons at the train station, which contained all the property of refugees from central Poland. They hastily loaded their spoils on automobiles and transported it somewhere, and they threw everything they thought was extra into piles and burned it. News of this quickly spread. The owners of the property began to run to the train station and tried to show receipts for the goods, but they were quietly led to the side and shot. The looting reached a climax when soldiers broke the door of one wagon, in which there were boxes of alcohol. A wild drinking frenzy began, from time to time someone drunkenly shot into the sky, and only then did the police run over and stop the rioting. On the Lviv's streets one could now observe amazing scenes. You couldn't imagine a Polish officer carrying a bag of potatoes on his back, and a baby bath or even a toilet on his head, but Soviet officers carrying such treasures were seen like that every day, pushing wheelbarrows with a dresser or writing desk confiscated from a bourgeois. For the Polish soldiers, these items were common everyday things, and no military patrol ever witnessed such a humiliating picture of the military elite.

Leah returned from a walk through the city and was full of impressions.

"Do you remember Mr. Zumpf's shop on Okhoronok Street?" She asked.

"Of course," I said. "I used to go there often as a child. It looked like some kind of Turkish or Egyptian market inside, and from the moment you walked in, the scent of spices and sweets tickled the nose."

"Yes... At one end of the counter tall cones of sugar in blue cardboard boxes were piled high like the snow-capped peaks of the Himalayas, next to that clear crystallized lumps of sugar sparkled in the sun like diamonds, and it was impossible to watch without sadness when Mr. Zumpf used a hammer to chip off small pieces of that beauty and pack them in paper."

"Then there were entire mountains of every kind of baked goods, jars filled with various candies, colorful lollipops, toffee, chocolate in cardboard boxes: long rectangles of "Danusya," "Eos" white chocolate, "New Fortune" chocolate—"Syanka," "Taras," and "Odarka ...."

"The second half of the counter," Leah dreamily uttered, "even sagged under the weight of large pieces of butter, balls and blocks of cheese, cans of sardines, pickled herring, and cans of tea, coffee and cocoa, jars of spices on the shelves on the wall...."

"Mr. Zumpf presided over it all. He had every button buttoned and always wore a polite smile. Mr. Zumpf, short in stature, with small, lively hands with sausage fingers. Mr. Zumpf, 'I kiss your hand, how may I serve you?' He'd open his notebook and enter the purchases, and then customers who enjoyed his trust could pay for everything once a month... And what else? Why have you mentioned him?"

"I was just there. I walked past the shop and looked inside. Why did I do it? I ruined part of my childhood memories." It was evident she was unnerved, and though she turned to the window, I noticed tears in her eyes. "Now there's nothing left... absolutely nothing... a herring barrel now stands there. A large cardboard box of matches. Several jars of vinegar. That's it... Although no... There's still salt. A large wooden box of salt, which you scoop up with a little slipper and wrap in newspaper. By the way, they also pack herring in newspaper. Both in Polish and Ukrainian ones."

"And Mr. Zumpf?"

"He's still smiling like before, but the smile is no longer the same... there are bags under his eyes, and he no longer says, 'I kiss your hands, how may I serve you?' Now he says nothing when he sees customers, just looks questioningly... but he recognized me... 'Ahh, Miss Leah... nice to see you... how's your mom?' Then he approached, took my hand and whispered: 'They took everything... everything... they came at night with three trucks and took everything... and brought this.' 'Who took it?' 'The police. For themselves...' They behave like highway bandits. They take over housing that they like and drive out the people. They confiscate furniture and belongings. I also met my dear school friend Dvoira. She told me about Rebecca, the daughter of Salomon, the innkeeper... Do you remember her?"

"I sure do!"

"Rebecca ran to her in the middle of the night. She escaped from a train en route to Siberia. Her father and mother didn't want to escape. Dvoira's hiding her at her place. She asked me for some clothes. I'll go drop them off in the evening. Salomon's tavern is now a 'Snack Bar.' Do you know what happened to Wolodyslaw Zalewski, who owned a confectionery store on Academician Street? He is a 'confectionery worker'—his duty now is to monitor the chocolate in the kettle. And at Mr. Torba's "Fryzierna" salon on Horodotska Street, where you went for a haircut, they wrote 'Parik... makhyer... skaya.'[99] Is that really the same?"

---

99 "Parikmakherskaya" is the Russian word for a beauty salon or hair dresser, while fryzierna was the Ukrainian word for it in pre-Soviet times in Galicia.

22

Her father was a heavyset man with a big round head, shaped like a ball, which he carefully shaved. On his short neck one could see a massive gold chain, and on one of his fingers—a gold signet ring. The daughter clearly took after the mother, who was still quite beautiful and preserved her figure and luxuriant hair. Both walked in as if entering a museum and immediately began to look around on the walls; it was unclear what they expected to see there. When they sat at the table, the conversation actually began with the weather and further moved on to politics; the future father-in-law complained about the government. He had voted for them, but what they're up to now... But everything was still ahead for him, so he would not advise them to rush into the marriage, because if he's renewed at his post, he'd be able to arrange a job for Marko. After all, information technology people are needed at the customs office too. To Marko's surprise, everyone liked this idea, even Danka shrugged her shoulders. Yarosh nodded and murmured something about the fact that the Lenten fast was coming, and during the fast one shouldn't... Then the conversation switched back to politics, because Danka's father couldn't calm himself down. Because his ideals were so cruelly betrayed, he was forced to become disillusioned in what he believed, though he always kept his hand on the pulse of the time and was a member of all pro-government parties in the order that each came to power, yet he still remained a patriot....

Yarosh listened to him the way a doctor listens to a patient. When he finally grew silent, Danka's mother leaned over and asked if he would not mind showing her his garden. Yarosh immediately agreed, suspecting that this probably was part of a scenario previously agreed to in advance with the father, because the latter immediately very enthusiastically began relating that because of his customs job, he used to go hunting in the border zone where mere mortals were forbidden to go.

"It's really nice here, peaceful," she said, walking among the trees. "You know, Danka is too emotional ... I would even say impetuous. She's had many infatuations. Although perhaps it might be difficult to call them infatuations. In a word, she flies in and says that she met someone who's so... so... so... And a few days pass—and that's it, she's sitting in the house, doesn't answer her phone. It's continued on that way since her school days. You know, we never interfered in her affairs. Sometimes maybe we prompted something, gave her advice. But she quickly became disenchanted. We don't mind if she gets married to Marko, no... But knowing our Danka... Once she said to us that she's not planning to marry. She'll go into academia and for a scholar marriage is death. That's what she said. Death!"

She came to the old apple tree and stroked the rough trunk.

"How I love these kinds of old trees; they remind me of my childhood. From them a special warmth emanates because they have seen so much in their lifetime. Am I wrong? Was this garden planted long ago?"

"Yes, in the thirties. I was going to chop down that pear tree that is already half-dried up and ceased to bear fruit, and I even cut off a dried-up branch, and it took and began to bear fruit again."

"My grandfather always used to frighten trees that did not bear fruit with his axe. Surprisingly, it helped. I get the impression that the trees hear something...." She paused for a moment and then said: "You know... I really wanted to get acquainted with you. I've heard so much about you from her. She's delighted with your lectures. Can you imagine that she even recorded them on tape and then listened to them again at home. And her passion for the Arcanumian language... This is so exciting! Really! I myself have a philological education. True, I never worked because I got married too young. But I've also become passionate about it... This amazing nonexistent world that emerges before you only partly like the tip of an iceberg... and most of it remains, as always, under water... Once, when she had the flu, she had a high fever... last winter ... she was terribly worried that she would miss your lectures and persuaded a classmate to record them for her... So... one night while I was asleep next to her, she started to say something in an incomprehensible language, something so strange, similar to German, though I don't know German well... Maybe it was Arcanumian... I don't know...." She fell silent again, took a few steps, tossing the fallen leaves with her toes, then turned and said in an already drier tone: "Why am I telling you this?... Danka is entirely into scholarship. She's different. Not like us. And I understand her. She is my unrealized self. But all the same she is still not me. She won't sacrifice herself to a family. Because she knows that it would bury her as a scholar and as a translator. We women are delicate beings... We find it hard to survive in everyday conditions, in cages... We waste away there and turn into brood hens." Again, there was a pause, and also—the rustle of the wind, the chirping of a magpie, the apples falling soundlessly, her eyes directed at Yarosh and her conclusion: "I don't know if she will be a good wife for your son." There was a pause, a rocking on her heels, her hand on the trunk of the cherry tree, silence, the wind quieted down, probably also listening, and: "Most likely she won't. It's somehow hard to believe that she can change and sacrifice her scholarship to quiet family happiness."

Yarosh listened to all this, entirely agreeing with her in his soul. Although Marko was his son, the reality really was not so rosy. Danka is different. And recently she proved it. She has doubts, she's hesitating... And that kiss? What was that about? Did it really happen? However, as a father he should have said something... What?... 'Time will tell?'"

"Time will tell," he muttered. "No one is pushing anyone into anything. They only started dating so recently...."

"Yes, some six months... although ... although I dated my husband only for two months... But that's me... I have what I wanted. And I am happy in my own way. But people like my daughter... somewhat excitable... should go through a long period of dating and courtship... Am I wrong?"

Yarosh nodded mechanically, but frightened that he might be exposed added:

"We don't know yet... I don't know, maybe my son is capable of sacrificing himself... to scholarship... that is to his scholar wife... Doesn't that happen?"

"I hadn't heard. I know one thing: almost all female writers, painters, artists, and scholars are lonely. At best, they are divorced single mothers. Well, there are exceptions... the exceptions who cast their lot with someone who is close to them in spirit... But these still are exceptions. Then are those who pretend to be decent wives and mothers, but they drag themselves abroad and continue to collect their amours." With this she gave Yarosh such a penetrating look that he blushed: was she referring to his former female student, who became a writer and described their relationship? Maybe she read it and understood who was who? Well, never mind, what does it matter, he makes no claims.

V

The bazaar behind the Opera Theater was not only called Krakidaly, but Paris, God only knows why. It never lost its importance or name even during the war. Forming two rows, residents of Lviv sold all sorts of things there. Buyers—mostly Soviet officers, rank and file soldiers, government officials, as well as their wives, who here "in Paris," turned into European ladies—walked back and forth between them. Among the vendors you could also meet theater actors, bank directors, and distinguished professors. Each one would bring out something from his or her home to sell, and each one would loudly praise his or her goods. Some needed money for food, and others collected money to bribe the liberators, to save someone assigned for deportation to Siberia. But the Krakidaly Bazaar drew people for yet one more reason—this was the place for socializing and a source of political news and rumors. Certain middlemen gadded about here, who knew how to arrange contact with the Cheka secret police and with prison workers; here you could find out the latest news from the London radio and the date and time of the next militia roundup, buy a German passport, and find someone to guide you across the border.

At the market from morning till evening shouts echoed of "Liquor, booze, hooch," "Bachevsky, Bachevsky, Bachevsky!," "Booze, booze, booze!," "Local liquor and imported stuff!," "Saccharin pastilles! Real Wyborowa Wodka!"[100] One cheerful man shouted out at the top of his voice: "Selling a cure for bedbugs, fleas, cockroaches, and all kinds

100 One of the oldest and most popular brands of Polish vodka, the

of utter bastards. Death to fleas, death to male lice and female ones too!" Soon after that a fellow approached him and wanted to know whom he had in mind, his mention of "all kinds of utter bastards" disappeared.

The enterprising women of Lviv collected a great big heap of shining multi-colored buttons, crowns, ribbons, belts, gloves for cotillions, artificial flowers, colored hairclips and combs, décolleté nightshirts and robes—and they carried out all this to sell to the greedy Soviet ladies, who had never seen such great wonders. Besides what they had collected from their houses, Lviv's ladies also sold what they had made themselves, because there wasn't a single lady of the house who didn't know how to bake tortes, sheet cakes, and cookies. It wasn't surprising that at the Krakidaly Bazaar you could see Mrs. professor,[101] and Mrs. learnedbarrister, and Mrs. haughtypants herself, who, without any complaining, peddled their goodies. Ah, how the ladies from the Soviet paradise savored them! You could see the chomping traps of the officers' wives bespattered with cream and crumbs with every step.

Milya peddled her mother's cookies and even grumbled about it:

"Because of this Krakidaly Bazaar I just get fat and nothing more. 'Cause when no one buys the cookies, I'm bored, and so I eat them. And then momma complains that she doesn't feel bad about the cookies, but she doesn't see any money from them."

It's not strange that the Soviets, shortly after arriving in Lviv, immediately became interested in how to get to the

---

production of which began in 1823. Its name means "select vodka."
101 See footnote #10.

Krakidaly Bazaar, or rather, as they said it, "to Krakodily" [The Crocodiles], because they could buy wonderful things really cheaply there. Acquiring used European suits and coats, they changed their clothes at the gate quick as a wink, and only then would walk out into the city. But that didn't save them from crooks who promptly figured out the liberators' ignorance and sold them the most wide-ranging, odd, useless stuff, convincing them of its exceptional value. The four of us joined in with this profitable gesheft.[102] Yas managed to get enema pipes and plastic covers for rubber syringes from the drugstore which had been smashed to bits during a bombing. All these devices had a small valve that opened and closed, which allowed you to control the flow of liquid from a vessel. As first we weren't able to comprehend Yas's idea, but he convinced us that the goods were first class and would sell if we marketed those pipes to the Red Army boys as an outstanding achievement of contemporary technology in the field of smoking. And it happened that we tried to convince them, explaining how such a "mouthpiece" was perfected by world science for smoking, twisting the valve in various directions before the eyes of the bewildered solider.

"Here's some great technolology! If you want to—you smoke, if not—you don't."

After he said that, the soldiers with glee and fascination smoked reeking cheap tobacco cigarettes made from rolled-up newspaper, jamming them into the "mouthpieces," continuously turning those little valves. After our sup-

102 In multicultural Lviv it was common for German, Polish, Yiddish, and other foreign words to be adopted into the local dialect of Ukrainian. "Gesheft" comes from the German word "Geschäft," which means business or deal.

ply of little pipes was gone, we managed to sell more than ten printing machines as a form of technology for printing money. We did this, of course, in the semidarkness, so the client wouldn't guess he's being duped. Afterward, Yas related that at Lucia's place he discovered a large box with broken watches and alarm clocks that were left after her watchmaker grandfather had passed away. Wolff took an interest in that news and had a burning desire to sell the treasure.

"But who will buy a watch that doesn't work?" We asked.

"Just about anybody," Wolff said. "All you need to do is break off the second hand, so it doesn't hinder us, then you lift the watch up to the soldier boy's ear and click your teeth. Like this: click-click-click!"

"Well, just look out that it doesn't click you," Yosko started to laugh, and we agreed to keep an eye on Wolff's activity, promising to join in if the business worked well. And what do you think? It worked! And how! It's possible that it may be difficult for someone to believe but imagine a person who never had a watch and never heard one ticking. One should say that the Soviets were just wild about watches. It's true, they had a very unique notion about beauty and reckoned that a watch must be big, the bigger the better, that's why they wore these impressive onions, while some even tied alarm clocks to their wrists and then rolled up their sleeves, so it was obvious what kinds of braggarts they were.

One day something extraordinary happened. Golda rushed over to us gasping and told us that a corpse was lying in their house. My mother just threw up her hands, and my granny immediately poured some kind of herb into boiling water to give the frightened Golda something to drink, because she couldn't catch her breath at all and kept waving her scarf near her face. From those fragments of phrases that she stuttered and whispered, we understood just one thing: the body belonged to an NKVD[103] guy, who on more than one occasion had tried to court Leah, and now he tracked down when she would be alone in the house and tried to force himself on her. Defending herself, Leah smacked him over the head with a frying pan, but because she smacked him not with the bottom, but the side, it sliced through his temple. He lay there like an elongated pancake, his face covered in blood and not breathing. Golda and Yosko found him in that unattractive position after they had returned from the store. Everyone looked my way once again, allowing me to understand that my role as savior had not yet been accomplished, and new achievements and new ordeals awaited me.

"Well, all right," I sighed. "Go there and wait for me, and I'll run over to Mr. Knoflyk. Maybe this time too he'll be able to save us.

At Mr. Knoflyk's funeral establishment a red flag was flapping, and a fresh inscription could be seen on the sign: "Red Kharon."[104]

"What do you think?" Mr. Knoflyk nodded in the direction of the sign. "That's my *oberih*[105] protective charm now. More than one soldier boy has peeked in here and asked in Russian: "Where can I find comrade Kharon?" I always

---

103 The Russian initials for the Soviet secret police, The Peoples Commissariat for Internal Affairs.

104 Kharon is the Ukrainian and Russian word for Charon/Kharon, the Greek ferryman of Hades.

105 The *oberih* in the Ukrainian folkloric tradition is usually a handmade charm made of straw, dried flowers, and other items from nature that is placed in the house to protect the hearth from evil.

answered in the same way: "Comrade Kharon's at a meeting in Moscow." And I'm left in holy peace. A few days ago, some Soviet Jewish guy dragged himself over and asked in Russian: "Isn't that Grisha Kharon, who was the director of the Zhytomyr NKVD?" I nodded. Then he says: "Say 'hello' to him. If you have any problems, I'm in the State Supply Office. I deal with all issues."

"But I've come to you again regarding a very delicate matter," I quieted my voice, and Mr. Knoflyk immediately took me to his office and got ready to listen to me. "Golda Milker has got into a new mess, this time because of her daughter. When a certain NKVD guy came to visit her, Leah decided to treat him with an omelet. She took a frying pan in her hands and just as she intended to put it on the stove, the NKVD guy got a burning desire to hug her, but he slipped on a spot of cooking oil and cracked his head on the side of the frying pan. He was so unlucky that now he's lying belly up, and his spirit is wandering somewhere over High Castle Mountain.

"Ugh!" Mr. Knoflyk shook his head. "Now that's a mess! We have to bury him properly. And you're incredibly lucky, because at the moment I have a really comfortable coffin—a deep and wide one. We prepared it for his Grace, who was at his deathbed, and was really obese, so fat that he wouldn't fit through this door. But he changed his mind about dying and he's alive and kicking, wolfing down honey nut pastries with marzipan. And the coffin is just sitting here. You know what we'll do? We'll put your guest on the bottom, and we'll put Mrs. Topolska on top. I'd guess he wouldn't mind if he has to lie under a lassie?"

"Of course not! He was quite a guy on the make. He couldn't pass up a single skirt."

"Well, that's super. You just bring him here to me."

"Wait a minute, would Mrs. Topolska's family have a problem with it?"

"What family? She doesn't have a family. She was a single lassie, a spinster, but she had a lot of foresight and didn't forget to set aside money for her funeral. In her will she wrote: "I want to lie comfortably, with lots of room and on a soft bed." All three requests will be honored. But tell me: was that guy of yours in a military uniform?"

"Sure, and with a pistol too."

"Then you have to get a suit for him. Over here in a box is Mr. Tsyepa's beautiful suit. When they put it on him, it burst at the seams in the back, and the family decided to buy him another one, though I tried to convince them that for Mr. Tsyepa it made no difference, because no one in this world now will see his back. But do you know how they answered me: and how about in the other world? And I shut my trap. So take it!" He shoved the package into my hands, but still didn't let go of it because the thought came to him that it would be worth putting makeup on our guest—what if along the way I meet one of his buddies? So Mr. Knoflyk also gave me a red beard, a gray hairpiece, and a box with paints for his cheeks.

What can I tell you? The deceased looked better now than he did in life. His formerly high-cheekboned blood-covered mug, becoming peaceful, now resembled an old uncle, calmed-down and satisfied with his former life. The perfectly tailored black suit fit him well, and a white rose stuck out of his breast pocket. His black glasses completed the picture. When "buddy" appeared in the wheelbarrow that Yosko and I pushed straight ahead as we were whistling, all the passersby politely nodded their heads, smiled, and some even took off their hats because "unk" looked like he was alive, and it would be a sin not to give a greeting to such a pleasant type. Even Mr. Knoflyk admired him and smacked his lips with satisfaction. He helped us pull the corpse out of the wheelbarrow and put it in the coffin. Nearby Mrs. Topolska was waiting for her turn on a table. She had some meat on her and was dressed in a dark-blue dress with white lace. One could see that she had prepared it especially for such a solemn moment. Her wax-like fingers were holding a small icon, and her dry, tightly pursed lips resembled ones that had never been kissed. Just as I was thinking this, suddenly all our hairs, except Mr. Bouchek's, stood on end, and Mr. Knoflyk clutched at his heart, because our "buddy" suddenly came to life and sat up in the coffin. He held onto the sides with his hands and looked around everywhere in surprise, without comprehending where he had ended up. Then he felt his face, took off his glasses, looked all around one more time, and muttered:

"Where the heck am I?"

Exchanging glances with Yosko I started looking all over for some kind of good cudgel to send "buddy" back in the direction in which his sinful soul was moving, but somehow the old devil had been turned back in order to give us even more grief. However, Mr. Knoflyk stopped me:

"Wait," and then turned to address "buddy": "We found you unconscious in the street. Do you remember who you are and where you live?"

The NKVD guy shook his head and began to search through his pockets, though there was nothing in them.

"Did I have documents on me?" He asked in Russian.

"No," we answered simultaneously. "There wasn't anything. Maybe you escaped from the hospital.

"From which hospital?"

"We've got a hospital where they keep people like you who've lost their memory."

"No, I don't remember anything. What's happened—have I died?" He asked in Russian.

Here Mr. Knoflyk delightedly rubbed his hands together and dialed the number of the Kulpark Mental Hospital and informed them that they should come and pick up a crazy guy who had certainly must have scampered off from their grounds.

"We'll come for him right away," they whispered to us.

"Can I lie down a bit more?" The "deceased" asked in Russian and again lay down in the coffin, crossing his arms over his chest. That is how the hospital attendants coming from the loony bin found him. Mr. Knoflyk told them that we picked up this man when he was unconscious, thinking he was dead, but he came to life and now had lost his memory. The doctors bent over the coffin and nodded their heads:

"We know him. That's the dummy Hilko. He escaped from us about five years ago. Well then, get up," they started to make whooping sounds at him.

The NKVD guy sat up again and, dumbstruck, glanced at all those present:

"Wha-a-at's my name?" He asked in Russian.

"Don't play dumb, Hilko, 'cause I'll stick you with a needle right now that'll make you remember the time your granny was a young maiden," one of the attendants said. With those words they lifted him up out of the coffin, grabbed him under his arms, quickly dressed him in a straitjacket, and dragged him to a car without any windows. The NKVD guy screamed out something indistinct, but no one was paying attention to him at that point.

"Aha," Mr. Knoflyk concluded. "Our Mrs. Topolska has lost her boyfriend. As she had never lain underneath a guy in life , so in death she won't lie on top of him either."

23

On Wednesday after the lecture Danka approached Yarosh and said almost in a whisper that she must talk to him, and Yarosh blushed but nodded:

"Good, let's meet in an hour at the Masoch Cafe.

What was she planning to say to him? He felt agitation and indecision. When he came to the cafe, Danka was already waiting for him, having taken a table on the street:

"I ordered some Spanish wine for us. Maybe something else?"

"No thank you. Your mother made a very positive impression on me. She seems to be your devoted friend."

"That really is true. You also made a positive impression on her. It seems we managed without any particular damage to get ourselves out of a delicate situation." Here she coyly looked at Yarosh, and a coquettish, meaningful smile began to play on her lips. Yarosh pretended that he didn't notice. Wine was brought to them, and he raised his glass:

"To Arcanum?"

"To Arcanum," Danka said, having a sip, and immediately went on to the matter at hand: "By the way, this is the topic of our conversation. Yesterday I had a very strange meeting. The secretary told me that the Dean wanted to see me. I went. Besides the Dean one other man was sitting in his office. When he stood up to greet me, the Dean said he'd leave us alone and left the room. That guy informed me that he was from the SBU security service."

Yarosh couldn't restrain himself from a surprised shout:

"Ha! He's also gotten to you?"

"So you know who I'm talking about?"

"Lieutenant Colonel Knysh?"

"Yes."

"What did he want from you?"

"For me to keep him informed about all our research related to Arcanum, as well as how the translation is coming along...."

"BoD?"

Danka laughed:

"He simply got under my skin with that 'BoD.' He's some nut job, doesn't it seem to you?"

"Unlike you, I've had many more opportunities to study these kinds of people. I can tell you that we take to be true at face value is just a game that they have to master perfectly. All the more so for Knysh, who judging by his age had to have worked for the KGB."

"He's an incredibly unpleasant type. You get the impression that when he looks at a person, he's undressing her."

"Well, it's pretty normal for a man to undress a beautiful woman with his eyes."

"Have you undressed me with your eyes too?" Danka laughed.

"It was on the Devil's Cliff," Yarosh answered with a smile. "I undressed and dressed you back. Right now, you're dressed; you don't have to be self-conscious."

"Oy, thank you, because I was getting uncomfortable." Suddenly she leaned over to Yarosh and whispered: "I'll tell you something, and you laugh and don't look up. Let's pretend we're intimate. Over there, a man is walking around and pretending to talk on his cell phone, but in fact he's waiting for a table to free up. He's been following me since I left the university." Then she sat up straight and continued:

"When I announced to that Knysh I'm not planning to do anything, he said that I should first consult with my father. I asked what this had to do with my father. He answered that because of my obstinacy, my father might not ever find himself in public service again. Do you understand?"

Yarosh looked at the street. The man with the cell phone was really walking back and forth, but soon one of the tables freed up, and he rushed to take it.

"I think," Yarosh said, "we can safely ignore that character. Like this one at that table. Why should we be afraid?"

"Knysh demanded that I promise to keep our conversation confidential. I refused. He literally said the following: 'Well, then... It's not necessary for you to be a student to satisfy your Arcanumian interests. To the contrary, the university only takes away your precious time.' I left and slammed the door, but just now figured out what he meant. Can they expel me?"

"I don't think it will come down to that. You haven't had any problems with your classes?"

"No. Well, except for physical education...I just got out of it, or rather, my father got me out of it."

"Maybe we should talk about something more pleasant? Have you already chosen a topic for your senior thesis?"

"Of course. You have three guesses."

"The writings of Lucilius on the background of the era?"

"Uh huh. And you're my advisor."

"Well, it won't be Knysh then!"

They both laughed. The character at the table looked at them askance and lit up a cigarette.

"On Sunday, Yarosh said, "I was too anxious... or nervous ... I didn't read your translation of Lucilius' biography by Alceste very carefully. But yesterday I finally read it attentively... It seems to me your attitude to the text is too serious... Alceste is really being ironic... deriding him... he was never Lucilius' friend and always saw him as his rival... It's the same relationship between Shevchenko and Kulish.[106] Kulish wrote the long poem "Taras in Hell" where he made fun of both Shevchenko and Kostomarov. In hell Shevchenko has a barrel of *horilka* attached to his neck, but he can't drink it because he can't reach it. We see something similar in Alceste. His stories about Lucilius are actually a kind of parody of saint's lives... Seemingly from the words of Lucilius, Alceste narrates various incidents from his life, even from his childhood. But there you can clearly see the irony. If Lucilius had told him something, it wasn't in this form. Well, for example, can you imagine a son speaking of his mother as a royal concubine?"

"I suspected something like that, because there are too many details of the kind that one wouldn't be mention out loud...."

"I permitted myself to edit your translation... that is, my intrusions were not so essential, but perhaps they at least reflect what Alceste wanted to express. That is, I cleaned up all the pathos and splendor.

"Oh, can I take a look?"

"Unfortunately, I didn't plan this meeting... I thought Friday, when we have our seminar...."

"But I can't hold out until Friday! I know what you'll say: I'll send it by email. No, I want to hear the edited transla-

106 Ukrainian writers and cultural activists of the nineteenth century: the national bard Taras Shevchenko (1814-1861), the writer and translator Panteleimon Kulish (1819-1897), and the historian and socio-political activist Mykola Kostomarov (1817-1885).

tion from your lips. I'm going to hold my translation in my hands and compare it to your editing. And do you know where we'll turn this into a reality? In your orchard. Under that old pear tree that you wanted to cut down. My mother said there are still plenty of pears there. I hope our heads will be safe?"

She said it with a laugh and her eyes shone and glimmered in the sun. Yarosh stared at her, and before he realized it, he agreed.

"Do you what we'll do?" he said. "Here's some money, take it and go over as if you're going to the bathroom, but really just pay the check. And then quickly go to Pidvalna Street. I'll catch up to you. When this character figures it out, he won't be able to settle his bill fast enough."

Yarosh enjoyed watching the unknown guy rush when he saw that he had stood up, and begin to wave to the waiter, but before the latter came, Yarosh was already around the corner. On Pidvalna they got into a taxi and within a few minutes were in Kryvchytsi. Yarosh brought an old mattress out of the house and put it under the old pear tree, on which both of them made room for themselves with the wine and the manuscripts. In the neighboring yard, Mrs. Stefa was tying up her asters, but she couldn't resist glancing in their direction from time to time with a satisfied smile.

"Well, should we start?" Yarosh said and began to read his version of the translation. "The Executioners and the Victims." I left your title, even though the original was "Liceu and olo"—"Knights and Heads." I'm not sure which variant is better. So, let's proceed...."

"During his childhood, his mother went with Lucilius to the royal palace. She left him in a huge hall there, ordering him to wait until she returned. Lucilius readily agreed to wait, because the walls were painted with fanciful plants and animals. It seemed that you were in an incredibly dense virgin forest. Big boughs with leaves, ferns and climbing stems hid the bodies of leopards. Only upon carefully looking closer, could one recognize their supple shapes, or catch the flashing of their ferocious eyes. Colorful birds that no one had yet seen in Arcanum fluttered above. Lucilius, slack-jawed, looked at this wonder and was not bored at all.

During that time his mother was in the king's arms. The king had many concubines, but none inflamed his desire like Anastasia. The first thing that drove him to a frenzy was that she was not ashamed of her nakedness and allowed him to examine her from every possible position. She undressed the king, laid him down on the bed, and kissed him from head to toe so intoxicatingly that he closed his eyes and felt like he was up high above the clouds. His other concubines didn't have a bit of that fantasy.

Interestingly, at home Anastasia behaved very modestly and more closely resembled a timid, quiet woman. Her husband, the governor of Thulium, was mainly away on campaigns. He rarely stayed at home, and in addition, was twice as old as his wife. His trusted servants took care of Anastasia like the apple of their eye, and when they saw that she was going somewhere by herself, they immediately came forward to accompany her. That's why she took little Lucilius with her to put a damper on the vigilant servants. The little boy never doubted that his mother was taking care of the royal daughters' hairstyles. He heard precisely that explanation from her lips, together with a request not to talk about it to anyone. Fortunately, Lucilius knew how to keep silent and did not bear away any impressions other than memories of the wondrous virgin forest on the walls of the royal palace.

Once Lucilius walked up very close to the depiction of a doe lying on the grass; blood trickled from a bite on its throat. He touched the wounds with his fingers, as though he wanted to heal them. His hand involuntarily pressed against the wall, and a door suddenly opened. Lucilius, without hesitation, stepped into a dimly lit room. What he saw then he would remember for a lifetime. In the middle of the room stood an oak table with seven knights seated around it. They all froze motionless with their right hands extended, holding wooden tankards. On the table something unknown turned black and green in bowls, sprouting wild greenery.

Lucilius carefully passed the knights and pushed the door open on the opposite wall. This time he saw a hall, littered with severed heads. However, unlike the knights, the heads didn't lie motionless. They rolled their eyes, blinked, scowled, bared their teeth, laughed, howled and snorted. When they saw Lucilius, they suddenly began to hiss, growl and gnash their teeth as though on command, and some even rolled over to the boy trying to bite his legs.

Somehow, he got the idea that these heads were cut off by those sleeping knights. Not waiting for the sharp teeth to grab onto his leg, Lucilius rushed headlong from the room and slammed the door. Cursing and swearing could be heard following him. Running past the knights, the boy got caught on someone's sword that reached to the floor and fell right on a knight's foot. Suddenly all seven came to life and began very slowly to lift their tankards to their lips, but right at the moment the tankards touched their lips, their right hands froze again and no longer stirred.

Lucilius ran out of the room. And just in time—right then his mother appeared.

'Mother! Mother! Look what I've seen!' The boy screamed.

'Quiet!" She touched her lips with her finger. 'You can't make noise here. You can tell me everything on the way home.'"

"Well, you see," Yarosh concluded the reading. "It seems the same, but it isn't. In the original there's no hint that it's written from the words of Lucilius, but twice after the name of Lucilius you used the word 'says'... That's true, the character 'KT' can be read as 'kayate'—meaning 'says'... But only when there's a line over it, because otherwise it is "kayayate"—meaning 'approached, came close'...."

"Ahh, I thought that line referred to that hieroglyph that's over 'KT'... Those lines above and below the hieroglyphs look the same."

If you take a closer look, you'll see that lines above are narrower than those below. Because of that a few more errors have crept in."

"It's because you printed those characters as tiny as poppy seeds. You need a magnifying glass to read it," Her feelings hurt, Danka pursed her lips. "I translated Lucilius's poems without mistakes, because you didn't make them so tiny."

"I was striving to convey not only the text but also the way it looked on the original tablet. The poems were written on narrower tablets, so the hieroglyphs fit there easily. But here there were wider tablets. Maybe you really should wear glasses?" Yarosh smiled.

"Are you making fun of me?" Now she really looked offended. But only for a moment, because again she chided: "Why did birds of 'paradise' become 'colorful birds'?"

"What kind of paradise could exist in the imagination of a pagan?"

"But those birds are called 'of paradise'...."

"They are now, but in those times it was impossible. The Arcanumians had no concept of paradise."

"But I'll tell you," interrupted Mrs. Stefa, who suddenly appeared right at the fence: "there, in paradise, my place is ready. I've seen it many times in dreams. It's too bad that I won't meet with my late husband there."

After these words she hobbled deep into the orchard, and Yarosh and Danka, casting glances at each other, made their way into the house.

"I'm hungry," the girl said.

"I don't have anything ready, but I can fry you some potato pancakes. I have some wonderful soured milk."

"Potato pancakes? That takes too long!" Danka grimaced.

"What do you mean long? About twenty minutes."

"No way. It takes my mother about two hours."

"Well, if it's a large family...."

"I wish! Only three people."

"I'll make them in twenty minutes."

"Well, I'll time you. If you don't manage to do it, then you'll let me read a book of my own choosing."

"And if I manage to do it?"

"Well, then... then... Then you'll get something you don't suspect. You'll see what cannot be seen, hear what cannot be heard, and imbibe what cannot be imbibed."

"Another one of your mother's sweet cakes?"

Danka laughed and shook her head:

"You'll never guess. Ready, go."

Yarosh chose four large potatoes, quickly washed and peeled them with a special knife with an adjustable blade that he brought from the US. The little knife obediently moved across the surface of the potato, shaving off long strips so that in a jiffy the potatoes were peeled. Once again, he washed them and grate them into fine bits, pressing firmly. Thanks to this the potatoes became small and disappeared right before your eyes. Then he put two cast-iron frying pans on the burners, poured in a little oil, and in the meantime he added an egg and a tablespoon of flour to the grated potatoes, salted it, mixed it up, and started to spoon out the pancakes. At high heat, they were fried just for half a minute on each side, and in less than twenty minutes, the bowl with the potato pancakes was on the table. Danka was stunned.

"You need to go on a cooking show like Jamie Oliver."

"You also watch his show?"

"I'm entranced by the way he makes everything so deftly. Although I don't cook, I've gladly watched his entire series. You won. And now you'll get a surprise.

"Great. But maybe let's have a bite to eat first?"

Yarosh poured out the kefir into cups, and they crunched the potato pancakes. Danka's entire demeanor showed how much she savored them:

"My mother's are a bit different... They're also tasty, but different...."

"Incidentally, this is one of the biggest mysteries: why do every cook's potato pancakes come out differently? I even once wondered what should I dedicate myself to? The study of dead languages or research on potato pancakes?"

"Oh my God!" Theatrically Danka wrung her hands. "After defending a dissertation on potato pancakes, you'd have to teach in a culinary college, and we would have never met."

"Why not? You would have met Marko. And Marko would have introduced you to me."

"But how could a potato pancake specialist or rather, a potato pancakeologist interest me?"

"Aha, I only interest you as Arcanumologist?"

"Not only. But about that later," she said with a mysterious smile.

When they finished eating, Danka collected the plates and washed them, and then disappeared in the bathroom. Yarosh poured himself some wine and drank it in a single breath, feeling his pounding heart. Something made him worry, something would happen in a moment, and the foreboding of this unknown frightened and made him doubt whether it was worth it to give in, whether there was still time before it was too late to tear away... to flee, to hide in a corner....

At that moment, Danka walks toward him slowly with a joyful smile playing on her lips, and he sees her breasts and the outline of her hips under her dress, and he isn't able to look away. She doesn't stop, comes up close to him, entwines his neck with her thin hands. Again, he feels a kiss on his lips, but this time the kiss lasts for a long time. He responds to it, his arms embracing her waist, pressing her to himself. Her tongue penetrates his mouth, quivers and tickles. He feels her breasts against his chest. She presses her stomach even more tightly against him, and he becomes rigid, placing himself straight into that valley between her legs. Then his hands slowly descend along her back without any obstructions, because she was wearing nothing else under her dress. His palms lay on her buttocks. He cups them with his hands, and then she suddenly, hanging on to him, lifts her legs and encircles his body. And he carries her to the bed without unlocking their embrace, their lips, their hands, their legs, and they fall onto the bed. She frees his member and accepts it into her heat, her honey, her paradise. And then he finally receives what he couldn't guess, saw what could not be seen, heard what could not be heard, and imbibed what could not be imbibed.

W

Lviv became a real Babylon. The population doubled thanks to fugitives from Poland and colonizers from the Soviet Union. More and more frequently, you saw the NKVD agents' blue and green hats. Red Army soldiers, who looked like tuberculosis patients with gray faces, scurried along the streets. They looked dull and sepulchral. They all wore heavy and dirty boots. The older ones are dressed somewhat better and look better fed, but now they all busy themselves with only one thing in mind: to amass things that were always in short supply and that they had never seen their entire life. The restaurants and pubs that have become crowded "snack bars" and "tea houses" are full of Bolsheviks who just chew, chew and chew all day, they devour everything without exception. It's not surprising, because when they tied the Russian ruble to the Polish zloty, dinner for only two and a half rubles seemed like a dream come true. Besides, Soviet women cannot cook, so almost all the families eat in the dining halls. In Lviv's cafes and breakfast rooms a particular odor prevailed, which was not previously there. Poisonous tobacco smoke hung there and loud chomping, munching and gulping echoed. Someone blows their nose right on the floor, holding one nostril with his thumb. Another spits while eating his meal. Almost everyone wipes his greasy lips on his sleeves. They belch heartily and pick their yellow teeth with their dirty fingernails. The Galicians try to avoid such places so the cacophony of sounds doesn't spoil their appetite. They prefer to go a little farther from the downtown, where in small alleyways you can come across a little "snack" place not ruined by tarpaulin boots.

The Soviet people who arrived in Galicia elicited considerable surprise in us. They're totally different. They're not used to greeting people on the streets or tipping a hat or cap. They don't apologize when they push someone. Anywhere there's a line or a larger gathering of people, they behave like savages; they swear and are rude. The most popular word among police officers, janitors and even any Soviet official is "move": "move back," "move forward," "move on." They address everyone using an informal "you," regardless of the person's age. Upon entering a Galician's house, none of them take off their hat. They mistake manual laborers for engineers or even for the bourgeoisie, because they are dressed much better than their workers.

"Have you ever noticed what their wives look like?" Ruta asked one evening when our entire gang was sitting in the Atlas Restaurant, which was living out its finest hour, and we shared our impressions about our liberators. "All of them wear red berets, pulled down all the way to their eyebrows. They have unfriendly demeanors, thin lips, gray and sleepy eyes, scraggy disheveled faces, a long narrow skirt, jacket, and boots. Affiliation with the intellectual "class" is marked by short-cropped hair and roughly painted lips. Our Galicia seems to be a fairyland to them. One Jewish woman from Ukrstrakh [Ukrainian Insurance Company] settled at our place but she didn't know a single word of our language. She had a small suitcase—if you could have seen it!—rags were in it that we would have used to wash the floor. There were two pairs of knee-length cotton drawers, rather mysteriously called "bloomers," in a solid, cornflower blue. As it later turned out, the ones she was wearing were also the same color. But the particular feature of these drawers is the fact that instead of a rubber waistband they have a long cotton drawstring that she had to wind around her waist three times. Can you imagine what luxury that is for a girl! Garter belts are made from whitewashed linen, and they don't have bras at all. Her stockings are so shiny that they even hurt your eyes. They aren't sewn closed at the end, so at the tip they have a hole through which the toes can be seen. Finally, I felt so bad for her, I gave her a few pairs of undergarments. She pulled them to her face and couldn't have been happier. Yesterday our class was taken to the theater to Korniychuk's[107] play *Bohdan Khmelnytsky*. The theater was overflowing. There were a bunch of different clerks and Red Army sergeant majors. Many Soviet women were also there who already smartened up in our stores. But you should have seen how they all looked! Some wore long dresses, grazing their tarpaulin boot tops, others wore bright pink muslin dresses. Not a single one of them guessed that they were in women's nightgowns! Yet others dressed themselves in "milyanez" embroidered nightshirts that displayed a wide décolleté. With the absence of bras, you can get an unforgettable view especially if you see all this from the balcony. And when one of the lady comrades in such a "dress" happened to be in a brightly-lit space, you could see what she had on underneath. Most often, it was not delicate Polish underwear, but Soviet knee-length pantaloons."

"Our new teacher who arrived from Kharkiv bought different outfits and every day now she struts in something new," Leah picked up. "One time she came in a chiffon dress, another—in a new robe, a third—in a sailor's top and

107 Soviet-period Ukrainian playwright Oleksandr Korniychuk (1905-1972). The play on the Ukrainian Hetman Bohdan Khmelnytsky of the Zaprozhian Sich Kozaks was published in 1939.

a pleated skirt like a schoolgirl. But of course, the pinnacle of her wardrobe was a floor-length evening dress with a slit all the way down her back to her waist. When she moved too abruptly, the edge of her powder blue pantaloons peeped out from the cutout. We all couldn't refrain from giggling, but the poor woman couldn't understand why and just grew nervous."

Each of us found something more to relate on this bountiful topic.

"I heard that some 'executive officials' who settled in the Hotel George once came to a restaurant for breakfast in their pajamas. The waiters politely asked them to leave with restrained malice. Now every one of us, even the poor proletarian, began to perceive himself to be a Kulturträger in comparison to the savage Asians."

"Have you heard the joke? Why do Bolsheviks wear red berets? So lice will have their own 'red corner.'"[108]

"It's a joke but I'm telling you the truth, I saw it with my own eyes. They ask one Bolshevik: 'Do you have flour?'—'Yes, a lot!'—'How about sugar?'—'Oh! As much as you want!'—'And kerosene?'—'Yes, lots, lots!'—'How about Copenhagen tobacco?'—'As much as you want!' They ask a second, 'Do you have oranges?'—'Yes, for sure.'—"Where do they make them?—'In factories.'"

"I was, riding in a tram, and asked a Red Army soldier: 'Can I buy cosine anywhere here?' He didn't hesitate: 'Yes, it's sold in the shops.'—"Well, how much is it?—'Three rubles a pound.' This morning I'm walking past the monument to Jan Sobieski. As you know, all the Soviets think it's a monu-

108 Red corners were stands or special reading rooms that promoted the Bolshevik revolutionary cause. Thanks to Olha Tytarenko for pointing this out to me.

ment to Khmelnitsky and take pictures with it in the background. I'm walking, and I hear one say to the other in Russian, 'Just look, here's another monument to Khmelnytsky!' To this a Pole answers in Polish: 'It's not Khmelnytsky, it's Sobieski'—'Well, of course, the Soviet Khmelnytsky, the Soviet. Everything's Soviet here.'"

"Yoy, listen to what happened to me today! That stupid captain who took up lodging in my building threatened me with a revolver and accused me of sabotage. I say what's wrong? And he takes me to the water closet, pulls the chain and screams that the water doesn't come out all the time, so he can never manage to wash his hair."

"You're not the first person to say that they use a toilet bowl for a washstand, and they even drink water from it and complain to boot that it's too low. An officer's family settled next door, and his wife invited me for tea. We're sitting there, jabbering about something. Finally, she gets up and says she's going to boil some water, and sets off with the teapot for the water, but not to the kitchen. In a minute she carried out a full teapot from somewhere and brought it to the kitchen. It seemed suspicious to me and I asked where she's getting the water from. 'Well, there in that little room.'—'Do you have a faucet there?'—'Yes, from the little water fountain.'—'What water fountain!?'—I was stunned. She takes me to the water closet, and, except for the white bowl, there's nothing else there."

"Yes, but at the same time they consider the level of culture in Galicia to be very low, because there are no delousing stations. They simply do not understand how the inhabitants of Lviv could do without such a valuable institution. Nowadays, it's impossible to resolve any administrative case without a certificate of successful delousing. Have any of you been in the delousing station on Rutovsky Street? Because I heard that everyone who has gone there curses to high heaven because of the terrible damage to clothes by the awfully stinky disinfectants and hot steam."

"Listen, these are some real Mongols. Anything they don't understand

they destroy. Just think, the slicing machines in the butcher shops that cut up ham, sausage and cheese upset them. 'Who thought this up to cut so thin?' Then the machines disappeared."

"A Red Army soldier comes up to me and asks: 'Are you an engineer?' Oh, no, I say. 'But you're dressed so well?' As you can see, I'm wearing the same thing now as I was then–a sweater."

"What can you say? Our poorest maid looks more richly dressed than a Soviet officer's wife. When we didn't have enough money to pay our maid, our Virunka went to work for a Soviet colonel. Upon learning that her maid had a whole bunch of boxes of shirts, dresses and shoes, his wife could not believe she acquired it by herself and accused her of pilfering from her previous mistress of the house. Virunka had to call us, and we confirmed that our servant bought everything herself. Then the dame raised up a scandal to her husband because she, the wife of a colonel, owned just one torn shirt. She screamed like a monkey in the jungle. The colonel got so angry that he chased her out of the house. Then he married our Virunka, and she's now the colonel's lady."

"One officer brought his wife to the market and she took an interest in hats that were being sold at a deep discount.

The hats were already out of fashion, but the officer's wife didn't care because she had never seen anything like that in her life. The seller tried to help her choose a hat and with that gave her advice in Polish: 'That hat is nice, but Mrs. is very *blada* (pale).'[109] The officer, understanding just the last word, drew his revolver and flipped out. They barely calmed him down."

"They've gotten used to the fact that everything [in the Soviet Union] is in short supply. Yesterday at the Kradidaly Bazaar a soldier approached an old woman selling rolls and asks her: 'Can I buy one?'—'Why not?' The old woman responds.—'Go ahead and buy one, please.' The soldier suspiciously approaches closer, timidly takes a roll and then asks: 'May I?' Then he pays, but in a minute returns and asks: 'May I buy one more roll?' 'You may,' says the woman. He stuffs the second roll in his pocket and asks: 'May I buy a third one?'—'You may buy a third and fourth, even all of them.' The soldier's eyes bugged out and he slowly muttered: 'So that's how they live here. You can buy as much as you want.'"

---

109 The Polish word for pale (blada) in the feminine adjectival form sounds all too similar to the Russian word "bliad'" (whore).

24

The general turned off the tape recorder, leaned back in his chair, lit up a cigarette, looked through light puffs of smoke at Lieutenant Colonel Knysh, and sighed:

"Well, I understand that the matter has not progressed any further. Neither Kurkov nor the professor has told you anything worthwhile."

"We're working on it. We're also working on his student and an old Jewish guy. We've had conversations with all of them."

"It's all going very slowly. I keep getting more reports of people who suddenly begin to recall something from their previous lives. The worst part is, it coincides exactly with the war and postwar years. They've even called from Kyiv asking what the hell is going on. We have a new policy now, so to speak. We're smoothing over all the rough edges with Russia, but here we go again—Katyn, the executions of prisoners, the Bolshevik terror... And all this from eyewitnesses! Where is it coming from?"

"It's all that music. We try to isolate these people... well, the particularly active ones... There is a separate room for them at the Kulpark psychiatric hospital. Let them reminisce in their own circle. They have a "Sector A" and "Sector B." In the "A" group, they are undeniably crazy, including three Wandering Jews (also known as Ahasuerus), two Nostradamuses, one prophet Vernyhora and one Mykhalda."

"Who are those last two?"

"Vernyhora is the legendary prophet who lived in the nineteenth century and Mykhalda a prophetess very popular before the war. They also tell different stories from the past that they saw with their own eyes. In "Sector B," there are people who know who they are, but they only remember what they experienced in a previous life."

"By the way, I recall an interesting case," the general said. "It was sometime at the beginning of the sixties. We receive a letter from a psychiatric hospital, from a certain person who says, 'I, Kalyesnichyenko, Vasily,[110] a lieutenant of the NKVD... in December 1939 due to injury I lost my memory and was in a hospital for the insane in the Kulpark, admitted under the name Ilko Dubnevych. Subsequently, my memory returned to me, I remembered who I was, but they do not believe me.' Well, we checked—there indeed was a Vasily Kalyesnichyenko, who went missing in December 1939. It was believed that he was tortured to death by the partisans in the underground. We went to that patient, interrogated him... He named for us all his previous superiors, his colleagues, he described the location of offices in the Moscow commissariat. In short, everything coincided."

"And so? Was he released?"

"Why? Almost all the people he remembered from his service were either shot or killed at the front. And he crossed his heart, admitting his love for Stalin. What could you do with that? We left him in the nuthouse. But now I'm thinking: wasn't this a similar case?"

The general stooped down, opened the small doors in the desk, took out a bottle of Martel, poured out two glasses and handed one to Knysh:

"Without a hundred grams you won't figure it out... This

---

110 The name is given last name first, which is typical of military men and those in the secret services. It as well is written here in Ukrainian transliteration, mimicking the Russian pronunciation of it.

is how I understand it. Let's call it that miracle-making melody of 'Tango of Death,' it was played right before the people in their previous lives died. Right?"

"It turns out yes," Knysh nodded, exhaling alcohol-laden air.

"And it was played in the Yaniv concentration camp. Right?" Knysh nodded and concentrated, striving to catch the direction of the general's thought. "And Jewish musicians performed this melody. Right?" Knysh again nodded and lit up a cigarette too, so as not to betray his emotions. "It was performed when the Germans liquidated the ghetto. That means...," the general poured out a second glass for them both. "Does that mean that those people who heard it right before their death, and now hear it again and remember their previous lives, are all Jews?"

Knysh finally got the gist and tenaciously held onto that thought. The general grew silent waiting for an answer.

"No, not necessarily. You know, I have studied this question thoroughly. Nationality has nothing to do with it. Only gender plays a role. A person can be reborn later as anyone, even as a student from Zimbabwe. There is just one nuance. Some power in the next life draws together people again who communicated in a previous life or were close friends or relatives. They are not conscious of it. They again contact each other, become friends, or fall in love."

"How about age? Does age play a role?"

"No, as strange as that might be. A man can meet his previous wife in the image of someone the same age, or much younger. A mother can meet her son who is older than she. I don't know why it works this way."

"So do you have married couples there?"

"No, you forget that in order for one of these people to have a revelation, he must hear the melody. If he hears it alone, then only he will have a revelation. He is not able to recognize a loved one from a previous life until that person also has a revelation."

"Until they also hear that melody?"

"Yes."

"And all these data..."

"I already reported to you about Kalkbrenner's treatise."

The general nodded and then filled the glasses with brandy.

"But where does the music come from? Who performs it? Where can you hear it? Have you figured it out?"

"Not yet. We're getting conflicting information. For example, we learn that the tango was performed in a particular restaurant, we question the musicians, take their sheet music—it turns out to be the wrong melody. People who, let's say, had a revelation after hearing this melody, can't remember exactly where they heard it. The fact is that their previous life is suddenly dumped on them—all the knowledge and memories. For many this is a shock, and they don't remember what happened over the course of the last few hours. Some recall walking down the street and suddenly hearing the melody they heard just before their death, and—bam!—he's no longer the person he perceived himself to be. Moreover—he begins to confound those close to him with unbelievable information. In addition, he also seeks out those like him, for an incredible longing is born in him for those who were dear to him, whom he left on the day of his death. These kinds of people are the most dangerous."

"Does it happen that someone remembers not just his last previous life, but also other previous ones?"

"Of course, though that's rare... Then the person suddenly discovers that he/she also understands a language other than his/her mother tongue or starts using words that have fallen out of use."

"Did you tell the professor about these cases when you spoke to him?"

"No, what are you saying! I just told him about one woman who ended up in the Kulpark asylum and began shouting in Spanish. But that's all we've managed to extract from her. We can't put together the exact notes to conduct a successful experiment by ourselves."

"And the treatise?"

"You see, we haven't yet deciphered all of it. There are a couple of notes that defy decryption. Specifically, two out of twelve. And without them the effect is only partial. Incomplete. And besides, only an extraordinary virtuoso can perform the notes, and no one can discern them."

The general leaned forward in surprise:

"What do you mean—no one?"

"I mean—not consciously... These notes are something like a subliminal message. If you so desire, it can be built into any melody. But Untersturmführer Rokita loved the tango, that's why they attached these notes there. Right now, we have a professor as our target, specifically, his work on the "BoD." Maybe the solution is hiding there."

"What does he say?"

"He says he hasn't completed his research. Though he might be lying."

"You know that we must always keep track of him... and intervene at the very moment when he finishes up his work. Not a day later. Of course, all his achievements should end up here. At any price. Are you aware that we interrogated him back in the days of the USSR?"

"No," Knysh was surprised. "I'm hearing this for the first time."

"I know. Unfortunately, all the records were transferred to Moscow in 1991. Back then we were already interested in his passion for things Arcanumian. Since this is a strategic problem, we advised him not to work on it any longer. He strove to explain that Arcanum, like the other ancient cultures, was his area of specialization. Back then we presented him with the first volume of *The Great Soviet Encyclopedia* and suggested he find the term 'Arcanum.' He didn't even look for it he knew well that it wasn't there. Then we said, 'If it is not in the *TGSE*—it doesn't exist at all. Nothing is written about this civilization in any Soviet book. How do you derive this information?' He explained that it was from earlier published sources as well as from abroad. Then we put the screws to him: 'What are those foreign sources? Who supplies them to you?"

"What did he say?"

"It turned out those sources were legal. Some research libraries were allowed to receive scholarly journals from abroad. Of course, these libraries weren't here, but in Moscow. Besides, those sources were only photographs of Arcanumian texts, nothing more, because nobody could decipher them. So, he ran back and forth and kept digging. In Moscow and Berlin, scholars have been engaged in researching Arcanum since the 1930s. People have struggled for years to decode the sources. However, then the goal was to decipher the texts and use them without publishing them. But he achieved everything, published his findings, got famous...

Well, now the situation is different. We have to seize it all."

Obviously feeling very self-important since the general himself was treating him, Knysh crossed his legs and lit a cigarette. Then he inclined his glass and said:

"We had a plan. Slip him a female student who a) is beautiful, and b) will have vulnerabilities that make it possible for us to put pressure on her. We found just the right female student through intense research. After that we studied his son. He likes to smoke grass. So, we nabbed him red-handed. Then we set a task for him: to score with the girl and get her closer to his father. In the meantime, we got her father, who worked in customs, fired. But there was a complication... he, that is, the professor's son, fell head over heels for her... However, the situation itself became resolved because she in turn fell head over heels for the professor. But we couldn't have any influence over her. Our conversation turned out to be ineffective. I even hinted to her that she might be drummed out of the university...."

"Well, you did that in vain. This is a different time now."

"Yeah, once upon a time! One phone call and the issue would have been resolved."

X

Soon the liberators began to liberate the Lviv residents from their homes and property. They would come with their entire families with only one or two cardboard suitcases and would acquire a home for themselves, usually using brute force with the police's help. The era of crowded living space began. Owners were left with just a single room, and the apartment was turned into communal property. That was the best case scenario, because when they started to transport people to the east, one didn't necessarily have to prove himself an enemy of the proletariat in order to get on the list for expulsion. It was enough to own a house or apartment that some higher-up official liked, or to have nice furniture. Then they kindly proposed to the entire family that they pack up a couple suitcases and slip away far from the downtown, even to a hut. Or they were taken away in the middle of the night, thrown into a freight car, and sent to Kazakhstan. On settling in a new apartment, the liberators first tossed the books into the basement—both those "in an incomprehensible tongue" and those "in a comprehensible one" but published by Ukrainian nationalists—which, later in the winter they burned in their stove. Mirrors that did not want to part with the reflections of their former owners particularly drew the hatred of the brothers from the East, and from time to time terrified them with unexpected visions, as if they were not of this world. But in reality they were from this one. More than one officer or his mistress became hysterical upon noticing the reflection of someone else's face twinkle in a mirror, or the figure of someone strange suddenly pop up from the depths and disappear only to slip in as a shadow again some other time. Pieces of furniture also joined in the passive resistance of mirrors and gave no peace: they scraped, loudly cracked in the middle of the night, driving the new occupiers into a stupor, forcing them to rise up and listen. Door jambs brazenly watched and cunningly stuck out their edges, into which people painfully would crack their shoulder or forehead; thresholds leapt up to grab a leg, water pipes and sewage lines got clogged; tiles in the bathroom became covered in slime, and barefooted feet slid on them. And sometimes menacing and unintelligible whispering could be heard in phone handsets, a whisper that then remained in one's ears for a long time and could not be aired out... Then, burning with a thirst for vengeance, the new residents broke up the parquet floors and used them to fuel the stove, smashed the furniture, and sold everything that was valuable in those homes, and thus, totally plundered everything. They moved in an already familiar way into a second apartment, but even there, traps lay in wait, and in their impotent rage they cursed this hateful world that they seized but did not conquer....

That's why it wasn't surprising that for residents of Lviv it was a remarkable consolation to get a tenant from the military or police who could help defend them if necessary. No one felt safe, but everyone thought that he was the only one who didn't have any reason to fear anything. We thought the same thing until Mrs. Konopelka came to us late at night and said that all three of us except for Yosko were listed in an arrest warrant. I was because I already had been detained by the Polish police on suspicion of attempted assassination, Yas—because they already knew he was a non-commissioned officer, and Wolff—because he's German. Everything was very simple. Mrs. Konopelka advised us to escape that night and informed us that a guide would be waiting for us at the station in Zymna Voda. My mother immediately starting bawling, but Mrs. Konopelka quickly got her to come to her senses and ordered her to gather up clothes, bedding and food. I was told to run to Yasko's and Wolff's.

Yasko's uncle drove us in a car to Zymna Voda. It was dawning. On the track stood a lonely railcar and near it a man in a gray cloak was waiting. He waved to us and we got into the car where there were several people with bags. In about an hour, the train arrived, they hitched the wagon, and we started to move. We rode for five hours, and when we finally stopped, we exited the car and paid for the ride. The guide gathered together the entire group and led us between cottages and orchards until we stopped to rest in some barn where we pulled out some food and had a bite to eat. Then we waited until it got dark, and then started off on the road, but this time we didn't walk for very long and finally ended up in a house where our guide's parents lived. The village was just on the other side of Yaroslav. We just needed to get to the other side of the San River. We couldn't go across the river because we didn't have passes, so our guide ferried people across in a rowboat, which locals referred to as "wings." Someone would be waiting to take us to Yaroslav there. Everyone made money on those transports and crossings—the railway workers, the guides, the transporters, the barn's owners, and even the guide's parents.

After spending the night in the barn, we learned that we would have to wait because the "wings" were not there yet. The lady of the house offered to peel some "krumpli" for us, that's what she called potatoes, and if we paid some more, she'd give us some meat, too. When it got dark, the guide ran over to us, ordered us to pick up our bags, and to follow him quickly. In the boat there was a pile of some kind of sacks, evidently with contraband, so the six of us barely fit into the boat with the guide. The guide took one pair of oars, and Yasko and I the other. Wolff was supposed to scoop out the water that got into the boat. When we landed, the guide ordered us to go straight to the bend and not look back. Beyond the bend, a man commanded us to follow him. Soon we met a German soldier, who exchanged a few words with the unknown guy, nodded to us and said: "Schnell, schnell, laufen Sie gerade zum Licht" ("Quickly, quickly, run right to the light").

We ended up right by some large building that was similar to a school. At the end of a long corridor an older gentleman sat behind a little desk conducting registration. We quickly signed a registry and went to a classroom where there were beds with pillows and blankets along with clean towels. We spent the night there. In the morning some people brought coffee, bread and butter, and omelets with marmalade. Then we boarded the train and were in Krakow and then entered into familiar petty hooligan geshefts after organizing contact with the Krakow ghetto. Maybe someone would try to blame us for profiting on someone else's misfortune, but we didn't acquire any great fortune. We had just enough to live, but in my opinion, we were doing good deeds because we were transporting food to the ghetto. In the winter of 1941, the police caught us in the act. Yasko and I managed to dash off, but our burly Wolff couldn't crawl through a lattice fence and got stuck. We tried to pull him through, but the other side had greater numbers.

A few days passed. We remained in hiding and never opened the door when our landlady suddenly shouted to us and informed us that a German soldier was standing at the gate and was interrogating the watchman, but when I looked out through the window, I recognized Wolff—he was in a military uniform. I called out to him, and in a minute, he was in our room. When the police learned that they were dealing with a pureblooded German, they quickly sent him to the military. At first, he'd go through training, and then they'd send him somewhere.

"How did you get so stuck between those latticed fences?" we inquired. "We saw that you could have gotten through!"

"Hey, I knew I could get out of it. What good would it have been if I had not gotten stuck? If I hadn't shielded you with myself? You would have ended up in a concentration camp. They were thrilled that they caught me and concentrated all their efforts on dragging me out."

"Hey!" Yas shouted out. "Son of a bitch, are you saying that you sacrificed yourself for our sake?"

Wolff modestly lowered his eyes and sighed. Yas and I looked at each other. Well, what can you say, we didn't expect such self-sacrifice from him. We said goodbye with tears in our eyes and continued our noble cause of saving Jews from death by starvation for the second time. But in May 1941 we were tempted by a real deal: a great opportunity fell into our laps to send a truck of rubber boots to the Soviet zone. It almost worked out, except on the other side our colleagues, if you can call them that, decided that it would be cheaper to hand us over to the police than to pay us. When we transported the last batch of boots by boat, they were already waiting for us on the shore, and in a few hours, we were already breathing in the shithole odor of Brygidky[111] Prison. This once spacious Polish prison was bursting at the seams from the large number of prisoners, most of whom were political.

At first Yasko and I were considered ordinary criminals, but the NKVD agents soon found evidence that I was arrested by the Poles on suspicion of an assassination attempt, so I became a political prisoner. I was transferred to a cell so packed with people that we were forced to stand all day long. At night under bright lights we sat down, stretched our legs, and between my legs a second guy say down, in between his legs a third. It was like that from wall to wall. Lice pestered us mercilessly. Most prisoners were Ukrainian: simple peasants, priests and teachers. Among us there were also several Polish policemen. They were all sentenced to death, and they all were given paper and a pencil to write requests for a pardon addressed to Stalin. They duly wrote them, believing that somehow it would help, but all of them were shot one by one to the roar of engines. There were also officers who tried to flee to Romania. They went into the cell in nice boots, but after the first interrogation came back in slippers.

The NKVD agent who interrogated me asked among other things where the best conditions were: in Polish or Soviet prisons. I answered that a prison is a prison and it's difficult to hope here for any kind of benefits, but in a Polish prison, we could not only sleep on plank beds, but also received newspapers and read books.

"What?" His eyes opened wide. "You even read books?"

---

111 See footnote #88.

Shaking his head incredulously, he slipped me a piece of paper and told me to describe how I ended up in the OUN (the Organization of Ukrainian Nationalists). I replied:

"It was a misunderstanding. The Polish police sorted that out and released me. I was arrested by mistake."

"Don't think that idiots are sitting here," he replied. "In their reports they write that they found no evidence of your participation in the assassination attempt. But that does not mean you are innocent. We are interested in your uncle. Was it he who led the gang? Did he plan assassinations? Speak! And Lucia? We know that she fired the shots. Where can she be hiding?"

"How do I know when I was arrested right at the border? I wasn't here."

"You say you didn't have contact with them? Your Leah told us a little."

I froze.

"Leah? You arrested her?"

"Of course. Membership in a criminal Zionist organization. Unfortunately, we couldn't find her brother. You had interesting company—all children of insurgents."

Subsequent interrogations occurred at night. Two times they really smacked me around until I bled and couldn't walk on my own. They carried me away and threw me to the floor.

Every Sunday, Father Myroslav, my uncle, quietly conducted a church service. Nowadays he didn't at all resemble the father-hooligan, whom I remembered from childhood. During prayer one of us stood at the door and covered the "visitor's window" with his back. Once we heard a calm female voice from the courtyard. I asked to be lifted up to the window and saw that female prisoners were walking, among whom was Leah, though I didn't immediately recognize her. She looked exhausted and sad, and her face was gaunt. I shouted: "Leah! Leah! "She looked back and fearfully searched for me with her eyes. She finally saw me and put her hand to her lips. What was that supposed to mean? A kiss through the air or a sign that she was silent and said nothing? I wiped away a tear and spent the rest of the day in deep contemplation.

I will never forget Sunday June 22, 1941 until my dying day. Right as the day was breaking, explosions reverberated; so many bombs began to explode that the walls began to tremble. Incredible agitation seized everyone. We jumped to our feet and tried to reach the window at least to see something. In the afternoon the cell doors started to shake. The NKVD agents began taking several prisoners at a time to the yard and shot them there, covering the noise with the roar of truck engines. Desperate cries echoed, pleas, requests for mercy. It was beyond one's strength to listen to those cries. They summoned all the Polish officers from our cell. They silently approached Father Myroslav, who was Greek-Catholic, because there was no other priest there. They kneeled and accepted his blessing. The NKVD agents tried to hasten them but were afraid to enter the cell, sensing that at that moment people might be capable of desperate actions. Then they summoned several seminary students. It became less crowded in the cell; now everyone approached father to confess without waiting to be summoned. We all were in a kind of stupor. We didn't speak among ourselves, just with God. In my thoughts, I put together a list of all my sins. Before me appeared those to whom I caused some unpleasantness. They looked me straight in the eye but were silent and I didn't know if they would forgive my sin or not. The sins came one after another, but the greatest one was not there. I consoled myself with the thought of the purity of my soul, when suddenly it hit me—perhaps your greatest sin hasn't yet occurred. Its grain is germinating right now and is going to grow, and when you again find yourself under interrogation, your greatest sin will crawl out of you like a serpent. I became terrified at that thought. All previous evil deeds immediately diminished. They obviously would vanish if I endured and gave no one up, because, if I thought hard, I could guess where you could find uncle and Lucia, and if I held out, then all past sins would be forgiven. But if I blurt it out, those sins compared to this, the greatest, will become invisible. I knew well that I wasn't a hero or a saint, and everything bad that I'd ever done didn't outweigh the sins that others had committed. Therefore, like everyone else, I suspect that I'm still a coward, at least in my dreams I am. For I haven't had a chance to test my courage in life or even to find out whether I have it at all. I tried to drive these cruel thoughts out of my head, because they tortured and punished me for who knows what. But the prospect of committing a crime haunted me and would continue to haunt me until I was summoned for questioning again and then I would test myself and find out who I am. I started to remember the harsh words that I threw in my family's face, that they quickly forgot and never held against me. Now I wanted to fall before them on my knees and beg for forgiveness. Also, fear gripped me for Leah, the thin, sickly girl with delicate features and soft hands. She might be interrogated in the same way as me, or abused and raped. The doors banged, and everyone became petrified. Father muttered a prayer and the killers shouted out several names, among them mine. I shouted without looking up: "Not here!" And I felt cold sweat pouring over me and my fingers trembled. One of them said in Russian "He's gone!" The doors closed. I didn't raise my head, not knowing with how my cellmates were looking at me, perhaps judging me. But so what? The lie could be revealed very quickly. I won from death only a few hours or minutes, perhaps. Thinking about death, I felt more at ease. Fear of death wasn't the most troubling, rather it was the fear in the face of torture. Regarding death, I would have preferred to choose which way to die. The best would be to die in combat while you were attacking, when some powerful force carries you forward, but I was not ready to die from a bullet in the back of the head.

Suddenly I realized that I had begun to listen to the sounds of a violin, which came from somewhere in the distance. These sounds interrupted the whining and bells of the tram cars and human voices, but the violin continued to play, and I recognized in those sounds the tango, which Yosko so often played, the tango of death.

During the night from Monday to Tuesday, a sudden silence reigned. Doors no longer slammed, footsteps didn't stomp. You couldn't hear the voices and the roar of engines. Outside in the yard you could hear female voices. Someone shouted that the NKVD agents had left the prison. Movement started. In all the cells the prisoners tried to break down the doors. We broke off the iron top of the wood-burning stove and pounded with it, but it was in vain. Meanwhile, in the corridor there was already a bustle, scurrying. I stood on my toes to reach the window and saw a bunch of prisoners in the yard. They were just hanging out and didn't have the nerve to approach the gate. Suddenly I noticed Yas. He and several prisoners were dragging an iron pry bar. In a minute they already broke through our doors, and we fell into each other's arms. But time was short, the NKVD agents could return, and outside it was already beginning to dawn.

"Where is Leah?" I asked after we had run into the yard.

"We smashed open her cell too. She's waiting for us at the gate on the other side of the street. Let's run out fast."

We ran out onto the street and saw two Soviet tanks. Shots flew over our heads. Someone rushed back into the courtyard, but Yas and I ran like the wind. It's better to die by bullet fire than return to that hell. We fly into the gateway at full speed. Leah's already there: "Come here, here!" She waves us over and takes us into an orchard, with a wooden fence at its edge. Next to the fence is a branchy acacia. We grab at a branch and hoist ourselves up into another small orchard, and from there through the gate we run to Brayerivska Street. There's not a soul. We're saved. The watchman of Yasko's building opens up the gate for us and whispers: "Into the attic! Into the attic! But be's quiet, cause the Soviet Zhydy[112] (Jews)... oops, Evrei (Hebrews) ... those—on the ground floor... haven't left yet, they're still arguing about whether to take off or not... Yasko, don't go to your place. I'll go to tell your mother you're here."

Having lost our strength, we fall on some bags and old furniture in the attic and look at each other. Soon we begin hugging each other, and tears fill our eyes. I control myself

112 The common Western Ukrainian (and Polish) word for Jew is "zhyd," which in Russian is a pejorative. Russians instead use the word "evrei" as the standard appellation.

and sob spasmodically. Leah strokes my head and I feel like our tears are uniting. Her body is shaking. I stroke my hand along her back and say:

"You can play Bach on your ribs right now," and we laugh boisterously through our tears and despair.

25

In the office of the chief doctor of the institution for the insane, a man about sixty years old was sitting in front of Lieutenant colonel Knysh. He was expressively agitated, crossing and re-crossing his legs, his eyes darting back and forth in a panic, but when they met the penetrating gaze of Knysh, they hid like snails under his eyelids. According to a really old habit instilled by his service in the KGB Knysh maintained a long pause and only after that opened the folder and read aloud:

"Vladimir Petrovich Tsybulko, year of birth 1950. Place of birth—Kolomiya. Place of legal residence—Lviv, 6 Prince Mstislav Street. Job—dance teacher. Married, two children. Is that so?"

"Yes," the man nodded and tried to concentrate, realizing that finally the real questioning had begun.

"So, tell me what happened to you. How did you end up in Kulpark? You've been diagnosed as having a split personality?"

The man winced and rubbed his face.

"What do you mean split? There is no split!"

"It's written here: impersonating Milker Zelman, a Jew who died in the Yaniv concentration camp."

"Uh-h, excuse me... it's not quite like that... No, I haven't stopped being Volodymyr Petrovych Tsybulko. I've just become enriched, if you can say it that way, by another consciousness... I suddenly discovered knowledge that I did not have up until now. I can tell you all the details about pre-war Lviv. I can tell you all the prices in all the stores, what they sold, and where they were. And if you want—I can take you to the location of the concentration camp and show you where which barracks were. Do you realize of what use I can be? So, I came to the city council with this. I'm ready to work, so to speak, to recreate the history of the city. Well, that's when it began... First, journalists, TV reporters, and then the orderlies... They took me away just when I learned that my nephew had survived...."

Knysh listened to him carefully and gradually knit his brows.

"Aha, so you believe that you are Zelman Milker?"

"No-no, what are you saying. I'm Volodymyr Petrovych Tsybulko. But Zelman Milker—this is my second "I." Well, you're the same way. Your first "I" is SBU colonel, and the second—a family man, a father. These two "I's" don't overlap, right? It's like that with me. They exist in parallel in me. And there's no conflict between them. I have countless evidence that I'm not lying. Here, for example... In September 1939, as a member of the Communist Party of Western Ukraine, I accidentally poisoned eight Red Army soldiers.

Knysh's eyes bugged out.

"Yes-yes, accidentally. I just decorated the room in which they were sleeping after a drinking bout with flowers. But there turned out to be too many flowers. So, we buried them in two graves as zhy (Jews)... sorry, evrei (Hebrews), as they say now. I can show you the graves. It's time to set up some kind of red pedestal there. And if you like, I'll read you a poem by Itzik Manger in Yiddish? I remember it from school."

The split Tsybulko even furrowed his brow and prepared himself to recite it when Knysh stopped him:

"Wait. Explain one thing to me. When your other "I" was led out to be shot, what did he hear right before death?"

"What did I hear?..." The little man thought about it. "What did I hear... Yoy! Screams and sobs—that's what I heard. There were several thousand of us. They shot us in groups, both women and children... Everyone was weeping, whimpering, they tried to calm down the children... Horrors...."

"And that's all you heard?

"There was machine gun fire. That's the last thing I heard."

"What about music? Was there music?"

"Uh-h, music? Well, of course—the orchestra was playing. But, you know, it played constantly without stopping. No one paid any attention to it. It was like the sound of the wind or the rustling of trees.

"Can you remember what exactly the orchestra was playing?"

"Some kind of marches... Our commandant Vilgauz was very fond of marches."

"Was there a tango?"

"Tango... there was a tango too... It was Rokita who insisted that they play a tango. My nephew Yosko was also playing there! If you just bring us together, then I'd immediately prove to you I'm not lying."

"Good," said Knysh, started smoking and tapped his lighter on the desk. "Now, remember the moment you became conscious of the fact that your second 'I' whisked in."

"I don't know. I'm walking along the street, then suddenly—bang!—And heck! I'm not the person I thought I was for so many years. That is, I am the person, but not entirely."

"Did you hear anything at that moment? Maybe some sounds...."

"Sounds... A jeep nearly ran me over. A Mitsubishi Pajero. When it beeped, I jumped. And, by the way, I crossed at the 'green' light. It knocked me off balance. Before that I felt completely relaxed. I was thinking about something pleasant. But when I crossed the street, I felt my blood pressure go up. I don't know if you heard that "pajero" in Latin American lingo means "pederast." I was all shaken up with rage. And when it happened I wanted to shout out after him: "You, pajero!" But I shouted something entirely different, "Mamzer[113]! Meshugenah!" Can you imagine? And then suddenly I sense something floating toward me... you know, so gently, something envelops me like a chrysalis of a silkworm ... I froze and then realized that a violin was playing. Of course, I love music, but I've never listened to street musicians. And then I froze, stood there and absorbed it into myself as if I were sunbathing."

"Who was playing? Did you see?"

No. A violin was playing somewhere from afar. I don't even know where the music was coming from—from the street or from an open window."

"Where did it happen?"

"Right next to St. Anna's Church."

"Closer to Kleparivska Street?"

"Yes, I had just walked across to the other side of the street. It was then, in fact, that I became a different person. Some force pulled me toward Zamarstynivska Street because I was convinced that I lived right there, but when I knocked at the door of my house, I saw strangers. Then I grasped that something was wrong. I apologized, left, rummaged in my pocket and, fortunately, found a receipt for an

113 The Yiddish word for an illegitimate child.

unpaid gas bill. Then I went in the direction of that address and ended up at home. Then all kinds of other problems hit me. So, do you see I'm not crazy? Talk to them about discharging me. If you insist, I can keep this new knowledge to myself. The only thing I'd like is to visit with Yosko. My favorite nephew."

"And what will you say to him? That you've been raised like Lazarus?"

Knysh got up, took the folder under his arm, and made his way to the door. The little man shouted after him:

"Don't leave me here! Don't leave me! I'm ready to forget everything! Do you hear? Everything!" But in a whisper he added: "Besides my favorite Yossel...."

Y

Now I'll use Yosko's diary and carefully copy all that happened in the city while I was sitting in the slammer. Yosko, who was supposed to be arrested just like Leah, hid in the attic and stayed there for a month.

"At the crack of dawn on June 22, 1941, as it did in September 1939, Lviv was again shaken by explosions. German planes began to rumble in the sky, and bombs fell on the train station and Snyliv Airport. Mikolyash Arcade was lying in ruins with two dozen spectators dead in the cinema. Although the pilots were aiming at the main post office, they missed. In addition, they destroyed the Church of the Holy Spirit next to the post office, and along with it another three hundred or so houses. The front had not yet approached the city when the super elite of the liberators rushed to flee, packing stolen goods—kilims, bedspreads, chandeliers, bedding, china, paintings, services, clothing—on their trucks... These trucks looked like pyramids, and because they were hastily packed, a lot of stuff falls off and breaks. "Move it! Move it! Move it! Move it!," echoes everywhere. Some spur others on, shout and curse. Their wives' insurmountable fear drives them to the east, and they are willing to even crush their own retreating soldiers, who prevent them from moving forward as do the trucks with ammunition covered with branches.

The major stationed at Zelman's uncle's paid him and told him to spend all his money on food. There was panic in the town. The water pumps were damaged and there was only enough water for two weeks.

Night is coming. Strips of light intersect across the sky. Trams aren't running.

June 24, Tuesday. Yesterday I stood on Kazymyrivska Street in front of Brygidka[114] and played the violin. No one bothered me because I prudently put on dark sunglasses and a crutch and hat lay at my feet. People threw me kopecks, and I played for Orko, Yasko, and Leah in the hope that they might hear me, so they wouldn't be as frightened. This morning Aunt Rivka ran over and told me the good news: Leah had been saved. Yas and Orko had also escaped. The Lord answered my prayers."

We left our hiding place on June 29, on the second Sunday in June during the war. On the streets there was incredible movement everywhere. Police booths emptied; cars stood in traffic jams. For an entire week continuous columns of Bolshevik troops stretched; cannons and tanks crawled. The soldiers' faces were tired and gloomy. You could read fear and indecision in their eyes; no one cast victorious looks on the crowds of Lviv's inhabitants. They didn't even want to start chatting. The army moved silently, and the people silently watched as they departed. Only once did we hear an exclamation from someone in the crowd, and it concerned captured Polish soldiers who were walking with shovels and picks on their shoulders. On their heads they still wore *rogatywka*[115] garrison caps that distinguished them from the others, because their clothes were dusty and faded, and their feet, wrapped in multicolored rags, hurt from walking without boots or shoes. "Why are you dragging them behind you? Let them go!" someone shouted. The guards who sauntered along on both sides of the prisoners paid no attention to the shouting, but they paid attention when one

114 The Brygidka Prison. See footnote #88.
115 See the following link for pictures of the hats: https://en.wikipedia.org/wiki/Rogatywka.

of Lviv's residents tried to give the prisoners a piece of bread or a cigarette. Then suddenly a bayonet flashed in the sun and you could hear the screams in Russian "That's forbidden! Back away! Back off!" And behind the Polish prisoners were boys from villages, who had been conscripted into the army yesterday; they were dressed in civilian clothes. Each one carried some kind of bag on his shoulders. Their eyes nervously flitted around as though they were seeking an opportunity to escape, but they were being guarded too.

The people stood on tiptoe and waited for the German prisoners to appear, but there were none. By the afternoon the crowd started to break up. Despite the heat and stuffiness, the windows of the stone buildings were closed, though no one ordered it, but recent experience suggested that it was better not to stick out, especially since gunshots and explosions reverberated in different parts of the city. Several days ago, when overly curious citizens watched the Bolshevik cars from their windows on Bilczewski Square, machine gunners showered them with abundant fire. Now there was only urban commotion on the streets and hooligans and thieves. They relished the risk, especially because a lot of goods remained in the stores. Antlike work was teeming on those quiet streets where the army wasn't present: iron sheets and bars were broken, doors and windows were pulled out, they broke in and dragged out everything they came across, and then they were also fighting and ripping stuff out of each other's hands. All of a sudden, they forgot that they were people and behaved like animals. They were pushing each other, scratching and biting. White flour was scattered everywhere, sugar and salt crunched underfoot, feet became entangled in rolls of fabric, they slipped on bars of soap, and then the people scattered. Cracked tables and shelves remained in their place. Some people also burned the merchandise to say farewell, as if they were expressing their rage caused by the Bolshevik occupation and prolonged standing in lines, and caustic smoke spread along the streets, and flames devoured everything they could. The soldiers looked at these flashes of fire and didn't intervene, thinking that everything was going according to plan. The enemy must not get the people's possessions. Closer to evening, the number of robberies grew, and those who didn't take part in them couldn't help but wonder where all these goods were coming from if they weren't available before. And if they were, they were thrown out for several hours, and again they disappeared. Those who started the looting returned with sacks, washtubs, buckets, blankets, and baby carriages, bringing their family along, both the elderly and little ones. First and foremost, they snatched the food, but barrels of beer and vodka would also not be wasted. Here and there, happy groups gathered next to such a barrel and took communion, pouring it for themselves in pots, vases, hats, and cupped hands.... Yas, Yosko, our moms and I also decided not to stand there gawking and began to drag out as much as we could—flour, buckwheat groats, pasta, soap, salt, sugar, and matches. Yosko dragged out an entire roll of calico and shared it with us.

On Monday June 30, the Germans entered the city. I went into town and saw people greeting them with flowers. Girls were handing each one a flower, even entire bouquets. They were hugging and kissing them, and not just the Ukrainian girls, but also the Polish and even Jewish women. I myself felt like shaking the hand of some soldier who freed us from the scourge of the Bolsheviks, but something kept me from doing that. Acclamations of greeting and applause echoed.

Behind the first divisions of German soldiers a Ukrainian division marched with a cheerful song on their lips. They were the young boys who had fled from Galicia before the arrival of the Red Army. All of them were like oaks, tall, healthy, and well-dressed. Each had a short rifle on his shoulder and those in front carried machine guns attached to their belts. In exactly the same way, the German soldiers looked unflinching and walked freely and naturally. They also were all young people, their light hair not covered by either caps or helmets; their collars were unbuttoned, their sleeves rolled up. No army had ever entered the city that way. They also sang something funny and cheerful. After the impression the Bolshevik army left on us, it seemed, that these soldiers were not going to war, but to a parade.

The people suddenly came to life. They dressed in festive clothing. Many attached blue and yellow ribbons to their clothes. No one was forced to pretend they were proletarian. Everywhere you could hear "Glory to Ukraine!" Blue and yellow flags appeared. Chemistry students from the Polytechnic University made yellow dye and dyed fabric because you couldn't get yellow fabric though you could still get blue fabric. Girls sat and sewed flags, and other students came to immediately hang them on the main streets.

But over the Ratusha City Hall a red flag with a swastika waved. Over the gate of the Ratusha, too, but right at noon two Ukrainian ones appeared on both sides of the German flag as well as at the four corners of the tower. On the Opera House there's a German flag. On the Hetman Ramparts they already managed to burn the monument to the Soviet Constitution.

A rumor instantly spread to us about prisoners executed in the prisons of Lviv. Aunt Olena told us the terrible news: it turns out Uncle Lodzio ended up in the prison on Lonska Street. They arrested him a few days before the war, and now my mother, my aunt and I run over to Lonska Street. There were hordes of people just behind the main post office. Ukrainian police with belts of ammunition and carbines stood right in front of the gate, and there was a cadaverous stench closer to the prison. People were telling stories of the horrors that took place. The Germans didn't forbid anyone from going onto the prison grounds and looking at the liberators' recent atrocities. You get the impression that you've ended up in hell or in a Brueghel or Bosch painting. There are mountains of executed prisoners, not just of men but also women, girls, and even children. All the girls were raped right before being killed, some were crucified on walls, their bodies attached on hooks. Several small girls were impaled on poles. Bottles stick out of girls' vaginas, along with iron rods and sticks. One of Lviv's priests lay there with his eyes ripped out, a second was nailed to the wall, his red innards dangling from his ripped-open stomach. I recognize our dear Uncle, Father Myroslav. And I can't be more amazed at how beautiful and calm his face is, even though he endured a martyr's death. As I look at him, I make the sign of the cross as though to a crucified Jesus. There are papers scattered everywhere. A draft whips through the windows and doors and tosses them around. Everywhere the heavy stench is overwhelming. Everyone coming here holds a handkerchief to his face. It's impossible to endure it longer than a few minutes, but people keep coming and coming, and not just from Lviv, but also from the villages. Some come with their carts and, after identifying one of their relatives, take him out and place him on the cart. The men do this silently and grimly, and the women cry hysterically. They damn the killers and ask God, "Why?" This time God again is silent. The carts drive off, the downcast relatives walking behind them. Lviv's inhabitants stop, remove their caps and hats and make the sign of the cross the way they do when they meet a funeral procession.

The Germans herded Jews over to carry out the corpses from the prison. I saw Yosko among them. There was such fear in his eyes that I approached a German officer and said:

"He's a musician and composer. His hands aren't suited for such work. Can you release him from it?"

The officer looked at me with a surprised smile:

"Physical labor has never harmed anyone yet."

From his pronunciation I realized that he was an Austrian, and continued:

"You should hear him perform Strauss! And Haydn!"

"You're a cunning guy!" The officer laughed. "You guessed I'm Austrian, and now you're trying to tug at my heartstrings? What would you do if I turned out to be Prussian?"

"Then I'd be a goner!" I said, hinting that Prussian music is known only to specialists.

"Okay, call him over."

When Yosko approached, I noticed his fingers shaking. The officer asked:

"So, you're a musician and composer? And you love Austrian music?"

Yosko immediately guessed what it was all about and nodded:

"I love it above all. It's so life-affirming, so bright...."

"And which of the Austrian composers do you like the most?"

"Ignaz Jakob Holtsbauer," Yosko proudly uttered, stunning the officer.

"Really? I never heard of him."

"He was born in 1711 in Vienna, was the conductor of the Vienna Burgtheater, and court conductor in Stuttgart and Manheim, where he died in 1783. He composed sixty-eight symphonies, twenty-one Masses, and thirteen operas, including *Son of the Forest*, *Gunther von Shvartsburg*, and *Tancredi*. Yosko chattered quickly as if he were reading from a script and perhaps would have continued on, but the officer, apparently stunned, stopped him:

"You can go. You have a good friend."

Yosko left, and at right about that time they stopped allowing people to enter the premises of the prison, because the Jews had already carried out everyone into the courtyard, and from there began to carry them out and pile them in front of the prison. People walked from corpse to corpse, trying to recognize someone, though it was hard because the dead bodies were horribly mutilated. A woman recognized her son only by the shoes that his father had made him; his face was swollen, and had no nose or eyes, and she falls on him and laments:

"Oh, my Lord! Oh, dear God! What did he do to deserve such torture! My baby Yura! Where are your shining eyes!? Where are your white little teeth! Where are your golden curls? Damned devils from hell! What you have done! May the earth spit you out, damn you!"

Wailing echoes everywhere, and curses, upon curses, upon curses... Suddenly, when all the bodies had been taken out of the courtyard, a scream split the air. In the yard they found a pit full of corpses, sprinkled over with dirt. People grabbed whatever they can with their hands, any tool that could scrape up the earth, and before their eyes yet another horror is revealed. It's not corpses, but human flesh naked and in rags, with their hands tied behind their backs with barbed wire—including girls as well. The Germans summon the Jews and again order them to remove the dead bodies from the pit and lay them in the yard, but no one can look at this calmly. Everyone gets to work including my mother and me too, because we didn't find our Uncle Lodzio, and in our soul there was still a glimmer of hope that he managed to escape. Again, hordes of people stream into the courtyard, and again examine each body, bursting into tears and pressing handkerchiefs, caps, or just their hands to their nose, because the stench overwhelms their nostrils. Someone can't take it and vomits. If it's impossible to recognize a person by their face, they examine the clothes, turn pockets inside out, because any kind of thing—a comb, a piece of paper, a handkerchief, a pencil stub—can be of use to identify them. We recognized my uncle this way, and we identified my mother's brother only thanks to a sweater that once belonged to my father, for which my mother had personally sewn leather patches on the elbows. Right then my aunt came by and also joined the chorus of laments that shook the prison walls. Only my grandmother, a professional mourner, cried silently at looking at the body of her son—Father Myroslav. For the first time in her life she cried silently and made the sign of the cross while we were removing the body of the crucified priest. But when we tucked his innards into his stomach and tied it up with some kind of cloth so they wouldn't fall out, her lament was the most powerful of all that she had performed in her life because all at once she had lost both her sons. Swallowing my tears, I ran to look for a cart. I found one quickly—right then a cart with the body of a young girl was supposed to be going to Yaniv cemetery. I talked the old man driving the cart into letting me put both of my uncles onto the cart. The old man agreed, and we arranged them all in sitting position, one beside the other, near the young girl, who had black lips. And when the cart shuddered on the cobblestones, a flowery kerchief that covered her shoulders and chest slipped off her, and I saw in place of her breasts terrible branded wounds. Her father walked next to the horse with downcast eyes and didn't look back. My mother wrapped the girl up again in the kerchief and tied the edges of it to the ladder beam so she wouldn't swing back and forth. At the cemetery there were many people like us. Corpses were brought from all three prisons. Gravediggers didn't have time to dig the holes. Relatives of the victims helped. Priests and monks conducted a mass and couldn't hold back their tears.

After those hasty funerals I returned home dizzy, leaving behind my mother and grandmother. I wandered around and staggered, and before my eyes stood the bodies of the executed, and that girl with black lips. I hadn't immediately recognized that girl because she was so bruised and bloody, but there in the cemetery, my mother and grandmother washed her with water from the hand pump before burying her. Then I recognized her and choked back tears of despair, because I had kissed those black lips and I had touched those breasts with my hands. "Lord, Lord," I whispered, "Why you? Why did they do this to you, Milya?" But I didn't tell her father that I knew her. I just helped him dig a hole and cover it with earth. And he in turn helped us bury my uncle. On the way home, I saw a scene that shocked me. A man recognized a Bolshevik secret agent by the Church of St. Anna and like a furious beast lunged at him and began to beat him. The secret agent ran into the middle of the street, but the attacker didn't back off. He caught up to him and had kicked him with his boot so hard that the agent failed to keep his balance and fell. The attacker already was kicking him in the head, back, and stomach; the agent tried to shield himself with his hands, coiled into a roll and screamed. People were walking along both sides of the road, some stopped to listen to the screams, to the irate words of the man giving the beating, and then moved on. No one dared to defend him, not even the German soldiers. They also glanced at the scene and kept smiling. And then I felt a beast awaken in me. A ferocious beast, thirsting for blood, thirsting for revenge to drive away my pain and my despair onto someone else.

26

As he was climbing up the stairs to Milker's apartment, Yarosh heard the sounds of an argument. The old man was swearing at someone. His voice was becoming louder, then weaker. A female voice replied somewhat timidly, as if making excuses, then her heels began to tap across the floor. The door to the stairwell abruptly slammed and a blushing, angry girl jumped out, clasping a violin in her hand. The following words flew after her:

"You can stop coming! Nothing will ever come of you! Better for you to go sell meat pies!"

Yarosh moved back toward the wall, and the girl raced past him like a whirlwind and stomped down the stairs, spitting out fragments of words and phrases. Milker met him on the threshold, breathing heavily.

"There's a goat! There's a goat! There's not a penny of patience. What is she thinking? That music is just a lark? Music is life! You need to give yourself to the music, not the other way around!" He screamed down the stairs, leaning over the railing. "It does not live for you, you must live for it! Breathe it, drink it and eat it! You must completely become the music! Completely! From head to toe! Until your last breath!" Then he nodded to Yarosh to come in, and then continued in the room: "Almost already! Almost! A little bit more! But she has no patience, she says she can't play any better. But I'm sure she will. Just a trifle remained. Just a few notes... The point is not only to replicate the tango, but when she is able to play those notes, she will become what she dreams of becoming—a master.

"So now what? Will you be looking for another student?"

"Why another? She'll come back. I've taught her well. She'll come back...."

Milker knew what he was saying because Yarka was in his thrall, in some kind of incredibly magical captivity. She knew a lot about him now, about his life, about friends he lost, and his family that perished. Strolling with him through the city before and after the lesson, she learned much that she didn't suspect. Although the lessons really tired her out because the old man forced her to play the same melody dozens of times, each time finding flaws that only he could sense. When he pulled out his old violin from its case, its surface resembling the face of a roughly scarred soldier, and handed it to her, and she slid the bow timidly, she felt that the violin emitted some wonderfully melancholy sounds unlike the ones born from her violin. And when she tried to play that same melody that she had already played countless times, inexplicable fear suddenly gripped her. She saw how the old man's eyes lit up, how his face brightened, how his hands folded as if in prayer as he apparently floated in dreamy clouds, lazily swaying like a feather in the wind. But instead Yarka felt light-headed. It seemed like she was losing her common sense. Her hand unwittingly scraped the bow on the strings and seemingly pulled out something sharp like a knife, something that cut the old man's heart. This was the moment he grew ferocious and screamed, she had the impression that with that sound she brutally tore some secret ravings out of him. She tried to explain that she hadn't yet gotten used to his violin, but he didn't listen, and that's when she ran out. Outside she hesitated, wondering where to go. Finally, she decided to go to a little square nearby and sat on a bench, thinking.

Twilight enveloped the street. Then the professor left Milker's and went toward the center of town. Yarka saw a short man emerge from the shadows across the street and at first follow the professor, but he suddenly stopped and cocked his head, and stared at Milker's windows, which were lit up. Yarka also looked up and saw something from which it would take her a long time to recover her senses. Behind the translucent curtains one could see a man's silhouette, holding a violin with one hand and sliding a bow, clenched in his teeth, across it.

Z

In the evening, someone knocked at the door. My mother went to answer and asked, "Who's there?" Ever since the war began, no one in Lviv opened their doors without asking this question. A woman's voice said, "It's me Feiga!" My mother opened it. Feiga was the wife of Ogrenshteyn, the shopkeeper, and Golda's cousin. She looked quite comical now, because despite it being summer, she was wearing a warm fur and even greeted us in a way that stopped our breath: "Glory to Ukraine!" She announced that she had come to request that my mother hide her fur, because there were rumors that Jews would be robbed, and following those words proceeded to take off three of them. My mother asked:

"What will happen if they take them from us?"

Feiga flicked her hand:

"Then so be it. But I'm sure you won't deceive us."

"Did anyone see you come over to me?"

"Do I look stupid? No one saw me. Be well. Glory to Ukraine!"

But the visits didn't end with that, because later the wife of Rittenbach the lawyer came running over and brought a basket of laundry which she also begged to be hidden for her, but when my mother asked whether there was only laundry there, Mrs. Lawyer hesitated and finally said that there were also a few silver utensils and "sort of golden trinkets," then my mother made her take it all out to show her. My mother carefully entered all the things in a notebook and only then took them for safekeeping.

"Wow," my grandmother sighed, "soon we'll have an entire warehouse of Jewish things.

The rumor that Feiga told us was confirmed: entire flocks of street lowlifes rushed to their noble work—to beat the Jews. They beat them all—both Ukrainians and Poles—they beat them because they had to beat them, because they had to pour out their rage against the Bolsheviks, to avenge someone for their own suffering, for their torments, for the deaths of their relatives, and for the fact that the press prompted by German instructions explained precisely who was to blame for all the Bolshevik crimes. Now it was almost like a sacred duty. Disheveled women stripped of their clothing were running through the streets. The scum tore everything off them, even their underwear, and forced them to run naked. The Germans laughed and took pictures. It was a comical spectacle for them. Countless inhabitants poured into the streets, stuck their heads out of windows and admired that enthralling sight. Someone shouted from a window:

"Why the hell are you undressing the oldest hags? How about a young lass! Or a girl so there's something's to look at!"

It soon became clear that the people for the most part were beating up the Jews who had come to the city along with the liberators and received apartments in the city center, not the locals. They dragged them out into the streets with great enthusiasm and drove their rage onto them. Those forced to move to the outskirts were particularly angry. They forcibly threw "the servants of the Soviets" out of their homes and chased them away with sticks like prodigal dogs. That those "servants" happened to be elderly and there were no girls among them led to the righteous indignation of some aesthetes.

Yosko, Leah, and their mother stayed a few days at our place, and it was right then when I actually proposed to Leah. She was quite surprised. She even protested profusely at first:

"You found the right time! You've wooed me so much and now you've finally gotten the courage to ask? When they're doing such awful things to Jews?"

"Precisely now. Maybe if you convert, that would be the best way."

"What? You want me to convert?"

And then on my poor head she poured a whole bucket of the Zionist propaganda that they were stuffing in her for so many years. But how effective can propaganda be against love? We loved each other, so after some short discussions Leah agreed to convert, but only for the duration of the war. And, we agreed, after the war, she would again be an orthodox Jewish woman on the condition that even when she becomes a Christian, I will not force her to work on Saturday, just when we, Christians, have the most work to do around the house. I tried to protest; because damn, does that mean that I'll be forced to beat the dust out of the rugs myself and cook dinner? No, she said, she'll cook dinner on Friday evening, but that beating the rugs is man's work anyway. And it came to pass as we planned, we took our wedding vows in the church of St. Paraskeva and just in time because the authorities finally introduced their infamous German order. On Thursday, July 10, the Commander of the city said that grocery stores should be open from 7 to 19 hours without interruption, and for Jews between 14 and 16 hours. The stockpiling of goods was prohibited. On July 12, an announcement concerning Jews was made by the commandant of the city in three languages . All Jews 14 years and older must wear on the right side of their chest a light blue Star of David. A Jew is considered to be anyone including the third generation, as well as those whose ancestors were both Jews, or who those who were married to Jews. And so I, Orest Barbaryka, the son of a Petlyura[116] soldier, became a Jew. My dear mom just shook her head:

"Who knows if I'll become a Jewish woman around you?"

However, neither Leah nor I wore a star. Yasko helped me fake a document that listed Leah as Ukrainian, after all, she didn't look Jewish. Unfortunately, for Yosko such a scam would end tragically: his thin face and big ears would cause suspicion immediately, and then it would have been enough just to give him the order to pull down his pants and disaster would have awaited.

From July 17 on, all Jews were to receive only a kilo of bread per week. Separate stores and dining halls were opened for them. During the night from July 25 to 26 an action was taken that seriously frightened everyone—two thousand Jews were deported to the Lonska Street Prison. What their fate was no one knew. And on Saturday August 9, the great Exodus began—the resettlement of Jews in the ghetto. Klepariv was included as part of the ghetto area, therefore, my mother, Leah, and I were forced to leave our home and move to a neighborhood on Brayerivska Street next to Yasko. In the ghetto terrible poverty was rampant.

116 Simon Petlyura (1879-1926). Ukrainian supreme commander of the Army of the Ukrainian National Republic, politician, and national leader, who was assassinated in exile in Paris in 1926 by Shalom Schwartzbald to avenge pogroms carried out against Jews by Petlyura's followers.

The people sold their last belongings to feed themselves. Leah and I visited Yosko and his family and brought them food. I didn't let Leah go anywhere by herself, but one day she didn't listen to me and went to the ghetto, because she just happened to get hold of a bag of millet. When she returned, she told me excitedly and even enthralled that she visited the synagogue and heard the rabbi in his sermon announce they were gathering those people willing to go to Palestine, and the Jews there rushed to sign up. Her entire family already had signed up. Yosko was hesitant, it's true, but his mother was already packing things.

"I think it's the best way out for us," she said to me. "We should go. From Palestine we'll be able to go to America. Nothing good will come out of it for us whoever wins this war."

"Wait. Do you know what happened to those Jews who were taken to the prison on Lonska Street?

"They are all in Palestine. The rabbi and chairman of the Judenrat showed us pciture postcards from them ... There was also an entire bag of letters there."

"In envelopes?"

"No. Why in envelopes? These letters did not go through the post office. They were transported by ship to Konstanz and from there by train here. Each letter had the name of the recipient written on it. Those from the Judenrat shouted out the names, people took their letters, kissed them and were happy. The letters were so joyful... My mother received a letter from Aunt Feiga. She wrote that she was living on the shores of Lake Tiberius in a spacious house and was willing to take us all in because there was plenty of space for us.

Something didn't sound right. I asked:

"Were there any photographs?"

"Yes, there were."

"Of Palestine?"

"No... There were pictures of people with suitcases in front of trucks, which they had to take to the train. Everyone was smiling, cheerful."

"Doesn't it seem strange to you that letters from Palestine are accompanied by images from Lviv? Why didn't your favorite aunt send photos with her spacious house in the background? Or at least under a palm tree?"

Leah frowned and bit her lip. I told her to sit at home and not to move, and I set off for Yas's place. I told him about my suspicions and dragged him over to the ghetto. A gray anthill prevailed there among the moving and noisy mass that jangled, buzzed, and reverberated with countless voices, among which you could even distinguish the original melody. The crowds of people continuously wagged their tongues, praising their products in stalls, at gates, in tents, on carts, on trays hanging on their chests, in baskets, buckets, sacks, boxes, and even simply on the ground, for one of the features of a true native of Lviv—regardless of whether he was a Ukrainian, a Pole or a Jew—was his exquisite avarice. One shouldn't even call it greediness, because that avarice has been brought to a highly absurd degree when any rubbish, any used thing elicited in the practical owner the hope that he at some point he would fix it, that it would still be useful, so therefore it found its place of honor in one of his boxes or packages and stayed there for years. Right after the death of the owner the thing could end up in the trash but not necessarily, if the grateful descendants decided its fate otherwise. But now when misery engulfed all, when new things were in short supply, all of Lviv became a gigantic flea market, and old things retrieved from dark nooks and crannies came to life. Not so long ago in Lviv you could come across yellowed collars of respected Austrian bishops emeriti, their top hats and waistcoats, monocles and brushes for waxing mustaches, worn ladies' elbow-length gloves, curly-toe shoes, color postcards, used purses, chewed-up pencils, glass corks, dried brushes, or such priceless relics as dried flowers from the grave of Juliusz Slowacki,[117] a leaf from the wreath on the grave of Markian Shashkevych, ladies' apparatus for casting bullets from the era of the Polish uprisings in old trunks. All this was sold and bought, because a Lviv resident, collecting stuff for his or her entire life, could not resist buying yet some other invaluable artifact of the old world that united him with his grandfathers and great-grandfathers and testified to the continuity of his lineage. That is why the wealth of diverse products blinded your eyes: pots, bowls, shoes, shirts, pants, overcoats, fancy displays of underwear, fake chocolates, colored candies, vegetables, herring. But mostly, there was all kinds of garbage, that only a really crazy person would want—broken toys with dancing figurines, glass balls, masks, smoky mirrors, mannequins without arms or legs, old gramophones, dismantled bicycles, broken printing and sewing machines, latches and keys, bent nails, rusted tools, old dilapidated children's strollers that could only be used to transport sacks of potatoes, torn books and old newspapers, broken furniture, yellowed prints, icons without frames and frames by themselves, clocks that would never work again, fake

117 Polish romantic poet (1809-1849).

gold and silver rings, wigs and a variety of rags, string and lace, drinks mixed in buckets with vinegar and saccharin, prepared meals in pots, and small boxes of pumpkin seed cookies. Under the open sky shoemakers, tailors, and master watch repairers worked; there were even tents, where huge pieces of meat were hung (mostly rotten horse meat), some kind of viscera, hearts and horse heads. Amid the din you could hear music: someone was playing a harmonica, someone else a flute, another a violin, and someone tried to sing something. Everywhere the odor of the Jewish ghetto dominated, the stifling mixture of sweat, old clothes, herring, onions, garlic, and *kvargli*[118] cheese. You could buy illegal alcohol and documents here. A man laid out aprons with the Star of David on the table, shouting out: "Aprons! Aprons! Made of paper! Made of material! First class!" An old Jew stopped next to him, unable to decide which to select, to which the vendor says to him: "Take the one made of fabric!" But the Jew shook his head sadly: "Will I survive longer than the fabric? No, give me the paper one," and after paying departed, hunched over as if all the evil in the world were piled on his shoulders.

I was surprised that all the bazaars in the ghetto and beyond were always overly crowded, even though they presented the most danger, because the Germans repeatedly staged traps there, and then innocent people ended up in deftly placed nets. At first a column of covered military trucks drove right in front of the bazaar so close to each other that it was impossible to slip between them. Usually no one paid any attention to this column because the trucks drove past every day, but these stopped, and armed soldiers jumped

118 See footnote #49.

out of them, forming a human chain while the gendarmerie ran out at the same time from all the alleys, and in this way the trap was set. Then an incredible panic enveloped the bazaar. You could hear desperate screams, swearing, someone gave someone else signs, called out, someone responded, people left their wares to fate and rushed off, looking for any way out. Vegetables crushed under their feet, grain was scattered, pots of soup, boiled potatoes, and giblets turned over, feet slipped, someone fell down, people tripped over him, and the Germans meanwhile formed a few exit corridors and allowed all those who had documents to pass, and those who did not were put on a truck and in the best case were driven off to forced labor, and in the worst to a concentration camp.

We found Yosko as he was getting ready to go to "Bristol," where he played in the orchestra every night. He laughingly showed us the orders of the Reichsmusicführer that related to dance music. Mr. Reichsmusicführer was particularly concerned by the fact that music thoroughly permeated with Jewish-Bolshevik motifs of Negro jazz echoed at institutions of mass recreation. Therefore it was necessary henceforth "to ban the compositions in which the foxtrot rhythm, so-called "swing," is more than 20% from the repertoire of stage and dance orchestras. In orchestra repertoires, preference should be given to compositions in a major key as opposed to a minor, and the lyrics should reflect optimism and the joy of life, not the typical Jewish pessimism particularly evident in slow compositions called the 'blues' which adversely affect innate Aryan discipline. The music of the barbarian races awakens dark instincts alien to the German people. This also applies to Jewish-Masonic instruments from which shrill squealing echoes and drum solos (so-called 'drum breaks') and the plucking of strings on a contrabass (so-called 'pizzicato') instead of playing it with a bow. We recommend that all orchestras restrict the use of saxophones, replacing them with cellos, violins, and other folk instruments." Then Yosko showed me the same order the Soviet Ministry of Culture distributed in early 1940, in which jazz had been called a provocation of the enemy, and then they hung a poster in their restaurant: "Today you are listening to jazz, tomorrow you will sell out your Homeland." Who would have thought there was so much in common between Stalin and Hitler!

Golda meanwhile baked some meat pies for the road, singing something filled with optimism. Yosko confirmed everything that Leah said. Feiga's letter, handwritten with her inherent verbosity, did not trigger any suspicion. Auntie chose that area in particular because she had already been there once on vacation and knew the neighborhoods.

"Really. Might you be able to read us the letter out loud?" I requested, thinking that the letter would be in Yiddish, but what a surprise it was for us when it turned out that Feiga had written her letter in Polish!

The letter was long and packed with information that could hardly elicit ardent interest even among the family, especially the description of the dinner, to which the immigrants were treated before the train departed. But there was no description of the journey, which was to take a long time with many transfers. The house where Feiga settled with her husband and children was located right on a lake close to the spot where the Jordan River flows in, and from the windows you could see the city of Tiberius. "It's a great place for living and relaxation," Feiga wrote. "We are waiting for you, take only the most valuable things with you, do not drag along a lot of clothes with you because everything here is very cheap, and they give out a lot of clothes for free."

"My mother immediately rushed to the *Jewish Encyclopedia*, found the lake and for an hour examined the locality where we would be living," Yosko said smiling.

"Orko! Yas!" Golda hollered from the kitchen. "You should come with a cart and take some things for yourself. Because we can't take everything. I think the furs will be of no use in Palestine. And there is a stack of good china. How would I be able to bring them? And you, Yas, can take the rocking chair that you like so much."

We asked Yosko to show us the *Jewish Encyclopedia* and really wanted to revel in the place where they'd be moving. In its shape the lake resembled the African continent.

"Look,"Yas nudged me. "The Jordan doesn't feed into the lake from the south, instead, it flows out of it. And from the windows of the house on the south shore of the lake, you can't see the city of Tiberius... it's on the west coast."

We raised our heads and saw that Yosko had turned pale because he couldn't figure out how he hadn't noticed this, even though he had already examined the map. Then a terrible conjecture depressed him: without a doubt the wise Feiga found no other way to warn the family that the situation was a crooked business. When Yosko approached Golda with the encyclopedia and tried to explain to her about what we had just ascertained, she wouldn't listen to him, screaming something that we didn't understand. She finally clasped her face in her hands and began spasmodically to sob in despair. Her entire rosy plan lay in ruins. But what would happen to grandfather Abeles, uncle Zelman, and our other relatives, who signed up to leave for Palestine tomorrow? Yosko calmed her down, promising not to go that evening to "Bristol," but instead to visit relatives and friends and tell them about Feiga's letter, and perhaps, look over other letters in which similar hints might appear.

Upon returning home, I told Leah the news that Yosko and her mother were not going. She fell into deep contemplation and didn't speak to me, and when we went to bed and I embraced her, she silently gave herself to me without making a sound.

The next day we learned that only a small fraction of those whom Yosko tried to convince believed him. All the others, encouraged by the functionaries of the Judenrat, gathered together with their suitcases, got into trucks, and drove off into the unknown. No Germans or policemen were there. So why wouldn't the people trust them? They also trusted their rabbis when they urged them in September 1939 and in June 1941 not to flee from the Germans—an intelligent, highly cultured people who would always remember how many Jews were among their most prominent figures of culture and science and were therefore no danger to Jews.

"Our trouble is that we have always been very well organized and law-abiding," Yosko sighed. "We listened to our rabbis and never allowed ourselves to doubt."

"Listen," Yas said to me. "I have a Volksdeutsche acquaintance who works at the prison on Lonska Street. Though he's about as Volksdeutsche as I'm a Moor, it's just that his name is Ruffer. Maybe we can learn from him where those Jews were taken. Every night he goes to the 'Hooked Herring' Pub."

I knew that pub. It was popular because of its location in the Union of Brest market square, where every day the crowded bazaar teemed. In the evenings, when speculators and bazaar vendors left for home, the best of society gathered in the saloon—actors, writers, and even the authorities. All this occurred because Vasyl Naida, the owner of the tavern, handed over its management to the students Ivan Veresiuk and Taras Myhal.[119] The former had a nice baritone voice and was a soloist at the opera house and the latter was a writer. Thanks to them the artistic community began to gather at the inn. In addition, both were endowed with entrepreneurial talent. I often talked to Taras because he quickly found an in with the food committee, which oversaw food rationing cards. The cards that were used, which salespeople attached to a sheet and returned to the committee, were to be destroyed. But officials found a way to resell those cards on the black market. They unglued the cards from the sheets and used them a second time when buying food in stores designated for the Germans. In this way the black market flourished. Myhal always had these cards, and he knew how to swap them for reuse from his butcher friend, the meat shop owner Masyukevych on Stefan Batory Street. So, I bought the cards from him at half price.

In the pub we actually did find Ruffer, who was already a little bit tipsy. From Taras I surreptitiously bought a bottle of Baczewski *horilka*, grabbed some herring sandwiches, and we endeavored to get the Volksdeutsche plastered. I managed to find out word by word that those two thousand Jews were brought to the prison on Lonska Street on July

119 Myhal (1920-1982) was a Ukrainian writer and author of the autobiographical novel *The Hooked Herring Tavern*. [author's note].

26. They were fed dinner, then each family was handed a printed certificate with a seal, which indicated their new address, area of accommodation, number of rooms, and so on. On the wall they hung a large map so that each could have a good look around and see in which area they would be living. Immediately a fuss ensued, because it turned out that someone wanted to be closer to relatives, and someone else to the contrary, but they were all told that they would sort it all out when they were settled in and that it wouldn't be a problem. England and America bought them thousands of homes and required they immediately settle in them; Germany simply was forced to abide by the agreement and was also interested in sending them all to the promised land as quickly as possible. They therefore advised everyone to write letters to their families so that they wouldn't worry, but the writing had to be only in Polish, Ukrainian or German, because, they said, government administrators would examine the letters since a war is going on and someone might pass along some spy messages. Also, they had to write as if they already were in Palestine, giving detailed descriptions of their houses. The reason given for this was that letters from Palestine would take a really long time. Also who knew if then—maybe in half a year—those accommodations might not be captured by the Arabs. Then it wouldn't be known whether it would be possible to form a new caravan, because trucks and cars could be sent to the front, but right now there was a great opportunity. Some people doubted whether it was worth writing such a letter, but several rabbis oversaw the process and harshly punished irresponsible citizens who did not want to help their families.

After that everyone was put on trucks and where they were taken—Ruffer didn't know. The only thing that we managed to squeeze out of him was that the trucks, returned in the evening spattered with mud and filled with suitcases. When Ruffer asked some driver why the Jews didn't take their suitcases with them, he laughed and said that where they went, they don't have only sausages on trees and rivers of honey, then why the hell would they drag all this junk with them? Later all the bags were unpacked, rifled through, and sorted. An entire tub of just jewelry was collected.

"Evidently, a true paradise is waiting for them there in Palestine," said Ruffer. And I thought, is he really that stupid or just playing the fool?

Over time it became more difficult to survive. Fortunately, Wolff, who could only stay for a few days in Lviv, lived with us, because his mother had been taken to Kazakhstan, and he couldn't even get into his apartment. It was taken by a Soviet functionary who didn't disappear under the Germans and still worked in the commandant's office. Before starting off to the East, Wolff told us an interesting thing: a gram of gold in Warsaw was worth 200 zloty and in Ukraine 60 rubles. The zloty and ruble still had equal value. We only had to exchange glances to know we needed to get new jobs. If we could earn the necessary amount, we'd be able to buy Portuguese passports for Yosko, his mother, and Ruta. We had to hurry up, because soon it became known that the Jews who were supposedly taken to Palestine were instead taken to the Lysynetsky Forest, or, as they say, "to the Sands" and shot there in the sand pit. Then I remembered that chorus I had written for Yosko:

And when I am no longer with you,
Sands will cover bodies
We will meet where poppies flow like a river
There, where their shadow fell.

Thus, these words began to come true—sand covered the bodies, and on the sands poppies blossomed....

27

The manuscript broke off at this spot. Still under the impressions of what he had read, Yarosh had a burning desire to publish these diaries. He visited Milker again and asked if he wouldn't mind.

"No," the old man said. "I would more than happy. But there's no ending."

"That's nothing, you can tell me what happened later. And these words… about poppies ... did they really enter the text of the 'Tango'?" Yarosh asked and quoted: "we will meet where poppies flow like a river, where their shadow has lain."

Milker carefully looked into his eyes, as if he wanted to say something, but confined himself to a nod.

"This is how you explain all your poppies?" Yarosh continued. "The meeting should be held in their shadow?"

Milker silently poured himself a glass of beet kvass and said:

"They're just word... words and nothing more… do you want to know what happened later?"

Yarosh nodded and turned on his tape recorder.

"I lived in the ghetto, but had a pass, and while playing at the "Bristol" I could see Orko and Yasko. In March 1942, Untersturmführer Rokita appeared at the Yaniv concentration camp. He was a little over fifty. A flattering smile never disappeared from his round red mug. Once he was a violinist in various pubs in Katowice and Zakopane, but this didn't get in the way of him mocking prisoners, treating them like cattle. When Maximilian Shtriks, a talented conservatory student, ended up at the camp, his father Leon, who used to play with Rokita in pubs, tried to save his son. But Rokita said that if he wanted to see his son more often, he should organize a camp orchestra. Shtriks quickly assembled an orchestra comprised partly of prisoners and partly of free musicians. That's how I ended up there.

In the late summer of 1942 they decided to reduce the area of the ghetto and Kleparivska ended up outside the Jewish zone. My mother and I moved to Zamarstyniv. Soon they banned Shtriks and other free musicians from returning home. We became prisoners with the difference that we had special rights and lived in a separate section. We were treated a little better, and Rokita was concerned about us being decently dressed.

We were ordered to sew a yellow star on our shirts. Ukrainians wore blue, and the Poles—red. Nothing was sewn on those who were to be executed.

The orchestra played for the prisoners when they set off to work and when they returned. It also played during the selection of prisoners. When they were taken away and examined to see if they were sick or unfit for work, they were taken to the Valley of Death and shot there, and we played to the rattling of machine guns and automatic rifles. As I mentioned, Professor Strikhs from the conservatory, Cuba Mund, the conductor of the Lviv Opera and I wrote the score for "Tango of Death." We inserted Kalkbrenner's notes from the manuscript.

Twice a week, the orchestra performed a concert at the square for the SS and their families, as well as at parties that the camp commandants SS Obersturmführers Vilhauz and Rokita arranged in their luxurious homes for guests. These parties lasted often until the morning, and the orchestra just hurried from there to the plaza to play for the prisoners who were waiting ready for the march.

One day I experienced something terrible. When I saw Leah and Ruta in the camp for women, I managed to exchange a few words with them. I learned that all of our relatives were already dead—my mother, grandfather, my uncle Zelman and my aunt—all of them were shot there in the Valley, and we had played for them... Eventually, each member of the orchestra experienced the same horror. After about a month I saw Yasko and Orko among the prisoners who gathered at the plaza. After that I saw them every day but I didn't have the opportunity to talk to them. They were losing their strength, wasting away before my eyes. Their clothes were turning into rags. How could I help them? And how could I help Leah and Ruta? These thoughts constantly haunted and tormented me.

But then Vilhauz decided that prisoners unfit to work should be moved beyond the camp's boundaries, and the committee that managed food supplies for the camp would feed them. They also allowed relatives to send them boxes of food. The Lagerführer chose a suitable place for these emaciated prisoners—a hall at the Jewish cemetery. The hall was huge but had a roof with holes and broken windows. The wind blew in freely from end to end, and many prisoners had ulcers that were rotting and stinking. Most of them preferred to lie outside in the cemetery rather than inside. Many of them died there. Then I actually had the opportunity to help my friends, because I saw that they were reaching the end. I met with Dr. Rapaport, who always listed the dead refugees in his reports. I asked that he write that Yasko and Orko were unable to work and should be sent out of the camp. From there it was easier to escape. He did that, so Yasko and Orko stayed in the cemetery for a few days. Their mothers brought them food, they regained their strength, and disappeared one night. Mr. Rapaport marked them as dead. It was right in time, because soon all those unable to work were taken to the Lysynetsky Forest and shot.

Unfortunately, I couldn't help Leah and Ruta in the same way. They worked in the sewing shop and were not so exhausted that they had to be removed from the camp.

At the beginning of May 1943, over the course of a week Jews were brought in from somewhere else and herded into the Valley of Death, where they were held for a week without food and water. More than eight thousand Jews were gathered there, and on May 8 all of them were ordered to strip naked, driven into a gap under the mountain and shot there. During that execution our orchestra also played, and I didn't even know that my beloved Ruta was among those killed... Only Leah was not there; she was still in the camp. I played for all of them for eternity....

In the first half of November the camp still held five thousand prisoners. Then a group of our weavers, realizing what fate was awaiting them, decided that they would not go as calves to slaughter. They convinced the camp guards to help them escape. The guards consisted of Ukrainians, who had come from Soviet Ukraine and had been captured. They didn't take Galicians to be guards because they might sympathize with local Jews and come to an understanding with them. Unfortunately, the plan became known to the camp commanders and the Germans on November 18 tried to capture the weavers, but they began to defend themselves and killed two Germans, and then the Germans decided to liquidate the entire camp. The Ukrainian guards refused to take part in the massacre and even helped some of the Jews flee from the camp along with several guards. Then the Germans disarmed the remainder of the guards, something like a hundred of them, and put them on a train in Klepariv to send them off to Lublin. The Jews zealously defended themselves by barricading themselves in workshops and barracks; they threw themselves at the Germans with knives and razors, pointed sticks and metal rods, cut their throats and smashed their heads. At this time my poor sister Leah took possession of an automatic carbine and began firing at the Germans until the ammunition ran out, and then bullets mowed her down.

The entire time the fighting continued we did not stop playing because Untersturmführer Rokita so ordered. Some couldn't hold out and sat down on the ground, continuing to play. At first, Rokita approached and kicked them, or beat them on the head with a switch, but eventually he abandoned the spot where we were and only watched from afar. Not knowing what force was holding me, I didn't fall or sit down. The music lifted me above the earth. I felt that I had become weightless. I played the violin for them all so that they would find themselves in eternity.

The battle lasted three days. Forty Germans were killed along with almost all the Jews. The corpses were taken by bus day and night to the Lysynetsky Forest sand pit. Executions had been going on there for a long time already, and they burned the corpses there. A special barracks was built for the Jews who worked at the furnaces, but it was emptied because a few days before the uprising the unit was eliminated in order not to leave any witnesses. Since there was no one left for whom to play, half the orchestra was taken away to be shot. About two dozen musicians and a dozen masons who did not participate in the uprising because they were outside the camp were taken to the barracks. They brought in Germans to guard them.

And then a miracle happened, because a miracle always lies in wait for us, and it's worth waiting for, even in times of the most despondency and despair. I saw Wolff! He just arrived in Lviv that day, two months after lying in a hospital after being wounded at the front. The rest of the camp guards were also newcomers and didn't participate in the camp's liquidation. They didn't exhibit the cruelty to which we had become accustomed. Moreover, when Wolff began to argue that we should all be released, they didn't even protest, but just thought about how to organize it. Then Wolff suggested that we all scram. We all escaped and fled in every direction. Altogether 160 Jews fled along with us during the liquidation. Some of them were later caught. But most of the Jews hid in the sewers. Many Jewish families hid themselves where the main channel of the Poltva River was. The odor was not the most pleasant, but a human being can get used to anything. In any case, the Germans didn't expect it.

Those who escaped from the camp had to live in the sewers for eight months until July 27, 1944 when the Germans left Lviv. Those who had settled there before lived in the sewers for almost two years in total. Lviv residents supplied them with food. Some brought it for free and others for money, because the Jews went there with their entire families and grabbed their valuables to take with them, so they were able to buy food. When the Germans left Lviv, and the Jews finally came out of the dark smelly dungeons, the children raised a terrible cry; because they were struck by the street noise and blinding sunlight. Then they wanted only one thing—to return back to the sewers....

First, Wolff and I hid in the channels along with everyone, but then Wolff asked someone for civilian clothes and went to see Orest's mother. He returned with food, clothing for me and for himself, and news. Yas at that time was in the Polish Home Army and there was no communication with him, Orest—in the UPA (Ukrainian Insurgent Army), but Orest's mother had contact with him through Lucia. At night we made our way out of the sewers and moved toward the Vynnyky Forest, where Lucia was waiting for us at an appointed spot to take us to the guerrilla camp. There I met several Lviv Jews who took part in the fight in the camp. But the greatest joy was when we hugged Orest. We laughed and cried, I for my sister, and he for his love....

When they accepted us into the squad, the commander was surprised that Wolff, a German would go over to the side of the guerrillas, but once he was told who Wolff's father was, he no longer had any reservations. He only said that we had to choose pseudonyms. I said, "Solomon." And he said: "Why not 'Queen of Sheba'?" And I said: "Because I'm Solomon." And Wolff, quite naturally, became "Wolf." We had several skirmishes with the Germans, but on the eve of the Bolsheviks' entry to the city, the Polish Home Army rose up against the Germans and drove them out of many neighborhoods to seize power in the city before the Bolsheviks entered, but then they were forced to retreat into the forest. We actually met up with Yasko then. His squad was defeated by the Bolsheviks. He had injured his leg and couldn't walk. Lucia took him to the village and after he healed up, the front was already far away. For Yasko there remained no choice but to stay with us. Afterwards, there were battles with the NKVD. In 1947 we decided to make our way through the Carpathians in the west, but winter was approaching. We split into separate groups and hid in secret hiding places. The winter was impossible for the partisans because our tracks would give us away. So, all four of us ended up in a single hiding place. Now there was a lot of free time to talk.

The day when we had to die approached as any day of death, with the only difference being that we anticipated this day very clearly and were ready for its arrival. We knew that we were going to die, that they'd kill us or we'd kill ourselves so as to not fall into their hands. Sitting in the snow-covered hideout in warmth and comfort, we felt like deep sea fish on the seabed. Sometimes at night, when the snow was shining and concealed our tracks, we came out of the hideout to the surface. One day, a local forester rode up on a cart and saw us. He immediately guessed who we were. Orko stopped him and warned him that if he gave us up, the other partisans would take revenge. The forester swore over and over that he wouldn't tell anyone, and we let him go. A few days later we heard a dog barking. The NKVD had surrounded our hideout and demanded our surrender. They even brought Orko's and Yasko's mothers to persuade us. They promised amnesty, but we knew that it wasn't true: either we would be condemned to death or given twenty-five years at a forced labor camp. Then Orko said, "For so long we've been unable to accept the act of our fathers who chose death rather than betrayal, and we too face a choice: death or slavery." However, we didn't discuss it. We knew that we had one choice. I started playing 'Tango of Death,' and then there was an explosion. I lost consciousness. I came to my senses in the snow. The NKVD scoured through the hideout seeking documents, but we managed to burn them. When I was lifted up and placed on a stretcher, I saw both mothers lying dead with bullets through their heads. But just before their death, they heard me play the violin.

"Was it this violin?" Yarosh asked, nodding toward the violin lying on the couch.

"No. I hid this one under the floor when we were kicked out of the house. It was the violin that I played in the concentration camp. Cuba Mund gave it to me. Unfortunately, it was destroyed in the explosion... Oh, later they gave me twenty-five years in a labor camp, of which I served ten. Five more years passed before I was allowed to return to Lviv. I had to rent an apartment because mine was occupied by someone else. Fortunately, the family that settled there sympathized with my life story. When he was offered a job in Kyiv, he quickly signed me onto the apartment. So, I found myself back at home."

Yarosh, coming out of Milker's apartment, bumped into Yarka on the steps. She was no longer seething with anger and even smiled at him.

"He has high hopes for you," Yarosh said to the girl.

"I know. But I don't have the endurance. Besides... besides when I play that tango...," she sighed and shook her head, as if gathering her thoughts. "When I play it something incredible happens to me... I think I disappear, I dissolve in space and then it becomes so terrifying... the last time I seemed to be lifted into the air and was swinging on an invisible thread... but when I tried to scream, I couldn't utter a sound... but played the whole time without stopping."

"Yes," Yarosh nodded. "I know that feeling."

"You've heard me perform it?"

"No, I heard the dance of the dervishes."

"What link is there between the dervishes and the tango?"

"What ties them together is those twelve notes that can be integrated into any melody or dance. The effect is the same."

"But I'm terrified. I have a feeling that something has to happen, something wonderful, something exciting, but also terrible."

"I have the same feeling too. But it seems there's no turning back. The meeting will certainly take place under the shadow where the hashhash blossoms."

"What does it mean?" The girl was surprised. "What is hashhash?"

But Yarosh was already down the stairs.

Yarka found Milker watering poppies. Upon seeing her, he smiled warmly and said:

"Yes-yes, you just lack patience, child. Just patience. A reward will be coming soon."

"What is the reward? I'm not looking for any rewards. That professor of yours is a weirdo. He told me something... about hashhash...."

"Hashhash?"

"It also casts a shadow... and, well, in that shadow...."

"...will be a meeting?"

"Exactly. What does that mean?"

"I'm saying—you only lack patience. And nothing more.

A meeting will happen... must happen... I feel it. Very soon. Can I serve you some tea? Before we go to the city...."

"To play for people again?"

"Not much longer remains," Milker poured some tea into a cup, added a spoonful of honey, and handed it to the girl. "You are close to the point where you'll play the melody as required. In fact, you need just to conquer two notes. They are, however, the most difficult, but you will play them. You must play them because they already dwell inside you. Here—he put his hand on her chest between her breasts and Yarka felt warmth spread through her body, but whether it was from the heat from the tea or his touch, she could not understand. The only thing that she realized was the touch of the old man's hand was pleasant for her, and she could hardly resist from stopping him as he pulled his hand away. He possessed her completely, and she made her peace with it.

28

In the evening Yarosh gave Danka the manuscript, which she volunteered to type into the computer, as well as to transcribe the recording of Milker's narration. Danka already read the manuscript and had the unprecedented impression that she was reading the notes of a close relative. Sometimes in her memory visions of something surprisingly similar rose up, something which she could see herself and feel, but apparently did not actually see. Her dreams now became bizarre and confused. She woke up in the middle of the night and could not remember where she was, not only when she spent the night at Yarosh's, but even when she slept at home. Mother was sure that Danka was overworked and tried to convince her to put aside the translations for a while, but Arcanum tenaciously held a grip on her just like the diary of the unknown stranger, Orest, and her feelings for Yarosh.

When she told her parents about their relationship, it surprisingly didn't cause a scandal. Her father, who was not reinstated in his job, had already let go of his honor as head of the family, because he only muttered: "Well, then, a professor certainly is better than that young scatterbrain," and her mother said:

"You know best. But you aren't planning on just remaining his mistress, are you? He still hasn't proposed to you?"

"No. He just proposed that I move in with him. I think that makes sense."

"I'm afraid our father won't understand that."

"To be honest, I'm really afraid of my feelings. I've never felt anything similar to this for anyone else previously. I can't live a day without him, without hearing his voice. Especially after I read those pre-war diaries. They've influenced my feelings in a surprising way. Whenever I type them now, I always want to be near him."

29

For the first time, Marko addressed his father as "Dad," and Yarosh felt excitement. He also wanted to say something in response but couldn't find the right words. He felt guilty and that constrained him, but Marko was quite amiably disposed to him and suggested they go somewhere for coffee.

"I have to confess to you," he said as he took a puff of his cigarette. "I was in dire straits. Half a year ago. They caught me red-handed with grass, threatened to slap a charge on me for the distribution of drugs, even though it was just ordinary marijuana. And then... then they demanded I do something for them."

Yarosh grew tense and prepared himself to hear some horror story, but what he heard amused him.

"I was told to put the moves on Danka and then introduce her to you. But it turned out that I liked her, and well, we started dating... this and that ... You know, I'm not too hot of a program developer... I needed to come up with something... So, when I heard that her father was Head of the Customs Office, I was immediately emboldened. You can judge me, but I don't take after you. Besides that, I thought that her father would get me off the hook. But then, immediately after I introduced her to you, Danka began to avoid me. It didn't take me much time to figure out this mystery... I realized that it really was not me taking advantage of her, but her of me. She wanted to get close to you and got what she wanted, and I was just a stepping stone." He smiled bitterly, remained silent for a bit, put out his cigarette in an ashtray and continued: "But I want to tell you that I'm not angry. In fact, everything turned out the way they planned. I did what they wanted, and we are quits."

"And what about the grass?"

"I cleaned myself up. I didn't really get into it—it was a slight dalliance for me. That's all I wanted to say. Just so you wouldn't worry about it. Because you were probably upset?"

Yarosh nodded:

"Everything happened spontaneously somehow... I wouldn't want to cause you pain."

"I believe you. I read in a certain book... called *Spring Games in Autumn Gardens*... I forgot the author. It's an awesome book. Have you read it? Well, I know you don't read those kinds of books. In it, some guy writes that you should knock a wedge out with a wedge. So, I knocked it out. I have a new interest. True, her father isn't a customs official, but the deputy chief of the railway also isn't chopped liver, eh?"

"Well—congratulations. You'll go far in life. What about your feelings?"

"I love her. Don't laugh. You know what love is? It's an illness. It lasts very briefly. And later... later comes the symbiosis of two beings. One is a palm tree and the other vines. The only question is which one will sap the other."

"I have a suspicion that you're going to be the one to do the sapping?"

"It's your fault. If you had studied to be a lawyer or surgeon, or at least had become a deputy minister, they would have sapped me." Noticing Yarosh's puzzled look, he laughed, then stood up and said: "No, I'm kidding. I've got to go. Let our families be friends, okay?"

30

The sound of wind rustling the trees came in through the open window. Branches fluttered and slammed into the window panes. After a moment rain began pouring and banging on the roof. Yarosh woke up and thought the rain would pour in over the windowsill. Carefully so as not to wake the girl, he stood up, closed the window, and then went downstairs to the bathroom. In the kitchen on the table he saw baskets of pears that Danka had gathered. He instantly thought about breakfast. He cracked eggs, flour and milk, added honey, and soaked slices of pears in the batter, then fried them in the skillet. Then his cell phone rang: it was Kurkov.

"Hey! I'm already in Lviv. We should catch up."

"Yes. I'm free. I'll give you a very cool book of memoirs about Lviv."

"What? It's already out?"

"You know about it?"

"I'm guessing. You gave me some pieces of it."

"Oh, I forgot. So where should we meet?"

"Well, what do you mean where? Where the hashhash blossoms under its shadow," Kurkov laughed and hung up....

Yarosh tried to reach him again, but he was out of range. Then his publisher called and told him that he was bringing over the books as he promised. Yarosh was amazed. It was surprisingly quick; the book had been printed in some four days. He called Milker and gave him the good news. The old man was incredibly thrilled.

"I'll be waiting for you at three. Before lunch I still have a few classes."

31

The last sounds of the tango descend and silence, frail and fragile, begins to reign. Yarka slowly lowers her hands, still clutching her violin and bow. The same melancholy melody continues to drone in her ears. It seemed that the melody penetrated all the walls and furniture; even the poppies recognized it and turned their gaping petals to the violin like sunflowers to the sun. Yarka stands facing her teacher, as if struck by thunder, for what she felt while playing terrified her at first and then triggered many questions, which she primarily had to answer herself, but did not know how. It wasn't like that feeling she had before; then there was mystery and uncertainty, but now everything was in its place, everything became illuminated and evened out. But her head was humming from the influx of emotions; words left unsaid pounded in her brain and swelled, shooting out stems.

"Is it really true?" She said through tears.

Tears also flow down Milker's face. Sadness and joy fill his eyes, his lips tremble, but not a word comes out of them. The poppies slowly lower their heads. Milker extends his hands to the girl. Obediently like someone dreaming, she approaches him and cuddles up into his chest. He strokes her head. She presses her nose into his neck and grows still, still holding the violin and bow in her lowered hands. For a few minutes both stand motionless, and it seems the entire old house out of respect for them became as still as a heron, grew silent and did not dare disturb them even with the slightest sound, not even a creak or rustle. The silence lasts until someone's steps echo on the stairs. The girl straightens up and looks questioningly at the old man. Josef nods, takes two steps back, and with his trembling hand takes the violin to his chin and glides the bow. The melody of the tango flies into the air, quivering slightly on the window panes, and slides along the books. The poppies again come alive and raise up their little heads. Their petals stir to the rhythm; a little bit more and they, breaking up into pairs, would start to dance. The sun moves from behind the trees and throws lavish rays into the windows. Long shadows fall onto the floor. The door opens and Yarosh enters with multiple copies of Orko Barbaryka's memoirs. Upon entering, he stops, then looks in surprise at Milker. The latter smiles at him as he had never done before, the way someone smiles, whom you really love, but haven't seen in a long time. And Yarka smiles, though through tears. With the music in the background, both of those smiles take his breath away. It seems that his heart can't endure such a frantic pace and will break out of his chest. Yarosh leans against the wall and listens to the melody that leads him through nooks and crannies of dreams and ravings into something unknown and sweet, joyful and anxious. His gaze fell on the floor where the shadows of poppies crossed; the shadows flicker, dance, whirl. His eyes get blurry.

"Lord!" He whispers and looks out the window, as if trying to make sure that everything is still outside, where he was a moment ago, and that really nothing has changed. Cars pass, people scurry by, a mustachioed old man with a string of colored balloons lingers at the entrance to the market. Grannies sit on a bench and whisper to each other. Suddenly, among the passersby he recognizes Mrs. Stefa. What's she doing here? Going to the market? It seems not.

She's turning into a gate. Into this or the next one? The balcony keeps him from seeing. And at that moment the stairs in the corridor begin to creak again, but not as much as under Yarosh's feet. The clicking of high heels indicates that a woman is climbing the stairs. Yarosh froze stock still and looks with dismay at the door. He suddenly realized that he is listening not only to the melody of the tango, but also to the words that Milker is whispering:

And when I am no longer with you,
sands will cover bodies
we will meet where poppies flow like a river
there, where their shadow has fallen.

The steps come closer. Yarosh breathes the air and feels his heart thumping mercilessly hard. The steps stop right here. Someone shifts from one foot to the other. Then the doors open, but very slowly, as if timidly, as if someone hesitates to enter or not to enter, and finally ventures to do so. Danka enters. She breathes with her mouth wide open as if she had run a long distance, but her lips are illuminated with a joyful smile, though in her eyes for some reason tears welled up. What is she doing here? Aha, they had agreed to go over together to the old man, but she called to say she would be late, that he should go alone, and that she would come soon after. He even wanted to give her the address, but she said that she knew where it was. He didn't manage to ask "How?" before she hung up, but then remembered that she had given him the address even though she had never been there. And the violin keeps playing and playing, and it seems to Yarosh, he is circling in a tango like in the dance of the dervishes, circling with shadows of poppies, but this time he doesn't close his eyes but rather takes in all that is in the room—the smiling Joseph Milker, the smiling Yarka, the smiling Danka, and the smiling poppies... Why are they all smiling at him so strangely? Do they know something more than he does? The steps creak again with someone's loud footsteps. This time more than one person was climbing up; it seemed like two, maybe even three. Yarosh's heart clenches. He tries to smile with quivering lips, though what he had just guessed was still phantasmal, shimmering and unfathomable to the end. He still doesn't believe it himself when he wants to say: "Danka honey!" But from his lips escapes the name: "Leah?!"

Yuri Vynnychuk was born in 1952 in Stanislaviv (now called Ivano-Frankivsk) in Western Ukraine. He is a man of many hats: prose fiction writer, poet, translator, journalist, editor, anthologizer, satirist, translator, comic stage performer, playwright, and culinary specialist to name several that come to mind. He was designated a Golden Writer of Ukraine in 2012 and is one of the country's most prolific writers. His works have earned numerous prizes including the BBC Ukrainian Book of the Year Award twice for his novels *Spring Games in Autumn Gardens* (2005) and *Tango of Death* (2012). During his undergraduate days in Stanislaviv, Vynnychuk fell under the watchful eye of the KGB. In part to escape that surveillance, he moved to the larger city of Lviv after graduating in 1973. He continues to reside there to this day and has become one of the major champions of his adopted city. Until 1980 he was blacklisted from publishing under the repressive Soviet regime but managed still to do so under various pseudonyms. After emerging from the underground, Vynnychuk rose to swift popularity in Western Ukraine (Galicia) with his singing and performance group "Don't Worry!" (founded in 1987), his fantastic stories and novellas in his collection of shorter works *The Flashing Beacon* (1990), and his pulp fiction erotic novel *Maidens of the Night* (1992). Since then he has published scores of fiction and non-fiction books, anthologies, children's books, and translations. Controversy has followed Vynnychuk throughout his creative lifetime: in particular for his overt male perspective on eroticism in his writings as well as for his satirical jibes at political and cultural figures both in Soviet and post-Ukrainian-independence times. In 2012 he was vilified by elements of the corrupt and now thankfully former Yanukovych regime for his satirical poem "Kill the Mother," which was circulated widely on the Internet. Vynnychuk's name more recently also was included in the infamous "List of 47," which consisted of 47 prominent Ukrainian cultural and political figures targeted for assassination by Russian-backed killers. The novel *Tango of Death* with the city of Lviv as one of its main heroes represents the pinnacle of Vynnychuk's craft and showcases his superb stylistic mastery.

MICHAEL NAYDAN is Woskob Family Professor of Ukrainian Studies at The Pennsylvania State University and works primarily in the fields of Ukrainian and Russian literature and literary translation. He received his BA and MA degrees from The American University and his Ph.D. from Columbia University. He has published over 50 articles on literary topics and more than 80 translations in journals and anthologies. Of his more than 40 books of published and edited translations, some of his most recent include *Nikolai Gumilev's Africa* (Glagoslav Publishers, 2018); Yuri Andrukhovych's cultural and literary essays, *My Final Territory: Selected Essays* (University of Toronto Press, 2018); and Abram Terz's literary essays, *Strolls with Pushkin and Journey to the River Black* (Columbia University Press, 2016).

In 2017 he published his literary essays in Ukrainian translation in the volume, *From Gogol to Andrukhovych: Selected Literary Essays* (Piramida Publishers). He has also published a novel about the city of Lviv *Seven Signs of the Lion* (Glagoslav Publishers, 2016), which also appeared in 2017 in Marianna Prokopovych's Ukrainian translation under the title *Sim znakiv leva* (Piramida Publishers). He has received numerous prizes for his translations including the George S.N. Luckyj Award in Ukrainian Literature Translation from the Canadian Foundation for Ukrainian Studies in 2013.

OLHA TYTARENKO received her BA and MA in English from Ivan Franko National University in Lviv, Ukraine, her MA from The Pennsylvania State University, and her Ph.D. from the University of Toronto with a specialty in Russian literature. She is currently an Assistant Professor of Practice of Russian at the University of Nebraska. With Michael Naydan she has co-translated Iren Rozdobudko's novel *The Lost Button* (Glagoslav Publishers), Abram Terz's *Strolls with Pushkin and Journey to the River Black* (Columbia University Press), Maria Matios' novel *Sweet Darusya: A Tale of Two Villages*, and Yuri Vynnychuk's novel *Tango of Death* (the latter two with Spuyten Duyvil).

Manufactured by Amazon.ca
Bolton, ON

24621195R00275